Exile's Challenge

PART TWO OF THE EXILES SAGA

"We can never go back to all we knew, to our old lives."

"Would you?" Flysse eyed him with amazement. "I'd not. We've a new life before us."

"Yes." Arcole nodded slowly, cautiously. "But it shall not be easy."

"Nor was our escape," she said. "Nor would have been life in the wilderness. We are fortunate, Arcole! We are safe from the Autarchy and the demons both; we are amongst good, friendly folk. How can you look so glum?"

"I suppose I'm afraid."

Davyd heard the last and chuckled. "Afraid? You know no fear, Arcole. And what's to be afraid of here?"

He looked at the young man and felt his smile grow genuine.

"Nothing," he answered, and shrugged. "Save that I'm a stranger in a strange land."

Also by Angus Wells

Exile's Challenge

Book Two of the Exiles Saga

Angus Wells

BANTAM BOOKS
New York Toronto London
Sydney Auckland

EXILE'S CHALLENGE
A Bantam Spectra Book

PUBLISHING HISTORY
Bantam trade paperback edition published December 1996
Bantam rack edition / January 1998

SPECTRA and the portrayal of a boxed "s"
are trademarks of Bantam Books,
a division of Bantam Doubleday Dell Publishing Group, Inc.

ISBN 0-553-57778-6

Published simultaneously in the United States and Canada

Bantam Books are published by Bantam Books, a division of Bantam
Doubleday Dell Publishing Group, Inc. Its trademark, consisting of the
words "Bantam Books" and the portrayal of a rooster, is Registered in U.S.
Patent and Trademark Office and in other countries. Marca Registrada.
Bantam Books, 1540 Broadway, New York, New York 10036.

PRINTED IN THE UNITED STATES OF AMERICA

OPM   10 9 8 7 6 5 4 3 2 1

Perhaps time runs out,
but never love—
so this is for Liz
and Laurence James:
always.

Not only a character or two
(unless she cuts them)
but also a great editor:
Thank you, Anne Groell.

And Jamie Warren-Youll:
The world's finest art editor.

And Steve for the covers:
Of course I put your depictions in!

And special thanks to Maggie Mann,
for being who she is.

Exile's
Challenge

1 Another Time, Another Place

The savage roaring of the Breakers' weirdling beasts echoed like frustrated thunder off the hills surrounding the Meeting Ground. Through that chorus, and rising higher-pitched above it, the dread riders sang their own blighted hymn, an ululation of thwarted bloodlust. From the trees surrounding the great expanse of meadow, birds frightened by the horrid threnody took flight, adding their own alarm-songs to the cacophony, and in the farther hills wolves howled, and coyotes. The night filled up with noise, rang in horrid lamentation, as the Breakers vented their disappointment on the bodies of the slain, mutilating the corpses of fallen warriors, or gifting them to their mounts like playthings to huge and vicious kittens.

It seemed, in that time the Breakers came down onto the grass of the Meeting Ground and found the People gone, that in all Ket-Ta-Witko only the Maker's holy mountain and the full moon of the Turning Year stood serene, allied in their defiance of the invaders. The moon silvered the grass—where it was not stained dark with blood—and the holy mountain towered white and dispassionate over all. Where the great arch of light had stood, the Maker-given gateway through which the last of the People had escaped, there was now only trampled ground. Of the People, and their horses and their dogs and their lodges, of the Grannach and all their possessions, nothing remained: they had gone away to another place, another time. Morrhyn's promise was fulfilled.

And the Breakers shrieked in dismay and frustration, their own promise of conquest and destruction denied them, their lust beaten like floodwater washed against immutable stone. Some, maddened by defeat, struck at one another; some turned their blades on themselves, drawing the blood they craved from their own bodies. They were not accustomed to defeat, these reivers of worlds: their habit was annihilation unthinking, massacre, and the overturning of everything stable; anything that was not them.

Then a clarion sounded, cutting like a knife through the tumult, and even before the echoes came back from the hills, silence fell. Riders fought their strange mounts to stillness; blades were sheathed, and the self-mutilators wiped at their wounds and sat their beasts and waited.

From the northern perimeter, where the Commacht had held the cliffs and the fighting had been fiercest, a figure armored magnificently in gold rode down. Curved spikes thrust like defiant talons from the armor, the gauntlets ended in vicious claws, and sharp-edged wings extended batlike from the helmet that concealed the rider's face. A great sword hung on chains from the waist, its bloodred scabbard rattling against the skulls that decorated the saddle, which in turn sat upon a mount no human creature had ever ridden. It was unlike the other Breakers' beasts, for it wore the delineaments of a horse, only larger, and with a hide of midnight blue. Horns sprouted from its red-eyed skull and about its flaring nostrils, and its snarling mouth exposed fangs no mortal horse had ever owned. Its muscular form was somewhat disguised by the plates—gold, like its rider's armor—that decorated the chest and neck and cruppers, and as its clawed hooves pranced across the grass, they seemed to leave imprints of flame that matched the exhalations of its breath. It was not so large as the lion-mounts, but as it drew near they pawed the ravaged ground and bowed their heads and mewled acknowledgment of this beast's superiority.

Nor less their riders of the golden-armored figure. They parted silently, shaping a pathway down which the two came as if in bitter triumph to where the arch of light had stood. None spoke as the rider halted the obscene, horned horse and the helmeted head bowed in slow contemplation of the ground, all tracked and trampled on the one side and on the other nothing, save where Breakers had been.

The helmet rose, turning in the direction of the Maker's Mountain. The same moon that lit the great peak bathed the armor in its bright light, but the golden plates appeared to absorb that radiance and dull it and change it, so that the armor, instead of shining, seemed to throb with a fiery life, as if its wearer stood before a blaze, or the metal ran with blood beneath its surface. It was as if the figure defied all natural laws, defied even the Maker.

Slowly, the wickedly clawed gauntlets lifted to the helmet's latchings and raised the pot. The rider shook his head, flinging loose a great spill of long, darkly golden hair. It seemed to glow redly, as if fire danced about the handsome face. And was it fire, then it was matched and met by the glow of his eyes, which burned bright and savage as his steed's, as if blasphemous furnaces burned inside his skull, fueled by the blood of all his slaughtered victims. He cradled the helm against his armored thigh and tugged the horned horse's reins so that the creature danced and snorted.

"They have denied us our prize."

His voice was deep, a musical bass that carried over the Meeting Ground almost as if he sang the words. In the hills, the wolves ceased their howling; the coyotes ended their calling; all the birds fell still. It was if his voice imposed some dreadful and obscene order.

Into that silence he said, "They have escaped us."

He spun his mount around, clawed hooves scratching up great sprays of dirt, the beast snarling.

"None have escaped us before. None!"

He slowed his mount's circling, lowered his head a moment, then raised it up to fix the waiting horde with a smoldering gaze that only a few dared meet.

"This is not the way. We are the Breakers, we are the unmakers of worlds. We are the dark side of light, the shadows that haunt men's dreams when they think of betrayal and dishonor. We are created to punish sin: we destroy. But . . ." He shook his head and it seemed that tears the color of blood escaped his eyes. "We have failed our duty here. These cringing things escaped us. How could that be?"

Armor rattled, paws scraped; all nervously: no answer came.

"Will none answer me?"

He turned his awful horse around its slowly prancing circle again, red eyes like torches on the horde.

And one replied: "They owned magic, Akratil. Great magic."

"Ah!" He halted the horned horse, facing the speaker, wide mouth parting in a smile. "Bemnida alone has the courage to say it. Come forward, Bemnida."

The speaker hesitated and Akratil nodded encouragingly, beckoning, still smiling. A lionbeast pushed from the throng. Its rider wore armor the color of a summer sky, her hair the pale gold of the summer sun. Her lovely face was delicately beautiful, marred only by the cuts she had carved across her cheeks and nose. Blood still oozed from those, and her pale gray eyes were stormy with frustration. She halted her mount before Akratil and urged the beast to kneel, her own head bowed.

Akratil said, "Rise up, Bemnida. It seems that only you of all my followers have the courage to speak the truth."

Bemnida raised her head and obeyed, urging her mount on until it stood alongside his.

"So, Bemnida," he said gently, "tell me of this magic."

Bemnida looked a moment confused. Akratil smiled at her, and motioned that she speak.

She licked a thread of blood from her lips and said, "It was as if they knew of our coming and rallied against us." Then paused, nervous under that red-eyed contemplation. "As if they owned such magic as warned them. And showed them how to escape." She gestured at where the gate had stood.

"Some did know of us. Those who'd hear us and take our way, whose ambition chooses the dark path." Akratil's smile was feral, like a wolverine savoring a kill. "Some I . . . spoke with."

"Yes." Bemnida ducked her head in agreement. "But the others, those we fought here . . . They *knew*. Why else did they gather here?"

"Perhaps those little dwarvish folk warned them."

"How?" she asked. "What few we left alive were surely trapped in their tunnels, in the hills. How could they have brought word? They used no riding animals and this is a wide world—how could they have traveled so far in time?"

Akratil nodded. "Indeed. So, how did the others know? Save they do own some scrying."

Bemnida, encouraged, said, "And more. Such magic as enabled them to fashion that gate and flee our wrath."

"And that," Akratil said. "Which was surely great magic."

Bemnida nodded.

"Great as mine?" asked Akratil.

"No!" Bemnida shook her head vigorously, soft golden hair flying in a cloud about her bloodied face.

Akratil spoke as if she had voiced no denial. "Great as that Power we serve?"

Again Bemnida shook her head, her denial louder now. "How could that be? Is the day mightier than night? I say, no—that the darkness conquers light, and that we are the darkness of all the worlds' light, and the Power we serve is surely the greatest of all."

"But they escaped us." Akratil's voice softened, a vocal caress, as if he whispered endearments to a lover. "We came to this world and have conquered all until now. Until we came through those hills and fought these folk. None others have stood against us, none others have escaped us."

Bemnida said nothing.

Akratil said, "Think you some other Power aided them, Bemnida?"

"It is not my place to say." She bowed her head.

Akratil reached out, setting a talon to her chin, raising her head until she looked into his eyes again. A droplet of bright blood welled from his touch, trickled unnoticed down her slender throat. "It would seem that you alone own the courage to speak, to think. And now that you have begun, I'd hear the rest."

Bemnida's eyes flickered around. The surrounding horde stood silent, attentive as a wolf pack awaiting the kill. The moon was westered past the Maker's Mountain now and shadows flung from the hills, the serried peaks bathed in patterns of silver and jet. Into the silence an owl hooted three times. Bemnida said slowly, "Perhaps there was a Power; perhaps they called on it."

"Perhaps." Akratil chuckled softly. "After all, is there that Power we serve, why not another?"

"Yes." Bemnida essayed a smile that failed to reach her troubled eyes.

"And that Power effected their escape?" Akratil said.

Bemnida said, "I suppose it was so. How else could they flee?"

"Save aided by a Power great as ours." Akratil nodded thoughtfully. "Save aided by magic great as mine."

Bemnida sat on her strange mount in silence.

Akratil said, "Which cannot be. There cannot be a Power greater than that we serve, nor magic greater than mine. Are we not that dark side of all beliefs—counterpoint to the feeble imaginings of the creatures we destroy—were we not created to reive worlds in dark judgment of betrayal and dishonor? Was it not dishonor and betrayal called us here?"

"So it is," Bemnida agreed, lowering her head. "It is as you say."

"Even so, they did escape us!" A man, torn-faced and bloody, urged his mount from the throng. He wore armor dented in battle, carmine in color. "And to me that suggests such a Power as Bemnida speaks of. Think on it, Akratil: are they protected by some Power equal to our own, then surely it were better we leave them go. We were never defeated before—only now—and we've not the means to chase them. I say we let them go."

Akratil said, softly, "Is that your true thought, Yuell? That we leave off our duty, forsake our honor?"

Yuell shifted nervously in his saddle. His mount pawed the trampled ground. He said, "It is. You saw the gate they made, and you know we cannot follow them. Whatever Power guards them must surely be great as ours, and has closed that pathway."

Akratil said, "Perhaps," and looked to Bemnida. "What think you?"

"That we have a duty," she said, "and can we pursue them, then we must."

"We lost many here!" Yuell gestured about the Meeting Ground. "Too many! I say we look to other worlds."

"I'd have these folk," Akratil said, a gauntleted hand closing as if it crushed some soft thing. "I'd not so easily admit defeat, nor betray our cause."

"They're gone!" Yuell argued. "We know not where— only that they are gone beyond our taking."

"How say you?" Akratil asked Bemnida.

And she answered: "That you are our leader, and I shall follow you down all the roads of time and space, to all the worlds."

"Then kill me this upstart."

Bemnida's blade swung clear of the scabbard in a fluid motion that delivered the edge to Yuell's neck in a swift, sweeping arc that severed the skull from the body and sent it rolling across the grass.

From the arteries of Yuell's throat thick columns of blood fountained high, black in the moon's light, lesser spoutings from the veins. His body jerked, dead hands tightening on his beast's mane, so that the creature roared and bucked, tossing the corpse clear of the saddle. It landed heavy and still, the carmine armor all streaked with gore. The head came to rest against a tussock that held it staring sightlessly at Akratil, the blank, dead eyes fixed on his. The mouth was stretched wide in a rictal smile that seemed adoring.

Akratil, too, smiled, and touched Bemnida fondly. "That was well done."

"Thank you." Bemnida sheathed her blade, and gestured at the snarling lion-thing: "Calm it."

A Breaker whose armor was all jet black save for the crimson sigils on chest and back ran forward, bearing a long pike. He prodded the animal, shouting, and it ceased its rumblings and retreated slowly.

"Take that away." Akratil pointed at the corpse, the head. "Feed it to the animals."

He waited until that task was done, then faced the horde again and said, "There was magic employed here, that these folk escaped us. But there exists no magic greater than mine. Nor any Power greater than that we serve."

He danced his weird horse around, and from the horde came a great shout of agreement. He let it ring awhile, then raised a gauntlet, motioning his followers silent.

"These folk have escaped us—for now! But amongst them

are some I've spoken with in dreams, some who take our way. Some, I know, have chosen our path. They're mine: I've their scent in my nostrils, and I can find them. I can find them in the night, when they sleep; and when they dream of conquest and vengeance, they leave their spoor on the shadow trails, along all the roads of blood and darkness. They shall show us where they are, and bring us to them."

He smiled a horrid smile, his face still handsome but also torn and burning, as if the malign purpose that made him what he was shone through, the skull beneath the skin exposing its deformity.

Bemnida stared at him, adoringly.

"We shall leave this world, to find the other where our prey has gone. They shall not escape us! Set up the pavilions here, and feed the beasts on the fallen. We wait here until I find the way. But know this—I *shall* find it! It matters not where they are, or when. We *shall* find them and destroy them. We shall reive them and their new world; we shall give it all to death, that they know the price of betrayal and dishonor."

2

Sanctuary

Arcole held his musket across his chest, thumb ready on the hammer, finger tensed against the trigger. For all these folk appeared friendly—and surely Davyd felt no doubt of their benevolence—they still looked to him altogether too much akin to the demons, and had Colun betrayed him and Flysse and Davyd, then he'd sell his life dear. They could not escape, not with the mountains at their back and their Grannach escort and these others there in such numbers as must surely overwhelm them, but he'd not die easy: he'd come too far, chanced too much— he'd take as many as he could with him, should they prove hostile.

"They're friends." Davyd's voice was urgent, nor less the hand that clutched Arcole's, pinning it still that he not fire. "Listen to me! They're friends, I tell you!"

Arcole glanced sidelong at the redheaded youth. There was an authority born of conviction in Davyd's voice, as much in his green eyes. He seemed no longer the boy, ever willing to follow, but a man now, commanding in his certainty.

Behind him, Flysse said, "I believe Davyd is right, Arcole."

Her voice was soft—not quite emptied of nervousness, but still calm, as if she would accept Davyd's judgment, as if she elected to his belief rather than her husband's suspicion. Arcole looked at the silver-haired man whose eyes shone bright as a winter sky, whose mouth was stretched in a smile, as if old friends came at last to home after too long away. He seemed only welcoming, and Davyd was a Dreamer, whose talent had brought them safely here.

"You're sure?"

Davyd said, "I've dreamed of him," and turned confidently to the man. "Morrhyn?"

The white-haired man lowered his head in agreement and touched his chest and said the name again, then pointed at Davyd and spoke his name. Davyd laughed before he nodded answer. Morrhyn opened his arms, and—to Arcole's great surprise—Davyd stepped forward into the embrace as if the father he had never known came back from the sea to greet him.

Arcole frowned, confused, and turned to Flysse. "This goes beyond my understanding."

She smiled and hooked an arm through his, which made it quite impossible to use the musket even had he deemed it necessary, and said, "Do you trust no one? Surely Colun's proven his friendship; surely Davyd's proven his dreaming."

Arcole shrugged, guilty now, and said, "Yes. But even so, they *are* much like the demons."

"Davyd explained that," she said. "Colun told him they all came from the same place, no? But these folk are enemies of the demons, and it was Colun's Grannach saved us from them. And nursed you back to health."

Arcole nodded. "I know, but . . ."

He had no opportunity to say more, for Davyd was standing before him, the man called Morrhyn at his side, and all the rest clustering round, speaking amongst themselves and to the newcomers as if this was some great and anticipated event for which they had been waiting.

Then Morrhyn raised a hand and silence fell. He spoke with Davyd, the words quite incomprehensible to Arcole or Flysse, so that Davyd must translate.

His young face creased as he struggled with the unfamiliar language. "This is Morrhyn." He ducked his head toward the white-haired man. "He welcomes us to this land, where we shall be safe from . . ." He shrugged. "This is difficult, but I think he said from the demons or anyone else who chases us."

"Difficult?" Arcole frowned. "I hear noises like water over stones, or the wind in the trees, but you understand? How?"

Davyd's face assumed an expression that was both embarrassed and delighted. "I don't really know," he said, "except . . . I think Morrhyn taught me in dreams." He shrugged.

"Like in the Grannach caverns? When I could almost understand Colun? It's as if . . ."

He hesitated, faltering for the words. Morrhyn touched his shoulder, spoke, touching his forehead and Davyd's, gesturing at the high hills, his hands moving in a pattern that was itself language.

Davyd chuckled and ducked his head as Arcole watched in disbelief, aware he witnessed some kind of communication that lay just beyond his comprehension.

"You remember I told you I'd dreamed of a man like Morrhyn?" Davyd said. "Well, I did; and he dreamed of me. Of us. He knew we were coming—that's why the Grannach were waiting for us, and Morrhyn's people. They're called . . ." He hesitated, stumbling over the name so that Morrhyn repeated it slowly. "Matawaye. They live here, the Grannach in the mountains."

"I understand none of this," Arcole said.

"Nor I," said Davyd. "Not really; only that it happened and I *can* understand them. Or most of what they say, at least." He frowned. "I've much to learn, but Morrhyn says—I think—that I shall. And you, in time. But most important, we're safe here. The demons cannot pass through the mountains."

"Nor Wyme's Militia?" Arcole asked.

Davyd chuckled. "Through the mountains? Didn't you say they'd not even come into the wilderness?"

Arcole nodded. There was magic at work here, such as he failed to comprehend. He was familiar with the hexing powers of the Evanderan Autarchy, knew somewhat of prophetic dreaming, but this was something else: as if the passage through the mountains imbued Davyd with the gift of tongues. Or it was as the young man said—that Morrhyn had reached out in sleep to teach this odd and guttural language to the youthful Dreamer.

For surely Davyd understood sufficient that he might play the part of interpreter: urged on by Morrhyn, he began to introduce folk.

The tall young man whose black hair was fastened in two long braids with silver brooches was named Rannach, and he was some kind of leader. He was very handsome, his features aquiline and somewhat stern until he smiled, and then only sunny. Arcole held out a hand, which Rannach stared at in confusion; then Rannach touched his own to his chest and extended it palm outward. It was, Arcole supposed, the manner of greeting in this unknown land, and he aped the gesture, at which Rannach and the others beamed in approval.

The fat man—though Arcole guessed muscle lay beneath those generous folds of flesh—was named Yazte. He was older, his dark braids paled with strands of gray, his eyes twinkling as he gave the newcomers greeting.

Then Kahteney—whose hair, like Morrhyn's, was unbound, his eyes deep-set, like pools of blue water in the weathered cragginess of his face—smiling grave greeting. Arcole noticed that neither he nor Morrhyn bore weapons other than belt knives, and as the introductions were made he thought that Davyd said these two were *wa-can-eeshas,* which appeared to be some title that set them a little apart from the others.

Finally there was Kanseah, whose hair was braided like Rannach's, dark red as a fox's brush. He was, as best Arcole could judge, of an age with Rannach, but lacked that one's authority, smiling shyly as he welcomed them and quickly retreating, deferring to Rannach and Yazte, who in turn appeared to defer to Morrhyn and Kahteney.

Arcole sensed some subtle order here. Rannach and the other—*ak-ah-mans,* he thought they were called—carried weapons: long-bladed knives and hatchets. Without any suitable frame of reference, he could think only in terms of his homeland, assuming the ak-ah-mans were military leaders and the wa-can-eeshas like the Inquisitors, owners of such magical powers as rendered sharp steel and powder unnecessary. Save neither Morrhyn or Kahteney seemed like Inquisitors, who were, in Arcole's experience, cold and arrogant men. These two seemed only kind, and he obeyed as Morrhyn beckoned, indicating that they follow him down the valley.

Colun and his Grannach fell into cheerful step beside, like an honor guard of animated rocks whose marching song appeared to be "Tiswin," accompanied by a great smacking of lips and much laughter.

Arcole felt Flysse take his hand, and looked, bemused,

from where Davyd walked in lively, if not entirely understood, conversation with Morrhyn to her eyes. They danced
with excitement, blue as cornflowers in the summer sun. She
was smiling happily, her blond hair dancing loose about her
lovely face. "We've come amongst friends," she said. "Oh,
Arcole, I believe we are safe at last."

He looked from her back at their escort and nodded.
"Yes," he allowed, "I think we have."

Surreptitiously, he eased the musket's hammer down, the
striker plate clear of the pan. Then wondered if it was the
slight sounds of those mechanisms or something else that
prompted Morrhyn to turn his head and smile. Arcole smiled
back and slung the gun from his shoulder.

Morrhyn said something to Davyd and the youth turned.
"Morrhyn wonders what our muskets are," he said. "I think
the Matawaye have no such weapons."

"I'll show them, does he wish," Arcole replied. "But if
they've no powder, we'd best reserve what little we have. In
case . . ."

He let his voice trail off, shrugging and smiling: he'd lived
too long with fear of pursuit. In case of what? For fear Governor Wyme send Militia after them? Wyme must surely assume them dead, slain by the demons besieging Grostheim or
the wilderness beasts, starved or drowned. Grostheim might
no longer exist, nor its governor live, and it was unlikely in
the extreme that even did Evander retain its foothold in this
new, strange land much effort would be expended on the
capture of three indentured servants. He touched the scar
burned onto his cheek, the *E* that marked him for the Autarchy as an exile, branded that all know him for a felon, condemned to lifelong servitude in the western territory across
the Sea of Sorrows. He looked back at the sky-assailing
mountains that divided what Evander claimed from this new
land beyond and laughed. Save Colun's Grannach allow it, no
Militia could pass those peaks; nor the demons surmount that
cloud-challenging barrier. No: save for hunting, they'd not
need conserve either powder or shot. They'd come amongst
allies here: it was an odd sensation to feel safe.

"What do you laugh at?" Flysse asked.

"Our good fortune," he replied. "That we find sanctuary at last."

They came down from the neck of the valley to its girth, where the pine-clad walls spread out around a swath of lush grass, a stream laid like a blue ribbon along the center, alders and silvery birches clustering the banks. Four tents stood there, unlike any Arcole had seen before, high structures of tanned hide painted with bright colors that as they came closer he saw were idealized depictions of animals. One was decorated with horse heads, another with wide-winged eagles, the third with what looked like turtles; the fourth was undecorated. Farther down the grass, horses grazed, their forelegs hobbled that they not wander too far; and before each tent stood frames that were hung with round shields and leather quivers that held bows and arrows, long lances propped against the wood. Smoke rose lazy in the summer sun from a central fire that was surmounted with a spit on which the butchered carcass of a deer hung ready to eat. The slight breeze skirled around as they approached, bearing the odor of the roasted meat, and Arcole sniffed, feeling his stomach move in anticipation.

He had been so intent on the scene he'd not realized Colun walked beside him until he heard the Grannach chortle, and looked down to see the rocky little man rubbing his stomach and beaming, pointing at the meat and then his mouth, then slapping Arcole enthusiastically on the back. Or as high as he could reach—which still set Arcole to stumbling. The Grannach were small and it was easy to forget how strong they were.

Colun said something that sounded encouraging, for all Arcole could not understand—God, would he ever comprehend the language of his new home?—so he nodded and smiled back, and walked toward the tents.

It seemed to him, as they all took places on the grass around the fire and the meat was carved, that this was a temporary camp, such as hunters or scouts would make. There were no women or children, nor any signs of long habitation. Instinctively, he counted the horses: one for each

Matawaye—had he got that name right—and six more. He assumed three were pack animals, so likely the remaining trio was for him and Flysse and Davyd to ride.

He swallowed juicy meat and looked at Morrhyn, at Davyd: Could they truly have known how many horses to bring? Where to come, and when? From the look of the grass, he guessed they'd not been here longer than a few days. So—had Colun sent word? Or was it all done sleepy, in dreams? Davyd was a Dreamer, but his nocturnal sendings were all of warnings or safety—of where danger lay and where refuge. Which was gift enough, Arcole thought, to have brought them safely out of Grostheim and then along the Restitution River to the wilderness. And then to hide them from the demons (had Colun not said they were called Tack-in, or some such word?) and—God, it was still hard to believe—persuade them to climb that blank-faced cliff with no possible hope of escape and arrows striking sparks all about them until the blank rock opened and the Grannach pulled them in to safety. And now this welcoming party, as if it was all ordained.

He realized he was staring when Morrhyn smiled and spoke with Davyd, who said, "I think I'm not lonely here. I think Morrhyn is a Dreamer, and Kahteney. I think that's what *wakanisha* means."

His young face was lit with excitement as he spoke, and wonder danced in his eyes. Hardly surprising, Arcole thought, for God knew but Davyd had lived the better part of his life frightened of his talent, terrified it become known and he be taken by the Autarchy, to be burned at the stake. The Autarchy was ruthless in its persecution of all those not its servants who were gifted with magic. That he found himself come amongst folk who cheerfully accepted the dreaming talent must seem to him like passing welcomed through the portals of heaven.

"That's good," Arcole said, "that you're with friends. Perhaps you'll be a wakanisha."

He meant it as a joke, but Morrhyn—seemingly understanding the gist of it—nodded and touched Davyd's shoulder, saying, "Wakanisha," then more that he accompanied with gestures. It seemed to Arcole that he said Davyd *would* be a wakanisha in time. Davyd only smiled, somewhat embarrassed now.

"And the others?" Arcole asked. "They are . . . ak-ahmans?"

Again it seemed that Morrhyn understood the meaning of the unknown words. He was, Arcole decided, a most intelligent and perceptive man. He said, "Akaman," nodding, and indicated Rannach, Yazte, and Kanseah, appending to each other words that sounded like Kom-acht, La-kan-tee, and Nigh-chee. Arcole could not tell whether he gave them surnames or further titles and looked helplessly to Davyd for explanation.

"I think," Davyd said after a further exchange with Morrhyn, "that those are the names of different . . . I'm not sure . . . perhaps families, or people . . ." He groped for the correct word.

"Tribes?" Arcole wondered. "Different clans?"

Davyd spoke again with Morrhyn, who answered slowly, with much gesturing, pointing at each akaman in turn and then at the tents—or, Arcole guessed, at the symbols painted on the leather—repeating the unfamiliar names. When he was done, Davyd said, "I think that's it, that they each lead a clan. Rannach is akaman of the Commacht, Yazte of the Lakanti, and Kanseah of the Naiche."

Those discussed listened attentively to all this, and when Davyd fell silent, nodded encouragingly and spoke all at once, Colun and his Grannach joining in, so that for a while there was a babble that sounded to Arcole somewhat like the noise of a squabbling dog pack.

He leaned close to Flysse and whispered, "Shall we ever understand them?"

"Likely in time," she answered cheerfully. "We'd best, no? For we'll likely spend the rest of our lives with them."

A sudden chill gripped Arcole then, for Flysse had calmly stated a truth that he had not yet entirely accepted. He had planned to escape the clutches of Evander, to escape his life as a branded servant, largely in reaction to indenture. That they might well live out their lives in the wilderness had been a dream that he had not properly faced; indeed, he had not truly thought far past the fact of escaping. Now they were come far beyond the aegis of the Autarchy and stood on the doorstep of a new life amongst their saviors. He knew there could be no turning back, but the immensity of what lay ahead for a moment daunted him. These folk—these Matawaye, had he the name aright—appeared, for all they were friendly, to be little more than savages. Looking at their primitive weapons, their hide tents, he doubted they built cities, thought they likely grubbed some kind of existence from the land. There would be no gaming salons where they lived, nor soirees, nor grand balls—none of those things he had, unconsciously, associated with freedom.

He felt the muscles of his face grow taut, the dead tissue of his brand seeming to burn an instant. Exile to Salvation had been enormity enough. God knew but he'd objected to that, but even so . . . Grostheim, for all it was a poor facsimile of what he had known, was at least a city of a kind. It had been populated with folk who spoke a language he could understand, and in the governor's mansion there had been some small measure, even for indentured servants, of those things he accepted as normal: a glass of wine, albeit stolen; the sound of music, even could he not ply the keys; a pipe of pilfered tobacco. There should be none of that here, he thought. Nor any turning back now: freedom, he realized, had a price.

"What ails you?"

He turned toward Flysse. Her pretty face was become solemn and she touched his hand. He stared at her a moment, then essayed a smile. She was with him, and that was compensation for all loss.

"That we leave much behind," he said, remembering that promise he had once made her, that he would conceal nothing from her. "That we can never go back."

"To Grostheim?" She frowned and shook her head so that the westering sun bounced light all golden off her curls.

"To all we knew," he said. "To our old lives."

"Would you?" She eyed him with amazement. "I'd not. We've a new life before us."

"Yes." He nodded slowly, cautiously. "But it shall not be easy."

"Nor was our escape," she said. "Nor would have been

life in the wilderness. We are fortunate, Arcole. We are safe from the Autarchy and the demons, both; we are amongst good, friendly folk. How can you look so glum?"

Almost, his old self spoke, to tell her that she and Davyd would likely fit this new place better than he. Davyd that he found himself with other Dreamers, without risk of persecution; she because she was born in the countryside and knew its ways. Whilst he was of the cities, a gambler and a duelist, a gentleman. But that was the man he had been, prideful, even arrogant, before the Autarchy set the hot iron to his cheek and sent him across the Sea of Sorrows into exile. That was an Arcole that no longer existed. So he said, "I suppose I'm afraid."

Davyd heard that last and chuckled. "Afraid? You know no fear, Arcole. And what's to be afraid of here?"

He looked at the young man and felt his smile grow genuine. Surely Davyd was no longer the frightened boy he had seen herded terrified onto the *Pride of the Lord,* seeking his protection. He had grown, physically and emotionally. His was the talent that had brought them safe through the wilderness to this new place. He accepted it now, and that acceptance of responsibility matured him. Indeed, it seemed to Arcole that Davyd became their leader here, and perhaps that was the reason for his uneasiness—that he could now only follow. He was not accustomed to feeling helpless.

"Nothing," he answered, and shrugged. "Save that I'm a stranger in a strange land."

Davyd laughed and said, "But a kind land, I think."

Arcole realized the Matawaye and the Grannach had fallen silent as they spoke, and were watching them. He looked at their faces, the Grannach like friendly boulders, the Matawaye like hospitable hawks. He nodded: "Yes."

It was impossible to tell whether Morrhyn had understood his words or merely read the emotions on his face, but the wakanisha reached out to grasp his wrist, and spoke in his odd, guttural language. Kahteney added something, and Arcole looked to Davyd for translation. But Davyd only shrugged and waved his hands in indication of ignorance. Rannach said something, and Colun clapped his hands and repeated it eagerly: "Tiswin!"

Rannach climbed limber to his feet and disappeared awhile into the tent painted with horses' heads. He emerged holding two containers of beaten metal, squatted smiling, and solemnly handed a flask to Arcole, the second to Colun.

The Grannach tilted the pot and swallowed deep and long. Arcole drank slower, remembering the fierce liquor from his sojourn under the mountains. It sat both sweet and tart on his tongue, somewhat like gin, but pleasantly smoother, with an underlying fire that radiated out from his belly to fill his veins and imbue his whole body with a delightful warmth. Perhaps these folk were not so savage, could they produce such a drink. He lowered the flask and hesitated, not sure to whom protocol demand he pass it. Morrhyn nodded to Flysse, who took the container and sipped delicately before handing it on around the circle, favoring Davyd with a warning, maternal glance that was answered with a grin and a swallowing almost enthusiastic as the Grannachs'.

The sun was descended below the western hills by now, the eastern sky become a slowly stretching panoply of blue velvet pricked out with stars and the slim crescent of a new-born moon. A warm wind skirled through the trees flanking the stream, rustling the leaves in a gentle susurration that softly echoed the murmuring of the water. A nightingale sang, and overhead a flight of crows winged roostward, calling noisily to one another. The scent of pine sap drifted on the breeze and a horse whickered softly, answered by its fellows. Arcole took the flask from Kanseah, who smiled shyly, and drank again. He felt the tiswin warming him, more than just his belly, but also his mind, so that his doubts began to drift away and he relaxed, smiling at these newfound companions.

He chuckled as the flask came round again, and drank eagerly. The moon seemed brighter here, the stars more brilliant, the sky even wider than over Salvation. The night hummed with sounds he could barely recognize, like unfamiliar music, and the wind was aromatic with strange perfumes. He beamed at Davyd and said, "You brought us to a good place."

Davyd nodded and said, "Yes." Arcole wondered why he nodded so slowly, and why his own head felt so heavy. Surely he'd not taken more than a swig or two from the flask?

Then Flysse said, "This tiswin is strong, no? Perhaps we've drunk enough."

Davyd shook his head no faster than he'd nodded. Arcole turned his to stare solemnly at his wife. "Shall we go to bed then?" And wondered why she assumed that expression of fond disapproval.

After a while, he was dimly aware of Morrhyn speaking with Rannach—great, good friends, the both; nor any less plump Yazte or diffident Kanseah, or stern Kahteney. And Colun was truly an ally, even was his squat and stumpy figure difficult to make out in the waning light, seeming to waver and shift like a boulder shining with moonlight and cloud-drifted shadow. He wondered why a ghost Davyd sat beside the fleshly reality.

"I think," he said with grave apology, taking care to articulate the words clearly for all they were curiously difficult to shape, "that I am become a trifle drunk."

Flysse said, "Yes," and looked for help to Morrhyn.

The wakanisha smiled and nodded, raising the flask he held and rolling his head, his eyes deliberately crossed. Flysse laughed and pantomimed sleep, folding her hands and resting her head against them. Morrhyn spoke to Rannach, who in turn spoke to Yazte, and both rose smiling to lift Arcole to his feet. Arcole felt both embarrassed and amused, leaning against the two Matawaye with a wide smile and eyes that refused to focus properly. They smelled comfortingly of well-worn buckskins and horse sweat, of the tiswin and more odors that he could not identify. Their arms were strong around him, and he hung his across their shoulders, aware he was drunk and knowing them good, true friends—the which he proclaimed, for all his tongue tripped on the words and they could not understand him. It seemed not to matter. Kanseah and Kahteney helped Davyd up, and Flysse followed as the two men were brought slack-footed to the unmarked tent.

It was shadowy inside, scented sweet with leather and pine sap, and three thickly haired hides were spread around the confines, blankets of bright colors folded on top. The Matawaye lowered Arcole and Davyd onto the furs, and Morrhyn indicated to Flysse where a waterskin hung from the lodgepoles. Kahteney delivered their gear, setting the packs and muskets down at the center of the tent. He seemed nervous of the muskets he carried.

Flysse said, "Thank you," and the Matawaye smiled and gestured and left them alone.

The flap covering the entrance was lowered and the tent grew instantly dark. Outside, Colun chuckled. Flysse spread a blanket over Davyd, who was already snoring softly, and hauled a hide to where Arcole lay. He sighed gustily as she lay down, and reached for her. She fended off his hands as she spread the two blankets across both their beds, and then held him, both still full-clothed.

He rose up on one elbow and stroked her lips, her cheek. "Forgive me?" he asked. "I'm drunk, but I still love you."

Flysse said, "Yes, I know; and I you. Now best you sleep, eh?"

Arcole nodded and groaned. And fell back, instantly asleep.

3 Welcome Friends

"Strange folk," Yazte murmured, and belched softly as he passed the flask to Kahteney.

The Lakanti Dreamer smiled faintly and glanced at Morrhyn. "Are they as you dreamed them, brother?"

Morrhyn shrugged. "Yes and no. As I've told you, only the young one was clear, for he's the only one with the talent, and I saw the others only through his eyes." He chuckled fondly. "He perceives the one named Arcole as a great warrior, and the woman as the most beautiful in all the world."

"She's somewhat skinny for my taste," Yazte offered, "but I suppose she's pretty enough. As for the man . . ." He looked to Colun. "You know them better than any of us, my friend. Is he a great warrior?"

Colun drew blunt fingers through his beard before he answered. "He fought Chakthi's cursed Tachyn bravely enough. With those fire-spitting things they carry. We watched them from the cave," he glanced at Morrhyn, "just as you told us. It was Davyd urged them climb, and Arcole who came last, as befits a warrior. He took an arrow—a nasty wound—but even then his thoughts were for the woman and the boy. Yes, I'd say he's a warrior."

"And Davyd a Dreamer?" Kahteney asked.

Morrhyn nodded solemnly. "I saw him like a torch burning through a foggy night. He's surely the gift, but must learn its proper usage."

"He's young yet," Kahteney said. "He's time to learn."

"Yes." Morrhyn nodded again, his bright eyes clouding an instant. "And the Maker knows, but we've need of Dreamers, eh? You and I, brother, are the only wakanishas the People have now. I've not named my successor, and . . ."

Rannach spoke for the first time. "There's time aplenty for that naming. You sound almost as if it were a thing imperative. As if . . ." He shook his head, eyes hooding.

Morrhyn chuckled, interpreting his expression. "The Maker's not ready for me yet, Rannach. But even so, that time shall come and I'd not leave the clan unguided."

"You'd name this stranger your successor?" Yazte frowned at Morrhyn, turned questioning eyes on Kahteney. "A stripling boy, not even born of the People?"

"Why not?" Morrhyn laughed. "We are all strangers here, no?"

"And he's the Maker's gift," Kahteney added. "And as my brother says—we've need of Dreamers."

Colun, blunt as ever, asked, "Why is it that you have no more Dreamers? By the Maker, I can remember when old Gahyth took Morrhyn for his pupil; and Chazde named Kahteney; and Bakka . . ."

Morrhyn quelled the recitation of names by passing the Grannach the flask. "Things change," he said. "Perhaps the People began to forget the old ways, and so the Maker denied us the talent. Or perhaps it was some doing of the Breakers. I know not; only that amongst all the People there is now only young Taza has the least sign of the gift."

"And he's willful," Kahteney said, eyes clouding as he frowned. "I'd not name him, save he calms."

"Taza's an unbroken colt," Yazte said. "All pride and vanity."

Kahteney nodded. "Nine times now he's come to me, asking that I name him. No," he corrected himself. "*Demanding* that I name him. It seems he cannot understand it is not like that."

"*Will* not," Yazte said. "He dreams and therefore believes himself a Dreamer. He needs a lesson in humility. Ach!" He shook his head. "I'd almost ask that you accept him, that he not wear the warrior's braids and I not get the task of disciplining him. He reminds me somewhat of Chakthi!"

At further mention of that hated name Rannach's face stiffened. His eyes grew bleak; like a hawk's, Morrhyn thought, studying its kill. It was hard for the young akaman, knowing Chakthi had murdered his father; harder still for Rannach to grant Chakthi his life and send the Tachyn akaman into exile beyond the mountains with his lapdog wakanisha and those of his clan who remained loyal after so great a betrayal.

Rannach drank before he spoke, as if he'd wash a sour taste from his mouth. Then: "What news of them?"

The question was directed at Colun, who shrugged and said, "The Tachyn roam the foothills, but this summer went away. I think Chakthi perhaps took them off to fight."

"Fight who?" Yazte asked. "Are there folk past your mountains?"

"There must be," Rannach said, impatience hidden under a soft tone. "Else where did these strangers come from?"

"Indeed," Colun agreed. "Though none of my folk have seen them."

"Then how do you know?" Yazte was become a little slowed by the tiswin.

Or age, Morrhyn thought, for the Maker knows we all grow older. How long have we been in this new land, two years? It seemed a lifetime and yet no time at all. Ket-Ta-Witko seemed both a dream and only yesterday; the Breakers both a distant memory and a daily threat. He was of an age with Yazte: they could not be so old.

"The Tachyn," Colun said with all the ponderous patience of the long-lived Grannach, "have spent themselves against the hills since first we took them east. We brought them through the high passes as was decreed at that first Matakwa, and delivered them to the land beyond the mountains. Then the golans sealed the passes, that none come back." He chuckled hugely. "I remember Chakthi's parting words: 'I shall return one day and slay you all.' Ach! I'd have slain him then, had young Rannach not set the duty of mercy on me. It should have been better, I think—to put my ax in his head, and Hadduth's."

"There was enough blood shed in Ket-Ta-Witko," Rannach said.

Morrhyn clasped his arm, smiling approval. That moment—when he sensed the future of the People in this new land hung on Rannach's decision—had been a proud moment in Morrhyn's life. He had known then that Rannach had learned to judge and weigh and think before acting. Known that the wild young warrior who had slain Chakthi's son, albeit in a fair fight, had matured, that he understood the nuances of the Ahsa-tye-Patiko, the Will that bound all living things into their place in the Maker's great design. And Morrhyn had known then that he would make a fine akaman. Rannach did not smile back.

"Whatever." Colun took up his account again. "He looked for ways. Ach, but he set men to climbing the cliffs and dying when they fell. Sometimes that cur dog Hadduth found our secret openings, and then tried to unlock them. He failed, of course, and more Tachyn died in the attempt—when rocks fell on them, or the stone changed shape and there were no longer any holds." He smiled with malicious innocence. "They gave up after a while, but always they patrolled the cliffs and the foothills. Like scavenging coyotes seeking an easy kill. Ach, it gives me great pleasure to contemplate Chakthi's frustration. Almost, it's better than killing him."

"We made a pledge," Rannach said uneasily. "That we'd not bloody Ket-Ta-Thanne. Not break the Ahsa-tye-Patiko again; not kill a brother."

"Chakthi's your brother?" Colun's deep voice was carefully neutral. "When he took his followers away did he not abrogate those bonds? How can he and his followers be still of the People?"

Rannach hesitated; Morrhyn waited on his reply.

"The Tachyn were created by the Maker," Rannach said slowly, the words emerging painful from his mouth. "They are Matawaye, no matter what Chakthi did, no matter what Hadduth did. No matter that they forget the Will, I promised them life."

"Chakthi promises you death," the Grannach returned.

"But to do that he must cross your mountains," Rannach said, and smiled. "So why do you believe he fights?"

"They went away," Colun said, "all of them. For a while the foothills were empty. I took men down to look, but there were no Tachyn there. It was too early for the summer hunting, and I thought perhaps they'd given up. But then Morrhyn sent word we should watch for the strangers and the Tachyn came back—in smaller groups." He shrugged. "Then these strangers came, and as best I can understand Davyd, they fled a battle. I may be wrong: it is only what I suspect."

He looked to Morrhyn, who took up the story: "I told you of my dreaming—that folk came from across a great water, such as I've never seen, on vast canoes with huge sails. I've dreamed of a strange place built all of wood, where they live all the time and never roam. They chop down trees and burn the grass so that they can seed strange plants. They are not like us."

Kanseah said, wary, "The Breakers?"

"No"—Morrhyn shook his head—"not the Breakers. As best I understand Davyd's dreams, and his words, these are folk come from a faraway land. I suspect that Chakthi resents their presence in what he considers *his* country, and that Colun's right—he brings the Tachyn against the wooden place. I've seen Davyd's dreams of fire and battle, and I think that these strangers have escaped this wooden place. Still, there's much I need learn about them; much we all need learn, now we know we are not alone."

"These strangers can no more cross the Grannach's mountains than Chakthi's Tachyn," Yazte said.

"Likely not," Morrhyn allowed. "But they are very different to us, and some, I think, own magic of a kind. So best we learn—in case."

"What do you say?" Yazte asked. "That you'd go seeking others?"

"Perhaps not that." Rannach shrugged. "But Morrhyn thinks these new-come folk are divided amongst themselves, in a way I cannot properly understand, and are there more like these three, I'd know of it."

He spread his hands in a gesture of incomprehension and Yazte turned to Morrhyn for explanation.

"I think that some are lesser than others," the wakanisha said. "This is a thing I've seen in Davyd's dreams, but I cannot explain it properly. It is something to do with the marks they wear on their faces."

"The woman, Flysse, has such a mark on her shoulder,"

Colun offered. Then scowled as Yazte's brows rose speculatively. "Marjia saw it and told me."

"I thought that was decoration," Rannach said.

"Ach, strange decoration!" Colun snorted. "Those are such marks as hot iron makes. I've seen such marks on our smiths, when they've burned themselves."

"What manner of folk would set hot iron to their own faces?" Kahteney's tone was horrified. "Are they mad?"

"I do not think they did it themselves," Morrhyn said, "or wanted it done. I think it is something to do with rank, or . . ." He hesitated, seeking to wrap his mind around a concept alien to the People. "The ownership of human beings; like the markings a man puts on his horse."

Yazte's plump face creased in a mighty frown, disgust and disbelief mingled there. "You say these strangers *own* one another?"

"I think it is something like that." Morrhyn sighed. "Understand that all I know of them is what I've gleaned from Davyd's dreams, and what little of his language I can understand."

"Do they claim ownership of one another," Yazte said, his tone one of horror, "then they can be not much better than the Breakers. How can one man claim to own another?"

"I know not," Morrhyn said, "but I think these folk do."

Kahteney said, "The youngster, Davyd, learns apace—likely we can find out from him."

"Yes." Morrhyn ducked his head in tentative agreement. "But I've the impression he knows less of their world than the man, Arcole. Davyd looks up to that one like a child to his father. I think it's from Arcole that we shall learn more."

Rannach looked to Colun. "What more can you tell us, old friend? They spent a while with you, and you must surely have learnt somewhat about them."

The Grannach scratched his bearded cheek thoughtfully. "Arcole's back is striped," he said, "all cut and scarred. As if someone had lashed him."

"No!" It was Kanseah who spoke, his eyes wide with horror. "Are these people monsters?"

Colun shrugged. "As Morrhyn says—they are different. I

tell you only what I've seen. But they were not such marks as a man gets by accident."

"What else?" Rannach urged.

"Ach, hand me that flask that I might loosen my tongue." Colun waited for the pot and drank deep before he spoke again. "Davyd is bright. He's mightily curious, and he accepted our ways easier than the others. Flysse stayed mostly by Arcole's side—remember, he was sore wounded—and Marjia took a great liking to her, which says much. She's brave." He chuckled, shaking his shaggy head. "You should have seen her coming up that cliff! She'd have turned back to her man, had Arcole not urged her on and we seized her."

"Their courage," Rannach said, "is not in question."

"No," Colun agreed, "but still a point in their favor. Is Morrhyn right, then they fled this wooden village like untamed horses the corral. And made their way through Chakthi's land, which must have taken some doing."

"They'd Morrhyn for a guide," Rannach said.

"Yes." Colun nodded. "But even so, I doubt that was an easy journey."

Morrhyn smiled, thinking of that journey he'd made with Rannach, from the high hills all across Ket-Ta-Witko, with Breakers all around and the Tachyn, too. He felt a kinship with these refugees: their departure from all they knew into the unknown world of the Grannach caverns, to Ket-Ta-Thanne, seemed a like pilgrimage. And there was that about Davyd that excited and troubled him, for a destiny lay on him like shadows seen past the fire's glow, all shifting and unguessable. Strands of those many dreams he'd known on the Maker's Mountain wound about Davyd, so complex he could not unravel them but only admit the absolute conviction that Davyd was linked inextricably to the fate of the People, their fate to his. He could not explain it to the others, not even Kahteney, not past the need to honor Rannach's promise of sanctuary for all exiles. But in the marrow of his bones and the certainty of his dreaming, he *knew,* and so the People accepted. He was still the Prophet in their eyes, and for all he'd not own that title, they took his word as if he were Buffalo Father come back out of the First Days to advise First Man and First Woman. It was a burden he could not reject for all its weight and all his doubt: the People looked to him for guidance, and now, even when he claimed a lack of clear knowledge, they laughed and reminded him of what he'd done to bring them to Ket-Ta-Thanne, and trusted him implicitly and totally as babes their parents. And so he could only dream and seek to untangle the tortuous strands of that oneiric web, and say that Davyd and the others must be brought safe to the Promised Land.

He heard Rannach say, "Tell us about their fire-sticks," and set aside his musings and gave his attention back to the discussion. Those things were surely interesting.

Colun frowned. "Those," he said, "are strange things. I've studied them, and they appear to be constructions of wood and metal, but not such as we make, and I can barely understand how they work. There's a black powder they pour into the metal tube, and it burns when they strike the metal pieces together. Flame and a loud sound like thunder come from the tube and spit a metal ball a great distance—farther than any arrow flies. But there's much to-do about pouring in the powder and the ball. A bow is a better weapon, I think; it makes less noise, and it works much faster."

"But they killed Tachyn with these things?" Rannach asked.

"Yes," Colun replied. "And when the Tachyn were hit, they did not get up again. It was as if they struck with thunderbolts, and the metal balls made great holes in them."

"How much farther than an arrow?" Rannach asked.

"I did not measure the distances exactly," Colun said, somewhat disgruntled by the interrogation, "but perhaps twice the distance. Why?"

"Because if these three have such weapons," Rannach answered, "then likely all these strangers do."

"So?" Yazte reached for his blanket, draping it about his wide shoulders. The night grew old and colder, and this weighty conversation seemed to damp the warmth the fire and the tiswin gave. "What's that to us?"

"Do you not remember the fight at the Meeting Ground?" Rannach looked about the firelit circle of faces. "When the Breakers' magic sent their shafts farther than ours? Should they find us . . ." He shaped a sign of warding, glancing around as if he momentarily anticipated attack. "Then such far-firing things would be very useful. And if these over-the-mountains people come against us . . ."

Kanseah said, "I saw Perico fall then. I could not flight a shaft so far."

"These folk are not Breakers," Yazte said.

"No." Rannach's face was planed grave by light and shadow. He looked, Morrhyn thought, as Racharran had when he thought grave on the future, the father reflected in the face of the son. "But it would seem they set hot iron to men's faces and the shoulders of women; and that they lash men as we'd not animals. And they possess fire-sticks that throw thunderbolts farther than arrows can fly. And Morrhyn believes some of them own magic."

He paused and Kahteney asked, "What do you say, akaman?"

Rannach thought a moment, even now not entirely comfortable with that title, with that weight of duty. Then: "I say that before Morrhyn dreamed of these three strangers we believed ourselves alone in Ket-Ta-Thanne. That the People lived secure behind the mountains, and that only the Tachyn dwelt to the east. Now we know it is not like that—that others than the Tachyn live there, and seem to own strange powers. I know that they are not Breakers, but what if they are *like* the Breakers? What if they, too, seek conquest?"

"Then we fight them," Yazte said.

"It was a hard fight against the Breakers," Rannach gave back, "and too many died. The Maker knows, but we are few here. I'd find out all I can about these others—how many there are, and how they live; what strength they have; what magic. I'd not see the People attacked all unsuspecting again."

Morrhyn stared at him, sensing where his thoughts went, and said quickly, "That's wise, but first we'll bring these refugees home, eh? See them settled amongst us, and learn to speak with them properly, so we understand them, and they us. Learn what we can of their world and its ways."

"Yes." Rannach nodded. His face was somber; Morrhyn wondered if he knew how much like his father he became. "But then . . ."

"I'll look for dreams," Morrhyn said, cutting him off. "Seek answers there."

Rannach looked at the wakanisha out of eyes older than his face. "You've tried that, no?" He smiled: a thin expression. "And only dreamed of Davyd, of what he knows and sees. Did you not tell me the mountains divide us from this other world so firm your dreams cannot climb them, but become all confused?"

Morrhyn nodded. Around the edges of his mind he felt clouds gather like the building of a storm. For an instant, he wondered if he had done the right thing, bringing these exiles to Ket-Ta-Thanne. It was surely fulfillment of the pledge Rannach had given, that he'd wholeheartedly supported, but did it bring fresh tribulation to the People? Did Rannach contemplate what he feared, then perhaps all his dreaming only delivered the People to more conflict, or a few to death: he'd not see any more. He had not seen Racharran die—he felt he should have; should have dreamed of that betrayal: the guilt lived with him—and he'd not see Racharran's son slain. He thought he could not face Lhyn with that awareness, not more guilt.

"Best that we seek answers of the Maker," Kahteney said into the sudden silence. "That before we decide aught else. We bring these strangers home, and then . . ." He glanced at Morrhyn. "Pahé?"

Morrhyn nodded. "Yes: pahé. And I'd give the root to Davyd, also."

The Lakanti Dreamer frowned, eyes narrowed in surprise. "He's not yet of the People, Morrhyn, even less a wakanisha. What of the rituals?"

Morrhyn hesitated, pondering awhile before he spoke. "Save they elect to live apart from us, they shall be adopted into the People," he said at last. "And are we to learn of their world, then we must be able to communicate with them. What understanding we have so far is got through dreams— through what I've seen of Davyd's, and what mine have planted in his head. So, does he take pahé, I believe he'll learn our tongue the quicker."

"Perhaps." Kahteney stroked his hawkish nose, not yet convinced. "But he cannot know anything of the Ahsa-tye-

Patiko. Does he even know of the Maker? You'd take a
stranger and introduce him to our mysteries—what shall the
People make of that?"

"Young Taza," Yazte murmured, "will be furious."

"It's a thing unprecedented," Kahteney said.

"I know." Morrhyn smiled. "As were the Breakers, our
coming to this land. A new land and new times, brother."

"Even so." Kahteney shifted uncomfortably. "I am not
sure it is the right thing."

"Does the Ahsa-tye-Patiko deny it?" Morrhyn asked
gently.

"No." Kahteney shook his head, fixing troubled eyes on
Morrhyn. "But still . . ."

Morrhyn lowered his head, thinking. The others waited:
patience was a virtue of the People, and they did not expect
or need instant responses, but allowed a man time to gather
his thoughts that he might express them clearly. Morrhyn
hoped he did the right thing: he believed it was necessary.
Since first he had encountered Davyd's mind wandering like
some lost soul in the Dream World, he had felt destiny gathered about the unwitting youth. What, he could not discern,
save that it should influence the People. But still he trod
dangerous ground: it was, indeed, as Kahteney said, a thing
unprecedented, and there would surely be those objected.
Nonetheless, he felt certain it was needful. The very appearance of Davyd and his companion refugees spoke of a
strange, unknown world beyond the mountains. Surely it was
wisest—safest—that the People gained knowledge of the
strangers. And how else than through speech? And how
swifter to obtain that goal than through the oneiric communication the pahé root allowed? And if Rannach contemplated
what he feared, then best communication be established fast
as possible.

When he had the shape of his thoughts defined, and the
words to express them formed, he spoke.

The others listened. The akamans deferred to Kahteney—
this was a matter primarily of concern to the Dreamers—and
it was the Lakanti who answered first. "I cannot argue your
reasoning," he said, "but still I am not sure in my heart. Do
we make a compromise?"

Morrhyn nodded his acceptance.

"Then let us bring them to the People," Kahteney suggested. "Do they choose to become Matawaye, then you and I should seek answers of the Maker in our dreams, and do our dreams confirm what you wish, then I shall support you and Davyd shall take the pahé."

Morrhyn said, "That is fair," and looked to the three akamans for agreement.

Rannach said, "I abide by your decision."

"And I," Yazte echoed.

Kanseah nodded, murmuring a soft affirmative.

"Then it is decided," Morrhyn said. "Tomorrow we depart the hills and bring them to the People."

"That settled," Colun said, "have you any more tiswin?"

4

Flysse smiled as Arcole groaned, and passed him the waterskin. He muttered, "Thank you," and spilled a flow of tepid water down his throat.

"Perhaps the stream would refresh you," she suggested.

He began to nod, but thought better of it. His head throbbed, and the warmth the tiswin had delivered seemed curdled into a sour pool that weighted his belly and filled his mouth with the taste of ashes. He licked his lips and glanced around the confines of the tent. The entry flap was thrown back and morning sunlight shone in painful lances against his eyes: he groaned again. Davyd lay snoring beneath a blanket; Flysse looked to have already visited the stream. Her face was bright with excitement, and wet tendrils of golden hair curled on her slender neck.

"It's strong," he said thickly, "that tiswin."

"Taken to excess," she answered with censorious solicitude, "I suppose it would be."

Arcole scowled, then saw the mischievous smile she wore and found its match. "You mock me, woman."

"I?" Flysse folded demure hands to her breast. "Would I mock you, husband? Why, I was just about to bring you breakfast, thinking you'd likely be hungry. A portion of cold venison from last night's dinner; there are still some cuts left—fine, greasy cuts, all larded with fat. Perhaps some marrow."

"God, no!" The notion was unpleasant enough Arcole forgot not to shake his head and winced at the pain. "Food is the last thing I want."

"What do you want, then?"

"Sympathy," he replied, mournfully.

"Bathe first," she said, laughing now. "And when you're clean I'll give you sympathy."

"Flysse, you are a stern wife." This time he remembered not to move his head. "And I love you for it."

"And I, it would seem, love a drunkard."

"Not me." He took her hands, his voice earnest. "You've my promise I shall take this brew only in moderation from now on."

"And I'll take your word," she said. "Now, do you take Davyd and go bathe?"

He sighed and crawled to where Davyd lay.

The lad opened his eyes and smiled hugely. "God, but I feared I'd dreamed it all." He sat up, throwing off his blanket, gesturing about the tent. "Isn't this wonderful?"

"Yes," Arcole said, envying the recuperative powers of youth. Perhaps he grew old. Surely Davyd had drunk as much as he, but appeared to feel no ill effects. No, he told himself as Davyd rose, I was wounded and lay healing whilst Davyd drank Colun's tiswin and got used to it. Surely that's the reason: it must be. But even so, I'll drink wary from now on.

"Shall we bathe?" he asked.

Davyd nodded eagerly. "Where's Morrhyn?"

"I don't know: I just woke up." He beckoned Davyd to follow him. "Come."

They quit the tent for a morning all filled with sunlight and birdsong. A warm wind blew down from the encircling hills, scenting the air with the smell of pine sap and fresh grass, and all across the valley bright yellow flowers waved heavy petals in the breeze. Contrary to Flysse's threatened promise, the carcass of the deer was gone, and only embers smoldered in the stone-circled fire pit. Colun and his Grannach sat there, drinking tea and spooning up some kind of porridge. Arcole smiled faint thanks and waved more enthusiastic negation as Colun raised a bowl, pantomiming the act of eating. Morrhyn and the one called Kahteney sat in earnest discussion outside the horse-head-painted tent, nodding as they went by, and farther along the three akamans were working on the horses with combs of carved bone.

Davyd hailed them all like old friends, and was answered

in like fashion. Arcole nodded politely, not moving his hurting head too much, and followed Davyd to the water.

They found a place where alders overhung the stream with a green panoply, the twisted trunks hiding them from view, and stripped. Davyd entered the water with a merry cry, Arcole more cautiously. The stream was chill even under the heat of the summer sun, and he gasped as he plunged beneath the surface. Then it was only invigorating; he dunked his head and felt the cold water wash away the aftereffects of the tiswin, and when he emerged he was able to offer Davyd a genuine smile.

"Do the—how do you say it?—Matawaye all live like this?" He scrubbed himself with sand. "In tents, out in the open?"

"I don't know."

"I thought . . ." Arcole shook his head, pleased that it no longer hurt.

"Thought what?" Davyd asked, clambering onto the bank and rolling in the grass like some young animal.

"I don't really know." Arcole followed him. "That Morrhyn had told you all about them."

"No." Davyd sat up, his face serious now. "I know that we shall be safe with them, but how they live . . ." He shrugged again.

"Yet you speak with them," Arcole said.

"Somewhat, but not really so much." Davyd tilted his head to empty water from his ears, brow creasing as he sought to express himself. "It's as if Morrhyn taught me in dreams, but the words—the sounds—are different when they're real. It's like . . ." He pursed his lips, eyes narrowing. "Listen, there was a fellow I knew in Bantar, a pickpocket called Short Thom. He had a dog called Sam, who did all kinds of tricks on Short Thom's word." He chuckled at the memory. "Short Thom would set Sam to dancing, or somersaulting, and while folk watched, Thom would lift their purses. He claimed Sam understood everything he said. God, but he talked to that dog more than he did people! But I think Sam just learnt what the sounds asked him to do, and didn't really understand. It's somewhat like that with me. Do you understand?"

"I think so." Arcole nodded. Then: "What happened to them?"

"To who?" Davyd asked.

Once Arcole would have corrected his grammar. It seemed pointless now and so he only said, "Short Thom and his dog called Sam."

Davyd's smile faded. His eyes went a cloudy green. "The Militia arrested Thom," he said bitterly. "Sam went to his defense and a Militiaman stuck him with a bayonet. Thom was sent to the prison barges."

They all had such memories, Arcole thought, and perhaps Davyd more than he or Flysse. Evander was a dark and gloomy country, the Autarchy a cruel parliament; he wondered vaguely what hierarchy governed this new land. He set a hand firm on Davyd's shoulder.

"All that's behind us now. We're free and amongst friends, no?"

"Yes." Davyd nodded, brightening again. "And I'm hungry. Do we see what's for breakfast?"

Arcole hesitated, then felt his stomach answer. Best eat hearty, he thought, suspecting a long ride lay ahead of them, and that it would be no easy journey. Then: God, have Flysse or Davyd sat a horse before? He nodded, and they dressed and made their way back to the camp.

Flysse was settled by the fire, surrounded by Colun and his Grannach and the five Matawaye. She was pointing at things—a kettle, the tripod that held it, the bowls—and her hosts were naming the items while she dutifully repeated the words.

She laughed as Arcole and Davyd approached, holding up a dish of beaten metal and saying something that sounded to Arcole like a cough. He saw Morrhyn touch her shoulder and correct her pronunciation, then nod his approval as Flysse repeated the word. It now sounded to Arcole like the sound of a dog's bark, and he wondered if he could ever learn this odd language.

He smiled as the Dreamer gestured, the hand signs easy of

interpretation, found a place at Flysse's side, and took the offered bowl.

The porridge was thick and restorative, salted and laced with wild honey. He washed it down with tea, and after he had eaten two bowls, proclaimed himself filled.

Rannach spoke then, and when he was done, Davyd announced that he thought the akaman said it was time to leave. This Arcole found easy to understand, for the Matawaye and the Grannach all rose briskly and set to cleaning the eating implements, then kicked out the fire and set to striking the leather tents. Arcole was impressed by their efficiency: the tents were down and bundled in moments, packed onto the spare horses, and the others readied. Morrhyn gestured at the exiles' gear and spoke to Davyd, pointing at the packhorses. Davyd said, "I think he'd stow our stuff with theirs."

Arcole studied the horses they must ride. The animals were smaller than those of his homeland, lean and muscular, with a look of speed and agility. They had no stirrups, he saw, and only thin saddles of lightly padded leather, each animal guided by a single rein that was woven into a simple halter around the muzzle. He could ride; indeed, he had been considered a fine horseman, but he wondered how he would manage with so basic a harness. And he doubted Flysse and Davyd could manage at all.

He nodded his agreement and watched as packs and muskets were lashed amongst the tents. The Matawaye, he noticed, stowed their quivers and shields on fastenings behind the crude saddles, thinking that he must learn to carry his musket thus—or learn to use a bow from off a horse's back, which he thought must surely be very difficult.

Then Colun and his folk were clustering around, bidding them what Arcole guessed were farewells. He clutched the Grannach's hand and offered thanks for all his help and hospitality. The words of both went knowledgeless, but the meaning was understood: a bond existed that had no need of words.

Then Arcole gasped as Rannach drove his lance into the ground and vaulted astride a bay stallion. Then again as plump Yazte did the same, and Kanseah, like limber gymnasts. Morrhyn and Kahteney mounted less dramatically, but still athletic, simply taking hold of saddle and mane and springing astride.

Arcole said, "I think this shall not be easy."

Flysse said, "Why not?" And went to the roan horse Rannach held for her, and leapt onto the saddle.

Arcole gaped. The Grannach and the Matawaye laughed at his expression.

"I was born on a farm," Flysse said; somewhat smugly, he thought. "I learnt to ride horses long ago, with no saddles on them."

He nodded and looked to Davyd, who was staring at the buckskin Morrhyn held for him with an expression that reminded Arcole of his looks before the sea serpent came to attack the *Pride of the Lord*.

"I've never been on a horse before," he said.

"It's not so hard," Arcole returned.

"It's big." Davyd's voice was wary as his look. "I'll fall off."

"We all do," Arcole said. "I did, at first."

Davyd's expression suggested that he doubted this, and Arcole saw that he was torn between embarrassment and disinclination. He felt sorry for the youth, remembering his own first equestrian ventures. The pony had seemed gigantic, the ground too far below him. And that little animal, he reminded himself, had been equipped with proper saddle, stirrups, and full harness. Then Flysse heeled her animal closer and smiled fondly at Davyd.

"It's really not so difficult."

Davyd refused to meet her eyes, his cheeks growing red. "How do I get on?"

"Mount," Arcole said unthinking. Then frowned—how, indeed, without Davyd be subjected to further embarrassment? He said, "I'll help you. Look, take the rein and the mane . . ." He set Davyd's hands in place and cupped his own, stooping. "Now put your foot here."

Davyd obeyed and Arcole took his weight, seeing him settled astride the buckskin.

"Hold with your knees."

The horse turned and Davyd swayed precariously, crying

out as he lost his seat and fell to the ground. His shout was followed by a stream of curses that fouled the morning air.

Flysse said, "Davyd!" Then, "Are you hurt?"

"No." He clambered upright, rubbing at his shoulder. His face was flushed and sullen. Arcole was grateful neither the Matawaye or the Grannach laughed. "Do we try again?" he asked.

Davyd hesitated, scowling, then nodded and came warily around the buckskin. Morrhyn brought his own horse alongside, Kahteney on the other flank, so that the buckskin stood quiet and the two wakanishas were positioned to support Davyd. Or catch him, Arcole thought as he lifted the youth back onto the saddle. This time Davyd kept his seat.

Arcole turned to his own animal. It was a rangy-looking gray that swung its head to study him as Kanseah passed him the rein. He stroked the animal's muzzle, murmuring softly as he braced himself to mount. I can do this, he told himself. I must, for I'll not be helped into the saddle like a child. Even so, he was less than confident. He took the rein and the mane as he'd shown Davyd and launched himself up. The gray snorted and skittered as he landed, and he clamped his thighs tight on its ribs, aware of the Matawaye watching, and Flysse. He gritted his teeth, determined to retain his dignity, and was thankful he stayed astride. Managing the horse, however, was another problem: the simple saddle was surprisingly comfortable, but he found the absence of stirrups disturbing, and could not at first decide how the single rein could guide the animal.

Then Kanseah touched his arm, smiling shyly, and showed him how the single length of rawhide might be drawn to the left to turn the horse in that direction, and how its laying against the neck turned it the other. Heels came into it, but such nuances he would leave for later—for now he was satisfied just to remain seated.

"You see," he heard Flysse call, "it's not so difficult."

The gray had begun to curvet and he was concentrated too much on holding his seat to answer, so he only offered what he hoped was a nonchalant smile until the beast calmed, accepting his weight and unfamiliar smell. He looked to where Davyd sat, still flanked by the Dreamers, and wondered how far they would travel this day, and how the youth would feel at journey's end. Pained, he guessed, and likely he not much better: it had been a long time since he'd sat a horse.

Then Rannach spoke, pointing to the east, and the Matawaye called to the Grannach and the Grannach answered. Hands were raised in last farewell and the horses heeled forward. Arcole chanced a last glance back, and saw Colun wave even as the squat little man roared laughter.

Rannach and Kanseah took the lead as they rode slowly down the valley, and Yazte the tail. Morrhyn and Kahteney held the nervous Davyd in his saddle, talking the while. Arcole and Flysse came behind. Arcole thought she rode better than he.

"I'm not used to this," he said.

"You're a gentleman." Flysse chuckled. The wind coming down from the hills blew out her golden curls and her eyes sparkled: Arcole thought she looked lovelier than ever, as if this wild free life suited her. "You're accustomed to fancy riding."

"I'm accustomed to civilized tack," he returned, aware he sounded a little grumpy.

"And a stableboy to groom your horse at day's end," she gave him back, "and hand you a stirrup cup, and pull off your boots."

He affected an expression of puzzled solemnity. "Shan't you tend to those matters? Are they not wifely duties?"

Flysse said "No!" and pranced her mount close, threatening to dislodge him.

"God, woman!" he cried, his alarm not entirely feigned. "Shall you knock me down?"

"Do you expect such services of me," she answered, smiling, "yes."

His face grew serious a moment and he reached to touch her hand, then snatched it back as the gray skittered. "Those things are gone," he said. "I'm not that man now."

"No." Flysse beamed and shook her head, so that sunlight danced in her hair. "And better for it, I think."

"Yes." Arcole nodded. Then indicated Davyd, ahead of them. "But I believe he'll need tender ministrations this night. Do I recall my first venture ahorse, I could not believe so much of me ached."

"Yes, poor Davyd," Flysse said, her expression grown solemn. "I hope our new friends carry balms with them."

The People lived largely on horseback, and children were set astride their parents' mounts when first they began to walk; for them, riding was natural as walking. What was a man without a horse? It had not occurred to any of them, that there could exist any folk other than the Grannach who did not ride, or would suffer pain from the experience.

Davyd did. Indeed, had Morrhyn and Kahteney not ridden beside him, and the pace not been slow, he would have flung himself from the saddle simply to escape the agony of the buckskin's bony spine driving like a hammer against his buttocks, whilst its ribs heaved between his legs, threatening to stretch his thighs and split him apart. He could not believe riding was so painful, or so uncertain. It seemed to him as unnatural as committing a ship to the unknown depths of the sea, and through all that long day he need tell himself he had overcome his fear of water, and therefore must surely overcome this newfound torture. Besides, Flysse was witness to his efforts, she apparently quite at ease on horseback, and it embarrassed him that he was so ungainly and felt so nervous. He'd not look a fool in her eyes, or in Arcole's, and so he struggled to ignore his discomfort and learn to master this unlikely new skill.

The pain helped in that: it consumed him, so that as the morning passed into afternoon and they did not halt, he began to forget his apprehension in the encompassment of the overwhelming ache that possessed his entire body. It was not so much the falls—for despite all the ministrations of Morrhyn and Kahteney, he still tumbled from time to time—as the unnatural position and the constant collision of his body with the horse's. He thought he would prefer the swaying deck of a ship to this, and that likely he should never learn to ride with the casual elegance the Matawaye displayed. But he gritted his teeth and determined not to give in to the pain, and must he sometimes blink tears from his eyes, then at least he did not cry out—save when he fell—and told himself he was not a child to whine and whimper at discomfort, but a man who would suffer his fate in silence.

Still, he was mightily glad when they halted. He watched the Matawaye spring lithe from their saddles, Flysse and Arcole dismount slower, and endeavored to emulate them only to find himself seemingly paralyzed. His legs would not move; they seemed melded with the horse's ribs, and he fused in place like some animate equestrian statue. His left hand was locked around the rein, his right in the buckskin's mane, and try as he might, he could not force his fingers open. The buckskin whickered, tossing its head impatiently as it saw its fellows unsaddled and turned out to graze. Davyd mouthed a curse and closed his eyes as the others gathered round. He felt his cheeks grow hot and knew he blushed, and when he opened his eyes and still could not move, and saw Flysse frowning solicitously, he experienced a terrible chagrin. God, but she must think him a useless boy, a fool!

"Stiff, eh?" Arcole set a hand on the buckskin's neck. "Me, too; and I've ridden before. The first time is always the worst."

Davyd nodded silently, quite unable to speak for the mortification he felt. The pain was nothing compared to this humiliation.

Arcole chuckled and slapped Davyd's thigh, which somehow Davyd did not feel, and said companionably, "I remember my first time—two grooms had to lift me down. Shall I help you?"

Davyd nodded again.

"Then let go the rein." Gently, Arcole prised his fingers open. "And the mane, eh?"

Davyd made his unwilling hands obey.

"Now ease your legs and swing down. I'll catch you."

Davyd tried to follow the instruction, succeeding in pitching sideways off the horse so that the buckskin snorted and skittered. Arcole caught him, grunting as his own back protested, and lowered him to the ground. Davyd swayed, the world spinning around his head for a moment. His legs seemed not to be there, or the fleshly columns unboned: he sagged, thinking he must fall down. Arcole held him upright and he clutched helplessly at the older man, who set a supportive arm around him and said, "Let's walk a little, eh? Until you've your balance back."

Davyd doubted most sincerely that he could walk—perhaps might never again—but Flysse came up on his other side and put an arm about his waist and offered him her shoulder, so he took it and ground his teeth and forced himself to pace out the painful steps.

He was surprised that in a while a measure of normal feeling returned and he could walk unaided, albeit like some frail ancient. He ached all over, and could not understand why his arms and shoulders hurt so. The rest was obvious—human legs were not designed to enwrap the barrel of a horse's ribs, nor buttocks to suffer the assault of the animal's spine. But why did *all* of him ache so? As they walked slowly back to where the Matawaye were already setting up camp, he noticed that they were all somewhat bowed of leg, and wondered if they were somehow designed by God to fit astride their animals, or grew on horseback. He, he knew beyond doubting, was not.

Morrhyn smiled with puzzled sympathy as they approached, and held up a pouch, speaking.

Davyd was altogether too immersed in discomfort to attempt to understand, and it fell to the others to explain as best they could.

"I think," Flysse said, "that he's some ointment might help you."

"I think nothing can help me," Davyd moaned in reply. Then cursed himself for acting the child and straightened his back—which sparked fresh shivers of agony. "I'll be all right."

Arcole said mildly, "My first time, I lay in a hot tub for hours. Then my mother rubbed me with liniment for another."

"Did it," Davyd asked, hoping he did not sound too desperate, "work?"

Arcole nodded solemnly: "After a few days."

Davyd said forlornly, "Oh, God!" And then miserably, "There's no hot water here. Not for a tub."

"Even so." Flysse nodded in Morrhyn's direction. "Likely our new friends have medicines that will help."

Davyd nodded and walked stiff-legged to Morrhyn.

They had halted in the lee of a tall bluff where a cascade sprang out from the rock to arc down into a stone-encircled pool before spilling over to feed a stream that ran swift to the west. A mountain meadow spread green below the cliff, wind-sculpted pines and green ash trees rustled in the breeze, and blooms of yellow and blue quilted the grass. Swallows darted overhead and the descending sun lit cliff and meadow and water with mellow radiance. Morrhyn took Davyd's arm and led him past the pool, around a spur of overhanging stone to another basin.

This was not fed by any cascade, but rather from some internal source that agitated the surface with gaseous bubbles. The air shimmered there and smelled of sulfur. Morrhyn pointed at the pool and spoke. Davyd listened, struggling to understand, but what knowledge of the People's tongue the Dreamer had instilled in him seemed blurred by his pain. Still, Morrhyn's gestures made clear that he wished Davyd to undress and climb into the water. Davyd looked around. The steaming basin was hidden from the campsite, but even so he hesitated, thinking that Flysse might come seeking him and find him naked. The notion was simultaneously alarming and exciting, and he blushed afresh.

Morrhyn spoke again, pantomiming the ache-boned stance of a man in pain, bending his back and rubbing at his buttocks with such an expression of feigned agony that Davyd must laugh. The bright blue eyes caught his and twinkled, then Morrhyn pointed toward the camp and shrugged, and patted his buttocks again. Then thrust a finger at the pool and held up the pouch, straightening his back and sighing in exaggerated parody of relief.

Davyd understood, even without the benefit of language: he nodded and began to strip. And as he did, he wondered that he trusted this silver-haired man like no other, save Arcole. It was as if the dreams had bonded them: he could not doubt Morrhyn.

Save, perhaps, for an instant as he entered the water. It was so hot he thought his skin must sear, and as he disturbed the surface he inhaled a lungful of thick, sulfurous air that set him to coughing, his eyes watering. He spat, looking to Morrhyn, who gestured that he immerse himself. There was such calm confidence in the Dreamer's eyes that Davyd felt his doubts assuaged. Morrhyn would not, he somehow knew, allow him to come to any harm. He felt the wakanisha marked him for some purpose he could not yet properly comprehend, nor would until they were able to speak properly; converse as . . . not equals, for he recognized that Morrhyn owned such knowledge as he could only guess at . . . but as if he were Morrhyn's pupil, and all that knowledge his for the asking.

So he lay down in the vaporous water and felt it ease his aches, the fumes no longer stinking but soporific. He sighed happily and closed his eyes, stretching out until only his face rose above the water. He would have slept there—should have been quite content to spend the night in that comfortable embrace—but Morrhyn touched his shoulder and spoke, and when he reluctantly opened his eyes, handed him a pinch of some herb. He swallowed the stuff, and in a while felt a vague and pleasant numbness pervade his limbs, as if the combination of the hot spring and the herb dismissed the day's pain.

He was reluctant to emerge, save that his belly began to rumble and he saw the sun fall down below the western hills. Morrhyn indicated that he should dry himself and dress. So he climbed out, marveling that he could move limber again, and followed the wakanisha back to where a fire was lit and the evening meal cooking.

Flysse looked up as he approached and smiled. "You seem recovered."

"I am," he answered, returning her smile, "thanks to Morrhyn. And there *are* hot baths to be had."

"Where?" Arcole asked eagerly. "Lead me to it, I beg you."

Davyd laughed, all discomfort forgotten. This was, he thought, a fine land.

5

Morning delivered a sky of pure blue striped with windblown ribbons of high white cloud. A breeze rustled over the lush grass of the meadow, the ripples like the swell of some green land-birthed ocean spread with a wrack of bright flowers. Birds sang a welcome to the rising sun, and from downslope a fox barked. Davyd emerged rested from the tent to find the Matawaye already preparing breakfast. He went to join them, smiling, his aches quite forgotten.

Arcole and Flysse rose slower. Both had availed themselves of the hot spring, but neither had enjoyed the benefit of Morrhyn's restorative herbs, and both felt somewhat the rigors of the previous day.

"I grow old," Arcole grunted as he laced his breeches.

Flysse laughed, combing her hair, studying the result in the mirror Marjia had gifted her. "You grow thin," she said. "You need some fattening—padding for that saddle."

"I surely need some kind of padding," he returned. "God, what did Morrhyn give Davyd, that restored him so?"

"Shall we ask for some?" she wondered, her eyes bright with amusement for all she put a solemn and solicitous expression on her face. "Can you not manage?"

"No," he said quickly, "and yes. I shall doubtless get used to this before long."

Flysse nodded gravely, marveling at the vanity of men, which they named pride. Davyd, she thought, had been consumed with agony this last day, and would not admit it for fear he lose some notion of himself in the acceptance. Arcole, for all he had withstood the rigors of the journey better, was still in some discomfort, but would not ask for help, lest she or the Matawaye think the less of him for it. She found that difficult to understand—surely it was no loss of self-respect to ask help of friends? She finished her toilette and suggested they eat.

"Best flesh out those thin, old bones."

Arcole scowled at her, then laughed. "Do you not suffer at all? Not even a little?"

"No," she answered. "But then I'm accustomed to riding so. I'm not a lady, remember."

He looked at her, no longer laughing, and shook his head. "You are, and do you deny it, I shall take offense."

"Then," Flysse rose, curtseying as best she could in leathern breeches, "I accept your compliment, 'sieur."

"Good." Arcole took her arm. "I'd not have a wife who argues with me."

"That," Flysse said, "I cannot always guarantee shall be the case."

"Nor would I have it otherwise," he replied, grinning. "Now do we go eat?"

Breakfast was again porridge, and some kind of hard bread that came in flat, round loaves, washed down with tea. It was not, Arcole thought, the height of culinary refinement, but undoubtedly filling, and he felt satisfied as the animals were saddled and they started down through the hills.

Davyd seemed happier today, more at ease on the buckskin, though Morrhyn and Kahteney still rode close to either side, poised to aid the lad should assistance prove needed. He will learn, Arcole thought as he watched Davyd swaying in the saddle; already he learns to move with the horse, and does it hurt, still it's a needful lesson.

For his own part he grew steadily more accustomed to the primitive harness, though he still found it hard to understand how these folk could fight from horseback. As best he understood it, they *had* fought with the invaders of their first land, who seemed—as best Davyd had been able to describe them—terrible warriors. But surely to fight effectively from the back of a running horse, a man needed stirrups and a firm seat. How else could he own a solid platform from which to use his weapons? These Matawaye carried the accoutrements of war or hunting—all save the wakanishas had lances and bows and axes stowed about their saddles—but how did they use them without stirrups, or high-mounted saddles?

He got his answer as they came down from a defile flanked by two tall hills, onto a plateau where the broad shelf spread all grassy to the drop beyond and it seemed the world fell away into distance like a steep beach meeting a great green ocean.

A small herd of deer grazed the plateau, sentried by a high-antlered stag. The wind blew from the south, carrying the scents of horses and men away from the deer. Rannach raised a hand to halt the little column and turned, smiling, to Kanseah. Arcole saw the shy akaman nod, and then both men take bows from their packs and nock arrows. Morrhyn gestured that none move, but Arcole could not resist bringing his horse a little closer to the front, that he might see the hunt clearly. He thought that were it left to him, he would work his way slowly down on foot and belly until he had a clear shot— which should be difficult, because likely the stag would sight him and take his harem away.

Rannach and Kanseah had no such doubts: they heeled their horses and charged; and Arcole could scarcely believe what he saw.

The deer scattered at the first sound of the pounding hooves. The stag belled and ran away toward the timber edging the plateau, his harem running swift after him. Rannach and Kanseah galloped in the same direction, intent on cutting off the herd. Neither held their reins, but left them loose across their mounts' shoulders, guiding the horses with their knees alone, both their bows full strung as they closed on the panicked deer.

A doe ran laggard, clearly aged, and hampered by some old wound. Arcole thought that her meat would likely be toughened by the years she carried, and that he would have selected younger game, but neither Rannach or Kanseah seemed to share that thought. They ignored the younger animals and closed on the limping doe. Both sighted and loosed their arrows, and the shafts flew straight and true, thudding hard into the doe's chest, just behind the left foreleg, so that she was killed on the instant and fell over with the feathered poles jutting from her side.

Rannach sprang from his horse as it still ran, landing loose with a long blade in his hand, that he drove deep into the deer's neck and slit her throat for all she was surely already dead. Then he fell to his knees and stroked her throat, and Kanseah joined him, and both men raised their hands to the sky and said something that Arcole could not hear, for the wind carried their words away, and he would not have understood them anyway. But he thought that they gave thanks for the kill to whatever god they worshipped, and that he had never seen such horsemanship.

Then Yazte slapped him on the shoulder and he must steady the prancing gray as he looked at the plump man, who pointed at the felled deer and then at his mouth, and then rubbed his ample belly, grinning hugely. Arcole nodded and smiled back.

"I think," he said to Flysse, "that we shall eat well tonight."

Flysse nodded, staring at the two akamans, who were already beckoning them forward that they might stow the deer on a packhorse. "I've never seen such riding," she said, her voice awed. "They're like . . ."

"Centaurs," Arcole finished for her. And promised himself that he would learn to truly master this simple style of horsemanship: the admiration he saw in her eyes rankled somewhat. "Like the legends."

"I wonder," she said, "if we've not stumbled into a legend."

He smiled at that, and squeezed her hand. Had he felt confident enough of his seat, he would have leant to kiss her. But he was not yet so able, and so only smiled. Then they were moving again, down to where Rannach and Kanseah waited, and the doe was loaded on a packhorse and they all, laughing, rode down off the plateau.

The trail grew steep here, narrow between high walls of roseate stone, and Arcole feared that Davyd should find it too difficult. Neither wakanisha could any longer ride beside him, but must go ahead and behind and leave Davyd to his own devices. The which, Arcole was pleased to observe, he managed well enough. He did not fall off, and was his face somewhat pale as they came out onto flatter ground, and his hands clasped like determined limpets on rein and mane, still he smiled proudly and called back, "I think I get the hang of this."

"You do," Arcole returned, "and well."

Morrhyn caught his eye, smiling, and he wondered how fast the Matawaye would have traveled were they not hindered by their inexperienced guests. They showed great patience, he thought, and took pains to make three strangers feel so welcome; which prompted him in turn to think that these were kind people, such as he had never known. He looked up at the wide sky, all sun-burnished blue now, with the clouds fading like old dreams, and felt the wind on his face and laughed for the sheer wonder of it all.

This seemed a marvelous land, vast and verdant—he saw the hills falling away around and before their path, like great descending steps that cupped meadows and woods and streams within their huge and magnificent embrace; behind, the mountains stood sentinel duty, broaching the sky itself, snowcapped guardians dividing Ket-Ta-Thanne from Salvation. And ahead, where the lower steps ran down, he saw an infinity of blue-hazed distance that must surely stretch out to the ends of the world. Or perhaps go on forever: he could not know, only wonder at the enormity of it all.

"God, but this is surely a wonderful country!"

He had not realized he spoke aloud until Flysse answered him: "Yes, I think it is." And Yazte brought his horse closer and beamed and waved a hand as if to embrace all of it, and welcome the newcomers. And Arcole nodded and reached out unthinking to clap the fat man on the shoulder, at which Yazte laughed and spoke in his odd guttural language, which Arcole could still not yet understand for all the words seemed daily to border on the comprehensible. Perhaps, he thought, some magic worked here, past those dividing mountains, that gave newcomers the gift of tongues. Surely it was a magical place.

■   ■   ■

That day they halted around noon to butcher the deer and pack the cuts. Morrhyn gave Davyd more of the herb that numbed his aches, and they continued down through the foothills. For a while, they followed a tumbling stream that danced away between stands of tall timber, larches and aspen that dappled harlequin patterns of sunlight and shadow over the ground, then the water turned and went off northward as they continued to the west, descending through the trees and over grassy hummocks. The woodland was loud with bird-song, and unseen animals crashed away through the under-growth at their approach; plump rabbits watched from the hummocks, bounding for the safety of burrows as the horses came near; overhead, hawks circled the sky, and swallows darted, crows flew noisy, and magpies chattered announce-ment of their coming. It seemed to Arcole a land filled with life, untamed and quite unlike Salvation, and its inhabitants as different.

As the sun fell away to the west they made camp where a ring of ridgepole pines surrounded a meadow. There was no hot spring, but neither Flysse or Arcole felt overmuch need of that solace, and Davyd bore up well, even did he grimace as he seated himself and eagerly take the herbs Morrhyn offered.

Arcole noticed that the wakanisha offered neither him nor Flysse that cure, and wondered if that was compliment of their equestrian skills or indication of the herb's scarcity. Or—as Morrhyn and Kahteney again engaged Davyd in a busy conversation that existed as much of handsigns as words—of the importance they attached to the young man.

Certainly, they paid him the greater part of their attention, mostly leaving Rannach and Yazte and Kanseah to communi-cate with the other newcomers. It was as if, Arcole thought, they would impress their language on Davyd as quickly as possible. And then he thought that that was surely the obvi-ous course—the dreams had already imbued Davyd with far greater understanding than he or Flysse owned, and so it was logical the youth be taught first, and become translator for them all. Or was there something else? Some other reason, that lay beyond his comprehension? He recognized now that these folk were not savages—they were too kind, too courtly—and had he at first believed them primitive, he now

began to see that it was only a different way of life they
followed, which did not make them less than his own people,
but only different.

That night he joined with Flysse in awkward repetition of
words as the three akamans patiently spoke, holding up a
variety of items and carefully intoning the names. It was not
easy. The language of the Matawaye was deeper than his own
soft Levanite tongue, even deeper than Flysse's Evanderan,
and much of it clicking glottal stops or what seemed to him
an entirely unnatural joindure of tongue and teeth. But he
learned to say the words for knife, and meat, and deer, and
fire, and began to believe that he might—in time—converse
articulately with their hosts. And that, no less than the kindness shown three refugee strangers, persuaded him he and
Flysse might find a life amongst these folk. It was an after-
thought to realize he already assumed Davyd should have a
life here, as if the youth and Morrhyn had already reached
some mutual treaty of adoption.

That night he slept well, and was it frustrating to lie so
close to Flysse and not be able to hold her as he wished for
fear they wake the softly snoring Davyd, then still it was good
simply to be there, safe.

They went on down through the foothills, lower and lower,
wending along ravines and gullies that turned and twisted,
mazy as some rocky labyrinth, as if the mountains dug claws
of stone into the land, reluctant to let go their hold. Three
days they traversed the breaks, and then the stone leveled and
fell away, like exhausted waves foundering on some impon-
derably vast beach. Save that beach was all green grass, and
more akin to an ocean. Arcole had never seen such a plain: it
spread out to the limits of the horizon as if it held all the
world within its grasp, lushly painted with a myriad shades of
green that rippled, shadow-shifting, under a soft wind. Stands
of timber stood like hazy islands in the vastness, and as they
rode through the knee-deep green sea he saw ahead vast,
darker shadows that moved slowly over the verdancy, like
great shoals of fish. He looked up, but the only clouds in that
enormous sky were random billows of cumulus, too high and

not large enough to lay such shadows. He wondered what they were.

A half day out onto the great grass sea he saw. The riders drew closer and the shadows resolved into individual shapes: great shaggy beasts, with massive shoulders, all hair-hung and dwarfing the horned heads that turned suspiciously toward the riders. Some snorted a challenge and ran a little way toward them, horns tossing in warning, but when the horsemen offered no answering challenge, only hooved ground and returned to their grazing. Rannach pointed at them with his lance, making a thrusting motion, and said a word Arcole could not understand, then the word for meat—which he could—and that for leather, and more that were incomprehensible.

"What are they?" Flysse asked. "Some kind of cattle?"

"I think so, but wild," Arcole replied, indicating the herd's guardians. "Those are surely bulls. And ready to fight."

He watched them warily, grateful the Matawaye steered a course around such massive beasts. For all the guardian bulls grazed, still they tossed their heads and watched and stamped their hooves, and there were so many of them. He calculated there must be some several hundred, perhaps even a thousand or more. If that herd charged, the riders would surely be swept under their weight like debris beneath a surging sea.

"You fight bulls in the Levan, don't you?" Flysse asked.

"Yes." Arcole nodded. "But not creatures like that. The bulls of the Levan . . ." He shrugged, kindling memories from a life that now seemed so distant it grew hazy as the horizon. ". . . They're smaller, and with wider horns. They're fast, but their shoulders are not so huge. I'd not much want to fight one of these—I think it would be impossible to get the sword past those shoulders. Surely, I'd not want to try."

"*You* fought bulls?" Flysse was surprised.

"Have I not told you?" It was his turn to express surprise: surely he had told her everything about his life there. Certainly he had confessed his affairs and his duels, his gambling. They had agreed there should be no secrets between them, and since that night she had found him copying Wyme's maps in secret—a betrayal of her trust—he had hidden nothing.

Likely, he had only forgotten this: it was a small part of his past, unimportant for its foundation in the vanity he had learned to lose in her company.

Flysse said, "No; tell me."

Arcole looked at the watchful animals—had Rannach said *buffalo?*—and then at Flysse. "Three times," he said, and grinned. "The first was to see if I could."

"And could you?" she asked.

He could not tell whether she approved or not; her face was unreadable. He said, "Yes. I'm alive, no? I was frightened." He felt his grin fading. "God, but my legs were shaking and my mouth was dry. But I put the sword in and slew the beast." He remembered, then, the cheers of the crowd, and added, proudly, "I was granted the ears." Then, humbler when her expression did not change, "But it was only a small affair, in a private arena. And the bull was only a three-year-old, not the mature bulls the professionals fight."

"Why?" Flysse asked.

Her voice was empty of intonation. Arcole had thought she'd be impressed—the bull might have been immature, but still it could have killed him—but neither her tone or her face suggested that. He shrugged and said, "A friend—Antonym de Chevres—bred the bulls for the ring, and wagered me five hundred golden guineas I'd not fight one."

Still Flysse's expression did not change. "And the other times?"

"Those," he said, "were for wagers resulting from that first—Antonym bet me a thousand in gold I'd not do it again, facing a full-grown bull. But I did." He chuckled, remembering. "I hired a fighter called Manolito to train me, and we split the money. Antonym was amazed."

Flysse said, "You might have been killed."

"Yes." Arcole shrugged. "But a wager's a wager, no? And it was the bull that died."

He thought that surely that must impress her. God, but the bull had been massive, and even did they not fight bulls in Evander, still they knew of the Levanite tradition—how could she not be impressed? But her face remained impassive, even less expressive than the heat-hazed blankness of the mountains behind them.

"And the third time?"

"That was a bull called Escovar. No one wanted to face him because he'd horned two fighters; one died, and the other never fought again." Surely she must be impressed with *this*. Even had she not heard of that battle, it must impress her. "Colign Murrie wagered five thousand, and I won."

"Won?" she said.

"Yes." He frowned. "I killed the bull: I won."

"You put your sword into the bull and killed it," she said.

Arcole said, "Yes," wondering why she seemed not at all impressed with his bravery.

"After the—what are they called?—the picadors lanced the bull?"

So she did know somewhat of the ritual: he nodded. "Escovar gored two of their horses."

"Did they die?"

He said, "One, I think," no longer confident in his pride, feeling it slip away. "I'm not sure."

Flysse looked at the impossibly distant horizon and sighed, nodded. "And then the—the ones with the little lances came in on foot."

"The banderillas," he supplied.

"Yes. They put those sticks with ribbons into the bull's neck, no?"

"To weaken it," he said. "So that it drops its head enough you can get the sword over the horns."

"And kill it."

"Yes."

"Did you eat it?" Flysse asked.

He shook his head. "God, no! That meat's too tough for eating."

"So you killed it for money. Or to prove something?"

"Both, I suppose," he said. God, why did he suddenly feel so embarrassed? Why did he want her approval so badly, that she turn her face toward him and smile; grant him . . . absolution? He spoke of a life left far behind, when he was different. He waited nervously for her response.

"I think," she said at last, slowly, "that you should only kill animals to eat. Not for sport, or to prove anything. Only to eat. The Matawaye"—she pronounced the title better than he—"don't kill like that."

He thought on the doe they'd been eating and nodded: she'd been the slowest of the herd, and likely to fall to wolves or age, and Rannach and Kanseah had singled her out from the tenderer meat, leaving the younger, stronger animals to run free and breed. A natural culling, he thought; and felt ashamed of himself.

"I was young then," he said defensively. "I'm older than that now."

"Yes, I think so." Now she did turn her head, but still her eyes searched his face. "But would you do it again?"

"You do not approve," he said.

"No."

"Then I'd not."

She shook her head. "Not for my approval, Arcole. Rather because . . ." She gestured at the vast, wide land around them, at the shifting, slowly moving herd of buffalo. "Because you should not kill for sport, but only in need."

"I've things to learn yet," he said; meaning it, suddenly aware he stood on the threshold of an experience perhaps even greater than the land around them. As if contact with the Matawaye introduced him to far more than only a new country. Davyd understands it, he thought, and Flysse; and I must learn to. I must shuck off these old notions that belong to the past, and learn to live with this new country and its thinking.

He said, "I'm sorry."

Flysse looked at him and smiled, and he felt suddenly like a child excused punishment.

"So do you forgive me my past sins?"

She ducked her head again, and he laughed; and said, "I learn from you, all the time."

And they rode out around the great herd of buffalo, out across the wind-shifted grass, Rannach and Yazte and Kanseah drifting their horses rightward to form a living screen between the riders and the warily guardian bulls, Morrhyn and Kahteney escorting Davyd, Flysse and Arcole following.

∎   ∎   ∎

Four more days they traveled across the prairie, living off the deer meat, which lasted them to the Summer Ground of the People, where all of them—the Commacht and the Lakanti and the remnants of the Naiche and the Aparhaso, and those few Tachyn who had forsworn the heresy of Chakthi and Hadduth—were gathered together in one great camp until the Maker or his prophet, Morrhyn, should tell them to scatter and spread over this new country.

It was not, Morrhyn thought as he rode toward the great camp, an easy destiny. Neither for him nor the strangers; but the Maker had shaped it, and so it must be. And doubtless the Maker would, in time, reveal it.

And meanwhile, he would do what he could. Which first, he was confident, meant giving Davyd the pahé root.

6

Like Coming Home

The People had not split into clans and scattered through the vastness of Ket-Ta-Thanne, as had been their habit in the lost homeland, but remained in a unified group, as if all their time here was Matakwa. The memories of disaster yet held strong, and no one clan would risk annihilation or the weakening of all to seek out individual territory. Even did Morrhyn assure them he owned no dreams of Breakers or other enemies, still they demurred, like buffalo frightened by a wolf pack and herding defensive.

Yet they had found a fine place, close by their entry point into Ket-Ta-Thanne, and was it not overlooked by the Maker's Mountain, they had raised a cairn of stones to mark the gateway. It stood twice a man's height, surrounded by poles bearing the clan totems, the base all spread with the thanks-offerings of the People—a monument in the great grass sea. The camp itself was spread out along a shallow valley that cradled a wide, slow-running river, the water the color of Grannach steel between the grassy banks. Lush grazing lay all around, and the valley walls were heavily timbered, the woods and the grass rich with game. Buffalo no different to those of Ket-Ta-Witko wandered the plains, and the warriors went out at need to hunt them. The People wanted for nothing here, not for the present—in time, Morrhyn supposed, they must deplete the stock of game to such extent that they be forced to wander farther afield, and then he anticipated they would separate, returning to the old ways, with each clan choosing its own grazing. By then, he hoped, they would know themselves safe.

For now, it seemed enough to live in peace, and he smiled

as they came down into the valley's eastern entrance and all
the lodges of the People spread before them, turning in his
saddle to observe the expressions of the newcomers.

They looked amazed, as if they stared at some great marvel
beyond their comprehension. It was surely a marvelous sight,
and for all there were not so many lodges as had graced the
Meeting Ground of lost Ket-Ta-Witko, still they spread nu-
merous over the grass, the symbols painted on the hides de-
noting the placement of the clans. The horse head of the
Commacht and the eagle of the Lakanti were predominant,
the Aparhaso wolf and the Naiche's turtle mingled together
in lesser numbers; and scattered through them all were lodges
decorated with newly painted symbols where those Tachyn
who had forsworn Chakthi's heresy were adopted into the
remaining clans. Morrhyn wished he commanded sufficient of
the strangers' language that he might ask their impressions.

"By God, it's a city all of tents." Arcole shaded his eyes
against the sun. "Like an army bivouac; save I've not seen so
large an army."

"Nor one so peaceful, I think." Flysse pointed to where
children played and dogs wandered. "Look."

She directed his gaze to the southern flank, where women
moved industriously amidst thickets heavy with red berries,
plucking the fruit to deposit in woven baskets. The breeze
carried snatches of song.

"And there." He in turn pointed, down the valley, where a
vast horse herd grazed. "God, so many horses."

"It's bigger than Grostheim," Davyd said, staring enrapt,
"and there are no walls."

Then he laughed, amazed at himself, thinking that not so
long ago he had felt at ease only behind walls, be they Grostheim's wood or Bantar's stone. At home behind walls and
afraid of the open country—but no longer: he had changed,
and this felt like coming home.

Still chuckling, he heeled his buckskin alongside Morrhyn's horse, too filled with wonder to remember that scant
days ago such ambitious movement had terrified him.

"It's marvelous." He flung out a hand to indicate the valley. Then clutched abruptly at the buckskin's mane as the horse snorted and pranced—as yet, a gentle trot was the best he could manage. "It's . . . wonderful."

Morrhyn nodded, beaming, Davyd's expression, his tone, interpreting the words. "It's our home," he said.

Davyd, in turn, nodded. "Yes, home."

Then gasped as the realization he had understood clearly struck him.

Morrhyn spoke again, and Davyd frowned, the words no longer clear. "Dream" he recognized, and "pahé," which he guessed was somehow linked to dreaming, but little else. He shrugged, shaking his head in frustration. Morrhyn smiled and touched his arm, speaking again; but the words again stood just past a veil that clouded proper comprehension. He saw Kahteney watching them, his lean face grave, and wondered why he thought the Dreamer doubtful.

Morrhyn caught Kahteney's eyes on him and turned his smile to the Lakanti. "How else, brother?"

Kahteney shrugged and shook his head.

Morrhyn said, "Not yet, but in a while. I'd see them comfortable amongst us first, and only then give Davyd the pahé. And we dream first—as we agreed."

Kahteney ducked his head. "As you will." Almost, he added "Prophet," but he knew Morrhyn felt no great liking for that title and so bit back the word. But still he wondered how the People might accept the introduction of a stranger, an unknown refugee from another world, to the sacred rituals of the wakanishas. Most, he supposed, would accept it because it was the Prophet's will—and Morrhyn, no matter his feelings on that subject, *was* the Prophet—but some would doubtless resent it. Chazde had selected him even before he received his manhood name, long before he was old enough to think of the warrior's braids, and that had birthed some measure of resentment amongst his companions; long gone now . . . but then childhood friends had eyed him as if he were a stranger, set apart from them by Chazde's decision. And he had grown in knowledge of the Ahsa-tye-Patiko. . . .

He smiled at the memory of childhood's hurt, his own brief resentment of the honor that made him different.

"What if he'll not accept the duty?"

"Then he refuses." Morrhyn shrugged. "The Maker shall decide, no? He'll tell us when we dream."

Kahteney had known Morrhyn most of his life, since that Matakwa when the Dreamers had named their chosen successors, and they both younger than Davyd. They were old friends; but Morrhyn had always been the stronger Dreamer, and now . . . now he was a Dreamer such as the People had never known. Kahteney wondered if he would welcome such communion with the Maker as Morrhyn had, or if that duty should destroy him. Sometimes he wondered if Morrhyn lived still entirely within this world, or set his feet in both the Dirt World and the Spirit World, like the Grass Dreamer who showed First Man and First Woman the bridge between the spheres. Surely he was changed by his sojourn on the holy mountain—and Kahteney would not argue overmuch with his decisions: he was, after all, the Prophet. And would he give Davyd the pahé root and name the stranger his successor, then so be it.

So Kahteney grunted agreement and held his tongue tight-reined against his doubt and looked toward the valley where all the lodges of the People spread out in glorious array, and set his mind to thoughts of coming home again.

And when they came down the long, wide slope of the valley's ingress, Rannach took a bugle of buffalo horn from his saddle and blew a clarion call that had horsemen thundering to greet them. The women picking berries set down their baskets and ran across the grass, and dogs barked, and all the camp gathered, wondering at what—or who—the Prophet brought to them.

It was an alarming sight, to see so many horsemen come charging toward them, all racing their animals as if to battle, whooping and shouting. None bore weapons, and their cries rang with glee rather than menace, but still Arcole glanced back instinctively to the packhorses, thinking of the muskets stowed there. The gray began to prance and he fought the horse calm, almost losing his seat. Beside him, Flysse turned her roan, looking from him to the approaching riders to the beaming Matawaye around them. She seemed less alarmed than excited, and he told himself no harm was intended, but only a welcome.

Davyd felt no doubts: Morrhyn's smile told him this was only greeting. But even so, the buckskin snorted and set to plunging, and for all he clamped his thighs hard on the horse's ribs and locked his right hand in the mane, and tugged on the single rein with left, still he felt himself bucked off.

He shouted as he fell; cursed volubly as he hit the ground. And then, even as he lay winded and embarrassed, there were unshod hooves all around him, and tan faces looking down, smiling, some—to his chagrin—laughing. He cursed some more, ignoring Flysse's admonition, and clambered to his feet, irritably dusting his shirt, rubbing at his shoulder, which ached abominably from the sudden contact with the ground. It seemed to him a most ignominious meeting, and he could not help scowling at the surrounding Matawaye as one took up the rein of his horse and leaned with careless, casual grace from his saddle to pass it to him. He took it with sullenly grunted thanks and wondered if he might retrieve his lost dignity by vaulting into the saddle.

He thought not—more likely he'd fall again and they laugh again—and so stood red-faced, holding the buckskin still, and wondered how he would get back up. God!

"Ach, but these strangers you bring us are not very good on a horse, Rannach."

"No, but they have other powers." Rannach looked at the speaker with disapproving eyes: it was not meet to laugh at guests. "There's much they can teach us. Much we need learn from them."

"But not horsemanship, eh?"

"He's a Dreamer. Morrhyn says he's a great Dreamer." Rannach hid his smile as Tekah's faded. Mention of the Prophet's name was a mighty tool: it stilled so many arguments. He glanced sidelong at the wakanisha, wondering if he abused their friendship. But Morrhyn sat his paint horse with solemn mien, only looking gravely at the welcoming riders, so he went on: "Do you help him up? His name is Davyd."

Tekah nodded and slid limber from off his horse. He went to where Davyd stood and said, "I am sorry, Davyd. Please forgive my rudeness. I welcome you to our lodges. Shall I help you mount?"

When Davyd only frowned, he said to Rannach, "He doesn't understand me."

"How should he?" Rannach asked. "Do you understand *him*?"

"Then what do I do?"

Tekah stared around, confused. The laughter shifted from Davyd to him. Rannach said, "He's not used to our horses, so offer him your hands to climb on, like a step."

Tekah frowned. "He's not a woman with child."

Rannach said, "No," sternly.

From the corner of his eye he saw Arcole readying to dismount; guessed he was about to help Davyd, and motioned that he not. He wondered if the stranger would understand the importance of this small ritual. That a man fall from a placid horse was indignity enough: was Davyd to be respected by the People, some precedent of importance must be established, even did Tekah resent it. Save Davyd be accorded respect, all Morrhyn's hopes should likely be dashed down abruptly as Davyd's tumble.

Morrhyn looked on in silence, clearly pleased with Rannach's response. No less than Yazte's as the Lakanti reached out to touch Arcole's wrist and indicate he remain in the saddle.

Then was delighted as Kanseah swung to the ground and cupped his hands and said, "Shall I help you up, Davyd?"

Rannach said, "You see? The akaman of the Naiche helps our guests."

"And I," Tekah said; hurriedly, moving to offer his hands alongside Kanseah's, so that Davyd was sprung back astride the buckskin horse so swift he almost tumbled off the farther side.

Tekah clutched the mane, that the horse not buck or

prance and disgrace Davyd further. He said, "Forgive me," ducking his head slightly. "I intended no insult."

Not properly understanding all that had gone on, but guessing the man apologized, Davyd smiled and said, "Yes."

Tekah nodded, and looked to Rannach. "Don't these people have horses?"

"I don't know," Rannach answered. "The man and the woman can ride, so I suppose they must. But I don't think Davyd had sat a horse before we put him up."

"Strange." Tekah shook his head in puzzlement. "People who don't ride?"

Looking down from his own mount Rannach said, "The Grannach don't ride."

"No," Tekah agreed. Then grinned. "But the Maker never saw fit to make horses their size, whilst these strangers"—he indicated the newcomers with a sideways turning of his eyes—"seem in most ways much like us."

"In many ways I think they are," Rannach answered. "And in others, not at all."

He glanced at Morrhyn, thinking this was a thing better explained by the wakanisha; but Morrhyn sat his horse silent, only smiling calmly. Rannach quelled a frown, wondering if Morrhyn tested him in some fashion. It seemed often that way: that when a word, an explanation that would ease a situation, might readily come from Morrhyn and be accepted by all, he left it to Rannach to explain. It was as if he guided his akaman just so far, and then left Rannach to his own devices; and it was not always easy. Rannach had inherited the mantle of his slain father—was now, here in Ket-Ta-Thanne, become all unassuming the paramount chieftain, as if he took the places of both Racharran and old, dead Juh—and he knew himself young and inexperienced in the ways of leadership. He supposed Morrhyn forced that duty on him for want of other candidate, and was still unsure he welcomed it. Yazte, after all, was older than he, and—he thought—wiser. But even Yazte looked to him, likely because, he thought, Morrhyn was wakanisha of the Commacht—the Prophet— rather than because the Lakanti believed him a great leader. But there it was: They looked to him for the final word. And

Morrhyn sat his paint silent and benign as an owl perched waiting for the movement of a mouse.

So Rannach said, raising his voice so that all the outcome riders should hear, "But whatever they are, they are welcome among us. They are escaped—like us! And we are pledged to welcome them, no? So, do we bring them home as honored guests?"

The answer was a great shrill shout of agreement; a waving of hands and bows; a dancing of horses. And from the women on the hillside and the folk in the camp, an answering yelling that set birds to flocking in alarm from the timber, and the dogs in the valley below to barking, the horse herd along the valley to snorting and running—as if all this new world belled a welcome that was entirely unnerving in its enthusiasm.

"God, they howl like banshees." Arcole fought his horse alongside Flysse's. Riders surged around them, whooping and circling, melded to their mounts.

"Yes," Flysse answered over the din, "but are they not magnificent?"

Arcole looked at the ringing, milling horde and could only nod his agreement. He had seen the armies of the Levan face the forces of Evander. He had been an officer of cavalry, and seen the squadrons of Evander's horsemen attack; but not like this. These people—these Matawaye—seemed at one with their mounts, as if they grew on horseback. He envied them their control, and shouted over the thunder of the hooves, "Yes! They are!" And could not resist urging his gray horse to a gallop.

Flysse matched him, stride for stride, on her roan, the two of them racing down the slope of the valley's mouth with Rannach and Yazte and Kanseah anxious beside, fearful their refugee guests fall off and harm themselves as horsemen came like grounded thunder all around them, screaming encouragement. Arcole felt his heart beat faster and whooped in response as he and Flysse heeled their horses to greater effort, looking to outrun their escort. Which, of course, was pure ambition and quite impossible; but it seemed to earn them respect—as if the Matawaye recognized kindred spirits—and they came swift and escorted into the camp.

Davyd saw his friends go charging off and wished he might match them. Almost, he tried, but sense prevailed and he came on slower, not daring more than a trot for fear he tumble again and again become the butt of laughter. Morrhyn and Kahteney rode to either side, and the one called Tekah hovered about, nervous. Davyd guessed some reprimand had been delivered the man—and thought, as Tekah watched him solicitously, that should he slip, then Tekah would likely come charging in to catch him. He wondered if the wakanishas would have joined in that mad gallop, were he not there, and what Rannach had said to Tekah.

But it seemed as if the man appointed himself guardian, for as they came down onto the flat and halted amongst the tents, it was Tekah sprang first to the ground and took the buckskin's bridle, holding the animal still as Davyd clambered awkwardly from off its back. He spoke—Davyd could not understand, but his tone was amiable—and Davyd smiled in answer, and then Morrhyn spoke and Tekah nodded dutifully and led the buckskin away; and then for a while all was confusion.

Folk milled around, staring, all speaking at once, with Morrhyn and Rannach and the others of the escort answering, so that the noonday was filled up with sound and Davyd felt his ears battered by the noise. Arcole and Flysse came to stand beside him, smiling and bewildered.

"What in God's name are they saying?"

Davyd shook his head in answer to Arcole's question. "I don't know. I think they welcome us."

"Like a pack of baying hounds." Arcole grinned and shaped an elegant bow as a man tapped the scar on his cheek. "Shall I ever understand them?"

Davyd began to say, "Yes," but then a figure wormed through the throng and stared at him with such . . . He was not sure; *anger* was the word that came to mind, or even *hatred*. But how could a stranger hate him, what could he have done to anger someone he had never met? He smiled tentatively and saw the other's lips thin furiously, the dark eyes smolder.

It was a youth of about, he estimated, his own age. They were of a height and similar build, save for the slight bowing of the other's legs. He was dressed in breeches and shirt, and his raven hair swung loose about his vexed face, backdrop to the anger there. He spoke, stabbing a dark finger at Davyd's chest and then at his own. The only words Davyd understood were "wakanisha," his own name, and that of . . . it seemed his accuser: Taza.

Taza spat on the ground between Davyd's feet.

Kahteney and Morrhyn spoke together then, sharply, and Taza scowled and turned away, disappearing back into the crowd. Davyd noticed that he limped.

Arcole said, "I know not why, but you've an enemy there: best watch him."

"How?" Davyd tried to find Taza through the crowd, through the shouting bustle of friendly greetings. "What have I done to make him an enemy?"

"Nothing that I know of." Arcole shrugged. "But even so . . . Watch your back around him, eh? I've seen that look before, in the eyes of men who sought my death."

Then he laughed as Davyd's face fell, and hung an arm around the young man's shoulders and said, "But I'm still alive, no? By God, we're all alive—against all odds—and come amongst friends."

Of that, save for Taza, there was no possibility of doubt: they were crowded round with cheerful faces and before long found themselves seated by a fire on which meat roasted, flasks of tiswin passing round, and they the guests of honor.

They were introduced to Arrhyna—Rannach's wife, as they understood, and who was, Davyd thought, almost as beautiful as Flysse, with red hair like his own, save hers was darkly burnished copper and his bright as a new-picked carrot. She was sweet and gracious in her skirt and tunic of soft hide, with dark, doe eyes that swooped lovingly on her husband and were answered with glances no less adoring.

Davyd wondered if he should ever find such a union.

And then there was Lhyn, who sat between Morrhyn and Rannach, and was older, with silver in the gold of her hair and lines on her smooth cheeks and about her eyes. For all her smiling generosity, she had an air of contained sadness, and also of pride—as if she had lost things or people but also won, and was not sure which were better. And Yazte came with his fat and beaming wife, Raize, who was plump and rounded as her husband and no less cheerful, and plied them and her husband with food and tiswin—like, Davyd thought, some busy Bantar tavern wife who'd see her customers eat and drink their fill. And also Kanseah, who seemed to have no wife, for he sat alone; and Morrhyn and Kahteney, who neither came with women. And a warrior called Dohnse, who also sat alone within the circle, and seemed shy as Kanseah. . . .

It was happiness and confusion, mingled. Davyd ate and drank, and wondered where the future might lead.

Morrhyn—he was sure—had spoken of dreaming together: of some oneiric union beyond his immediate understanding, which should gift him with . . . he could only think of revelation . . . some order that lay like God's will somewhere beyond his immediate comprehension, like the light of the rising sun dispelling mist and night, promising the clarity of a sunlit day. But yet it was as if, even as he sat with succulent meat in his mouth, a cup of tiswin at his elbow, and friends all around him, there existed a dark dawn none there, not even Morrhyn, could see.

He was not sure of it, himself; only that it came: of that, somehow, he was certain. Suddenly, as he sat with these new-won friends and ate their meat and drank their tiswin he *knew* that he *would* see it, and that it was his future, and Flysse's, and Arcole's, and Morrhyn's, and—he looked around the circle of smiling, laughing faces—Kanseah's and Yazte's: all of them. . . .

He had seen it in Taza's eyes: it came. He felt it in the surety of his blood. It was in the laughter of the Matawaye and the color of Arrhyna's hair, the shade of the sky and the lines on Lhyn's face. But he could not name it, or—without proper comprehension of their language—explain what he felt. What he *knew*.

So he waited for further explanation, afraid he had it wrong and unsure what to say—even had he the words to explain it—save thanks for the food and the tent he was brought to when the feasting was done, which was his alone. Flysse and Arcole were given another, which was a kindness to them and chaos to him, for he needed to talk but was embarrassed to interrupt what they might—surely!—be doing, now they were at last alone.

And he would have gone to Morrhyn, save that the wakanisha had left the circle in company with Lhyn, and he was unsure whether they were lovers or old friends. And Rannach had surely gone eagerly with Arrhyna, so there was no one he might properly talk with.

And likely, for all what he felt, it was nothing—so he told himself. Surely if it was anything, then Morrhyn or Kahteney would have dreamed it: surely they were far greater Dreamers than he.

But still, as he lay down on the furs of his gifted bed and watched the play of firelight on the hides of the lodge, he could not forget Taza's eyes, or the doubt he felt.

7

The Inquisitor

Tomas Var had not thought to see Salvation again.

On his return to Evander he had delivered Andru Wyme's messages to his commanding officer and given his own report, then gone about his duties thinking he had seen the last of the New World. Grostheim and its occupants held no great attraction for him, and did he occasionally wonder what fate befell Arcole Blayke, he surely felt no desire to again cross the Sea of Sorrows. He had found himself posted to garrison duty in the Levan and assumed, with the countries conquered in the War of Restitution now pacific, that he might look forward to a slow rise through the ranks. He found himself thinking, for the first time in his life, of settling into some permanent posting. He had met a woman, Krystine d'Lavall, and contemplated engagement. Consequently, he had been surprised to find himself recalled to Bantar, where he must reiterate all he had observed in Grostheim to a committee of senior officers, Inquisitors, and officials of the Autarchy. They plied him with questions and then—to his far greater surprise—announced his immediate promotion to the rank of major. And his new commission.

An expeditionary force of two hundred and fifty marines accompanied by infantry, artillerymen, and engineers was to set sail for Salvation under the command of the Inquisitor Jared Talle. The newly appointed major was to be Talle's second-in-command. Their immediate task was to secure the city of Grostheim, after which they would exterminate all hostiles and see a chain of forts established along the perimeter of the explored territory. Salvation then pacified, the full force would scour the wilderness and, should Inquisitor Talle deem it beneficial, extend by main force the boundaries of the known country.

It was elevation undreamed of for Var, but for all he was delighted with his promotion, still he could not deny he felt some reservations. For one thing, he doubted Krystine d'Lavall would wait for him—after all, he had no idea when he might return. But he was an officer in the God's Militia and did not question the orders of the Autarchy, so he penned a swift letter to Krystine and prepared to leave. It occurred to him as he wrote that he might never return, and thought abruptly of Arcole—perhaps now they shared the bond of exile. For another, he realized that he was second in a line of command that effectively replaced both Governor Wyme and Major Alyx Spelt, thereby rendering him one of the most powerful men in all the New World. He felt somewhat uncomfortable with such abrupt elevation over older men: he wondered how Spelt and Wyme should take it. That they would accept, he did not doubt—neither provincial governors or military officers argued with Inquisitors—but he anticipated resentment, such as might well brook problems affecting his designated tasks.

He had said as much—cautiously—to Talle as the *Wrath of God* sailed westward. And Talle had coughed out his whispery laugh and dismissed Var's reservations. Was the major not his second-in-command, he asked, and was he not an Inquisitor? Therefore who would dare argue? And did any colonials resent this imposition of Evander's authority, then they would answer to him; so Var need not worry—only obey his orders.

So far as Talle was concerned that resolved and ended the problem; Var was less sure. There would not be open disagreement, but it should be mightily difficult to execute his orders without the full cooperation of Wyme and Spelt, or the wholehearted support of Grostheim's garrison. And he was loath to impose his authority by recourse to the Inquisitor. Were Governor Wyme's worst fears realized, he must fight a campaign in unfamiliar territory and knew that victory would depend on concerted effort, shared purpose rather than enforced obedience.

Worse, he could not like Jared Talle, nor respect the man.

The Inquisitor enjoyed the exercise of his power too much, relished his position too much. He seemed to gloat on the prospect of usurping Andru Wyme, and seemed to expect Var to enjoy the same pleasure at thought of Spelt's demotion; nor less at thought of exterminating whatever hostile forces existed in Salvation. Var wondered—traitorous thought—if power corrupted Talle. Also, he smelled. Which was a small thing—God knew, Var himself had often enough gone stinking into battle—but still there hung about him a sour odor of must and sweat, as if he lived in a state of perpetual excitement, galvanized by that talent that made him an Inquisitor. He bathed seldom, and for all the long crossing had not, as best Var could tell, changed his clothes. It was not easy to sit with him in the small cabin, the air heated fetid, the windows never opened, as if Talle enjoyed the inhalation of his own body odors. Var preferred to spend his time on deck, or on the other ships, which bore the infantry and the light cannon of the artillerymen, or even with the engineers. That was to him an escape—from Talle's acrid excretions and the Inquisitor's oppressive presence, both.

Sometimes, as the flotilla proceeded westward, Var wondered if he was a fit officer for such an enterprise.

But still it was advancement beyond his dreams, and he was ordered to the conquest of a world by an authority he had never doubted. Were they successful, he and Talle, then he knew he might well find himself promoted colonel, or even marshal—military commander of all the New World. So he hid his dubiety and played the diplomat as he smiled at Talle and endeavored not to choke on the man's sourness, which seemed as much spiritual as physical.

He smelled it now, as squadrons of gulls mewed raucous welcome and he leant against the forrard rail, staring into the hazy blending of summer sky and lapping sea that rendered Salvation's coast a misty line across the horizon.

He turned as Talle approached, thankful for the breeze that did a little to subdue the man's fetor.

"Ere noon, eh?"

Talle took station at the rail alongside Var. His long black hair seemed too weighted by oil for the breeze to shift from his sallow face, and Var could not help the impression of a

carrion crow dressed in frock coat and breeches that sprang
to mind. He nodded and said, "Soon after noon, I think.
We've Deliverance Bay to cross yet."

The Inquisitor grunted and fixed bright black eyes on Var.
"You seem none too happy at the prospect, Major."

"I've my orders." Var met his stare expressionless. "My
happiness is surely of no account."

"No." Talle smiled, exposing yellow teeth. "But better that
you enjoy your work, eh?"

Var said stiffly, "I serve the Autarchy, Inquisitor. Now—
with your permission—I'd see my men ready to disembark."

"Yes, of course." Talle waved a languid dismissal and Var
turned away. As he went across the deck he felt the Inquisitor's eyes on him, as if an overheated sun burned against his
back. None of this, he thought, should be easy, and likely
none too pleasant. He resisted the urge to glance back and
went to his officers.

The *Wrath of God* reefed sail, slowing that the three accompanying vessels might take station astern. It had been Talle's
suggestion that they approach Grostheim in formal array, so
as to impress those waiting ashore, and Var must admit they
did make a gallant sight. He wondered what reception they
should receive, and how Grostheim fared. Wyme's reports
had spoken only of hostile attacks on inland farms, and the
governor's fear that the demons grew stronger. Might they
have grown strong enough to attack the city itself?

Var saw his men readied for landfall then went forrard
again, arming himself with a spyglass.

At least the city stood, but not without damage. The glass
showed him the signs of burning, blackened wood about the
walls, and watchtowers contrasting darkly with the pale scars
of fresh timber where repairs had been effected. Folk came
from the seaward gate: he picked out Wyme's sedan chair
surrounded by the scarlet coats of Spelt's soldiers. He passed
the glass to Talle, who surveyed their destination, grunted,
and returned the device without further comment.

The *Wrath of God* came alongside the wharf and Var accompanied Talle down the gangplank. The *Lord's Pilgrim,* the

God's Vengeance, and the *Fist of God* stood to offshore, awaiting the disembarkation of Var's marines before disgorging
their own military cargoes. The sun stood high overhead and
the air was warm: summer came earlier to this western land
than to Var's home. He adjusted his tricorne and saluted as
he halted before Wyme's chair. Alyx Spelt stood beside the
governor, his eyes widening slightly as he recognized Var and
saw the insignia of his new rank. Wyme commenced an unctuous speech of welcome, and Talle raised a hand, less in
greeting than to halt the governor's rhetoric.

"I am the Inquisitor Jared Talle." He spoke as Wyme's
effusive litany spluttered into silence. "I am come to rectify
your . . . problems. You already know Major Var, I believe.
He is my aide, answerable to me alone."

His tone brooked no argument, nor left room for discussion. Var saw Wyme's florid features darken to a purplish
hue, Spelt's lips purse tight as his eyes narrowed. The practice
of diplomacy seemed not to occur to Talle, nor did he appear
to notice the resentment his abrupt declaration produced.

"Later, you will apprise me of the situation," Talle continued curtly, "and I shall decide what measures I must take.
Meanwhile, I'd find my quarters."

Wyme seemed a moment lost for words; Var doubted he
had anticipated this when he requested Evander send him an
Inquisitor. Then he cleared his throat, struggling to retain
some semblance of dignity. "Yes, of course, Inquisitor Talle.
A room's prepared for you in my mansion—if you and the
major will accompany me?"

Var said quickly, "By your leave, Inquisitor, I'd see my
men billeted, and the other vessels off-loaded."

"Very well." Talle nodded in agreement. "That done, join
me in the governor's mansion."

He turned away, ignoring Var's salute, and beckoned for
Wyme follow him. Var looked to Spelt. "If you would assist
me, Major?"

Spelt hesitated, frowning irritably. He glanced toward
Wyme's chair as if debating the placement of his allegiance,
but the sedan was already in motion, the indentured bearers
striding alongside Talle, whose short legs carried him with
surprising speed toward the open gate.

"I'd be most grateful," Var said, hoping to disarm his fellow officer and perhaps undo some measure of the resentment. "We've a small army to see ashore."

Spelt stared a moment at the *Wrath of God,* blue-coated marines already forming ranks along the wharf, then out at the waiting craft. Var saw that his already-bitten nails were chewed almost to the quicks, his fingers stained dark with tobacco. He appeared older; his eyes, as anger faded, weary. He nodded and said, "So, a major now, eh? And aide to an Inquisitor, to boot." His tone was neutral, his voice harsh as if alcohol and tobacco roughened his vocal cords. "I suppose I must congratulate you."

"I believe my previous visit persuaded the Autarchy I've some small knowledge of Salvation." Var smiled apologetically, bowing to Spelt's greater familiarity. "And as Governor Wyme requested an Inquisitor . . . Well, I was fortunate enough to be chosen, and consequently promoted to suitable rank."

Spelt fixed him with cold eyes. "You'll earn it here, I think. What are your orders—to prosecute the demons?"

"To exterminate them," Var answered. "And establish forts along the wilderness edge."

"Exterminate them?" Spelt coughed out what might have been a laugh. "Easy for Evander to order; harder to achieve. You've your work cut out, Major."

Var heard something akin to despair in the harsh voice. "With your aid, Major," he said carefully, "I hope we shall be successful. I must rely on your knowledge in this."

"And I'm to answer to you, eh?" For an instant unconcealed anger sparked in Spelt's eyes, then was replaced with resignation. "Ah well, are those my orders, I must obey, no?"

"We are all under orders," Var said tactfully, seeking agreement between them, some kind of truce. "I had no choice in this."

"No, I suppose not." Spelt's mouth curved in approximation of a smile. "And you'll earn your rank out here, Major; no doubt of that. So," he grew brisk, "do we see your men safe ashore and settled in their billets?"

Var nodded. There was much he'd ask Spelt, much about the man's manner that disturbed him, but that must wait.

He'd see his troops settled first and then obtain a full account of the situation.

Time had done nothing to mellow Chakthi, nor banishment damped his rage: it ate him like a cancer, impossible to ignore, oblivious of reason, seeking only destruction. It defined him and made him what he was, which seemed now something other than human. Even Hadduth was afraid of him.

He had led his depleted clan away from Ket-Ta-Thanne under the watchful eyes of the Grannach and those warriors appointed by Rannach to escort the Tachyn to the mountains and beyond, and that ignominy festered: a new wound struck into the scar of the old. Had he thought he might prevail, he would have turned and fought, but the fighting in Ket-Ta-Witko and the desertion of so many—might whatever gods ruled here damn them!—left him with not enough warriors to chance the combat, and he could do nothing save obey the upstart Commacht. It had rankled, that the People listened to the slayer of his son, and he must go skulking away like a dog driven out from the pack, his tail between his legs and his pride sullied. That it was a fate of his own manufacture was obliterated by the heat of his anger and a consuming desire for revenge. It burned inside him like a fever, and he swore daily that the time should come when he would go back through the mountains, slaughtering the Grannach before he washed the plains of Ket-Ta-Thanne in the blood of his enemies. It was a sickness that devoured him from inside, so that even those still loyal walked careful around him, never sure of his rage's direction.

And to find that the land eastward of the mountains was claimed added fresh fuel to his hatred's fires. He had thought that land all his, and found some small solace in the knowledge that none of the People save his Tachyn rode there. He had thought of it as his kingdom—and then discovered there were others, firstcome.

So he had set out to destroy them. It was not difficult: they were sorry fighters, and mostly fled in terror when he sent his warriors against their strange wooden lodges. Then the red-coated ones had come, and they were better fighters, but still not hard to defeat. They tramped the grass like blind buffalo, clumsy and unaware of the land's ways, as if they knew nothing of the country they disputed and were afraid to enter the forests. Had they any power, it was in their strange weapons, which seemed to Chakthi near mighty as those of the Breakers. They had metal—which the Tachyn now lacked, save what they had carried with them, for there was no longer any trading with the Grannach—and they carried the long sticks that spat thunder and killed at a great distance.

"Muskets." He said the word aloud, savoring the sound and its secret knowledge. "Gunpowder."

"Master?" The thing tethered like a ragged dog outside his lodge stirred, eager to please.

Chakthi glanced at it and spat, the gobbet landing on the thing's face. It smiled and ducked its head as if in gratitude. To the Tachyn it was less than an animal, it was *owh'jika*—nameless and without honor, despised.

Once it had been a man whose name was Owan Thirsk. That man had owned a farm, had a wife and indentured servants: considered himself fortunate, even wealthy. Then the Tachyn had come and taught him better: now he was Chakthi's creature, alive—unlike the others of his holding—on whim of the akaman, and sickeningly grateful for that small scrap of what he saw as mercy.

Hadduth had shown wisdom, Chakthi thought, when he suggested they take one of the strangers alive.

"Listen," the wakanisha had said, wary of his akaman's reaction, "this is a new land and my dreams are very strange here, so that I cannot understand them all; not properly."

Chakthi raised his face from the fire at that and fixed Hadduth with burning eyes. "Your dreams were very clear in Ket-Ta-Witko," he said coldly. "You told me what to do there, and it brought us here. Kill Racharran, you told me, and the Breakers shall favor us. They will give you Rannach, and we Tachyn shall be mightier than any clan." He fingered the hilt of his knife as he spoke, his mouth stretching out in parody of a smile. "Ach! Tell me why I should not kill you?"

Hadduth felt his throat tighten at that, aware his death was a distinct and imminent possibility. Had Chakthi been wild in Ket-Ta-Witko, here he was like a wolverine maddened by a souring wound. The wakanisha answered quickly.

"It was Morrhyn spoiled that. Morrhyn! He climbed the mountain and so thwarted our plans. He spoke with the Maker there."

"You told me the Breakers were mightier than the Maker," Chakthi replied. "That they serve a greater god."

"They do!" Hadduth raised his hands, not sure if he extolled the might of the creature who had visited him in dreams or set a defense against Chakthi's simmering wrath. "How else could they cross the mountains of Ket-Ta-Witko, defeat the Grannach?"

"And be defeated," Chakthi snarled, "and all your plans come down in ruin, and we come here outcast."

"To a new land," Hadduth said, urgently. "Which we shall own—all of it!"

"Save we fall to the thunder-sticks," Chakthi said. "They are not true warriors, but they have that power. And we are few now. Thanks to you! And where are the Breakers now?"

"Waiting, I think." Hadduth thought fast: he sensed his life lay in the balance of Chakthi's fury. "I think that Morrhyn worked such magic as hid his trail, and therefore also ours. But they will find us: I seek them nightly in my dreams, that they come again and raise us up."

"And meanwhile this land is not ours."

"It shall be," Hadduth promised, hiding his fear and putting confidence in his voice. "Listen—we must find out what these strange people do, what they think. We must find out how many there are, and why they are here."

"How?" Chakthi asked, watching his Dreamer's face as he drew his knife, enjoying the alarm he saw. "How shall we do that?"

"We must take one alive," Hadduth said. "We must learn their language."

"I've heard them," Chakthi said. "They scream and shrill like frightened birds. How can we learn that?"

"Take one alive," Hadduth promised, "and I'll show you."

■   ■   ■

Like Major Spelt, Grostheim itself exuded an air of tension, as if the city awaited further attack. Folk met the long column of blue- and red-coated soldiery with cheers, as if rescue were come, but Var saw hollowed eyes and thinned cheeks, as if sleep and food were both in short supply. No less could he help noticing the signs of damage, where roofs or whole buildings had burned down, the charred remains often as not inhabited by people who appeared to live under the canvas pitched there. Also, the place seemed more crowded than he remembered, the sunny afternoon more redolent of Bantar's poorer quarters than this airy western clime. He inquired of Spelt just what had happened, but the older man was again become taciturn, waving a stained hand and suggesting Var wait until they gained the privacy of Wyme's mansion, where a full account might be delivered. After some moments of awkward silence Var asked after the billeting of the column.

"There's too many for the city," Spelt replied. "You're prepared to bivouac?"

"Of course." Var chose to ignore the insult implicit in the question. How else might he proceed against the demons? "We're equipped for a campaign in the field."

"Then best establish camp beyond the walls." Spelt gestured vaguely to the north. "Save you'd turn my men out of their barracks, and those not enough for all your force."

It was difficult to maintain an air of friendship in face of the man's morose humor, but Var refused to let his irritation show. Instead he kept his tone amiable and said, "I'd not see your men put out, and mine had best learn to live rough; so do you show us where, and we'll dig in."

Spelt grunted in reply and said no more as he brought Var to the north gate, where the Militiamen stationed on the wall stared at the newcomers with the expressions of wearied soldiers sighting a relief column. Var's curiosity grew, but he made no comment as Spelt took them through the gate and indicated where they might bivouac.

The area lay between the city walls and the Restitution River. Var recalled that timber warehouses had stood there, beside a series of riparian wharfs that served the river traffic. Now none remained, save as ruins, fire-blackened and fallen in.

Spelt said, "The demons," by way of explanation, then turned his head to observe the column.

Var saw that he crossed his fingers and spat. The gesture was surreptitious, but Var could hardly fail to see it. Spelt offered a shamefaced grimace and shook his head, as if denying his fellow officer's unspoken question.

"I'd best see to feeding them. After shipboard rations they'll doubtless welcome fresh meat." Spelt barked his odd laugh again. "Not that we've overmuch to spare."

Var sensed the man spoke to conceal his embarrassment. "You're short? What of the farms?"

Spelt shrugged. "Too many untenanted, or left to the indentured folk. Why d'you think we're so crowded?"

Var said, "I'd wondered," and was about to question Spelt further, but the major was already calling up an attendant officer, issuing instructions that supplies be issued the newcomers. Var found his reticence disturbing. He remembered Spelt as a brusque man, yet there was something about him changed, and Var sensed it went beyond resentment at his usurpation. But now was not the time to question him; Var hoped he should be more forthcoming in company with the governor and Jared Talle.

Wyme sat behind his ornate desk, a decanter at his elbow, a brandy glass clutched in his right hand. Sunlight fell slanting across his round face, and Var saw he sweated. The brandy rippled as Wyme's hand shook; Var wondered if that was the product of fear or Talle's presence. Perhaps for Wyme there was no difference—surely the Inquisitor was an ominous figure, settled like a black crow in an armchair, his eyes sharp, darting from Wyme's face to the two officers as if he accused them all of some unadmitted sin.

"The troops are settled?"

Var nodded. "And Major Spelt has arranged for provender."

He glanced at Spelt, seeking again to establish some communication between them, but Spelt's gaze was shifting nervously from Wyme to Talle.

"Then do we begin." The Inquisitor gestured at chairs as if it were his study, not the governor's, they occupied. "Sit."

"You'll take brandy?" Wyme indicated the decanter.

Before Var had chance to reply, Spelt nodded and found himself a glass. He filled it close to the brim, brows raised in inquiry as he looked to Talle and Var.

Talle only shook his head, fingers drumming impatiently on the chair's arm. Var said, "A measure, if you please." Did Talle disapprove, then damn him—surely they could retain some degree of civility. He smiled his thanks as Spelt passed him the glass.

"Now that we all are gathered, Governor," Talle's voice was soft, "do you advise us of the situation."

Wyme was clearly troubled as his garrison commander, save where Spelt was taciturn the governor waxed loquacious, reiterating his earlier reports.

Talle cut him short with an imperious hand. "We know all this. Major Var returned this news to Evander—that's why we are here. Do you speak of more recent events."

Wyme mopped at his beaded brow and gulped a measure of brandy. "Yes, of course. Forgive me . . . I . . . So much has happened."

"Then tell us of it." Talle's voice grew sharp: Wyme licked his lips. "Commence with events after Major Var's departure."

"More attacks." Wyme's eyes shifted from the Inquisitor's penetrating stare as if he sought some avenue of escape. "Refugees began to come in to Grostheim, quitting their farms."

"And you did not order them to return?" Talle's voice was cold with disapproval. "How shall this land be settled if every farmer comes running in to Grostheim at the first hint of trouble?"

"No. I . . . How could I?" Wyme shook his head helplessly, his cheeks glowing. Sweat ran into his eyes like tears and he produced a kerchief, dabbing at his face. "They were free folk."

"And you were the governor." Talle made the past tense sound permanent.

Wyme's flush deepened. "Save I ordered Major Spelt to force them back at bayonet's point, they'd not have gone."

"As well I'm here." Talle spoke softly, no louder than a murmur. "Things appear in a sorry state."

Wyme swallowed; Spelt emptied his glass and rose to fill it.

"Patrols were sent out," the governor declared hurriedly. "They found the signs of attack, but not the attackers. Only one man was left alive. The demons sent him back, that he bring a message."

He broke off, filling his glass. Talle said, sharply, "They spoke to him?"

Wyme looked to Spelt for support, but the Militiaman only sat slumped, staring blankly ahead. "They did, Inquisitor. They told him they planned to come against Grostheim; that this land is theirs."

"They spoke our tongue?"

"Yes."

"His name?"

Wyme looked again to Spelt, who said, "Captain Danyael Corm, Inquisitor."

"I'll speak with him later." Talle scratched his narrow nose, his expression thoughtful. Var was reminded of a carrion bird studying a carcass. "Go on."

"They made good their promise." Wyme's eyes met Talle's at last, almost defiant. "More holdings were destroyed and folk flooded into the city. Food grew scarce. I must find quarters for them all. . . ."

"Or send them back." Talle's lips curved in a mocking smile. "At bayonet's point, if necessary."

Wyme flushed. "They'd have fought," he protested. "God knows, but there'd have been rioting. And had they gone back, surely the demons would have slain them."

"And where was Major Spelt the while?" The Inquisitor's bird-bright eyes swung to the officer. "Why was no punitive expedition mounted?"

Wyme appeared grateful that attention was focused on Spelt, who shrugged uncomfortably and said, "It was discussed, Inquisitor. But I've only so many men—and enough lost already. You must understand . . . it was the governor's decision—" He avoided Wyme's angry glance. "—that it were best we hold Grostheim secure against the threatened attack. These demons are not such creatures as I've ever fought. They come out of nowhere and disappear like shadows . . . they're savage beyond belief. Had I taken my full force out—or even sufficient men to scour the land—I should have left Grostheim undefended."

"We believed ourselves alone in Salvation," Wyme added desperately. "We've never had more than a garrison here—not enough men to fight a *war*! And so many folk had come refugee, we deemed it best to hold the city secure. And as well we did!"

He paused, topping his glass as if the memory required the fortification of alcohol. Var studied his face, and Spelt's, and thought two very nervous men sat here. Doubtless both feared for their positions—nor did Talle's interrogation reassure them—but there was more. He wondered what these demons were, that they induced such unease.

Talle grunted and gestured that Wyme continue.

"They came in the night, with fire." Wyme shuddered at the recollection. "They burned those buildings outside the walls—the warehouses and the docks, all the boats there. Worse, they sent fire-arrows over the walls. In God's name, it was chaos!"

"I sallied against them," Spelt took up the narration as Wyme fell silent, "but I was beaten back. God knows, but it was all we could do to hold the walls."

"What of your hexes?" Talle locked eyes with Wyme.

"Not strong enough. It requires one of your strength to fix those secure."

He essayed a nervous smile that Talle ignored. "They breached the walls?" It was the first time Var had seen the Inquisitor disconcerted.

"They did," Wyme said. "We held them off for seven days, but then they entered. God, it was terrible!"

"It was a hard fight." Spelt looked to regain some measure of authority, of respect. "We fought them through the streets, and finally drove them back. But there were losses. . . ."

"Yes, yes." Talle was unconcerned with the fallen. "And then?"

"They sieged us," Spelt said.

"A month," Wyme added. "Then they quit. Between the

sun's setting and the next day's dawn, they were gone—praise God!"

"And then?" Talle prompted.

"We set to repairing the damage as best we could." Wyme dabbed anew at his face. "There's not so much timber left in the vicinity, so we sent armed expeditions south to the Hope River."

"South? Why south?"

"The demons would seem to inhabit the north and west," Wyme explained. "The attacks began there, along the wilderness edge."

"And did you find sign of them to the south?"

"None." Wyme shook his head. "Indeed, I was able to persuade a good number of the refugees to return in that direction."

Had he hoped this news would please the Inquisitor, he was disappointed: Talle only nodded, his face expressionless, and asked, "And those with holdings to the west and north?"

"Some have gone back. Under armed escort. Mostly those closest to the city. The rest—those with holdings closer to the forest rim—are afraid. They believe the wilderness spawns the demons."

"They'll return." Talle glanced at Var. "When the major goes out, he shall escort them home."

"They'll likely argue."

Talle frowned, his angry eyes prompting the governor to retreat back into his chair. "This land belongs to Evander," he snapped. "To the Autarchy! We shall not give it up."

"No, of course not." Wyme hastened to agree.

"And since this . . . siege . . . what further attacks?" the Inquisitor continued.

"None," Wyme said. "We've seen no sign of them."

"Save, of course, you do not venture very far." Talle pursed his narrow lips, staring at nothing, and for a while silence descended. It was clear who commanded here. Wyme and Spelt, for all their faces were dark with anger and indignation, made no sound, only waited on the Inquisitor as if fearful of disturbing his silent contemplation. Var sipped the last of his brandy, thinking that he should welcome venturing inland. Grostheim, he felt, would not be a pleasant place while Talle remained.

Finally Talle broke the uncomfortable silence: "I'd speak with this officer, Danyael Corm."

"Now, Inquisitor?" Wyme snapped a fob watch open. "My wife prepares dinner in your honor. She looks forward to meeting you."

Var doubted that anticipation should last long. From his recollection of Celinda, he suspected she and Talle were likely to find one another mutually distasteful. He thought that dinner should be a strained occasion.

But that dinner was, in any event, postponed. Talle looked at Wyme and said, "Now," and the governor swallowed nervously and motioned at Spelt, who rose as if grateful to escape.

No, there was no doubt who commanded Grostheim now.

8

Frightened City

Var could not remember Captain Danyael Corm from his previous visit and doubted, even had he, that he would recognize the man now. Corm's hair was stark white, paler even than his ashen face. His eyes were hollow and bloodshot, bagged with purple pouches that stood out against his pallor no less than the scarlet tracery of veins decorating his swollen nose. His tunic was crumpled and stained, the stock at his throat tied loose and dirty, his boots grubby. As he stood to attention, his lips trembled in time with the shaking of his hands, and his eyes darted anxiously about the room, resting longingly when they fell on the decanter. Var wondered how Spelt tolerated so slovenly an officer; Talle seemed not to notice the man's decrepitude.

"So you spoke with these demons."

Corm's throat flexed as he swallowed. He nodded dumbly, eyes closing as if to shut out a nightmare.

"Speak up, man." Talle's voice was commanding, empty of any sympathy.

"Sir . . . Inquisitor . . . I . . . Yes," Corm stuttered. Spittle glistened on his lips, swept up by a nervous tongue.

"In Evanderan."

"In Evanderan, yes."

"And they frightened you."

It seemed to Var that Talle savored the man's obvious terror, as a connoisseur might savor the aroma of a fine brandy.

Corm said, "Yes," in a faint and frightened voice.

"But they let you live." Talle's voice was speculative. "Why did they do that?"

"That . . . that . . ." Corm swallowed vigorously, eyes shifting wistfully to the decanter.

"Look at me!"

Talle's harsh order brought Corm's eyes back to his face; his own shone dark as he fixed the frightened man with a look so intense it seemed to bind their vision, denying Corm escape.

"That I might bring back their word," Corm said slowly, but no longer stuttering, as if Talle's gaze drew out the words. "That I tell our folk the demons were coming to destroy them, to destroy Grostheim. That the demons claim all this land for their own."

"And they said all this in Evanderan." Still the Inquisitor's fierce eyes held Corm transfixed.

"Yes. Not very well, but I understood him."

"Him?" Talle's head cocked to the side, though his eyes remained firm on Corm's.

"Their leader, I suppose." Corm shuddered. "He was . . . horrible. Like an animal. Like a demon come out of hell."

"Who speaks our language?"

"Surely demons would be gifted with tongues," Wyme suggested.

Talle ignored him. "Did you slay any?"

"Yes." Corm nodded without taking his eyes from Talle's. "We slew some few before they overwhelmed us."

"So, honest steel and musket shot kill them. Go on."

"They came out of the night," Corm said. "So sudden we had no warning. The shadows hide them, I think."

"Shadows hide a great many things." The Inquisitor turned his gaze on Wyme. "But they defied your hexes. Even weak, that should not have been possible. Still . . ." He nodded, a finger reaching absently to scratch at his nose. Var thought the nail came away grimed. "They speak Evanderan and they die. What did you do with the bodies?"

The question took them all aback.

"Well?" Talle was irritated at the delay.

"Burned them," Wyme said quickly. "They were gathered up and burned. What was left we buried in a pit, with quick-lime."

"So there'll be no remains. A pity."

"They were *demons*!" Wyme protested. "What else should

we do with them? By God, had we buried them, they'd likely have risen again."

"Perhaps." Talle shrugged. "But I'd like to have a body."

"In God's name why?"

The Inquisitor favored the governor with a look of utter contempt, as if the question came from an idiot child. "So that I might study one," he said calmly. "Dissect the thing— demon or man. Better still, I'd have one alive."

A horrid gagging sound came from Corm at that, and he shook his head vigorously. Var feared he might faint, or vomit over Wyme's carpet. Talle glanced at him and smiled unpleasantly.

"Does that disturb you, Captain?"

Corm swallowed, nodding. "Only destroy them, Inquisitor. In God's name! They're not fit to live."

"No," Talle agreed, "not whilst they contest this land. But still . . . a live one should be useful." He ducked his head, confirming his own thoughts, and waved at Corm. "You may go now."

Corm needed no further bidding: he sketched a shaky salute and spun on his unpolished heel, almost running as he quit the room.

"Excellent." Talle smiled, contentedly now. "For all the man's a drunkard, he aids me."

"How so, Inquisitor?" Wyme ventured.

Talle shook his head. "In time perhaps I'll tell you. But now . . . do we eat that dinner you promised?"

It was as awkward an occasion as Var had anticipated. The governor's wife was readied to play the perfect hostess to an illustrious guest, voicing effusive excuses for the simple fare she offered. She simpered, seeking to engage Talle in conversation, he returning curt monosyllables that before long brought a flush of anger and embarrassment to Celinda's plump cheeks. Nor did it help that what conversation ensued soon revealed that her husband was effectively displaced, that Talle was now Grostheim's premier authority. Var, feeling acutely embarrassed, did his best to alleviate the tension. But in face of Spelt's taciturnity and Wyme's obvious discomfort it was a vain effort, and the dining chamber fell silent save for the clink of glasses and cutlery as the branded servants mutely tended their masters.

Var was grateful for its ending. Talle consumed two portions of the sticky confection served for dessert and declined coffee, throwing his napkin carelessly aside and rising without preamble.

"I'll find my bed. Major Var, do you attend me at sunrise in the governor's study."

And he was gone, leaving Wyme anxiously calling for a servant to light his way. Var sipped coffee, determined to make some show of manners for all the Inquisitor had none. It was not easy: Celinda sat with angrily reddened cheeks and pursed lips, her husband and Spelt drank brandy—all in disgruntled silence. Clearly, they regarded him as Talle's man, and he supposed that he was. His instructions were to obey the Inquisitor, and was Talle a boor, still he was—by order of the Autarchy—Var's commander.

As soon as he might—politely—quit the table, Var made his excuses and left, explaining that he'd check his men. He anticipated that Spelt would accompany him, but the major only nodded a silent farewell and watched him go. Var thought that once the door closed on his back the conversation would grow animated. It was tempting to linger, eavesdropping, but a servant came with a candle and he had the man escort him to the outer door instead, warning that he should return later.

The night was warm, the sky all pricked with stars, the moon a slender waning crescent. The streets were quiet and dark, few windows showing light and the fires of the homeless banked to dully glowing embers. A dog barked at his passing, and from the shadows where canvas hung from charred uprights and lean-tos sheltered refugees, faces silently watched him go by. He heard a baby cry, and the soft murmuring of the mother; from an alleyway where splintered timber and ragged cloth roofed the dirt below, he heard the chink of bottles, the slurred mumblings of drunken men. There was much wrong in Grostheim, he thought, and wondered how bluntly Jared Talle would rectify matters.

The north gates were closed when he arrived there, and he must hail the sentries to open the sallyport.

Beyond, he was halted by pickets, starlight glittering on the bayonets they leveled. He announced himself and was escorted through the lines to the center of the bivouac. He was pleased to see the cannons were placed and work already begun on the rampart. It was an orderly encampment: no less than he expected.

He found Captain Matieu Fallyn, his second-in-command, still awake, stretched on a campaign bed and puffing industriously on a long-stemmed pipe as he read Pico's account of the Gavarian Wars. Fallyn set down the book as Var entered the tent, starting to rise.

Var waved him down, taking a stool. "How goes it, Matieu?"

"Well enough." Fallyn knocked the pipe on his heel. "They fed us, and I've arranged with the commissary for provisions. But by God, Tomas, they're a glum lot!"

"They're short of food." Var gave a brief account of events.

Fallyn ran a hand through his unruly curls. "And so we're a problem, eh?"

"So far as feeding us is concerned," Var nodded. "The sooner we take to the field, the better, I think."

"And how soon shall that be? I've already men asking when they might visit the taverns."

Var shrugged. "It depends on Inquisitor Talle."

"Ah, yes." Fallyn grinned mischievously. "How was your dinner?"

Var grimaced. "Inevitably, there's some resentment felt by the governor and Major Spelt."

"And our dear Inquisitor does little to placate them, eh?"

Var hesitated. He and Matieu were old friends—fellow captains until his promotion, and no envy after—but even so he was loath to voice openly his dislike of the Inquisitor. No matter his personal opinion, Talle *was* the representative of the Autarchy. So he only smiled and said, "He's surely his own way about him. But listen, Matieu, best we show the locals only courtesy. We shall need their cooperation, eh? So let it be known that I'll not have our men lording it over them. I want no trouble."

Fallyn nodded. "And what of leave? They're somewhat restless after the sea crossing. After all"—his grin expanded—"we're not all billeted in the luxury of the governor's mansion."

Var snorted, chuckling. "Had I any choice, my dear fellow, I'd be here with you."

"That bad, eh?" Fallyn assumed an expression of mock solicitude. "Still, orders are orders, no? And must you suffer a soft bed, servants, fine wines . . . Well, such is life on campaign."

Var answered his friend's grin. By God, but it was good to be able to relax. "Indeed. And as for leave . . . I think it best I speak with Major Spelt first. But meanwhile, do you draw up a roster. Small groups, eh? The city's already overcrowded with refugees."

"You shall have it tomorrow," Fallyn promised.

"Excellent." Var rose. "Then I'll leave you. All well, the Inquisitor should decide soon when we march."

Fallyn nodded enthusiastically. Var felt less sanguine: his friend had not witnessed Corm's naked terror or Spelt's grim resignation. It seemed to him that there was about both Militiamen, indeed, about the city itself, a fatalistic conviction that the demons could not be defeated. He wondered what Talle had made of Corm's account.

Owan Thirsk had sooner died, but he was not granted that benison.

He had seen his farm burned down and his wife slaughtered, and when he had fled the wreckage of his life he had been clubbed to the ground and woke to find himself a prisoner of the demons. He had thought they'd torture him, and prayed for swift and painless death, but that had not come. Instead, he had been dragged away and slung across a horse, lashed like a sack in a manner he'd not even have used against a branded man, and suffered the indignity and the pain and the far worse wondering . . . what did they want with him, that they kept him alive?

But they had fed him and given him water—just enough to sustain his body while his mind wandered wild—and taken him off to the wilderness woods, which now he knew were infested with demons because they had brought him to a camp where they lived like animals in leather tents, and none had houses or servants or any of civilization's accoutrements. But they had fed him and so he stayed alive because there was a tiny scrap of hope that he might survive, and that made him more afraid of death than of living. So even when they cut his heels that he not run away, even through his screams, he clung to the scrap, and accepted it when they tethered him like a wounded dog outside the leader's tent.

He had thought they tired of their sport and meant to poison him when he was dragged to a tent heated hot as an oven by the fire there, and the bitter potion had been forced into his mouth, and his nostrils pinched closed as his lips until all he could do was swallow. And find himself . . . he was not sure where . . . perhaps wandering in limbo, or gone to hell. It was like a dream; like speaking with the minions of the devil, tempting. . . .

But when he woke—he was quite unaware how long after—he found he understood the demon who sat with him and told him that its name was Hadduth, and that he could live if he did its bidding and served it.

It had seemed to Owan Thirsk that this demon assumed manly shape, for he could see little difference between its physical contours and his own, save that its skin was darker and its hair was long. He had asked what it wanted of him, and it had told him: "Your language. My akaman would know your tongue, that he might speak with your kind."

"And if I refuse?" Owan Thirsk had been surprised that he could ask that. "What then?"

"Why refuse?" the demon had countered. "I can feed you more of the pahé and you will tell me. Or Chakthi could take his knife to you again. What does it matter? Either way, you *will* tell us."

Thirsk had thought then of how the knife had felt, cutting into his heels, and how far away from home he was, and that he wanted very badly to live, and nodded.

"I'll tell you."

"That is good," the demon called Hadduth had said. "Chakthi will be pleased."

And so Owan Thirsk had taught the two demons, Chakthi and Hadduth, Evander's tongue and lived.

He had told them of what settlements he knew, and of Grostheim: of its walls and cannons and garrison. He had told them about muskets and gunpowder, and of the Autarchy—which they could not at all understand—and of how that authority would doubtless send troops against them.

And they had laughed and spat on him, and men and children had urinated on him as he lay tethered outside Chakthi's tent, and he could do nothing to protest for fear they kill him. Only hope that someday he be rescued: and wonder if his rescuers—who must surely come from Grostheim—not execute him as a traitor for all he'd told the demons.

He had obediently laughed when Chakthi spoke of the attack on the city, and after been careful not to ask why it had failed—the akaman was fond of inflicting pain, and Owan Thirsk knew that a misdirected question would earn him suffering—but he also knew that the Tachyn had withdrawn. Not entirely in defeat, but still denied the absolute destruction Chakthi sought. As best he knew, the Tachyn had pulled back into their forested stronghold, and waited to attack again.

He thought they would: he thought they would rally and go out once more until they burned Grostheim down and no farms were left, or mills or vineyards, or any other civilized things. And he was resigned to that. He was Chakthi's creature now and no longer a civilized man: only a thing, existing.

Sunrise found Tomas Var fresh bathed and dressed in a clean uniform, facing the Inquisitor across the width of the governor's ornate desk. Wyme was banished from his own study, curtly dismissed by Talle with the blunt announcement that he should be informed of his orders once the Inquisitor had spoken with Major Var. His face had darkened again, and a vein throbbed on his forehead, but he had not dared voice objections, only mutter that he would take his breakfast and retreat with what little dignity he could muster.

"A pompous man," Talle observed. "Worse, he's incompetent. In God's name, what possessed him to allow the farmers to stay?"

Var was uncertain it was a question, but then a black brow rose, like an arching caterpillar, Talle's small eyes fixing him inquiringly. It occurred to him, for the first time, that the Inquisitor was not so cognizant of military matters as he pretended.

"Likely as he said," Var answered, "that he feared rioting. And that the garrison lacks sufficient troops to patrol all Salvation."

Talle grunted, finding a pipe that he filled from Wyme's humidor. He struck a lucifer and drew deep, exhaling a cloud of sweet-scented smoke before he spoke again.

"He also said the attacks come from north of the river, so you'll concentrate on that area."

"When?"

The Inquisitor thought a moment. Then: "First, I'll see the city walls hexed secure. That should take me no more than two days, three at most. Do you meanwhile inspect the other defenses and report to me. How long shall that take you?"

"A day, I'd think; surely no more than two."

"Good." Talle puffed out more smoke. The day was already warming and the study windows were closed, the room stuffy with the mingled aromas of tobacco and the Inquisitor's own rank odor. "Then, when you're done, obtain maps from our pompous governor and have him mark you every untenanted holding. Plan your line of march in such a way that we can deliver the owners back."

"As you order," Var said. "But . . . what if they refuse to go?"

The Inquisitor smiled. "They'll not. My word on it."

Var nodded, holding his expression bland. He wondered if Talle's authority, his own show of force, could be enough to persuade the terrified farmers to return. Or would Talle work his magicks on them? That thought he liked not at all: he had come to Salvation to rescue its folk from danger, not impose tyranny.

"I shall issue a proclamation," Talle declared, "once our work here is done. Your men are ready?"

"They are. And with food in short supply here, we're a drain on Grostheim's resources. But meanwhile, I'd grant my men leave to visit the town—with your permission."

"Granted." Talle waved a careless hand. "Now breakfast, I think."

Var felt no wish to again suffer last night's awkwardness, and so he asked that Talle excuse him, explaining that he wished to inspect his men and commence the investigation of the city's physical defenses. Talle agreed, and with a sigh of relief Var quit the mansion.

His excuses were not unreasonable. Were they to march soon, he must soon prepare. Horses must be purchased or requisitioned to haul the cannon, and shortages or no, his men would need supplies to augment what they might find in the field. He anticipated problems, but even so could not deny the excitement he felt at thought of the campaign. It should be a novel expedition, against an unknown foe, and such as might well make his name. It was, for all his doubts, a heady prospect.

He went first to the garrison barracks, finding Spelt at breakfast, and accepted the man's ungracious invitation to join him. It occurred to Var, as he was served by a branded man, that the shortages afflicting Grostheim seemed not to apply to governor or garrison, and he experienced a small pang of guilt as he ate. He could not ignore the feeling that the servant's eyes lay hungry on his plate, and when Spelt pushed away his half-finished breakfast and gestured that the servant remove it, Var wondered if the man smiled somewhat in anticipation of the leftover food.

But such considerations were Grostheim's affair, not his, and he set them aside as he outlined Talle's orders and his own needs. Spelt was as uncommunicative as before, listening in silence until Var was done.

"Food we can manage," he allowed, "if you're prepared for short rations. Horses though . . ." He smiled sourly. "We ate most of the horses this past winter, before we started on the dogs. Most of those left were taken by the farmers for the spring planting."

"Surely there are some available." Var frowned at the prospect of manhandling the artillery inland. "I've twelve light cannon and three times as many swivel guns for the forts. Also the powder and shot; and we'll need wagons to carry our supplies."

Spelt drained his cup and dabbed fastidiously at his mouth. "How many in all?" His voice was flat, as if he already had his refusal prepared.

Var made a swift calculation. He had sooner taken extra horses, but if the animals were truly in such short supply and Grostheim so hungry as to eat dogs, it were better he settle for the minimum. He said, "A hundred, at least."

Spelt laughed, shaking his head. "Major, there's not more than fifty horses left alive in this city. And four of those haul the governor's carriage."

Var felt irritation tighten the muscles of his cheeks, even as he forced himself to maintain a pleasant smile. He had anticipated problems with Spelt—could not, in all honesty, blame the man for feeling resentful—but by God, he was come here on Wyme's request to salvage a situation Spelt had admitted he could not handle, and it seemed that all he got from the garrison commander was obstinacy and prevarication.

"Then those four, at least," he said, "will be accustomed to pulling their weight."

Spelt frowned, his eyes narrowing. "The rest are Militia animals, for my mounted infantry."

Var nodded. "But as you and your men will remain here, you'll not need them. Now, as to the remaining animals?"

Spelt shrugged, fidgeting with his waistcoat. "There are no more, not here."

"Then where?"

"On the farms," Spelt said, reluctantly.

"Then they must be requisitioned."

"But what of the plowing? The harvest? Grostheim could starve! By God, Major, we depend on the farms for our sustenance."

Var thought of the meal they'd just eaten and felt his patience dissipate. "What of the demons? What if they come again? Shall there be a harvest then? Or shall they conquer you?"

He saw Spelt's face pale at that, the frown deepening. But still the man argued: "The farmers will object."

"And shall you tell Inquisitor Talle that, Major? That he's not to have horses for fear you'll not have bread to eat?"

Spelt's face flushed—God, but mention of the Inquisitor elicited fear—almost, Var felt embarrassed; almost, but not quite. It was akin, he thought, to bringing in the threat of heavy artillery. And it worked: Spelt nodded sullenly and asked, "What would you have me do?"

"I'd have at least one hundred sound horses," Var said, "as soon as possible. More, if you can find them."

"Aught else?" Sullenly.

"How far's the closest farm large enough to provision my full force?" Angry now, Var could not resist adding, "Remember that most shall be on foot."

Spelt blushed and said, "On foot? Five days; thirteen more to the next."

"Then," Var said calmly, "we shall need provisions for five days at the least."

Spelt nodded, no less sullenly than before. "What else?"

"My inspection," Var answered. "The Inquisitor would have me check your defenses."

Spelt scowled. "Which shall I do? Find you your horses, or take you around my walls?"

"I think," Var said, "that a junior officer might show me the walls. Why do you not see to the horses? Doubtless the farmers shall take it better from you."

Spelt's scowl deepened, but he nodded, and Var marveled again at the power invested in mere mention of Jared Talle's name.

"I'm speaking out of turn, of course, but . . ." Lieutenant Jolyon Minns hesitated, glancing nervously toward Var, who leant against the northern wall, surveying his command's bivouac and the burned structures layered like discarded waste along the river's bank beyond. Var nodded, indicating that he go on. ". . . Well, it took us all by surprise. No one ʰught Salvation was aught but empty, and us the only ˑ. Then there came the attacks, and farmers coming in frightened, and patrols going missing. And then Danyael Corm came back, and not long after the siege began. It scared the governor, I can tell you; and Major Spelt. You'll not repeat this, eh?"

"On my word." Var shook his head.

"It was devilish hard." Jolyon chuckled grimly at his pun. "The demons sieged us fierce, I can tell you. Winter was on afore they quit, and scarce little harvest brought in for fear of their attacks. Nor the hunters going out, so it was a hungry time."

"Major Spelt said you ate horses and dogs."

"We did." The lieutenant nodded solemnly. "But worse than that—God, I've no objection to eating horsemeat. Why not? How's it different to beef or sheep, save we ride them?—it was like . . ." He broke off, shaking his head, nervous again.

Var said, "Go on."

"It was like," Minns said, "neither the major or the governor could believe it was happening—that they were attacked, that Grostheim was besieged. I think . . ." He shook his head, shamefaced.

"What do you think?" Var asked. And thought to add, "This shall go no farther."

"That they gave up," said the lieutenant. "That they drew back to Grostheim and left the rest of Salvation to the demons. And waited for you to come."

"Are they so terrible then," Var asked, "these demons?"

Minns ducked his head. "Yes! I thank God you've come, you and the Inquisitor. You'll drive them out, no?"

Var nodded. "Such are my orders, and I shall do my best to execute them. Now, do you show me the rest of these walls?"

They went on, past burned sections patched with innocent timber and places entirely new, the signs of attack left like old scars, memories of battle. But most was sound, and all the guns were in place, so that it seemed to Var the city had suffered no more than such siege as he had witnessed in the War of Restitution. Save then he had fought against men, knowing them men, and here it was clear they believed demons had come against them.

He concluded his inspection and went to find Jared Talle.

The Inquisitor was in the church, aided by a nervous and subservient vicar, busy mixing his hexing potions. A succession of Wyme's servants were delivering him those items he needed, such as paint and herbs, chickens' blood, the livers and bladders of certain animals, the spleen and claws and eyeballs of others. The brew seethed in its cauldron atop the altar, noxious, Talle's arms colored with the stuff, his hair lank about his downturned face, dripping. Var had witnessed Inquisitors at work during the War of Restitution, and for all he had benefited from their power, he could never like it much. It seemed to him a thing, delivered from God's dark side, that frail men might conjure occult strength where honest force of arms and purpose not prevail. But he was an officer of the God's Militia, and Jared Talle his commander, so he clenched his nostrils against the fulsome stink and delivered his report.

And Talle said, "Well done. How long shall it take Spelt to find us our horses?"

"I cannot say for sure." Var shrugged. "He'll bring them from the southern holdings, I'd think."

"Well enough." Talle drew his arms from the cauldron. He had shucked off his coat, and his shirtsleeves were rolled back to his thin shoulders. His arms were all red; he wiped them, depositing gory drips back into the steaming hex mixture. "You've checked Wyme's maps?"

"Not yet." Var shook his head.

"Then do it now." Talle wiped his hands across his shirt, coloring his chest. "He's skulking in his mansion, I think."

Wyme was, and Var was embarrassed afresh. He found the governor in his study, the windows open now, loosing the stale odors of tobacco and brandy and sweat. Wyme sat with a pipe in hand, a glass at his elbow, wearing a harried look that fused with concern and indignation as Var entered.

"I understand you ordered Major Spelt to find you horses."

Var doffed his tricorne, bowing slightly. "I *requested* that

Major Spelt obtain us animals for our campaign, Governor. Also such supplies as we shall need for the first few days."

"Difficult, difficult." Wyme shook his head. "Alyx told you most were eaten?"

"He did." Var sat uninvited. "But am I to progress against the demons, I've need of animals. Surely you understand that?"

"Of course; yes." Wyme smiled around his pipe, unctuously, reached for his glass. "But . . . how can I put this? Major Var, you are only recently promoted to major, and have seen Salvation but the one time. Can you truly understand our situation here?"

Var answered honestly: "No."

"And yet," Wyme said, "you come with Inquisitor Talle to . . . what? Usurp my position; Major Spelt's. To *command* us, to *bend* us to your will. As if we know nothing of this country."

"Governor," Var said, recommending himself to patience, "I am come here under orders of the Autarchy to exterminate your demons. Yes: I know nothing of Salvation, but I come at your request—as does the Inquisitor—and we are, all of us, bound by our orders. I'd not usurp Major Spelt or you: I only obey."

"And the Inquisitor?" Wyme asked.

Loyally, but doubting of his words, Var said, "Inquisitor Talle is servant of Evander—of the Autarchy. I doubt he wants your seat, only to rid you of your demons."

It was poor excuse, but sufficient for a desperate man. Wyme clutched it to him and accepted it, and offered Var brandy—which was refused—and then took out all his maps, which Var perused at length. After a while, because some hook of memory tugged at his mind, he asked, "The branded man—Arcole Blayke?—is he still with you?"

Wyme shook his head. "Him? No, he ran away, God damn him! He murdered my majordomo then fled with his doxy." He puffed harder on his pipe, expelling smoke in angry gusts at the memory. "Him and his doxy and a boy indentured to Trader Gahame. They fled when the demons attacked, and God willing, the demons slew them."

Var nodded, memories flooding back: but old and of another time. Arcole Blayke and the woman—what was her name . . . Flysse? And the boy . . . Davyd? He shook his head, dismissing them. Had they escaped under such attack as Wyme and Spelt described then they were surely dead. He wondered why he regretted that.

He asked politely, "May I take these maps, Governor?"

Wyme nodded, and Var took the charts to his chamber and set to studying them: planning his line of march, where he should deposit recalcitrant farmers, where establish forts, what troops to leave there, and how many guns. And all the time, like a nagging bee buzzing remorseless around his head, he wondered if Arcole Blayke still lived; because he could not—somehow—believe the branded man had died. Somehow that seemed impossible, as if hope and belief were taken away.

But Tomas Var could not properly understand that, and so he only went about his duties, and readied for the great expedition against the hostile demons.

9

Ungentle Persuasion

"Dammit, you can't force us!"

The speaker was a tall man, broad of shoulder and chest, his beard dense and red as a fox's brush, matching the angry color in his cheeks. His name was Niklaus Corwyn, and it seemed he was elected spokesman for the refugees. He stood a pace or two ahead of the crowd filling the square, glowering up at the dais where Inquisitor Talle stood, Governor Wyme was seated beside, Var and Spelt standing behind.

Talle said "No?" in a soft, almost mocking voice.

Corwyn shook his head vigorously. "Inquisitor you may be, and do you drive the demons out, then I'll be the first to bend my knee in thanks. But that first! Rid us of the demons, and then we'll go home." Dramatically, he flourished Talle's proclamation, crumpling the paper between large hands and flinging it to the ground. "Eh, neighbors?"

The crowd behind him—all the dispossessed, the refugees—shouted their agreement. Corwyn waited for the hubbub to die away, then: "You see? We're of one mind. Drive out the demons and then we'll go back. Not before!"

Var watched the Inquisitor take a step forward and then looked past him, out over the throng to the Militiamen ringing the square. They stood to attention, bayonets affixed to their upright muskets. Most of the refugees were armed—with pistols and swords, if not heavier weapons—and Var prayed earnestly that Talle not provoke a riot: that must inevitably end in bloodshed. God, he thought, when I was given this duty I believed we came to help these people, and they'd be grateful, but they look at us as if *we* are the enemy. And Talle does nothing but exacerbate their feelings.

He glanced sidelong at Spelt, wondering if the major's impassive features hid a triumphant smile, as if he relished these objections to Talle's diktat. He's no better than Talle, he thought. Him and Wyme, they all look for petty advantages, personal gains, when the fate of Salvation stands balanced and Evander might lose all this new world.

The long days of waiting for Spelt's men to gather his horses had allowed Var to form a clearer picture of the situation. From the maps he had studied, he had learned that most of the northwestern quadrant stood deserted, and from Wyme's tally books he knew Grostheim could not survive the year without the farms being tenanted again. From careful conversations with the refugees he had realized that a paralyzing fear gripped them, blinding them to the truth that they should starve did they remain, deafening them to persuasion. And Lieutenant Minns had been right: Wyme and Spelt looked only to hang on, to survive until Evander—in the form of Inquisitor Talle and Var's small army—salvaged them.

Grostheim, he had seen, was secure as any city; more, now that Talle had painted his hex signs on the walls and gates. But even so, for all they looked to be rescued, still both governor and garrison commander resented the authority imposed on them. What had they expected? Var wondered, and felt contempt at their petty jealousy.

He longed to be gone from this miserable city. He was a soldier, not a diplomat, and he had no time for these games. He was ready to leave. The horses were gathered and his men prepared to march; they were—grudgingly—supplied. He had secured the services of a hunter, one Abram Jaymes, who claimed to know the wilderness edge better than most. Young Minns—Var had come to trust his opinion—vouched for the man. Talle's proclamation had been posted, asking (Var's touch, that: the Inquisitor would have *ordered*) that the refugees present themselves in the square, preparatory to departure.

Spelt had suggested that they be gathered by Var's marines—they'd have the greater authority, he claimed—and Var had smelled a trap in that. He'd seen the proclamations torn down and tossed into the dirt, and knew the mood of the refugees, so he'd smiled and countered with the suggestion that surely Major Spelt's Militiamen represented authority in Grostheim, and therefore it were better *they* insure the refugees attend.

Perhaps, he had thought as he smiled and spoke softly, I do learn to be a diplomat. But God knows, I don't like it.

He brought his eyes back to Jared Talle. The Inquisitor stood on the edge of the platform now, head thrust forward to stare into Corwyn's eyes. Var could only see his back, but he could imagine how those eyes looked, and did not envy Corwyn.

He heard, very clearly, what Talle said. It was as if the Inquisitor's voice were a cold wind icing its way through the heat of the summer day. He did not speak loud, but nonetheless it carried out to all the refugees and the soldiers beyond them. Var thought that perhaps even the guards along the catwalks heard it, for it was like steel in flesh: undeniable and remorseless.

"This land is ours. *Ours!* It belongs to the Autarchy and Evander. It *belongs* to you, and to me—because we are Evanderan! Can you not understand that? Have you no pride, no care? Would you give it up to savages? Leave it to them?"

"Demons!" Corwyn gasped, staring at the Inquisitor, into his darkly sparkling eyes. "Demons who kill us."

"No!" Talle's voice rose to a shout, like a clap of sudden thunder. Even Var staggered back. "Not demons, but only savages. Vicious: yes; cunning: yes. *But not demons!*"

"How," Corwyn asked, swaying on his feet as if Talle's stentorian voice had loosened his limbs, his hold on gravity, "do you know?"

"Because I am an Inquisitor." Var could not see Talle's face, but he could imagine those thin lips curling in physical expression of the contempt larding the man's voice. "I do not need to see them because *I am an Inquisitor!*"

Corwyn hesitated, shuffling nervously, like a bull brought to bay. Var saw him tear his eyes from Talle's gaze, and marveled at the man's willpower. Yet when he spoke, his tone was less confident. "But I have seen them; and what they do." He turned slowly around so that he faced the crowd. Var saw his shoulders hunch, his back straighten, as if he drew on a reservoir of strength. "Eh, neighbors? We know what's out there, don't we?"

The crowd, silent until now, murmured a massed affirmative. It shifted, milling nervously as a herd of frightened cattle. Corwyn raised his arms. "And we know where we're safe, eh? Here, that's where! Here behind high walls, with the Militia to protect us. So I say we stay here. Are you with me?"

The answer was a sullen bellow of agreement, a waving of fists, in some cases of weapons. The Militiamen stationed around the square grasped their muskets firmer; the lieutenant in command looked toward Spelt. Oh God, Var thought, don't let this go wrong. He saw Spelt frown and wondered what thoughts went through the man's head. Wyme sat mopping his florid brow, eyes darting from the crowd to the Inquisitor. Then Talle, as if possessed of hindward-facing eyes, said, "Hold your men steady, Major. Leave this to me."

Corwyn, emboldened, turned to face the Inquisitor once more. "There, you see? Every soul here's a freeman, and we've decided to stay."

"Look at me!"

The command seemed unnecessary—Corwyn was already glaring defiantly at the black-clad man—but as the words lashed out, he stiffened somewhat and his gaze fixed unwavering on Talle's eyes. Var guessed what was coming—he had seen Inquisitors at work—and choked down the sour lump that threatened to clog his throat.

"Come here."

Talle beckoned and Corwyn took a stiff-legged pace forward, and then a second, his head tilting as he continued to stare at the smaller man. His eyes were unblinking despite the bright sun, the sweat that trickled down his forehead as if he were engaged in some tremendous internal labor. He halted when his belly touched the edge of the dais, standing rigid as any soldier on parade. Talle delved in one deep pocket of his frock coat, still holding Corwyn with his eyes, his hand emerging with a small silver-topped pot of some dark ceramic. He unscrewed the lid and dipped an index finger.

"Closer."

Corwyn bent from the waist, bringing his head nearer the Inquisitor, who in turn leant forward, reaching out with an odd delicacy to trace a pattern on the bearded man's forehead. He murmured as he painted his design, but too low that any save Corwyn himself might hear. Then he stood back, stoppering the jar. Absently, he wiped his smeared finger on the lapel of his coat. All the while, his eyes remained firm on Corwyn's.

The square was unnaturally quiet. Var heard gulls mewing, but that was the only sound until Talle spoke again, aloud.

"Now tell me what you intend to do."

"Go home," Corwyn said.

His voice rang loud in the silence—which ended with his announcement, a babble of protest and disbelief starting up amongst the refugees. Talle raised his arms and shouted "Quiet!" in the same thunderclap tone he had earlier used. The crowd fell obediently silent.

"Tell your friends," the Inquisitor ordered.

Corwyn turned to face the crowd. Var thought of automatons, and those frightened soldiers he'd seen hexed so that they raged into battle, careless of injury, like the berserkers of legend. From the corner of his eye, he saw Alyx Spelt cross stained fingers and spit.

"We must go home." Corwyn's voice was a rich baritone, full of conviction. "Our farms need tending, the mills repairing. We must think of the harvest, and the vineyards. We've let them go too long."

From within the crowd a man asked, "And what of the demons?"

"We've the Inquisitor to protect us," Corwyn replied confidently, "and all the strength Evander's sent us."

"The demons have slain Militiamen before," called a second protester. "Why not these? And us, after?"

Corwyn said, "The demons are only savages—as the Inquisitor says. Nor have they faced an Inquisitor before—they are chaff before his God-given power! And you've seen the soldiery Evander sends us—engineers to build forts, and cannon to ward them. All the might of marines and infantry and artillery! How shall the savages prevail against the chosen of God?"

"They did before," cried the hidden voice.

Talle smiled and said to Corwyn, "Name him."

Corwyn said, "Jerymius Thorne."

"Excellent. Lead me to him."

Talle sprang from the platform with an agility Var found somehow incongruous, all flapping black coattails and lankly swirling hair. Conscious of his duty for all he disliked the man, he cried, "Inquisitor! Is this wise?"

Talle spun around, as if performing some weird dance, and pantomimed a bow. "Fear not, Major Var. I am quite safe. Or do *you* doubt me?"

Var shook his head and Talle grinned; Var thought again of predatory animals. He watched as the Inquisitor touched Corwyn's elbow, for all the world like they were old friends, motioning that the much larger man lead the way.

Var looked to Spelt, finding the major staring wide-eyed at the incongruous couple who walked into the hostile crowd as casually as if they were making their way through the guests at some garden party. He could not be sure whether Spelt was genuinely amazed, or prayed that Talle be torn apart by the angry throng. Wyme, he saw, was gasping as if unable to breathe adequately, his pudgy hands knotting his handkerchief so tight the bundle loosed a steady dripping of moisture onto the white cloth of his breeches. It should look ill on the governor's record, Var thought with cynical amusement, if an Inquisitor were slain within his jurisdiction.

But it was, he knew, hard to slay an Inquisitor. They were the Autarchy's ultimate authority, and fear of reprisal was a powerful weapon, even without the strengths the Inquisitors themselves owned. And God knew, they were plentiful and terrible.

Even so, he must—albeit reluctantly—admire Talle's courage.

And so, it appeared, did the refugees; or they were confused by this strange turn of events. Whichever, they parted to let Corwyn and Talle through, forming a wide avenue to a brown-haired man dressed in a soiled shirt and grubby waistcoat. He wore a dusty tricorne, a belt supporting a holstered pistol, and in his hands he held a trade musket. The crowd moved back from him as it might from a felon, condemned, a circle shaping where the avenue ended so that Var had a perfect view.

Corwyn said, "This is Jerymius Thorne," and Talle beamed and aped his gangly bow again, and said, "Sieur Thorne, well met. I am, have you not already learned, the Inquisitor Jared Talle. I am come here on Evander's business, on orders of the Autarchy, to make this new land safe again."

Thorne swallowed, fingering the hammer of his musket, looking from side to side, finding no support there so that he must face the capering black figure before him. He looked at Corwyn.

"For God's sake, Niklaus! I've only followed you."

Corwyn said nothing. Talle bowed again, arms spread wide in parody of courtly greeting. "But now Sieur Corwyn is persuaded to go home—to do his duty. Are you not willing to do yours? Are we not all servants of Evander, of the Autarchy? Are we not all committed to holding this new land secure for Evander? Sieur Corwyn understands that now. Why not you?"

Thorne said, "You hexed him; *I'm* not bewitched."

Talle's laughter rang high-pitched. "You don't like hexes?"

Thorne shook his head nervously. His right index finger stroked the trigger of his musket.

"You don't like the hexes I've set on Grostheim's walls?" Talle spread his arms and bowed his head in parody of disappointment, spinning around in a swirl of black tails, weird as a dancing crow. "The hexes you'd hide behind? Shall those same hexes not protect you out there?" His prancing ceased, an arm flung out to the north and west. "Where forts shall be built, and soldiers be there to protect such cowards as you?"

Thorne said, "I'm not a coward."

Talle said, "You are."

Thorne said, "I've seen the demons. . . ."

"Savages!" Again, the thunderclap: denying argument, leaching antithetical will. Niklaus Corwyn stood nodding solemn confirmation. The crowd stood quiet, waiting; afraid. "No more than savages!"

Thorne sniffed and hung his head a moment.

As he did, Var saw that he set the hammer of his musket on half cock and dropped the strikerplate against the pan. He wondered what the man knew of Inquisitors, and what Talle saw and would do.

"Are you wed?" Talle asked at last, smiling his horrid smile.

Tomas Var saw it through the crowd and wondered where this discussion led. Likely, he thought, to Thorne's downfall. But still he must, in a way, admire Talle: as he might admire the approach of a soft-stepping spider to its prey: all slow and subtle until the fangs sank in to deliver the poison.

He saw Thorne nod, confused, and heard him say, "I've a wife and two children."

"Are they here?"

"Yes." Thorne shrugged. "Where else would they be? There's nowhere else safe in Salvation."

"Nor anything of Salvation left," Talle said, "save you and your kind go back. Would you see them safe, then, your wife and children?"

Thorne nodded.

"Then that," Talle concluded, "can be easily arranged. I shall have them branded, and indentured to folk in Grostheim. You think the city safe, no?"

Thorne gasped. "You can't! We are free folk."

"I can," Talle said. "I am an Inquisitor."

"No!" Thorne looked around for support: found none, and thumbed his musket to full cock. "You can't do that."

Talle said, "I can. I can do everything I promise. I can hex you safe from the savages, or kill you. I can send your wife and children into indenture, branded."

Thorne screamed *"No!"* and swung his musket down and round at the Inquisitor's chest, squeezing the trigger.

Var saw it all clear, as if time slowed and ran glutinous, so that it seemed all done in mime, unreal. He saw the hammer fall, driving the flint against the strikerplate, the resultant spark igniting the powder loaded into the barrel. He saw the musket buck in Thorne's grip and the gray-white cloud of smoke that erupted from the muzzle, lit by the flash of the explosion that propelled the lead ball into Talle's chest. He saw the Inquisitor stagger back and thought, God, no! He can't be slain! What shall happen now? He saw Niklaus Corwyn catch Talle in his arms and steady the stricken man. Then he saw Talle find his balance and stand upright out of

Corwyn's supportive embrace, smiling unpleasantly as Thorne gaped in naked disbelief.

"I am an Inquisitor, and we are hard to kill." The dark-haired man brushed at the frontage of his coat, where material smoldered, slapping out sparks. "And to attempt our murder is a crime."

Thorne stared at him; every eye in the square was on him. Talle adjusted his coat, tugging a moment at the waistcoat beneath. Then held up the ball that had struck him full in the chest. He examined the bullet and turned slowly around, holding the lead missile high—an exhibit in this impromptu prosecution.

"Would any here deny that this man attempted to murder me?"

Silence answered his question and he flicked the bullet away. It fell, dull, on the packed dirt of the square.

"Then by the authority vested in me by the Autarchy of Evander, I declare Jerymius Thorne guilty of attempted murder. The sentence is death."

From the rank of onlookers closest to Thorne a woman wailed. Thorne stared at his musket, at Talle, as if he could not believe the evidence his own eyes gave him. He shook his head, flung the musket away, and looked to Corwyn.

"Niklaus, for God's sake, do something! Help me!"

"I can do nothing." Corwyn faced his friend with an impassive visage. "The Inquisitor is right—you tried to kill him. You are guilty, Jerymius."

"No!" Thorne shook his head desperately. "No . . . I . . ."

Corwyn said, "Yes," in the same confident tone.

Thorne wiped a hand across the sweat beading his face, his eyes darting about, seeking support from the crowd: none came. Only frightened faces answered his unspoken plea, and the weeping of his wife.

Talle said "Look at me!" and involuntarily Thorne faced the Inquisitor.

Talle stepped a pace closer. "Jerymius Thorne, you have attempted my murder. You have betrayed Evander, your family, and your friends. How say you?"

Tomas Var was unaware that he balled his fists as he

watched Thorne struggle against the occult strength of the Inquisitor's gaze. He was, no less than any other present, unable to intervene, stilled by Talle's voice, by the aura of power the little man radiated: all the dread authority of the Autarchy at his back. Var could do no more than watch and hear out this sad drama, already guessing its end—not liking it, but bound by duty and magic to witness it.

Thorne's eyes bulged as he fought Talle's will. His head craned back—though his gaze was not able to sever the awful connection with Talle's—and tendons stood rigid on his neck. His lips stretched back from his parted teeth and saliva trickled down his jaw. Slowly, as if each syllable was dragged out unwilling, he said, "I am guilty."

Talle nodded, smiling as if a point in some minor argument were conceded. On his face, Var saw the same expression he had worn when interrogating Danyael Corm. It was a look of unalloyed pleasure, a delighted savoring of his victim's suffering.

"And your just sentence?"

Thorne's mouth closed, opened, his lips writhing. Talle raised an inquiring eyebrow, his head cocking to the side, expectant, hideously patient.

Thorne said "Duh . . ." and began to choke.

Talle waited.

"Duh . . ."

The Inquisitor nodded, a minimal ducking of his head that did not remove his gaze from Thorne's bulging, fear-filled eyes.

Then Thorne said, "Death."

"Which you deserve," Talle said.

Thorne's head wobbled on the stalk of his corded neck: "Yes."

"Then die."

Talle stretched out a hand to trace some arcane sigil over Thorne's face, and the refugee staggered back as if he were shot. His spine drew rigid, his arms flapping from the shoulder sockets like the empty sleeves of a scarecrow caught in a wind. His head lolled, rolling from one side to the other, loose. His feet executed an obscene jig as his features suffused with blood, purpling, his tongue extending black from between his wide-stretched lips, bloodying as his chattering teeth bit down. Then he made a mewling sound, much like the calling of the gulls, and fell over.

There was a ponderous silence, heavy as the weight of summer's heat, and just as still. Talle studied the body a moment, then turned to Corwyn.

"Well, Sieur Corwyn, justice has been done, no?"

Corwyn nodded. "It has."

"And shall we go on about our business?"

"Yes."

"Then do we decide what our next move shall be?"

"We must go home," Corwyn said. "We must go back to our holdings. We shall be safe now."

Talle smiled, motioned for the big, bearded man to follow him, and walked back down the avenue of dumbfounded refugees to the dais. Corwyn helped him mount the platform, then sprang up alongside.

Like a trained dog, Var thought, studying the mark scribed on Corwyn's forehead. It was fading now, as if the potion of the hex sign sank into Corwyn's flesh. He looked out at the crowd. It, too, was closing around the body, which only a few looked at, as if the refugees were afraid of similar retribution and would ignore the one who'd argued. Like sheep, he thought, ignoring their own dead.

"Now," Talle said, his voice ringing out far louder than his small frame had right to produce, "we shall prepare to leave. You outland folk shall go with all your goods and chattels to the north gate. You will wait there until tomorrow's dawn, when we shall escort you home.

"We shall take you back to your farms and mills and vineyards and reclaim this land for Evander! The savages shall be slain, and forts built to protect you—my word on it. No harm shall come you.

"Now go!"

No cheers answered his oratory, but the refugees began to move away. Most likely, Var thought, because they feared to die at the Inquisitor's hand, and would sooner take their chances on his promise in the outlands. Fear set against fear.

He started as Talle's hand clapped his shoulder.

"Smoothly done, eh?"

Var wondered if the Inquisitor sought his approval. Surely not; Jared Talle was a power entire unto himself, nor could Var forget the relish he had seen on Talle's face, heard in the man's voice, as the Inquisitor faced Thorne.

So he ducked his head and said only, "Yes."

Talle chuckled and gestured at the red-coated Militiamen escorting the refugees from the square. "And had they opened fire? Had these arguments gone on—persuasion and counter? stay or go?—what then?"

Var said, "I don't know."

Talle chuckled and said, "A moment, Major," and went to Niklaus Corwyn, who stood still as an ox resting in its traces, and clapped the huge man on his shoulder and said, "Niklaus, my friend, why do you not go with your fellows and see them settled. You are their leader, and I should appreciate your help in this endeavor."

Corwyn nodded and jumped from the platform.

"You see?" Talle said, not asking a question. "Their leader obeys me, and they are afraid of me."

"Is that a good thing?" Var asked, unable to resist the question for all the sour taste he felt at its answering. "Fear?"

"One man died," Talle said, "when there were hundreds ready to argue. Men and women and children—would you have seen Spelt's redcoats open fire?"

Var shook his head.

"Nor I," Talle said, and chuckled. "They're too valuable. Are we to take Salvation back from these savages, we need the settlers. Evander needs them in their farms and mills and vineyards. We need them to do our will, Major Var. To hold Salvation for the Autarchy."

Var ducked his head. He had no clear answer, only nebulous doubt that Talle's way was wrong.

And a last question that he could not resist: "How could you survive that bullet?"

Talle chuckled and loosed the buttons of his waistcoat, the grubby shirt beneath. He drew the cloth aside, exposing the hex signs daubed over his chest. A bruise flowered there, mingling with the sigils but already fading, becoming one with the pale skin. The hex signs were far brighter, as though they absorbed the wound.

"As I have said, Major Var, I am an Inquisitor. And we are *very* hard to kill."

10

March, or Die

Officially it was the Inquisitor Jared Talle who led the column out, but in fact it was Tomas Var, mounted on a fine black gelding that Andru Wyme had been mightily loath to part with, who rode at the head. Matieu Fallyn sided him to the right, on another of the governor's horses, and Abram Jaymes slumped to his left on a lop-eared mule. Immediately behind them—the spearhead—came half of Var's marines, on foot, the second half spread as flankers to either side. Talle rode a wagon, back down the column, where the light cannon trundled before the marching infantry. The supply wagons, the settlers, and the remaining infantry moved dust-clouded in the rear guard.

Var had sooner owned more horses, seen all his men mounted. All he had learned of the hostiles—were they demons, as the inhabitants of Salvation believed; or only savages, as Talle claimed?—persuaded him that his duties were best dispensed swiftly, and the war brought fast to the enemy. The settlers were sullen in their acceptance of Talle's instructions, and whilst none dared argue, Var feared that should the hostiles attack, the farmers would again flee back to Grostheim, and all their work for naught. Still, they were promised protective forts, guardians of the wilderness frontier, and he must see those built—and manned—before he could contemplate carrying the action to the hostiles. It was yet early summer, but from his perusal of Wyme's maps and his investigations, he could not foresee completion of all the forts before the snows came, and he was loath to fight a winter campaign in unknown territory. He had cannon and the lighter swivel guns, and sufficient force of infantry to withstand siege of the forts. But cavalry or mounted infantry—had he the horses!—might cut down fast on attackers; might come out from the forts to deliver swift vengeance and ride the perimeter, speedy, patrolling the defensive line.

But Salvation was short of horses and he must make do with what he had: and be grateful his threats had won him enough to haul the cannon and the wagons. He consoled himself with the thought that as each fort was built more horses would become available. And perhaps . . . He looked to Abram Jaymes.

"You've seen the hostiles, no?"

Jaymes spat over his mount's ears and ducked his head. "At a distance." He flourished the Baker rifle he carried, as if that explained the meeting. "I seen 'em, sure; but I got this long gun, and she fires farther'n your muskets—so I never needed to be close. Only leave 'em behind."

"Did they have horses?" Var asked.

"Yes." Jaymes nodded, expelling a cloud of flies from his buckskins. "Why?"

Var said, "I'd wondered if we might not capture animals from them."

Jaymes laughed and said, "I doubt you could capture anythin' from them, Major. Save maybe the heads o' the dead, or scalps—they take both, an' they fight fierce."

Var's faint optimism waned. "You doubt we might raid their herds?"

"Don't reckon so. Not afoot." Jaymes shook his head and spat a liquid stream of chewed tobacco, stabbing a thumb back toward the marching column. "Your soldiers aren't exactly woodsmen, an' the demons are quick as bobcats, an' as wary."

"What do they look like?" Var asked.

"Horrible." Jaymes rolled his eyes. "All painted up and dressed in skins, like savages—like what the Inquisitor says."

"Not demons?" Var asked.

"I don't rightly know what demons are supposed to look like." Jaymes reached inside his buckskin shirt to find a fresh plug of tobacco, sliced off a wad with a wickedly bladed knife, and sucked it into his mouth. "They don't wear horns—leastways, only animal horns—an' they don't breathe fire, or suchlike; an' they die when a bullet hits 'em. Much like any man."

"Then why," Var asked, "are the people of Grostheim so afraid of them? Why are the settlers so afraid?"

Jaymes dug awhile inside his shirt, chewing ruminatively. Then: "I suppose they're scared because they never expected to be. They all thought this was an empty land—there for the takin'. Then they found it wasn't so, and that put the fear in them."

Var nodded. It was an echo of what Lieutenant Minns had told him: complacency. "And what now?" he asked. "Are they gone? Shall they allow us to build the forts?"

"I'd reckon not," said Abram Jaymes. "I'd reckon they'll fight."

"And the settlers?" Var asked. "What of them?"

Jaymes chuckled and spat out more filthy tobacco. "I'd reckon," he said, "that the painted people'll fight you first. I'd reckon they'll look to wipe you out an' then go after the farmers, because they're not stupid—they know you soldierboys are the real threat; the farms are easy to pick off."

Var said, "They frighten you," somewhat surprised.

"Sure they do." Jaymes nodded cheerfully.

"Then why," Var wondered, "are you riding with us?"

"Lord God, Major," Jaymes laughed, "you're payin' me, no? An' all I need do is lead you on to where you want to go. I don't reckon they'll attack so many men; no, they'll wait until you split up—an' by then, God willin', I'll be long gone."

Var frowned. "I'd thought . . ." He shook his head.

Jaymes studied him soberly. "I agreed to guide you, an' I'll do that. I'll show you them places you want to build your forts, just like I agreed. But then I'm gone."

"And if I asked you to stay?"

"I'd tell you no."

"I could," Var murmured, "ask Inquisitor Talle to hex you. Then you'd have no choice but to stay."

"Yes, you could." Jaymes grinned. "But I reckon you won't."

"Why not?" Var asked; he was genuinely curious.

"Because you're not like that." The guide's grin faded, his

seamed features becoming thoughtful. "I saw your face when the Inquisitor hexed Niklaus Corwyn, an' when he did what he did to Jerymius Thorne. An' I saw you didn't like it."

Var said, "Even so, I . . ."

"No." Jaymes shook his head. "You an' the Inquisitor are cut from different cloths. You'd ask a man to follow you, but I don't reckon you'd force him to it."

Var opened his mouth to speak again, but the guide heeled his mule forward, calling back, "Reckon I'll go earn my pay, Major. Scout ahead some, eh?" and was gone.

Smiling, Fallyn brought his horse closer to Var's. "He's your measure, Tomas, has he not?"

Var scowled. "I *could* have him hexed," he said.

"No." Fallyn chuckled. "It's as our somewhat malodorous comrade says—you'd *ask,* not force him to it. Tell me, am I wrong?"

Var's scowl deepened as he shook his head. Then he sighed and allowed himself to smile. "No, Matieu, you're not wrong. But tell me, does that make me a poor leader of this enterprise?"

"It does not." Fallyn reached out to clap his friend on the shoulder. "It makes you a man worth following."

They went on, through the mounting summer heat, day after day at a pace that threatened to punish the weak and that left the strong weary at day's end. Var was anxious to reach his sundry destinations as soon as he might—not least the first farms, where he hoped to replenish his supplies—and Talle seemed indifferent to the pace or the heat, so when settlers complained and asked that they halt longer, and sooner, they were denied. And none dared complain overmuch, remembering what the Inquisitor had done to Jerymius Thorne, and knowing that Niklaus Corwyn would report their words to Talle.

It was an odd duty, Var thought as he stretched beneath a sky sprinkled with more stars than he had ever seen. He had perceived himself a rescuer when first told of the commission, and anticipated (he snorted laughter) a hero's welcome—the savior of Salvation, come with his legions to drive out the savages and deliver the land back to Evander. But events had taught him better. The resentment of Wyme and Spelt was reflected in the faces of the settlers, in the hushed and sullen mutterings he heard as he walked amongst their campfires. All of them, it seemed, had expected some miracle, some magical sweeping away of all problems. As if Talle could raise his hand and strike down the demons, and Var's battalions be there only to reassure the settlers with their presence. It seemed that none had anticipated a protracted campaign, and now that it was come, resented the deliverers. As if—Var laughed aloud, cynically—they saw little difference betwixt savior and destroyer.

"You're cheerful," Fallyn said.

"No." Var shook his head, still smiling. "Only amused. God, Matieu! I thought there'd be glory in this. Not . . ."

"Hatred?" Fallyn smiled back.

"Is it truly that bad? They hate us?" Var lifted up, looking to where the settlers' fires burned within the ringing flames of the infantry, those lights outlining the defensive cannon spread along the perimeter. Beyond, the glow reflected off the bayonets of the pickets between, watching wary.

Fallyn shrugged, reaching for a bayonet on which was spitted a chunk of venison delivered by Abram Jaymes.

"It's not that," the guide said. "Leastways, not exactly."

Var turned toward him. The man was of indeterminate age, in need of a bath and a haircut, his clothes in need of washing—likely in lye, Var thought—and his habit of chewing tobacco was undoubtedly disgusting. But Var liked him. He said, "Then what? In God's name, we've delivered half of them safely home to their holdings. We've even rounded up their indentured folk; and we've not taken more cattle than we need to feed ourselves. There's been no sign of hostiles, so what have they got to hate?"

He thought that Jaymes would repeat himself: reiterate that the settlers were afraid, would sooner remain behind Grostheim's walls until Var and Talle had swept Salvation clear of the demons, or the savages—whichever they at last proved to be—and hated those who'd forced them out from the city, back into the land they feared.

But Jaymes surprised him. He said, "This used to be our land. You understand that?"

Var shook his head; Fallyn set his venison back over the flames. It dripped fat that spat and sizzled, ignored.

"Evander conquered the Old World, no?" Jaymes said. "The War of Restitution saw us—I was Evander born an' bred—take the Levan an' Tarrabon, an' just about every other country worth the conquerin'. I fought in that war, likely as you two did, an' I saw the Autarchy take control of all those lands. I was—what?—thirty-somethin', when I heard about Salvation. A new land! Off westward, past the Sea of Sorrows. God, but when I heard what was there, I wanted to go! You know the story?"

Var nodded, followed closely by Fallyn: it was a common tale, scribed down in Evander's history, the history of the Autarchy. . . .

In the ninth year of the War of Restitution the brigantine, *Lord's Delight,* captained by Eban Patcham, was blown off course whilst seeking to elude two Levan warships—far enough that he encountered the Sea of Sorrows, and lost his pursuers. He survived—amongst few of his starving and thirsty crew—and found a bay that he named Deliverance, and beyond it a clean, clear land that he called Salvation. He was able to repair his ship, and take on sufficient water and meat that most of those who'd survived the initial journey came back alive to tell the tale—which inspired the Autarchy to colonize that westward land, and in honor of its discoverer, name it Salvation. . . .

"I was on the first ship," Jaymes said. "I'd seen the War, done my share of fighting—God knows, I killed enough men—an' I was weary of it." He laughed, wiping his hands. "You know when the War ended, how old soldiers were paid off or offered free passage out? Well, I chose to take the passage. I wanted a new land that was clear of war. I wanted to go someplace there wasn't war. So . . ." He reached into the flames to fetch out Fallyn's venison. "Mind that, it'll be hot."

Fallyn smiled and spat on his burning hands. Var only shook his head and motioned that Jaymes continue.

"I wasn't good for much," Jaymes said. "I'm surely not a

farmer—not got the patience—nor the head to be a trader; or the money you need to set up as either. But I'd learned to shoot, an' how to walk careful—the War taught me that—so I became a hunter."

"But," Var said, "you don't like war."

"No." Jaymes laughed. "What I said was I didn't like the War. There's a difference, eh?"

Var said, "I don't understand."

"Ain't that why you wonder about the settlers?" Jaymes asked; and laughed as Var shook his head. "Listen! I came out here to a free land. Most of them others did, too—the farmers, an' the millers, the vintners; everyone—to a *free* land. You understand? Not what there is back in Evander, but a place that was all ours. Not Evander's or the Autarchy's, only *ours,* where we could live free without priests or Inquisitors or the Militia watchin' us all the time. Can't you understand that?"

Var hesitated before replying. The tone of this conversation veered perilously close to sedition, and he wondered if he—an officer in the God's Militia—should take part, or bid Jaymes hold his tongue. Should Talle overhear . . . He glanced around, half expecting the Inquisitor to appear out of the shadows. But they sat alone; Talle was ensconced in the wagon he had commandeered, engaged in whatever arcane practices occupied him. Even so, Var doubted the wisdom of allowing the guide such latitude, and, conversely, felt he must grant that freedom—must understand the thinking of Salvation's inhabitants if he was to properly dispense his duty. So he said, "To a point. But Salvation has a governor appointed by the Autarchy, and a garrison to enforce Evander's will."

Jaymes chuckled softly. "Salvation has a governor who sits safe behind Grostheim's walls an' doesn't bother himself too much about the rest o' the country. An' you know by now how successful Spelt's troops are—why else are you here? No, the truth of it is that Evander keeps a hold on this land through the indentured folk."

"What do you say?" Var frowned. "You speak of living free, and then of dependence on branded exiles. They're hardly free."

"Indeed," Jaymes agreed, "but they're not citizens. The

folk who own them are, and they consider themselves free folk. Listen, most o' those settlers never had servants back home. But here? Well, here they get their pick o' the exiles, an' their choice o' land—more land an' more servants than they could ever dream of back in Evander. They become . . . gentlemen." He invested the word with contemptuous relish. "An' that's what ties Salvation to Evander, not loyalty to the Autarchy."

"But . . ." Var began, and fell silent as Jaymes grinned and raised a hand.

"There's never been an Inquisitor set foot here before. The law's pretty lax, an' folk mostly go about their own business without much thought of Governor Wyme or Evander or the Autarchy."

"Until they need us," Var said.

"That's true." Jaymes ducked his head. "But when you've defeated the painted people an' built your forts—what then? Shall you an' the Inquisitor stay? Or go back to Evander?"

Var shrugged. "I don't know. That will depend on what orders I receive."

"Which'll come by ship, no? Across the Sea of Sorrows, an' you know how long that voyage takes. There's naught but a handful o' ships come an' go each year—we're isolated here. We're an' awful long way from Evander, on the far side o' the world."

Var began to see the direction of his thinking. Jaymes chuckled again and went on: "An' year by year the farms prosper; an' the indentured folk bear children. Think on it, Major: things go on as usual, an' the time must come when Salvation won't need Evander. There's already food enough for all, an' about enough branded folk to serve the farmers. In time, Salvation'll be ready to stand on her own feet."

"God!" Var gasped. "Are you talking about some declaration of independence?"

Jaymes spat a stream of liquid tobacco into the fire. It erupted sparks, stinking. "I'm just pointin' out the obvious," he said mildly. "You asked me about the settlers' attitude, an' I'm tellin' you. Don't you see it?"

"I think," Var said slowly, nodding, "that I do. The settlers need us to defeat the hostiles; but they also fear that we shall bind them to Evander; that we shall be—what? Evander's police?"

"Somethin' like that," Jaymes agreed. "They're afraid o' that, but they still need you. So they don't rightly know how they feel about you. Neither them or Governor Wyme, I reckon."

Var took a deep breath; released it noisily. For a while he stared into the flames, then raised his head to study Jaymes.

"You know that I should report all this. That I should advise the Inquisitor of everything you've said."

"Yes." Jaymes met Var's eyes unafraid. "But I'll take a wager you won't."

"You have," Var said, "and likely the stake's your life."

"That's not worth so much." Jaymes cut a plug of tobacco and set it between his teeth, chewing loud. "An' I know where my money's placed."

"You've great faith in me," Var said.

Jaymes shrugged. "I trust you."

There was a long silence. The fire crackled, sparks rising as if in forlorn hope of joining the stars in the wide sky above. All around were the noises of a night camp: the voices of the settlers and their children, the conversations of soldiers, the calling of the pickets, the snorting of the horses. Where Var sat with Jaymes and Fallyn there was only a pervading, thoughtful quiet.

Then Var said, not sure why he did, "I'll not betray you."

"Nor I," added Fallyn.

Jaymes spat more tobacco. "Didn't think you would," he said calmly. "Else I'd not have told you."

Var saw the settlers in a different light after that. He tried to put himself in their position, to think as they did—which was not so difficult, their situations being not so very different. Was he honest with himself, he could imagine his duty lasting the rest of his life, that Evander would order him to remain even after the hostiles were exterminated. Likely as military commander of all Salvation—which was such promotion as he would not have dreamed of a year or two ago—but . . .

It was as Abram Jaymes had said: Salvation lay a world

apart from Evander, and when he thought on that, it did, indeed, seem an isolate land, vast for the exploring. Wyme's maps had shown him that, for all its size, Salvation was but a little piece of an unknown immensity. What Evander knew of it ended at those sky-topping mountains that sprawled across the western horizon, at the Glory River to the north and the Hope River to the south. It was, out here where the grass ran seemingly limitless and the sky spread vast above, a jigsaw segment in a country huge beyond imagining. And, save for the hostiles, open for the settling. He began to see the forts he was commanded to build as the clenching fingers of Evander's fist—which not long ago he would have applauded as defenders of the land—but now, with Jaymes's words sinking in like seductive claws, he wondered if they were not to become barriers, containing the inhabitants of Salvation that the Autarchy not lose them.

And why? he began to wonder. After all, Salvation *was* on the far side of the world. It exported nothing to Evander, and apart from such luxuries as the privileged imported (he thought of Wyme's furniture) and those metallic manufactures Salvation could not yet produce of itself, there was nothing Salvation could not make. And in time, surely, ore would be found, and metalworks begun, and then . . . Why then, Salvation might make her own guns, manufacture her own powder, and not need Evander.

Tomas Var wondered, as he delivered the reluctant settlers back to their farms and mills and vineyards, if he became a secessionist.

He told himself, *No!* That he was an officer of the God's Militia, his duty clear: to render Salvation safe for its Evanderan settlers. To secure the land for the Autarchy, whose servant he was. But he could not forget what Abram Jaymes had said that honest night, and when he saw Talle work his hexings on those reluctant to remain, he must bite his lip to not cry out in protest.

At least, when they came on farms burned down, he was able to persuade the Inquisitor it was in the best interests of Evander that they delay awhile, that the engineers and his own troops help rebuild the wreckage. And every holding, standing or new-built, was hexed by Talle, protection against attack. Sometimes the settlers even thanked him.

So Tomas Var saw his first duty done and set to the next. He swung his column around to find the treeline, the wilderness edge, where the Restitution River came out of the forest, and set building the first fort. It was by now midsummer and no hostiles had been sighted. Var wondered how long they would remain invisible.

11 The Owh'jika's Warning

"Bluecoats, eh?" Chakthi's kick took Owan Thirsk from his sad musings. "Tell me about them."

"Marines." Thirsk stirred warily on his tether. "Bluecoats are marines, Master."

"What are . . . marines?" The Tachyn akaman clearly found the word hard to pronounce.

"Elite warriors," Owan Thirsk said. "The chosen fighters of the Autarchy, the spearhead of the army."

Chakthi could understand that. Thirsk was grateful: he'd not relish another kick, his ribs were sore enough.

"And they wear blue?"

Thirsk said, "Yes."

"And the ones who wear green?"

"I think . . ." Thirsk paused, racking his mind, frightened. "Engineers, I think."

"What are engineers?" Chakthi pronounced the word *en-jin-ears*. "What do they do?"

"Build," Thirsk said quickly, anticipating punishment.

"Build what?" Chakthi flicked a rawhide strap across his face, as he often did when he could not comprehend.

Thirsk flinched. It was not a hard blow and he was thankful for that: his master was often unkinder. "Forts," he said. "Like Grostheim—the city you attacked."

The memory prompted another lashing and Thirsk cringed.

Chakthi asked, "Why?"

"I think," Thirsk said, "that they bring a terrible power against you. I think the akaman in the city has sent word across the sea, to bring soldiers against you. To take this land from you."

Chakthi nodded and asked, "Forts, are they all like the big wooden city?"

"No." Thirsk shook his head. "They are like little cities: small, but filled with soldiers."

"With muskets?"

Thirsk nodded eagerly. "And cannons."

"Tell me again," Chakthi said, "about cannons."

Thirsk spoke, the words tumbling out, anxious to please that there be no more pain, telling Chakthi all he knew of cannon and forts and the soldiers of the God's Militia. When he was done, Chakthi nodded and appeared too lost in thought to strike him again. Had Thirsk retained any belief in God, he would have given thanks for that, but his faith was lost with his tattered sanity and his only belief now was in survival. He was become something less than human, and so he smiled and gibbered his gratitude as Chakthi tossed him a gnawed bone and walked away.

The Tachyn akaman found Hadduth seated outside the wakanisha's lodge, grinding pahé root.

"The owh'jika says they are building things called forts," he announced, "that they will fill with their warriors. It says a thing called an army has been sent to drive us out."

Hadduth ceased his pounding, set the pot and the pestle aside, and wiped his hands on his breeches. "What will you do?"

Chakthi squatted, staring past the wakanisha to the dense timber surrounding the camp. It was strange to live so enclosed, not out on the open grass, but Hadduth's dreams had confirmed his own desire to stay close to the mountains, and in light of all he'd learned it seemed now a wise decision. He listened to the wind singing through the firs and watched the flickering of sunlight, aware that Hadduth waited on him to speak, not caring. Let the Dreamer wait: he had failed in his appointed task, and it amused Chakthi to see him squirm.

Finally the akaman said, "I am not sure yet. The scouts

spoke of a great many warriors—both the bluecoats and the red—and they have the cannon."

Hadduth nodded sagely. "The cannon are very dangerous."

There was no need to elaborate. Both men knew the carnage the guns along the walls of the big fort had wreaked, and the Tachyn were not so many now.

"But if they build their forts and put the cannon in them . . ." Chakthi scowled, letting the sentence trail away.

Hadduth nodded again, thinking that it should be hard to conquer one, and if the strangers built a series. . . . He pushed the thought aside and held his tongue, waiting on Chakthi.

Who asked him bluntly, "What do you think? Have you dreamed of this?"

Hadduth swallowed. As he had told his akaman, his dreams had been few and difficult of interpretation since coming to this new land. Had he not turned his face away from the Maker he would have prayed to the deity—but that was not possible now, and could only invite punishment. Nor could he pray to the Breakers, who were, he supposed, left behind in Ket-Ta-Witko, frustrated by Morrhyn's cursed magic. But Chakthi demanded an answer, and Hadduth knew it had best be one favorable to his akaman's wishes. So he shrugged and composed a reply he hoped would please Chakthi.

"I have dreamed of a great river that comes from where the sun rises, only it is a river made not of water but of men. The men are all strangers, in the warriors' coats, and the river washes all before it and spreads across the land. But . . ." He raised a nervous hand as Chakthi snarled. "The river comes against the forest and is stopped, and can go no farther."

"What does it mean?" Chakthi demanded.

"That we are safe here," Hadduth gestured at the enclosing timber, "and that the grass is dangerous."

"So we do nothing?" Chakthi's face darkened.

Hadduth shook a hurried head. "No—only be careful." He thought quickly: it was not so hard to give Chakthi what he wanted. "We must strike against them when they least

expect it. I think when they are building their forts, before
they are finished."

Chakthi ducked his head, the scowl becoming a smile.
"Your dreams prove my wishes right."

Hadduth returned an unctuous smile. "My akaman is a
great leader."

Var located the site of the first fort and saw his force bivouacked behind perimeter defenses. Trenches were hurriedly
dug, the displaced soil thrown up in makeshift walls with the
cannon set to command the approaches, the tents and live-
stock at the center of the square. Talle was impatient, but Var
succeeded in impressing on the Inquisitor the need to establish a basic command post before work on the fort proper
might safely commence.

"The wilderness is close," he gestured at the blue-looming
forest edge, "and is Abram Jaymes right, then the hostiles
might well be watching us even now."

"Then might we not attack them?" Talle stared malevo-
lently at the woodland, as if he'd pierce the shadows with his
gaze. "Might we not mount a preemptive expedition?"

"Better that we set up our defenses first." Var spoke carefully, marveling the while at Talle's apparent lack of understanding. "Are we to safely build all the planned forts, we
shall need this one as a stronghold. And are we attacked
whilst we build . . ." He paused, thinking that surely the
Inquisitor must understand the importance of a basic command post.

But Talle only shook his lank-haired head and frowned a
question. So Var continued: "We do not know the forest,
Inquisitor; but the hostiles do—it's their home—and were we
to venture into those depths too soon, why, they might well
deplete our force drastically enough we could not complete
our task."

Talle grunted, scratching at a nostril. "I must trust your
judgment in military matters," he said at last. "But how long
shall we delay here? I'd take the fight to the enemy."

Var turned, indicating the men laboring in the trenches,
those throwing up the earthworks. "It shall be some weeks,

Inquisitor. We'll need to enter the forest to fell timber, and that to be hewn to shape and raised for the walls. But we'll see it done."

"We'll do our duty," Talle returned. "And as quick as possible, eh?"

Var said, "Of course," and watched the frock-coated little man stalk away with a sense of palpable relief.

"He getting impatient?"

Abram Jaymes came up to stand alongside Var, who grinned ruefully as he nodded. "He'd go out against them now."

"They'll come soon enough, I reckon," Jaymes chuckled. "Maybe he'll change his mind then."

Var said, "I don't think Inquisitor Talle admits to changing his mind."

The owh'jika had said the blue-coated warriors were the finest, but Chakthi thought them blind as the others. Had he the men to match the numbers massed about the site of the fort, he would have risked a full-scale attack; but his clan was small now, and Hadduth had counseled against a frontal onslaught. Chakthi's confidence in his Dreamer waned, but in this he must agree with the wakanisha. Indeed, he must agree that Hadduth's suggestion seemed the most likely route to success. So he only watched the strangers, his warriors hidden in the long grass and the undergrowth, until he saw clearly what they did, and how.

Soon he saw that the fort would be like the big wooden camp at the mouth of the river—all built of timber. He saw that the green-coated ones planned it, whilst the redcoats labored alongside and the bluecoats played watchmen. As the owh'jika had promised, it would be smaller, but if it were finished, Chakthi could see that it would dominate the river and a wide area around. It came to him that if the strangers built such places all along the edgewoods, raiding out of the forest must prove very difficult. But to build the thing the strangers must have timber—and for that they must enter the forest.

Chakthi watched until he was satisfied with his knowledge of their ways, and then planned his raid.

Each day, between three and five of the odd vehicles the owh'jika said were called wagons were driven into the forest. They carried men with axes, who set to felling trees, and were escorted by a party of the bluecoats. The felled trees were later hauled back to the burgeoning fort: the smaller specimens on the wagons, the larger waiting for horse teams that dragged them like great travois.

Chakthi curbed his impatience and waited, allowing the strangers to grow more confident; besides, he wanted to kill as many as he could in the first raid. He deemed the time right when five wagons came down the trail, carrying some fifty men, with perhaps as many marines marching in escort.

The Tachyn waited in concealment, even though Chakthi doubted the strangers had the eyes to read the forest's signs. Their faces were painted for war, banded white and black and yellow, and on Chakthi's signal they attacked.

Matieu Fallyn commanded the detail, and he was deploying his marines about the perimeter of the cleared area when the arrows came in a terrible rain from amongst the trees. He felt a blow on his shoulder that numbed his left arm before he felt any pain. He saw men falling around him, shafts sprouting like deadly weeds from their bodies, and saw the arrow jutting from his own. He cursed, confused an instant by the pain and the suddenness of the attack, then drew his pistol.

"Form square! Two ranks!"

The order was redundant—his men, disciplined veterans, were already shaping the defensive formation, the wagons at the center.

Fallyn aimed his pistol at the shadowy timber. "Front rank, fire!"

The muskets exploded a volley into the trees. Dirty white smoke billowed across the clearing; lead shot thudded, snapping branches, sending great chips of rent bark flying. Fallyn wondered if he heard screams: it was hard to be sure through the din.

"Second rank, fire!"

Another volley: the timber was momentarily hidden behind the smoke. The front rank, kneeling, was already reloaded and Fallyn shouted that it fire again. He holstered his pistol and tugged at the arrow; then could not stifle his cry of agony.

"Likely barbed. Best leave it for now." Abram Jaymes was at his side, the Baker rifle cocked ready. "Less you want me to cut it out."

"No." Fallyn shook his head. "Dammit, where are they?"

Jaymes said, "In the trees. You won't see 'em unless they come at us head-on."

The muskets were silent, the marines awaiting Fallyn's order. More arrows came, as if the forest itself flung the missiles. Fallyn saw marines fall, an engineer scream, clutching at the shaft protruding from his chest; a horse shrilled, bucking frantically as it was struck in neck and hindquarters.

"Fire!" Then to Jaymes: "How many, d'you think?"

The guide shrugged. "A lot."

"Can we beat them?"

"Depends." Jaymes spat tobacco. "How much ammunition you got?"

"Every man carries a full pouch." Fallyn fired his pistol into the smoke. He could see no target, but it seemed necessary to do something. "Shall that be enough?"

"Might be." Jaymes had not yet fired his rifle. "Depends."

"Dammit, give me a straight answer for God's sake." Fallyn lost patience with the laconic guide. "Can we hold them off, or do we retreat?"

Jaymes said, "There's no straight answers with these folk, Captain. I don't know how many there are, so I can't say whether you got enough powder, or not. Might be they decide to quit, or . . ." He shrugged again. "Might be they don't."

Fallyn struggled to reload his pistol and found that his left hand refused to work. Cursing, he thrust the gun into its holster and drew his sword, forcing himself to think calmly. It was not easy: he faced an unseen enemy who fought by no rules of warfare he knew. Who hid from sight as if, just as he'd heard the settlers muttering, the forest had spawned them. He wondered what to do. Not advance into the trees—

certainly not that. Hold the square? Hope—pray!—the savages or demons or whatever they were would give up? Hope the firing was heard and a rescue column came? Or retreat? They were not too deep into the timber, and he doubted the enemy would follow onto the open grass, where the fighting would surely be noticed by the main force.

Arrows still flew, not in that terrible rain now, but individually, as if the unseen bowmen taunted the intruders and picked them off leisurely. Matieu Fallyn envisaged his entire command slaughtered man by man. God, if only the bastards would fight face-to-face!

Fallyn's experience was all of open warfare, of frontal attacks in which army clashed with army. There was no honor in ambush. But this was a new world and a new enemy, and Fallyn knew he must adapt or die. He came to an abrupt decision.

"We withdraw! We fight our way back! Fix bayonets!"

He bellowed the order, his marines holding the square as engineers and Militiamen cut free the slain horses and loaded the wounded men onto the wagons. His shoulder throbbed abominably now and he turned to Jaymes.

"Cut this damn thing away."

The guide nodded and lowered his rifle. He drew his big knife and hacked through the arrow, close to Fallyn's shoulder. The captain groaned as the shaft was moved inside the wound, and forbade himself to faint. Jaymes tossed the length of painted wood away and retrieved his long gun.

"Wagons are ready, Captain." A sergeant of the Militia came through the smoke. "What about the dead?"

Fallyn cursed anew, glanced toward the wagons, and saw there was insufficient room for the bodies. "Strip them of their weapons and leave them."

The sergeant nodded and was gone. Fallyn shouted for the marines to form around the wagons. It would be a difficult maneuver, the hindmost line marching backward over a trail rutted by the carts and the dragged timber. He prayed it would work: he could think of nothing else, save waiting here to die. He did not relish reporting his defeat to Inquisitor Talle.

They retreated, slowly, arrows still coming out of the trees, answered by the disciplined fire of the marines. Fallyn did not know he staggered until he smelled Jaymes's buckskins and felt the guide's arm around his waist. He straightened, pushing free of the man's support, and turned to survey his stricken command.

The arrow entered his mouth as he parted his lips to shout encouragement. It pierced the soft flesh of his throat and emerged from the back of his neck, his cry drowning in blood. Jaymes caught him as he fell and manhandled the stumbling officer to the closest wagon, heaving him bodily on board. Ahead, down the avenue of felled timber, the guide could see the open prairie. He doubted Fallyn would.

"It was a good fight," Hadduth declared. "You slew many strangers, and surely they'll be afraid to come back into the forest."

He gestured at the warriors dancing their victory. Tunics of blue and red and green were waved aloft, and hanks of bloody hair, and all the clan was gathered to watch and celebrate. Only Chakthi seemed dissatisfied.

"As many got away," the akaman muttered. "And they took all the muskets. I wanted to capture those."

"There will be others," Hadduth said. "And now these new-come warriors have learned to fear the Tachyn."

"Perhaps," Chakthi allowed. "But there are still many of them."

"But they must surely be afraid now," Hadduth insisted, "and even if they dare the forest again, we can attack them again."

Chakthi studied his wakanisha through narrowed eyes. "I think they want very badly to build their forts," he said, his voice so cold Hadduth flinched back, "and that one fight does not win our war. If *I* led them, I should come back with more men—so many none would dare attack me."

"The war is not yet won," Hadduth agreed quickly, "but still it was a great victory."

"It was a little fight!" Chakthi's voice rang with contempt.

"And I would win this war. This is *my* land, and I'll not share it."

Hadduth was about to speak, but Chakthi silenced him. "Listen, Dreamer! I have spoken with the owh'jika and he says his kind are many—far more than we Tachyn—and that they will send big canoes loaded with warriors to fight us. Like in your dream, eh? Before that happens, I want this land emptied of the strangers, so that the rest *are* afraid to come here. To do that, I need allies. Do you understand?"

Hadduth nodded. "You know I seek our allies in my dreams." His voice was nervous.

"Do better than *seek* them," Chakthi said. "*Find* them, and bring them here!"

12 A Choice Is Offered

None had objected when Morrhyn suggested Davyd eat the pahé root, and he had gone many times to the wa'tenhya and drunk the bitter brew and gone away into dreams. For days he had lain there, unconscious as broth and water were dripped between his lips, and then awoke understanding the language of the People. It was what Evander would call a miracle: he thought of it as Morrhyn's magic.

Nor less Arcole and Flysse, whose acceptance by the People was total. It was as if they came amongst friends who took them in and gifted them with clothing and a lodge, even horses, and considered the act of giving an honor. Lhyn and Arrhyna took Flysse beneath their wings and set to teaching her their language and their customs, whilst Rannach and Yazte performed similar services for Arcole. Both outlanders soon felt at home, as if Salvation were a dark dream left behind when they crossed the mountains, and could not imagine ever returning there. Why should they, when they dwelt amongst such hospitable folk? And did they entertain any doubts, they were not for themselves but for Davyd—for it was clear that Morrhyn discerned in the young man some great purpose, and looked to shape his future.

Davyd studied Morrhyn's face as the wakanisha spoke. It was dark as old leather, seamed like the sunbaked bed of a dry stream, and starkly planed, all sharp angles and hollows. It should—would, worn by any other man—have been forbidding in its ageless gauntness, but the bright-burning blue eyes radiated such compassion, and the wide mouth smiled so often, it was instead kindly and wise. It was easy to see why the People named him Prophet, for all he resisted the title, claiming he was only a Dreamer blessed by the Maker. But Davyd—even now he knew the story—still thought of him only as Morrhyn, his tutor and his friend.

"And shall there be a Matakwa this year?" he asked in the language of the Matawaye. He was fluent now, thanks to the pahé.

"Yes." Morrhyn nodded solemnly.

"Why was there not one held last year?" Davyd wondered if he saw humor sparkling in the blue eyes, as if Morrhyn held back some announcement that excited him. "Surely the Ahsatye-Patiko says the People should meet yearly."

"That is true," the wakanisha agreed, "since first Grass Woman and Buffalo Dreamer went to meet the Stone Boy, but I think the Maker forgives us the lapse. At least, I dreamed he does."

"But why did we not meet?" Davyd did not notice that he named himself Matawaye.

"Because," Morrhyn answered, smiling, "this is not Ket-Ta-Witko but Ket-Ta-Thanne, and things change."

Davyd frowned. "I don't understand."

"We are not long come to this new land," Morrhyn explained, "neither we Matawaye nor the Grannach, and we both need time to settle here, to find our way." He sighed. "We remember what that last Matakwa delivered, and that's a sour memory—the People were worried by that."

"But that's in the past," Davyd protested, "and in Ket-Ta-Witko."

"Even so." Morrhyn shrugged, the movement almost lost beneath his furs. It was the Moon of the Turning Year and the air was yet chill. "We had nothing to trade, nor the Grannach. The akamans went alone—a little Matakwa. Kahteney and I held Dream Council on the matter, and that was the answer the Maker sent us. Also, there was another reason."

Davyd waited, and when Morrhyn failed to continue demanded, "What other reason?"

The wakanisha grinned and said, "You, and your friends."

"Us?" Davyd was taken aback. "Why us?"

"Matakwa is for the People and the Grannach," Morrhyn

replied. "For those who understand the Will. It was not fitting three strangers ignorant of the Ahsa-tye-Patiko attend, and we'd not leave you to fend for yourselves."

Davyd opened his mouth to speak, bit back the words and frowned again.

Morrhyn chuckled at his forlorn expression. "You did not understand then," he said, "but now . . ."

"There shall be a Meeting this year?" Davyd was excited by the prospect. "Because we do?"

"Yes." Morrhyn nodded, his eyes twinkling. "And because it is time . . ." He hesitated deliberately.

Davyd refused to rise to the bait, playing Morrhyn at his own game, waiting.

"It is time you became truly Matawaye. Do you agree, the ceremonies shall be held at this Matakwa."

"I agree!" Davyd cried.

"And the others, Arcole and Flysse? They speak our tongue well enough now."

"They will!" Davyd nodded enthusiastically. "I know they will."

Morrhyn said, "That is good. Now, do you tell me of your dreams?"

The Prophet thought long on what he heard, and spoke at length with Kahteney of all Davyd told him. The Maker knew, but this youngster owned the talent in abundance. His conviction that Davyd was destined to become his successor was confirmed daily, even had he discussed it only with Kahteney. It was not yet time to make that announcement— Davyd was powerful in his dreaming, but still disordered, still affected by remembered fear. Sometimes, when Morrhyn shared the dreaming, he saw Davyd's visions consumed by flames, the image of Davyd chained to a stake and burning superimposing itself. Morrhyn could not comprehend a people that condemned Dreamers any more than he could comprehend the setting of a hot iron to a man's face, a woman's shoulder, that they be marked as slaves and sent into exile. He thought Davyd's people very strange.

They had explained those horrid customs, and the iron

rule of the Autarchy, and all who listened were horrified. Such folk as they described seemed monstrous to the Matawaye, alien as the Breakers. And across the mountains were hundreds, perhaps hundreds of hundreds, more who wore the mark of exile. Rannach had even spoken of crossing the hills to offer refuge to the indentured folk, but that was in the heat of his disgust and Morrhyn had persuaded him to set the idea aside. For now, at least.

"We are not long come to Ket-Ta-Thanne," he had told the young akaman. "Look at us—we live all huddled like a wary buffalo herd, nervous of the changing wind. Let us first find our way about this new land, find our clan territories and live like true Matawaye again. Then, perhaps, we can think of the wider world."

Rannach said softly, apologetically, "It was delay delivered the People to the Breakers."

"Then, yes," Morrhyn agreed. "But then all we wakanishas had dreamed of approaching danger."

"And not now?" Rannach asked. "Arcole says that all their warriors carry muskets, and they have the things he calls cannon, that are like giant muskets. He says they claim the land they name Salvation, and that council that brands men and women and sends them into slavery would conquer all the world. What if they decide to cross the mountains? Should that not be like the Breakers again?"

"It would," Morrhyn replied, "but I have not dreamed of that, nor Kahteney, and so I do not think it is a present danger."

Rannach grunted, dissatisfied. "It sits ill with me to know there are others like Arcole and Flysse and Davyd. It seems to me a sin against the Ahsa-tye-Patiko."

"For us it surely would be a sin. But they are not like us, eh?"

"Ach, no!" Rannach made a gesture of dismissal, as if the very thought of comparison was distasteful.

"Wait," Morrhyn urged. "I like none of this any better than you, but it is not the time to start a new war."

"I'd not go to war. Only steal away those who'd find sanctuary with us."

Morrhyn had reached out then to clutch Rannach's wrist.

He felt proud of the young man's ardor, and equally afraid the old, hotheaded Rannach should gain sway. "First you would need cross Chakthi's land," he said, "and that would not be easy. Nor the return, if you came with some number of refugees. And do these people claim to own the branded ones, then I think they would send their warriors after you. Better to wait, no?"

And that had contented Rannach somewhat, though he still spoke at length with Arcole of the strange folk across the hills, as if he would learn all he could of their ways. Which was, Morrhyn supposed, the mark of a wise leader—to think ahead, to learn about potential enemies and prepare to face them. The Maker knew, but that was what he had argued in Ket-Ta-Witko, and none but poor, dead Racharran listened to him. Did he now fall into that same complacent trap, he wondered? Surely he did not dream of danger from over the mountains, but then, before, the dreams had dulled and clouded under the malign influence of the Breakers. Could that same curse descend again?

He told himself no; surely the Breakers were left behind and no longer a threat. Surely it was common sense and not complacency that prompted him to urge caution on Rannach. But that the case, why did he dream as he did of Davyd? That the youth was vital to the future of the People he could not doubt—the dreams made that much clear, but not much else. They did not explain how or why Davyd was so important, and Morrhyn could only instruct him in the lore of the Ahsa-tye-Patiko and endeavor to train him as a Dreamer and wait for revelation. In his own good time, he told himself, the Maker will surely reveal all. And meanwhile, he did not want Rannach to cross the mountains: he thought he could not look into Lhyn's eyes were he to approve that venture.

Davyd's voice returned the wakanisha to the present.

"Shall I get my braids at the Matakwa?"

Morrhyn was startled: did Davyd not understand? Surely he had guessed what future Morrhyn planned for him.

"Only the warriors wear the braids," the wakanisha explained, thinking the while that Davyd knew this. "They are the hunters and defenders of the clan."

"I know," Davyd confirmed, "and the wakanishas wear their hair unbound."

Morrhyn looked at him awhile in silence. He was of an age to take the braids. Were he born of the People, he'd be named a man by now, and for all his youthful innocence he was no longer the gangly child-man Colun had brought down from the mountains. He had filled out, was becoming muscular, and sun and wind had joined the freckles covering his face in a uniform tan. He could ride now—perhaps not so well, but without fear—and Tekah had taught him to use a bow with some skill. Arcole tutored him in swordplay—which the Matawaye considered a strange way to fight—and pronounced him talented in that deadly art. He could both wrestle and use his clenched fists in the odd style Arcole explained was called pugilism, and could set a snare and build a trap, construct a shelter or raise a lodge. He owned the skills that could earn him the braids—and Morrhyn was suddenly afraid, filled with dread that Davyd should choose the way of the warrior.

"Can a man not be both?" Davyd asked.

"No." Morrhyn shook his head. "A wakanisha communes with the Maker, he guides the clan in the ways of the Ahsa-tye-Patiko. Only a wakanisha dreams, only a wakanisha may eat the pahé."

Davyd frowned. "You gave me pahé, and I am not a wakanisha."

Almost, Morrhyn said, "Yet," but he stifled that response—it must be Davyd's decision alone—and instead said, "That was in special circumstances, and only after Kahteney and I had dreamed on the matter. Even then, we must ask the approval of all the People. Do you not remember the council?"

Davyd nodded. "But I didn't understand much of what you said."

Morrhyn chuckled. "Because you'd not eaten the pahé then. Indeed, were you not so strong a Dreamer, I'd not have suggested it."

"Taza dreams," Davyd said, thoughtfully, "but you've not given him pahé. He'd be a wakanisha, but Kahteney refuses to name him."

"Taza . . ." Morrhyn's expression darkened somewhat. "Taza is headstrong. He's something of the talent, yes, but he's wild. He thinks not of the People, but of himself. He'd become wakanisha for his own glory. Save he forget his pride, he'll not be named."

"But still he dreams. Can he become a warrior and also dream?"

Morrhyn answered with a slight shaking of his head. "The dreaming talent shows early, in the young. Save the gifted eat the pahé then, the talent dies as they grow older. Is Taza not given the root soon, his ability will wane." He saw Davyd about to object and raised a hand to order silence. "Kahteney and I have discussed this at length, and with the akamans, and we are agreed that Taza is not fit to become a wakanisha."

Davyd nodded slowly. "He says I cannot be a wakanisha," he murmured, "because I was not born of the People."

Morrhyn smiled humorlessly. "I say you can," he said. "Whose word do you take?"

"Yours." Davyd answered without hesitation. "But even so . . ."

"At this Matakwa you will be adopted Matawaye." Morrhyn's smile grew warmer. "You and Arcole and Flysse. Then you must make your decision."

"To be a warrior," Davyd said slowly, "or a wakanisha."

Morrhyn nodded, studying his face. Your will be done, he thought, but, Maker, grant he takes the right path.

"Taza would be very angry," Davyd said, "if I became a Dreamer."

Morrhyn said, "I do not think Taza's opinion is important."

Davyd shrugged. "I'd not anger any of the People."

Morrhyn laughed, clapping his hands. "Already you think like a wakanisha. But listen, Taza is but one voice. There are many others would support your choice—no matter what it be."

"You'd make me wakanisha, no?" Davyd said.

Again, Morrhyn nodded. "But mine is only one voice, too. The decision is yours."

Davyd looked past the older man to the totem-ringed cairn

that marked the gateway's site, the holy place from which the People had come to Ket-Ta-Thanne.

Then he said, obviously choosing his words with great care, "From the first time I saw Arcole fight, on the ship that brought us to Salvation, I wanted to be like him—I wanted to be a warrior. I saw him with Flysse and I wanted a woman of my own. I . . ." He paused, embarrassment flushing his cheeks. "I wanted Flysse." He chuckled softly, laughing at himself. "I know better now. I know she belongs with Arcole, but even so . . . to never know a woman?"

Carefully, Morrhyn said, "The Ahsa-tye-Patiko does not forbid a wakanisha a wife. Some choose not to wed—as if all the clan, all the People, become our bride—but it has been done."

Davyd nodded. "But I could never wear the braids."

"That," Morrhyn said, "no." He wondered if it was sorrow or confusion he saw on Davyd's face, and felt a pang of guilt that he forced the youth to such decision.

"This is not an easy thing you ask of me," Davyd said.

Morrhyn answered, "No."

"Why?" Davyd asked. "Why me?"

"Because," Morrhyn said, "you have the talent, and I believe you would be a fine Dreamer."

"And if I'd be a warrior?"

"Then you would be a warrior," Morrhyn told him. "The choice is yours. I am sorry, but I cannot make it easy for you."

"No." Davyd's lips curved in a faint smile and he coughed a short laugh. "I suppose I knew, really—that you'd ask me this. Must I decide now?"

Morrhyn shook his head. "It is something you should ponder."

"Then I think," Davyd said, "that I should like to go away on my own, and seek the answer of the Maker."

"That," Morrhyn said approvingly, "is a very wise decision."

Flysse sat with Arrhyna and Lhyn, working a buffalo hide smooth. It was comforting, even now, to engage in such homely tasks—to go freely about her own affairs without fear of reprimand, and better still to live safe, not forever on the alert for danger. It was good to wear skirts again; indeed, she enjoyed the feel of the doeskin Arrhyna had gifted her, and found the soft leather boots of the Matawaye more comfortable than buckled shoes. The People lived to the rhythm of the seasons, and that reminded her in many ways of her childhood in Cudham. Save, she thought with amusement and only the very least pang of nostalgia, her parents would frown on her living in a lodge constructed of poles and animal hides, furs for a bed, and most of her cooking done outside, over an open fire. Yet she felt entirely at home, and no longing at all for squared walls and tiled roofs, wooden floors and cooking stoves.

She worked the scraper firmly over the skin as the two Commacht women had taught her, and glanced at the child playing busily with the wooden spinning top Rannach had carved him. Dressed in jacket and breeches of soft rabbit fur, he resembled a small bear.

Debo was a sturdy child, whose customary expression was a broad smile, and was his conception a matter of some doubt, it was never mentioned. He favored his mother in looks, save for the thatch of reddish brown hair and the angle of his nose, which belonged to neither his mother nor Rannach, but they both doted on him, and Flysse considered that a sign of their virtue, the innate goodness of the Matawaye. She had heard the story soon enough—how Chakthi's son, Vachyr, had kidnapped Rannach's new bride and raped her before dying on Rannach's lance point—and was it not surely confirmed, still it seemed that little Debo was Vachyr's child. Which mattered not at all to Rannach, or any of the Commacht. Flysse thought that a marvelous thing that set the People quite apart from her own kind. In Bantar the offspring of such an assault would have been aborted with the approval of the Autarchy, or did the mother seek to keep the baby, then it was her husband's right to divorce her or give the child up for indenture. The Matawaye, Flysse thought as she smiled at chubby Debo, were far kinder.

Arrhyna saw the direction of her glance and made a cooing sound that brought Debo trotting to her, holding up his toy as if for her inspection. Arrhyna planted a kiss atop his head and he abruptly sat down, chortling with delight. Flysse caught the mother's eye and Arrhyna offered her a smile happy as her son's. Flysse wondered when she and Arcole might have a child.

"What thoughts, eh?" Lhyn asked knowingly.

"I was . . ." Flysse blushed, then laughed. She had no secrets from these two. "I was thinking of babies."

"The thing to do," Lhyn advised with mock solemnity, "is to keep trying."

"Yes." Arrhyna giggled. "Rannach and I try very hard."

"Arcole is a powerful man, no?" Lhyn affected a questioning expression.

"He is." Flysse was by now accustomed to their teasing: the People were far more open than her own kind, and felt no embarrassment at discussion of such intimate matters. "And we do."

Lhyn nodded sagely. "Perhaps we should ask Morrhyn prepare you a potion."

"I think not," Flysse replied, smiling. "We shall have a baby, or not. It shall be as the Maker wills."

"Spoken like a true Commacht," Lhyn declared. "Which you shall be soon enough."

"The Matakwa?" Flysse raised inquiring brows.

Lhyn nodded, but it was Arrhyna who answered: "Rannach says it shall be held this year, when the New Grass Moon is full."

Flysse made a swift calculation. She had yet to properly master the People's calendar, which was based not on the arbitrary titling of months but their naming in accordance with their nature, with the climate they delivered. It was now the Moon of the Turning Year, when the last vestiges of winter gave way to the promise of better weather, and as best she could work out, the New Grass Moon would reach its fullness in about six weeks. She asked, "Where shall it be held?"

"Close on the mountains," Arrhyna told her, "that the Grannach have not so far to travel."

"They've not horses," Lhyn explained. Then laughed, slapping her forehead. "But I forget—you know as much of their ways as I, no? Surely you've spent more time with them."

"Yes," Flysse said. "It shall be good to see Colun and Marjia again."

"And be an easy journey," said Arrhyna, pride in her voice, "thanks to my husband."

"How so?" Flysse asked.

Arrhyna smiled. "When we sojourned in the high valley we saw the Grannach drawing a thing they called a cart," she said. "It rested on pieces of round wood that rolled over the ground smoother than a travois. Rannach remembered that, and showed the People how to make carts. We shall use them when we go to the Matakwa."

"My son is clever," Lhyn murmured.

They seemed so delighted with Rannach's borrowed invention that Flysse forbore to mention that wheeled carts were entirely usual in Evander. Most Evanderans, she knew, would consider the Matawaye primitive, uncivilized, but they were not—they simply lived a different life. Indeed, in many ways they were more civilized than her kind, surely far closer to the world they inhabited, living with nature rather than seeking to impose their will on immutable forces. Nor, she thought, absently stroking her shoulder where the brand sat, did they claim ownership of other human beings, or burn Dreamers at the stake. And so she smiled with Arrhyna and Lhyn and said, "And at Matakwa I shall become truly one of the People?"

"All of you," Lhyn confirmed.

"Arcole shall get his braids and be named a warrior," Arrhyna said. Then quickly added, "He is now, of course. But at Matakwa it shall be declared before all the People."

"And Davyd?" Flysse asked.

She saw the two Commacht women exchange a glance then, Arrhyna opening her mouth to speak but deferring to Lhyn. The older woman said, "Davyd must choose his path. He's the Maker's gift."

Flysse said, "The dreaming?"

Lhyn nodded. "Yes; and so he must decide which path he'd take."

Flysse thought of the enthusiasm she'd seen on Davyd's face as he faced Arcole at swordpoint, and the pride he took in his bowmanship, his delight when he finally mastered his buckskin horse; then she thought of the time he spent with Morrhyn, his pleasure in those lessons. He had sought to emulate Arcole for so long, and now, in Morrhyn, had found another figure with whom to identify—and it was as if he stood divided.

The object of her thoughts appeared then, his young face set solemn, his smile of greeting somewhat strained. He squatted, opening his arms to Debo, who ran smiling toward him. He picked up the child and held him high, Debo laughing all the while as Davyd studied his round face as if seeking answers there.

He set Debo down and said, "I must go away."

"Why?" Flysse was suddenly afraid.

"I've a decision to make, and I need to be alone."

Almost, Flysse reached out to take his hand—was tempted to urge he stay, to tell him she knew of the imminent branching of his life, the crossroads he faced. But Davyd was no longer a boy and she knew he must make his own decisions, so she only nodded and said, "As you will." And then could not resist adding, "But be careful, eh?"

Davyd chuckled and said, "What harm can come me?" Then: "Where's Arcole?"

"With Rannach," Flysse told him, "hunting. Shall you await their return?"

"No, I'd go now." Davyd shook his head, his eyes a moment regretful. "This is not a thing that can wait." Then he shrugged. "No matter; tell Arcole, eh?"

"I will," Flysse promised. "When shall you return?"

He said, "I don't know. It depends on the Maker," and rose to his feet.

Flysse watched him go, thinking that a heavy burden was placed on his young shoulders. She hoped he had the strength to bear the weight.

Davyd went to his lodge and gathered up those things he'd need; not much, for he intended to construct a shelter and set snares rather than drag the lodge behind his horse or carry food. He would need, anyway, to fast. He saddled the buckskin, packed his gear, and readied to mount.

"Where do you go, brother?"

Tekah appeared; like a self-appointed guardian, Davyd thought fondly, ever vigilant of my welfare.

He said, "I must go away awhile, Tekah; alone. There are things I must ask of the Maker."

Tekah frowned. Since that first day when Rannach had reprimanded him, he had elected himself Davyd's mentor in lay matters. "Shall I not come with you?" he asked. "Partway, at least?"

"No." Davyd smiled to soften the refusal, springing astride the buckskin. "This is something I must do alone. Trust me, eh?"

Tekah nodded, still frowning. Davyd laughed from the saddle and repeated what he'd said to Flysse: "What harm can come me?"

Tekah shrugged, his face still doubtful, but offered no objection as Davyd heeled the buckskin round and set the horse to walking through the great camp.

Neither he nor Tekah saw the figure that had watched them from the shadow of a nearby lodge, nor did any mark it as unusual when Taza saddled his horse and rode away.

13 Dangerous Dreaming

Taza had no particular plan in mind save to follow Davyd and see where his rival went, and why. The stranger had been with Morrhyn before he quit the camp, and from his expression Taza guessed he had matters to ponder. He thought he likely knew what. Word was out that Matakwa would be held this year, the strangers adopted officially into the People, and it was plain to see that Morrhyn would name Davyd his pupil. Against all precedent, the wakanisha had given the newcomer the pahé root, and spent the winter cloistered with him, instructing him in the Ahsa-tye-Patiko and the ways of dreaming.

The notion enraged him: it was unfair! *He* owned the talent—both Morrhyn and Kahteney knew it—but still Kahteney refused to name him, and Morrhyn supported the Lakanti Dreamer. Taza could not understand why. He had approached Kahteney when first he began to dream, and the wakanisha had agreed to consider him as catechumen, but then—in Taza's opinion—reneged on the agreement. He had gone to the wakanisha time and time again, pleading with him, even begging, demanding, but still Kahteney refused. Yet Taza owned the ability. He knew he could become a true Dreamer if only he received the training—the training he saw Davyd get daily. He ground his teeth in rage, feeling his face grow hot as he thought of the injustice. Why should this upstart newcomer—one not even born of the People!—be given that prize Taza coveted? Morrhyn fed him pahé like mother's milk to a baby, and that could only strengthen his talent while Taza's must wither and wane without the sacred root. Davyd, he thought, would grow ever stronger, and he steadily weaker, until the passing years leached out his ability and left him dreamless, his gift wasted. He would become no more than another warrior, ordinary. Or less, for his crippled leg denied him some measure of mobility. He could not run with the other young men, nor climb very well, nor walk without his twisted foot dragging.

None spoke of this, there was no laughter, but Taza was nonetheless aware of his deformity and was convinced the Maker gave him the dreaming talent in compensation. Therefore it seemed obvious to him that Kahteney *should* name him, that it was his right. The last time he had spoken with the wakanisha, he had lost his temper when Kahteney again refused him. It was unjust, and the sight of Davyd forever in company with Morrhyn was like a burr prickling under his tail.

So when he saw Davyd readying to leave, he decided to follow.

It was easy to quit the camp unnoticed. His mother had been slain by Chakthi's Tachyn in the summer raiding and his father had died fighting the Breakers. His mother's brother and his wife, themselves childless, had taken in the orphaned Taza, but his uncle was off hunting now, and his aunt was busy foraging for roots. He had—thanks to his temper—few friends, and there were no others to pay him heed as he gathered up his gear and stowed it on his chestnut horse. Even so, he rode out of the camp at an angle to Davyd's route, casually, as if he thought only to go hunting awhile. Then, out of sight of the lodges, he heeled the chestnut to a gallop and swung around in a wide sweep to pick up Davyd's trail.

It was not difficult. The stranger rode slowly—poor horseman that he was—and Taza trailed him at a distance: too far back that Davyd, even did he turn, could recognize him.

There was an oak wood Tekah had shown Davyd about three days' ride from the valley. A stream ran through the grove, and grass for the horse was plentiful. It was a serene place, as if the great trees imposed calm on the ground beneath, and he thought it an ideal spot to build his shelter and seek the answers he needed.

He rode leisurely, deep in thought and only half-aware of the landscape around him. He had known, he supposed, that this decision had awaited him, but put off its contemplation in the sheer exhilaration of living with the People. There was so much to learn, so much to do, and it seemed to him incredible that a former thief from the backstreets of grim, gray Bantar should come to this new land, this new life, as if reborn. He had clutched eagerly at the opportunity, glorying in the new skills he learned from Arcole and Tekah as much as in the lessons Morrhyn taught him, all part of his new life. It had been exciting enough, busy enough, that he had been able to ignore the clear implications inherent in Morrhyn's teaching. Why else would the wakanisha tutor him so, if not that he follow in Morrhyn's footsteps?

And there lay his quandary. Certainly, he wished to learn how to use his dreaming as the wakanishas did; but no less had he longed to become a warrior, to be like Arcole. Now, he knew, the time came when he must grow up and choose his path like a man. Save as yet he could not decide which trail he'd follow, and Morrhyn had told him he could not be both wakanisha and warrior, that he must choose the one or the other.

He sighed, for a moment idly wondering why life could not be simple, then laughed at himself for such foolishness. Life was what it was, and his was complicated by his gift, which he could not ignore, and so he must act the man and make his decision. The Maker, he trusted, would guide him. He would build his shelter and set fishlines in the stream, snares around the wood. He would lay up a store of food and then fast in search of the answer, and until then there was no point thinking overmuch about it. The dreams would show him what to do.

Reassured by that resolution, he began to enjoy the journey for its own sake. The prairie, long sere after the winter snows, was once again alive. The grass grew green under a bright, cold sun that shone from a cloud-patterned sky the color of gunmetal. The wind blew strong, rustling his shoulder-length hair, carrying the promise of rain before nightfall. Prairie dogs watched him pass, curious and unafraid, and overhead hawks swooped and circled. Far to the east he could see the shadow line that was the mountains dividing Ket-Ta-Thanne from Salvation. He wondered what went on there, but only vaguely—this was his home now, this wide land of grass and forest and hill, of rivers and ravines; this fine, free place. He ran his fingers over the scar imprinted on his cheek. In Salvation that was a mark of shame, a mark of servitude. Here it was a badge of honor that told the People he had crossed Chakthi's domain in search of liberty. To the Matawaye, the brand spoke of courage, and Davyd had grown proud of the mark.

Abruptly, he heeled his horse to a canter, for the sheer joy of it as much as in search of shelter before the rain came. Not so long ago, he thought, such speed had terrified him. Now he gripped the buckskin's ribs with his thighs and thought nothing of its swift gait. He began to laugh.

As the sun approached the western horizon, clouds gathered in massy banks of ominous gray, blown toward Davyd by the wind out of the northeast. Lit redly by the setting sun, dark above, they reminded him of the Grannach furnaces. Indeed, like the distant crashing of giant hammers, he heard the rumble of thunder carried on the wind. It was time to halt for the night.

He found a stand of hickory and walked the horse into the shelter of the tall, shag-barked trees. The wind was strengthening steadily and already the sky grew dark, the thunder drawing closer. He hobbled the horses and left them to forage, then set to constructing a makeshift shelter. There seemed little point in attempting a fire that likely the approaching storm would drown, so he contented himself with the jerky in his pack, squatting beneath a roof of branches and the tarpaulin brought from Salvation. As he finished his meal the storm arrived, and he sat watching lightning stab daggers of jagged brilliance at the ground before moving on like some vast and ethereal many-legged beast stalking the prairie. The thunder dinned awhile longer, like great drumbeats pounding a senseless rhythm on the skin of the sky, and rain drove hard against the trees and the roof of his shelter. Davyd stretched out dry, pleased with his construction, and composed himself for sleep.

∎   ∎   ∎

On the open grass, Taza sat huddled and miserable, his chest-nut horse pegged that it not panic and run away as the lightning danced and the thunder tolled. Such discomfort did nothing to improve his temper.

Davyd woke to a morning freshened by the rain. It dripped steadily from the limbs of the hickories, pooling on the ground below, where mist hung ethereal so that the two horses seemed to move on a drifting, insubstantial gray mere. The sun was only a little way up, a hazy disk against the brightening sky that promised a warm day. Cold yet, though, as he rubbed the animal dry and washed in the dew that bathed the grass. Then he ate more jerky, packed his gear, and rode on.

The storm had obscured Davyd's tracks, but Taza guessed he'd likely taken shelter in the wood, and knew it when he found the makeshift wickiup. Then the aftermath of the deluge favored him: the ground was soft and held the hoofprints preserved for him to follow. He trailed out of the hickory stand and rode onto the open grass.

Davyd reached the oak wood on the third day with a little daylight still in hand. The hurst was deep and wide, saplings thrusting up along the edge as if the timber sought to spread, contesting with the prairie's grass. He followed the stream to the center, where the oldest trees stood massy, their vast branches spreading a sheltering canopy overhead, the lowering sun flinging long shadows across the ground. Squirrels chattered at his approach and birds trilled an alarm, browsing rabbits scattering as he halted and looked around.

There was a solemnity to the grove that suited his purpose and he dismounted, stripping the horse and rubbing it down, setting hobbles on its fetlock before seeing to his own needs. He saw trout in the stream and baited fishlines, then set out his snares. This night, he thought, he'd eat well, and tomorrow construct a proper shelter and begin the fasting that would help induce the dream state he sought. He gathered wood for a fire and set up a lean-to against the trunk of a giant oak. Then he lit his fire and bathed in the stream, and as dusk fell, swiftened here by the overhang of budding branches, he found two rabbits caught in his traps. He skinned them, and spitted the carcasses over the fire as he checked his fishlines. Already three trout were hooked and he cleaned them and set them aside as the clearing filled with the savory odor of the roasting meat.

He ate both rabbits and, his belly pleasantly full, settled down to sleep.

He woke in the midpart of the night from a curious dream of watching eyes. Almost, he felt afraid, for the dream hinted at possible danger and he wondered if some predator stalked the wood—a lion, perhaps, or a wolverine. The moon was young yet, but stars lit the clearing with a pale light that revealed the horse sleeping peacefully. The banked fire glowed red and he could neither see or hear any animal or other sign of danger. He listened awhile, hand on his bow, an arrow loose on the string, and still heard nothing. Then a raccoon ambled across the clearing, studied him a moment, and hurried on. Davyd went back to sleep.

Taza thought it would be easy to slay the stranger. Clearly, he thought himself safe, and for all his vaunted prowess as a Dreamer he seemed unaware he was followed and watched as he slept. Taza thought that he could put at least three arrows in him before he woke properly, or even creep up and slit his throat, smash a hatchet against his skull. But he hesitated at that extreme, thinking that Morrhyn or Kahteney would surely find him out and he then face condemnation as a murderer. Better, he decided, to continue watching. He was confident now that Davyd sought the Maker's guidance on his future, and perhaps he would decide against continuing as Morrhyn's pupil. In that case, Kahteney must surely accept Taza. If not . . . The young Lakanti was not certain; he would wait for now and decide his course later. He crept silently away from the clearing, back to his horse, which he mounted and rode to the farther side of the wood.

Morning dawned clear, the oaks loud with birdsong, the wind a caress whispering through the branches that filtered the early sun in dancing patterns over the grass and the stream. Davyd rose and bathed, set the trout to smoking and, after checking his horse, began to gather the makings of a wickiup. He cut saplings that he drove into the earth, tying them off at the apex to form a small, inverted bowl shape. Then he wove younger shoots between the uprights and plastered the entire structure with mud dug from the stream's bank. As it dried to a hard shell, he dug a small fire pit and set stones to heating. The work took him the better part of the day before he was satisfied the wickiup was built as Morrhyn had instructed him, and his stomach protested its lack of filling. He ignored that discomfort and strung the cured trout from a branch, then filled his waterskin and set it inside the wickiup. He made obeisance to the Maker, asking that his questions be answered, and stripped naked before retreating into the shelter, covering the entrance with his tarpaulin. The stones were heated now and he spilled water over them, filling the wickiup with steam, then soaked thick chunks of moss and dropped them over the glowing fire. More steam billowed, fragrant, and Davyd lay down, endeavoring to drive all extraneous thoughts from his mind, seeking that oneiric void that was the doorway to communion.

Taza set up a store of food—rabbits and squirrels, some trout—that he be free to observe Davyd, and made his stealthy way back through the wood.

The stranger was building a sweat lodge—sure confirmation of Taza's beliefs—and the Lakanti watched from the shadows as he completed the structure and crawled inside. An idea took shape and Taza smiled to himself, then circled the clearing to approach downwind of the horses. They'd likely not give notice of his presence, for his scent should be familiar to them, but still he'd not chance revealing himself to

Davyd; at least, not yet. He crept to the big oak and cut the strings holding the trout and then, suppressing laughter, crept away with his stolen booty.

It was a small gesture, and likely Davyd would assume a raccoon or some other scavenger had taken the fish, but still he'd not fill his belly when he emerged from the wickiup. Pleased with himself, Taza slunk away to his own camp.

Time held no meaning inside the sweat lodge. No light penetrated the mud-chinked walls and the banked fire gave off only a faint glow through the billowing steam. Sound was dulled, and as hunger took hold what Davyd mostly heard was the pulsing of his own blood, the steady beat of his heart. He slept, and woke only to stoke the fire and add more soaked moss before drifting again into the limbo that was neither full wakefulness or true sleep.

And he began to dream. . . .

He stood on a mountaintop that was clad in snow, pristine under a sky of pure azure, the sun a blinding disk immediately above him. Cloud wreathed the flanks, but through the great white banks he could somehow see Ket-Ta-Thanne to the west and Salvation to the east. He turned and Morrhyn and Arcole stood before him, neither speaking, only watching him with wondering eyes. . . .

And then he was astride the buckskin horse and knew that his hair was tied in the braids and paint was on his face. A round shield of hardened buffalo hide was strapped to his left forearm and he held a nocked bow in his right hand, and knew he rode to war. . . .

And then his hair was loose and he sat within a lodge preparing the pahé root, his mind filled with a terrible dread, aware that awful danger came against the People, but not from where, or who the enemy might be. . . .

And then Taza's face filled his vision, laughing. . . .

And he saw a great army marching out of Salvation, blue-coats and red, with muskets and cannon, and he stood before the column with arms upraised and shouted that the Militiamen must fight for right, not conquest. . . .

And then another army, Matawaye warriors he knew must

be Chakthi's Tachyn riding horses that were dwarfed by the dread beasts the others rode, which seemed a commingling of creatures, as if lions and lizards merged, their riders clad all in glittering rainbow armor, with skulls strung from their saddles. And Taza laughed at him, and he held a musket and his hair was unbound and he fought. . . .

The images came swift, imposed on one another, mingling and interweaving until they became a vast conflagration that swept over the plains of Ket-Ta-Thanne and Salvation, and the mountains between shattered and melted. And he stood inside the flames and raised his arms and shouted and rain fell, dousing the fires, and grass grew again and trees, and Morrhyn smiled at him, and Arcole, and a soldier in a blue coat whose face seemed somehow familiar. And soldiers walked with branded folk and Matawaye, all smiling. . . .

And then an unknown face, sallow and cruel, its owner pointing an accusatory finger, beckoning him to a chain-hung pole around which was piled brushwood. And he was drawn to the pole by a force he could not resist, only stand helpless as the manacles were locked about his wrists and ankles and a torch set to the pyre so that flames rose about his feet and smoke clogged his nostrils and he screamed as the pain began. . . .

Davyd woke awash with sweat, starting up from the bare earth of the wickiup with a choking cry. Almost, he flung aside the tarpaulin to crawl outside, where the air was clean and not filled with the dream memory of his scorching flesh. But he had no answer yet—as yet he was unsure what the dreams meant, they seemed all confusion and chaos—and so he forced his racing heart to calm and voiced a prayer, and lay back. He was light-headed, and his belly felt like a vacuum, no longer hungry—beyond that—but drawing him inward, into himself, where the answer would be found. . . .

He saw the armies clash, the soldiers of Evander fighting the People; the weirdlings he knew must be the Breakers fighting the Evanderans, fighting the People; Matawaye fighting Matawaye: chaos. And then the imposition of a kind of order that, even dreaming, unconscious, he knew came from a source beyond himself. The images blurred and realigned, the struggling factions parting and then joining in alliance,

Matawaye and Militiamen siding together against the might of the Breakers and the renegade Tachyn, and he watching as if from on high, anxious to know the outcome. . . .

Which was not vouchsafed him, for the images faded behind a screen of flame that filled up all the world, and he was running from the conflagration, seeking a safe place he knew existed, but not where or how he should reach it. And suddenly he was pursued: Taza chased him, laughing, and the sallow-faced Evanderan, who held chains and a burning brand, and Matawaye whose faces he did not know, and Breakers in their glittering armor astride their horrid beasts. And he could only run. . . .

Taza listened to the sounds Davyd made and wondered what the stranger dreamed. Were his shouts a guide, it was nothing pleasant, and that pleased the young Lakanti. Perhaps Davyd would decide the life of a Dreamer was not for him; but Taza doubted that would be, and would sooner not leave that decision to chance, but tip the scales in what he thought must be his favor.

He would not harm Davyd—that should be too risky—but there were other ways to remove the upstart. He thought of the trout he'd stolen and grinned, another idea taking shape. He looked at the two horses grazing peacefully in the noonday sun and made his decision.

Davyd lay panting on the bank of a crystal stream. He could run no farther and knew he must either perish here or find the answer to . . . He was not sure what. Behind him the fire raged, coursing ever closer; across the stream the grass grew green and safe. He knew that if he waded the shallow water he should be safe, that the fire must halt at that barrier and leave him unscathed. He rose and looked back, and inside the flames he saw Flysse and Arcole, Morrhyn, Rannach and Arrhyna, Lhyn, Colun and Marjia, and knew that if he crossed, they all must perish. He cried out to the Maker, pleading for answers, and felt the heat sear him, his eyes watering, his mouth and nostrils sour with smoke. He fell gasping onto his hands and knees, head hanging over the water . . . and saw his face reflected, painted for war even though his hair hung unbound.

Abruptly, a great calm settled on him and he became aware he held things in his hands. He raised his hands, and in his right he saw that he held a hatchet, and in his left pahé root. Not knowing what he did, he brought his hands together, clasping them as if in prayer, and the root and the hatchet blended and became one: a tomahawk fashioned of pahé. . . .

Davyd opened his eyes. His limbs felt oddly light, unweighted, and when he tried to rise he began to shake and fell back, his head spinning. He groaned, smiling because he had his answer now, and closed his eyes and slept, and this time he did not dream.

He woke again and rolled onto his side. The fire was dead and the wickiup chilly. He was very weak. Laboriously, he crawled to the waterskin and raised it to his lips. It weighed heavy and there was not much water in it, but he drank what there was and struggled to the opening. He pushed the tarpaulin aside and looked out onto a clearing washed by the moon's pale light. He saw an owl watching him from the branch of the oak tree, the great round eyes solemn, and wondered if the bird omened wisdom or death. He took a deep breath and rose to his feet, staggering as the world spun wildly round. The owl took flight, swooping low and ghostly across the clearing, and when Davyd could see clearly again, it was gone. He felt no hunger, only an imponderable emptiness, as if a void existed where his belly had been. He wondered how long he had lain inside the sweat lodge, and knew that he must eat to regain his strength. He felt too weak to mount his buckskin.

On legs that felt both weightless and leaden, he went to where the trout were hung. Thought of the fishes filled his mouth with saliva, and when he reached the branch and saw they were not there, he groaned. He was mistaken, he told himself: light-headed, he became disorientated and had come to the wrong branch. Slowly, he circumnavigated the great tree, and still the fish were not there. He frowned, examining the branches until he found the cords that had held the fish and saw them cut.

He leant against the oak, wary of sitting for he was not sure he had the strength to rise again, thinking that without food he might well starve before he could reach home. He would need, he thought, to set his snares again, and drop his lines in the stream. He could surely last this one more night without food.

He went to where he'd stowed his gear in the fork of a low-hung branch. The snares and fishlines were there, his bow and all his clothes. Or had been: now they were gone.

For a moment, panic threatened. He could not understand what went on. The fish were perhaps taken by some scavenger more agile than most, but the snares, his clothes? He searched the ground and found no sign, no remnants or wreckage: all was gone.

He wondered if he dreamed still, if this was some extension of his oneiric quest, but he could feel the night air chill on his naked skin, the grass moist under his bare feet, the rough bark of the oak. He could hear the night sounds of the wood, the small noises of the hunters and their prey. Then it dawned on him that he could not hear his horse. Nor could he see it when he looked about. He fought a fresh surge of panic then, for he knew that he could not survive the journey home on foot: without a horse, he must surely starve.

Frightened now, he stumbled across the clearing, desperately hoping that the animal had merely wandered a little farther afield, but he could find it nowhere. Instead, close to the stream, he found the hobble—it had been cut.

For long moments he stared at the severed rawhide, struggling to comprehend. It was almost too strange, too enormous to accept, save the reality forced itself on him. As he had lain dreaming, someone had come to the clearing to steal his horse, his gear, his food; to leave him naked and alone, and—afoot—too far from home that he could hope to reach camp alive.

14

Fight to Survive

His mouth was very dry and he went weak-kneed to the stream, dropping on his belly to drink. Thirst slaked, he heaved to a sitting position, the movement setting his head to reeling again. He was afraid and at the same time oddly distanced, as if he observed himself objectively and wondered how he should survive. The waxing moon told him he'd been eight or nine days, perhaps more, in the sweat lodge. The camp was three days' ride away—six for a healthy man on foot to walk. He was unsure how long it might take a hungry man; longer, he thought, than he could endure.

Suddenly he began to laugh at the irony of his predicament. He had come here alone to seek an answer, and dreamed strange dreams of danger all oblivious of his own immediate peril. It should surely be a cynical jest if he were to die here, answered; to starve in Ket-Ta-Thanne after surviving Bantar and the Sea of Sorrows, indenture in Salvation and the dangers of the wilderness. He stifled his laughter as it turned to sobs, and he realized that tears filled his eyes. This was no way for a warrior of the People to act. He gasped, his chest heaving painfully, his belly abruptly reminding him it was empty, and forced himself to ignore discomfort as he assessed his situation.

Morrhyn had survived alone on the Maker's Mountain and come back through the snows to bring his warning to the People. Now Davyd sensed he owned a similar mission. He could not properly interpret his dreams, save for the one clear answer, but he knew he must describe them to Morrhyn, else dreadful threat again come upon the Matawaye. Or was that only vanity born of fear? The Maker had gifted Morrhyn with certain knowledge, and kept the wakanisha alive that he deliver the People, but would he look so kindly on Davyd?

"The Maker is like a wise father," Morrhyn had told him. "He guides us and guards us, but he does not indulge us. We should not expect him to pick us up each time we fall, for he'd leave us to take our knocks and learn from them. It is our duty to seek our own solutions before we turn to him and ask him to carry us through the hard times. Do we always run to him asking that he resolve our every difficulty, then we are less than he'd have us be."

So then, Davyd decided, he could ask the Maker for aid, but must also look to help himself. He rose slowly to his feet, swaying a moment as he shuddered, his limbs trembling as if his blood ran thin and all his muscles vibrated to some internal disharmony. He felt mightily weary, and feared he should fall down. He swallowed, taking deep breaths, willing his shaking body to stillness, and then turned to the four points of the compass as Morrhyn had taught him, intoning a prayer that the Maker grant him life, at least long enough that he be able to describe his dreams to the wakanisha.

Then he set to the fleshly preparations for survival.

First came a fire—the nights were chill in the Moon of the Turning Year, and rain was likely—naked and near starving, he could not survive without warmth. He wished he'd brought his tinderbox, but he had elected to perform the rituals in the traditional manner and lit his fire with dry wood and a fire-stick. Both were now consumed and he must scavenge the clearing before he could find suitable materials to start the blaze again. In time, he found what he sought and carried dry branches and kindling to the entrance of the wickiup. His hands shook as he turned the stick between his palms, and it took several attempts before the drilling sparked the moss in the ancient log. He leant forward, blowing gently, and saw tiny flames rise. He added twigs, adjuring himself to patience, and waited until the kindling took before setting larger pieces in place. Slowly, the fire built, the flames rising stronger, and he set a cone of wood in place, watching as the blaze sent flickering red light across the clearing.

He was tempted then to lie down close by that seductive warmth, and sleep, but he was not sure he'd have the strength to rise again. So he warmed himself and wondered how he could procure sustenance.

Tekah had shown him how a fish might be caught by hand, tickled from its watery bed were the fisherman skilled enough and swift enough. Davyd had caught a few in this fashion—after frustrating hours and many failed attempts—but now it seemed the likeliest way to gain immediate food. He might build traps, could he find suitable wood and pliant vines, but that should take much longer, and even then hold no promise of success. Fish, he decided, were his best option. He returned to the stream.

The surface was patterned with light and shade, the moon shining down through the overhanging trees so that it was difficult to locate the trout, their camouflaged backs blending with the pebbly streambed as they drifted in their piscine sleep. Catching them was harder still. He could barely quell the trembling that possessed his limbs, and too often that disturbed the water, sending the fish scattering, leaving Davyd moaning with frustration, his arm chilled by the cold immersion. And that chill grew to pervade all his body, so that the shuddering grew worse and he must crawl back to the fire, to warm himself again before his next attempt.

The moon passed across the sky and the light faded into the toneless gray that precedes dawn. The cold grew worse and he must go more frequently to the fire now, chanting prayers that he not succumb to sleep. Delirium threatened, and several times he found himself drifting, his arm submerged and the cold taking hold, sucking out what little energy he had left. Then he would start back—again frightening the fish—and curse himself for a weakling and damn whoever had stolen his gear and horse.

Almost, he gave up; almost consigned himself to death. But some spark of obstinacy still burned, some small flicker of determination, and despite his chattering teeth and the numbing weariness that filled him, he continued. And then, as the gray predawn sky began to brighten, his resolution was rewarded, as if the Maker tested him and now granted him a prize. It was a small trout, but it was enough: he carried it back to the fire, barely scorching the skin before he tore at the meat.

He felt somewhat better then. The fish was not enough to assuage his hunger—if anything, it served to remind him how starved he was—but he was proud of his success, and as the sun broke through the mist floating amongst the oaks, he returned to the stream. But this time he was disappointed, and by midmorning he admitted defeat and gave in to cold and weariness. He wrapped himself in the tarpaulin and allowed himself to sleep.

"Ten days!" Flysse faced Arcole across the lodgefire, her blue eyes both angry and concerned. "Is it not time to seek him out?"

Arcole shrugged. "You said he went seeking dreams, no? And he can look after himself. Likely he's made camp and looks to dream his destiny."

"And is he hurt? Has he suffered some accident?"

Arcole faced her square, a measure of guilt kindled by those burning eyes. He nodded and said, "I'll speak with Rannach and Morrhyn come dawn."

"And go find him?" she asked.

"He might not," Arcole said cautiously, "appreciate that. Is he on a dream quest, then likely he'd sooner be left alone."

"Left for dead; perhaps starving?"

"I'll speak with Rannach and Morrhyn," he repeated, "and do they agree, I'll go looking."

Flysse ducked her head in acceptance. "I'd not lose Davyd."

"Nor I," Arcole declared. "Do the others agree, then I'll go in search of him."

Flysse said, "Good," but even as she smiled and set their sleeping furs ready, she felt a terrible doubt that all was not well with Davyd, and wished he had not gone away alone.

The sun was westered when Davyd awoke and the fire burned down to embers. He rose—a little steadier now, the dizziness receded somewhat—and painstakingly gathered more wood, rebuilding the fire. When he was satisfied with the blaze and had a stock of dry branches in reserve, he returned to the stream. He was no more successful, and before the light faded he gave up, electing to search out what berries and tubers he could find before dusk came down. He ate the sorry results of his foraging raw as birds chorused farewell to the day and the night creatures came out. Bats fluttered amongst the trees, and he wondered if it was the same owl he saw perched on the far side of the stream, the same raccoon that wandered unafraid past his lodge. He was again light-headed, and the earthy roots sat uneasy in his stomach. He felt queasy and very weak, and when he drank from the stream his gut complained violently and expelled its contents. He dragged himself to the fire, his belly cramping, and painfully banked the flames before crawling inside the wickiup.

"Ten days are not so long," Morrhyn said. "I spent twice that on my first dream quest—the Maker decides the duration."

"And Flysse my patience," Arcole returned. "She'd have me go out in search of him now."

Rannach chuckled fondly. "Wives, eh?"

Arcole smiled in response, but still could not help feeling the doubts Flysse had set in his mind. He said, "Even so."

"A while longer," Morrhyn said. "Surely, had harm come to him, I'd have dreamed of it."

Arcole nodded and wondered how he might tell Flysse this news.

The next day Davyd woke a little after dawn and lay shivering, his mind wandering random, waiting for the sun to warm the clearing. He thought it should be near impossible to make his way home without provisions of some sort, and wondered if he could lay up sufficient fish for the journey, or fashion traps successful enough to catch rabbits. He wondered if he was missed, and who had stolen his horse. Had they been turned free, they'd no doubt make their way back to the valley, and then his clan—he smiled as he realized he assumed himself a Commacht now—would surely come seeking him. But why would the thief turn them free? His smile became a frown as he pondered the mystery. The clans were in alliance after the exodus, and there was none of the horse-taking Rannach had described so proudly: the People did not steal from friends. Only rivals or enemies took horses, and he could think of no enemies—save one. He thought on his dreams and remembered Taza's laughing face. He recalled Arcole's words: "You've an enemy there: best watch him." Was it Taza then, had sought to strand him alone and starving in this wood? Could the young Lakanti hate him so much?

It mattered less than surviving. He put Taza out of his mind and went looking for food.

The sun was bright this day, the rays that struck down through the canopy of branches blinding him and setting his head to aching, the painful throbbing a counterpoint to the hunger pangs that cramped his belly. Several times as he searched he doubled over, curling around the focus of his discomfort, his eyes screwed tight closed, and must force himself upright, to go on with his desperate hunt. He found more berries and realized they were not yet ripe enough to eat—he left them and concentrated on digging out edible roots, which he charred in the fire. This time he kept them down, and as the sun passed its zenith he decided he might survive. It would not be easy, but the hope alone energized him somewhat and he spent the remainder of the day fashioning traps of supple green wood and laboriously woven grass, and set them in the rabbit runs. That simple effort exhausted him and he collapsed into a deep sleep.

Too deep: rain fell during the night and doused his fire, so that he woke to an unfriendly morning, all chilly mist and dripping trees. His spirits fell then, and more when he found his traps empty. Most were destroyed, only one sprung, and all that held was the severed leg of a rabbit taken by some predator more skilled than he. It seemed a useless endeavor to rebuild the traps and he left the scattered remains where they lay. He felt gloomy as the day, but even so, for all his belly complained bitterly and the cold struck deep into his bones, he refused to give up hope. He rebuilt his fire and ate more roots, then inspected the stream again. It seemed the trout had grown wiser and fled that section running through the clearing, so he wandered on unsteady legs deeper into the wood until he found a place where stones and a toppled tree shaped a small pool where fish hung in the current like speckled clouds. Tekah had shown him how the People sometimes built fish traps to catch migrating salmon, and he thought to put that knowledge to use. The effort left him exhausted, but as the shadows lengthened he had the downstream end of the pool blocked with stones and branches, denying the fish exit.

That night he slept hungry, and in the morning wanted only to lie still, warmed by the smoking fire. But that was weakness and should bring him closer to death, which he was not yet ready to meet, so he steeled himself and rose shivering into another day of dull gray skies, shaking as the chill invaded, seeming to slow his blood, to dull his thoughts, so that he longed to curl beneath the tarpaulin and escape into slumber. He crouched a long time beside the fire and only when the shaking had abated did he return to the stream.

The sun was a pale eye in the gray, indifferent in its observation of his labors as it traversed the somber heavens and descended toward the western horizon. By then he had the upstream entrance to the pool blocked with a second makeshift dam, trapping the fish. It would be a little easier to catch them now, he thought wearily, but later—for now he was too cold, too weak to contemplate wading into the deepening fishpond. His head swam, lights dancing before his eyes as his teeth chattered, a ringing as of distant bells dinned in his ears, and all the aches possessing his body seemed to merge in a singular torment. He fell down as he returned to his campsite, unsure how often, not caring, seeking only the comforting warmth of the fire and sleep, unaware of bruises or cuts, finally moving on hands and knees like some wounded animal intent only on reaching its lair.

After the rain, his fire smoked abominably, but he was warm again and his spirits rose accordingly. He gave thanks to the Maker for the simple fact of his survival, and promised himself that the next day he would catch fish and eat well. He crawled into the wickiup and clutched the cold tarpaulin to him. And then he thought again of his dreams, and what they might presage, and knew that he *must* take word back to Morrhyn. He thought now that perhaps he could survive in this wood, like some hermit returning gradually to a primitive state. Could he take fish from the pond he must grow stronger, and then he could fashion weapons and hunt the larger creatures he heard moving in the night, make clothing from their skins, build a better shelter. He was still not sure he could make the journey home, not afoot and naked, and then he wondered if that was the intention of the mysterious thief. Had Taza—if it was Taza—taken his horse and his gear that he be trapped? Or perhaps the Lakanti had not believed he could survive, thinking he would starve. Davyd grew angry then, and determined to confront the youth.

But to do that he must find the People again, or they find him. He stared at the smoking fire, the sputtering flames seeming to mock his resolve. The moon was close to full now, its light filtered by the smoke that came in thick billows from the damp wood. He raised his head, staring intently at the gray-white clouds that drifted up, swirling about the over-hanging branches, rising dark against the stars. Then he smiled and thanked the Maker for another answer.

"I found it running loose by the little river to the north where the hornbeams grow," Taza explained. "I saw it was Davyd's horse, and I wondered if he'd fallen off, so I looked for him awhile. But I could not find him, and so I brought it back. He's not here?"

Rannach said, "No." Then: "What were you doing up there?"

"Hunting," Taza said, pleased with his dissimulation. "I looked to earn my keep."

"And you found it along the hornbeam river?" Tekah asked.

"Yes." Taza nodded. "It was drinking when I saw it, and there was sweat on it—as if it'd run a long way." He affected an expression he trusted combined both doubt and fear. "I pray he's not come to harm."

Arcole said, "To the north?"

"Yes: to the north." Taza nodded, and congratulated himself.

■   ■   ■

The next morning the sun shone bright, warm with the promise of the year's turning, and for all Davyd tottered like some ancient he went to the pool optimistic. The sun was warm, but the water cold; it seemed to envelop his legs in an icy blanket as he waded in, numbing his trembling muscles, driving shards of chill into his groin so that he moaned with the pain as he bent and reached for the frightened trout. He knew he could not withstand such cold for long and prayed as he fished, asking that the Maker grant him a catch, grant him the strength to carry word of his dreams back to the People. Only that, he asked, and must I die after, let it be; only not before.

It seemed the deity heard him, or he profited from Tekah's lessons, he did not care which—only that he succeeded in flipping two plump trout onto the bank. He clambered out and snatched up his catch. He could no longer feel his legs as he staggered to his fire and set fresh timber to burning. He luxuriated in the warmth, tearing at the raw fish with teeth that slowly ceased their chattering, careless of the slimy skins, sucking the last remnants of meat from the spindly bones. He felt bloated then, and sat awhile by the fire, smiling, pleased with himself, confidence returning. But two fish, he knew, were not enough: he must go back to the pool.

This time, he thought to build a fire before he entered the water, and then must return to the wickiup to fetch a brand, but the flames were a cheerful promise that justified such delay and he settled to his task with renewed vigor. The day was aged before he felt satisfied: four fishes lay on the bank, and as he crouched beside the fire he thought he should eat well this night.

He could manage only one before his belly protested this sudden munificence, and he carried the rest into the wickiup, unwilling to risk their loss. He doubted the horse thief remained in the wood, but there were other scavengers to contest his prize, and was he to survive he must regain somewhat of his strength.

He breakfasted well and returned to the fishpond on stronger legs. There seemed fewer fish in the pool and he wondered if animals—likely raccoons—had discovered this easy hunting. No matter, he decided, there remained sufficient for his needs, did all go well, and the day was warm, the breeze that rustled the infant oak leaves gentle, the sky clear blue, so that he felt a great goodwill toward the woodland creatures and did not begrudge them a share. He built up the fire again and spent the better part of the day tickling trout, then hid his bounty inside the wickiup, trusting that the fire and his own man-smell would deter thieves as he foraged for roots.

That night he feasted, and determined that come the morrow he would set in motion the plan that had come to him as he watched his fire. Did that fail, then he would strike out across the prairie. He thought now that he might survive the journey.

Soon after dawn he followed the stream back to the edgewood. The great grass sea spread out before him, and some distance off he saw a small herd of deer grazing. He thought of venison roasted over the fire and could taste it in his mouth. He thought that did he succeed, did he live, then he would not eat fish again for some time. Then he set to collecting wood, deliberately choosing the dampest timber he could find. He built what he hoped should be a large enough stack and returned to the wickiup, taking a brand from the fire there that he carried carefully back, lighting the second fire.

The sun was past its zenith now and he calculated that only a few hours of daylight remained. He hoped it should be enough as he watched the flames take hold and smoke rise in a thick column above the trees. If not, he told himself, he would rebuild the beacon the following day and, must he, every day until he deemed it time to set out on foot. He was undecided just how long he would wait, and determined he would not succumb. He would live to take back word of his dreams. That, and find the horse thief. He squatted, chewing a cold fish as he basked in the warmth of the smoking bonfire.

He waited through what remained of the day and then, disappointed, returned to the wickiup. For a while he contemplated transferring his camp to the edgewood, but that would mean a longer trek to the fishpond, and so he chose to remain where he was. He decided he would divide his time between foraging and the signal fire, and was he not rescued by the full of the moon, then he would strike out across the grass.

That night he dreamed of riders and warm blankets, of buffalo meat and venison, that he slept within a lodge, safe amongst the Commacht. He was uncertain, when he woke, if the dream was prophetic or merely the product of hope. He was not yet so skilled in the interpretation that he could decide, and when he came to the pool he forgot the dream as he saw disaster bright in the morning sun.

Like his traps before, the crude dams containing the fishpond had been destroyed. The timber, the rocks, he had so laboriously placed were all torn apart, the stream flowing free again. Part-eaten trout littered the banks, as if whatever beast had ravaged the dams gloried in wanton destruction. Davyd stifled a shout of disappointment, staring about as he realized he shared the wood with something more than harmless raccoons. He felt abruptly cold again, an uneasy prickling nervous on his back, as if furtive and hostile eyes watched him from the undergrowth. Instinctively, he snatched up a branch, and then examined the grass around the ruined pond.

He found tracks there, the spoor of something sizable and clawed. It was not a lion, he thought, but perhaps a small bear or—worse—a wolverine. He did not think a bear would kill fish and leave them, or wreck the pool, and his heart raced as he decided it must be a wolverine. Those beasts were rapacious predators, cunning and vicious—and willing to confront a lone man. He doubted he had the strength to fight off a wolverine, and knew his strength must surely wane again could he no longer rely on the pool to provide his food. He cursed volubly, in the language of the People and his own native Evanderan, foul gutter curses that expressed his sudden desperation. The wood took on a different aspect now, a place of shadows and danger. He studied the tracks, seeing where they disappeared into the thicker woodland around the pool. They went away from his campsite, but that was no guarantee the beast would avoid him, and he felt an unpleasant presentiment that a confrontation should arrive. Had he his bow, or the musket he'd left in his lodge back in the valley, he'd own a chance against the wolverine: defenseless and still weak, he doubted his chances. Therefore, he told himself, it was imperative he escape the wood soon—if not rescued then afoot. He gathered up the landed trout—even chewed by the beast they remained edible—and, still clutching the branch, returned to the wickiup and built the fire high. Even wolverines, he thought, must surely fear the flames.

Then he returned to the edgewood and rekindled the fire there. As the season turned, mellowing into the warmth of spring, it became harder to find damp timber. He lacked the means to cut green branches and the strength to break off any but the most slender, so he resorted to dumping what he could gather in the stream, soaking the wood that it give off smoke. It was a slow process, and the smoky beacon dwindled to a thin column. He watched it forlornly now, wondering what the night should bring, willing riders to appear out on the grass. None came, and he trudged back to the wickiup to fill his stomach with scavenged fish. That, at least, was a boon—did he eke out the trout, he calculated he could survive for five more days. But then he thought he should be too weak to contemplate crossing the prairie on foot. It was a quandary: it appeared he had a simple, brutal choice. He could take the damaged fish and walk away now, or he could remain, hoping his signal fire was spotted, and risk the wolverine. He examined the fish. They were badly chewed, not much meat on them, and while they would keep him alive did he conserve his energy, they were scarce enough to sustain him through the long walk home. Grimly, he decided his best chance was to remain. He sighed and went in search of a weapon of some kind.

The best he could find was a length of straight wood almost long as he was tall that he charred in the fire, chipping awkwardly at the tip with a stone until he had imparted a blunt point. It was poor defense did the wolverine attack, but save for gathering more stones to throw at the beast, he could think of nothing better. As the sun went down he prayed to the Maker and retreated inside the crude lodge.

His fire blazed high outside and for a long time he lay watching the flames, listening to the night. He heard the cries of questing owls and the chattering of raccoons, other sounds he could not identify, and wondered if wolverines called or roared or hunted silently. At last he slept, his makeshift spear clutched like a talisman to his chest.

"Where is he?" Tekah swept his lance in a wide arc, indicating the ground they'd covered and the land ahead. "Where would he go?"

"Taza said he found the horses this way," Rannach answered.

"And do you trust Taza?"

Rannach stared at Tekah, his eyes troubled. "What do you say?"

"That Taza envies Davyd, because Morrhyn would give Davyd what Taza desires most. By the Maker, I believe Taza has lied to us all!"

"That is a grave accusation," Rannach said.

"But still I make it!" Tekah stabbed the innocent earth in emphasis of his point. "I say that we go back and seek Morrhyn's advice."

Rannach looked to Arcole. "How say you, brother?"

Arcole stared at the landscape ahead. Beyond the river where the hornbeams grew it was mostly empty. Small stands of timber dotted the grass, but what he saw before him was largely a vast expanse of prairie devoid of woodland. Buffalo herds passed like shaggy shadows in their grazing, and he could see no place where Davyd might have gone on his quest. He wished he'd listened earlier to Flysse.

"I say we go back and ask Morrhyn's advice."

In the morning Davyd found tracks on the far bank of the stream. It was another bright day, as if spring came early to Ket-Ta-Thanne, and the spoor was lit clear by the sunlight shining through the trees so that he could see where the beast had emerged from the woodland and traversed the farther side of the clearing to the bank. It had not crossed, and he wondered if his fire had halted it, and if the flames would continue to deter the animal. Surely, he told himself, it must find sufficient prey within the wood, and then remembered that wolverines were curious and guarded their territory fiercely. The People loathed the beasts, for they were wanton in their habit of destruction, killing for only bloodlust even when their hunger was sated. Such memories depressed Davyd, and he told himself he was safe whilst the sun shone and could forget the danger for a while. It was poor consolation, for he knew that night must fall and then, perhaps, the wolverine would cross the stream. Leave worry for the darkness, he told himself, and went again to the signal fire.

It was burned down to embers and he must painstakingly rebuild, gathering more wood before the smoke rose once more into the sky.

Still no one came, and before dusk he hobbled back to the clearing, building up his other fire, resisting the temptation to gobble all the remaining fish, so that he slept hungry, his belly cramping. Tomorrow, he decided, he would attempt to catch more trout and dig for roots. He began again to wonder if he could survive.

The morning sun revealed tracks on his side of the stream. They circled his wickiup and went off along the waterside as if the wolverine followed his trail to the edgewood. He felt afraid, and walked slow and wary to the signal fire, wondering if he had made the wrong decision and should quit the wood to take his chances on the open grass. He was very hungry now, and weaker, and knew the few remaining trout would not sustain him must he walk. He thought he should likely fall to hunger on the prairie, and not find the means to light a fire but go chilled and without a beacon—though that seemed increasingly pointless, as this was the fourth day he'd sent up smoke and still there was no sign of rescue. He could no longer remember how long he'd sojourned in the wood, and cursed himself for a fool for failing to advise anyone of his destination when he left the lodges of the People. The confidence that had sustained him waned. His head ached again, his vision blurring, the tolling of distant bells again in his ears as his hands trembled and a terrible lassitude gripped him. It was, he mused, such a slender line between death and survival. Had he a horse, he could ride away; even starving, a horse would carry him home. Had he his bow or his snares or

his fishlines, he could eat and grow strong. Had he his
clothes, he'd not shiver so, not feel always chilled. But all
those things were gone and so death loomed imminent.
Again, he cursed the thief, but now he wondered if he would
ever know his identity.

He woke abruptly, realizing he had drifted not into sleep
but into a limbo of miserable contemplation. The sun was
close on the western skyline, layering the blue with bands of
gold and orange and red. The Moon of the Turning Year
stood in the east, almost full now, and the air grew chill as a
breeze transformed the prairie to a sea of swaying green.
Davyd groaned and levered upright, using the spear, and
slowly made his way back to his campsite. As he ate he remembered he had intended to fish. Tomorrow, he told himself, tomorrow I shall try, and also dig for roots. Now he felt
only weary, and could barely find the strength to enlarge the
fire, that it burn bright and protective through the long night.

Come daylight fresh tracks approached the wickiup, circling the fire to approach the mud-chinked walls: the wolverine grew braver.

Davyd ate the last of the trout and kindled his signal fire
once more. He endeavored to catch more fish, but his hands
shook and the cold of the stream pervaded his very bones so
that he could not bear to stand for long in the water. Instead,
he hunted for roots and gathered a few tubers that he turned
in the flames before eating. They were poor sustenance and
left his belly cramped and aching. He thought he should have
left the wood before he grew so weak, and knew he could not
now. He doubted he could walk a full day, surely not all the
long days back to the valley. Hope now seemed a luxury, a
foolish indulgence, and he accepted that he would likely die
here, alone.

That night he dreamed of a beast all clawed and fanged,
and filled with a dreadful rage, that ignored his fire and dug
its way through the thin shelter of his wickiup to attack him,
the intruder on the beast's domain.

■   ■   ■

"No sign at all?" Morrhyn asked.

"None." Rannach shook his head. "We rode out past the hornbeam river, but . . ."

"Taza lies," Tekah snarled, interrupting. "Let me question him."

"Why would he lie?"

Tekah stared at the Dreamer and said, "Because he envies Davyd; because he'd have what you give Davyd."

Morrhyn said, "Perhaps, but even so we cannot judge him on envy alone."

"But leave Davyd to die?"

"We cannot know that he does," Morrhyn said. "That is not our way—to mistrust."

"Then what do we do?" Tekah asked.

"Find him," Morrhyn answered. "Where do you think he might be?"

Tekah thought a moment, then slapped his forehead as if he'd reprimand himself. "I showed him a wood once—an oak wood—that he liked. Perhaps he's gone there."

"Then you go there," Morrhyn said. "Now, and swiftly."

Davyd woke with a start, trembling and sweat-drenched, and looked for reassurance to where the fire blazed. Then sound intruded, a busy scratching, and he turned to see black-furred paws, from which extended long, curved talons, thrust through the lodge's wall. His dream grew flesh as mud and wood were torn away and a blunt muzzle joined the paws, vicious fangs snapping down on a sapling, splintering the green wood in a single bite. Hot breath redolent of decaying meat gusted against Davyd's face and he shouted in shock and terror, scrabbling urgently to the wickiup's entrance as the snarling wolverine tore its way inside.

He rolled across moon-washed grass not knowing he still clutched his poor spear, and shouted again as flame seared his back and the wolverine exploded from the wickiup. As he looked into the cold dark eyes it seemed time slowed, each instant drawn out interminably as he saw the beast crouch, thick hind legs bunching in readiness to spring. He had not seen a wolverine before. Tekah and Rannach, Morrhyn, had described the beasts, but words did little justice to the reality. It was large as a young bear, its fur thick and dark, its limbs short and heavy with muscle, tipped with murderous talons. Its snarl exposed long, curved fangs between the bone-breaking jaws, and the eyes seemed possessed of a malign intelligence, lusting to kill. It launched itself at Davyd and he flailed wildly with his spear, flinging himself across the fire, careless of the pain, seeking only to escape.

He landed on his back and staggered upright, fear lending him a strength he had not known he possessed. The wolverine coughed out a snarling roar and charged. Oblivious of the flames that seared his skin, Davyd reached into the fire and tore loose a brand. He flung it at the attacking predator and the wolverine sprang clear. Davyd grasped his spear in both hands as the beast launched itself anew. He thrust out the pole as the ravening animal hurtled toward him. It seemed all fangs and claws and horrid determination, and he felt raw pain as talons scored his flesh and fetid breath befouled his nostrils. Its weight smashed him down and he screamed as the world went dark.

15

A Man Possessed

After Matieu Fallyn's death Tomas Var felt very alone, in ways to which he was not accustomed. In the Old World he had had friends around him, old acquaintances from the campaigns or the peaceful aftermath: familiar faces with whom he might relax and speak openly. Here in Salvation he had no one—and until Fallyn was slain by the hostiles, he had not realized how dear those faces were. Here he had no one save the oddest friend: Abram Jaymes.

They were quite unalike, the major and the scout, but even so a bond formed between them, slow and wary, but nonetheless firm. Jaymes had forgotten his declaration of departure once the forts were built and continued to scout for Var. Not for the Inquisitor Jared Talle—he showed a cheerful disregard of that eminence—but for Var; and Var was grateful and came to open himself, as much as he dared, to Jaymes. It seemed to him that the man was the embodiment of Salvation's pioneering spirit, more than the farmers and millers and vintners, more than the traders and bargemen and Militia, and he came to enjoy Jaymes's company, the scout's rough-hewn directness. Jaymes spoke honestly, and was he crude in his expression, still he spoke only what he saw as truth and Var respected that.

The forts were built and manned, garrisoned first by those Militiamen Var had brought with him from Evander, and then augmented by the troop ships that had arrived as the year aged toward winter. They were sound now—surely against such primitive weapons as the hostiles owned—with cannon and swivel guns and the muskets of the infantry. Each bastion was armed with case-shot and grape-, powder for the infantry, and kegs of musket balls. The wilderness perimeter was sealed from where the Restitution disappeared into the forests northward to the emergence of the Glory River into the sea. The engineers headed southward to repeat their efforts along the Hope River in the—as yet—unattacked lower quadrant of Salvation.

And as the year aged, Tomas Var returned to Grostheim to face a problem he believed might destroy him.

"He's crazy." Abram Jaymes leaned sideways to expel a stream of tobacco-darkened spittle into the cuspidor. "A winter campaign?"

Var glanced around, more nervous of disapproval, of listening ears that might carry such criticism back to the Inquisitor. Jaymes seemed entirely unconcerned, and not without reason: they sat alone, as if some invisible perimeter separated them from the tavern's other patrons. It was a further reminder of the hostility most felt toward Talle and, by association, his lieutenant.

Var said, "It's what he talks about; and for God's sake keep your voice down. Do you want to end up on the gallows?"

The first snow had fallen; not much, but enough to remind folk that the long months of winter descended. The harvests had been poor for the neglect of the preceding year, and the farmers and the vintners and the millers were not yet convinced the land was secure, so some fled back to the city.

Where Jared Talle hanged them.

The gallows was a permanent fixture of the central square now, its last victim left dangling until the next appeared in grim reminder of the new order, and Spelt's red-coated soldiers patrolled the streets to drive out those who would hide with friends or argue the Inquisitor's diktat. Under Inquisitorial rule, Grostheim lived in fear.

Talle himself was ensconced in Wyme's mansion, the governor banished to lesser rooms, and Var—to his intense embarrassment—was settled on Talle's order in the chambers of the governor's wife. He had sooner found quarters in the Militia barracks or gone out to the forts, but Talle would have his military commander close to hand—mostly, it seemed to Var, that the Inquisitor might insist on a campaign that seemed to him insane.

"He's convinced they must be easier to find and attack in winter," Var said. "He claims they withdraw with the snows; that they don't fight in winter. That they retreat back into the forests."

Jaymes shrugged and lifted his tankard; drank deep before replying: "Sure they do—into the wilderness forest. Snow's deep there, an' they know the trails. Unlike you. More likely your boys'll be slaughtered if you try to follow them in there."

"Even so, he wants you to scout for us," Var said. "Lead us to them."

Jaymes sniffed loudly. "An' if I say no?"

Var said, "He'll hex you. That, or hang you."

"An' lose himself a scout?" Jaymes grinned across his mug, exposing stained teeth. "You know there's not a man knows the wilderness like I do."

"I know that," Var said, wondering the while why he spoke to this draggle-haired tramp so honestly, "but does he? Or does he care?"

Jaymes shrugged again, emptying his mug. Var beckoned that it be refilled and waited until the indentured woman who brought their ale was gone before speaking again. A tavern servant, her flounced blouse hung down over her plump shoulders, exposing the brand there.

"He'll go out anyway," he said, "if he's decided on it. And I'll have to take my men with him. I've no other choice."

"You'll get lost," Jaymes said. "You'll wander around through the trees an' the snow an' likely never find 'em. Or they'll hear you coming an' slaughter you like they did Fallyn."

"I know." Var winced at the memory of his friend's torn body. "But even so the Inquisitor shall not leave me much choice. I must do what he orders."

"Why?"

Var frowned, taken aback by the unusual question. "Because I am an officer of the God's Militia, and Talle is an

Inquisitor, and therefore my commanding officer—I must obey him."

Jaymes repeated himself: "Why?"

The question was so direct and so bluntly put that Var was momentarily at a loss to find an answer. Old tropes came to mind, the ritual responses, but Jaymes's stare held him and fixed him to honesty, and so he said, "Because that is what I do."

"Obey orders?"

"Yes." Var nodded. "What else holds this world together?"

Jaymes shrugged and emptied his mug, belched loudly, and said, "Comradeship; friendship. Belief in what you're doin'."

Var said, "I do believe in what I'm doing. And I've comrades . . ."

Jaymes chuckled, shaking his grizzled head as he interrupted. "And that's why you're drinkin' with me? You'd sooner be with me than your *comrades*?"

Var thought a moment, staring into his mug. Then he raised his eyes to Jaymes's and said, "I'm drinking with you because you're honest. Because you tell me the truth about Salvation."

"And I drink with you," Jaymes returned, "because you're willin' to listen. Not like that damn Inquisitor."

"Careful!" Var let go of his tankard that he might gesture the scout to silence, to caution. "Are you hungry for the gallows?"

"No more than any other man he's hung." He snorted cynical laughter, then his face grew serious. "You don't like what the Inquisitor's doin' any more than I do."

"No." Var shook his head, wondering again why he opened his mind to this truculent, sweat-stinking scout. "But even so, I'm under orders, and he wants a winter campaign."

"Then I suppose," Jaymes said, "that I better come with you. You'll need a guide, eh?"

Var was surprised how grateful he felt. He began to express his thanks, but Jaymes waved him silent. "You'll get yourself lost otherwise. An' besides," the scout chuckled, "I got no stomach to hang around Grostheim all winter—I'd just get drunk an' fat an' bored. Better I take the Autarchy's pay. But," his grin disappeared, "understand that I'm not doin' this for Talle or the Autarchy. I'm doin' it for you."

Var nodded, meeting the man's level gaze, then gave Jaymes back the scout's own earlier question: "Why?"

It was Jaymes's turn to hesitate, to frown in . . . Var was not sure . . . confusion, perhaps, or embarrassment. He pressed the point, asking again, "Why?"

Jaymes hid awhile behind his tankard, then wiped foam from mustache and beard before replying. "Like I said—there's money in it, an' I got no stomach to winter over in the city." He no longer met Var's eyes.

"Those are reasons to obey the Inquisitor." Var shook his head. "Tell me the truth."

Jaymes scratched under his shirt, found something there that he cracked between his dirty fingernails, flicked it away, and raised his head to face the marine. "You're different, Major." He said it slowly, as if anxious to find the exact words, the precise expression of his sentiment. "You're not like Talle, nor Major Spelt or the governor. You're not quite like any officer I've met."

Var held an expression of bland friendship, wondering where this conversation led and if he should not curtail it now. He felt an odd presentiment, as if they trod the border of some forbidden country, each sentence a step farther toward . . . He was not sure what. He shaped a casual smile and asked, "You've met so many?"

"Enough." Jaymes waved his mug over his head, eliciting the attention of the serving wench. "Most were bastards; a few were decent men. You're . . ." He shrugged. "Decent, an' more."

Now Var felt embarrassed. He was, he believed, a good officer; he treated his men decently because he knew he must rely on them in battle. They were as much his comrades as gun-fodder for the Autarchy's imperial ambitions. Nor did he consider any man's life a casual thing to be spent carelessly. But he knew other officers who felt the same, and did not consider himself special—only sensible. How ask a man to fight for you, to perhaps give up his life on your command, if you were not prepared to do the same? But there was something more in the scout's words, something behind them, that he was not sure he wished to investigate.

He endeavored to gather his thoughts as the branded woman fetched them fresh mugs. He realized that Jaymes had not spat in a while, nor cut a fresh plug from his wad of tobacco, and that impressed on him the seriousness of the scout's observations. It was, he thought, as if Jaymes tested him, tried him for some purpose he could not yet discern precisely; only guess at, and shy away.

He was, after all, an officer in the God's Militia, as much representative of the Autarchy as Spelt or Wyme, even Talle.

So he looked the scout square in the eye and demanded, "Explain."

Jaymes shrugged and shook his head at the same time. "I mean you care about folk. You don't much like seein' them hanged, nor hexed into doin' what they don't want to do. You don't like to see lives wasted needlessly."

Var drank, feeling his footing shift loose beneath his convictions. "I obey my orders," he said.

Jaymes chuckled. "Sure you do: so arrest me."

"Why?"

"God!" Jaymes shook his head again, only now his eyes remained steadily fixed on Var's. "I've disrespected Inquisitor Talle an' every other authority in Grostheim. I don't go to church, an' I think it's a lousy deal that Evander puts a hot iron on folk an' ships 'em out here like they was branded cattle an' nothin' better. Is that enough? Now you going to arrest me like you should an' give me to Talle for hangin'?"

Var emptied his tankard and smiled. "No," he said.

Jaymes grinned. "Why not?"

"Because I need you to lead me and my men into the forests," Var answered. "Because you know the hostiles better than most. And you've said you'll do that."

Jaymes nodded. "Sure. But what else?"

"I don't know," Var said, biting back the "yet" that gnawed on his suspicions, "only that the Inquisitor wants a winter campaign, and you're the only scout I trust."

"I'm honored." Jaymes aped a mocking bow. "When do we go?"

"I don't know for sure." Var drained his mug and rose. "I'll speak with Talle and let you know."

"You do that, Major," Jaymes replied. "You speak with him an' let me know. I'll be waitin' on his word."

Var nodded and pulled on his greatcoat, settled the tricorne hat in place, and quit the tavern wondering at the conversation. It was surely not such as an officer of the God's Militia should have with a commoner, and there was something he could not quite recognize hidden behind Jaymes's casual disregard of authority. He should, he knew, report it to Talle, and knew he would not. God, he thought as he stepped out from the tavern's warmth into the night's cold, this is no easy duty.

The evening was chill, rime shining bright on moonlit rooftops, the mud of Grostheim's streets crunching frosthardened under his boots, ice glittering over puddles. The sky swept wide and starlit above the ragged city, the moon a cocked and judgmental eye observing Evander's foothold in the New World. Var buttoned his coat and tugged the wide collar up around his ears. Barely October, he thought, and winter already coming on. What chance of a winter campaign if the months follow this pattern? How soon before the deep snow comes? Shall Talle listen to sense?

He thrust his hands into the pockets of his coat and trudged on, toward the governor's mansion. A thin-ribbed dog darted from an alley, saw him, and snarled, spinning around to find the shelter of a raised walkway as if afraid he might offer harm. Var smiled bitterly; he had heard of dogs being eaten as food ran shorter. He was not sure: Governor Wyme said that all were fed who deserved to be, but he did not trust Wyme. Inquisitor Talle demanded that the outland farmers bring in their crops and that was done, but still food was not plentiful and Var could not like Talle or agree with his methods. There were—despite Talle's gallows—still hungry beggars inside the city, more lurking beyond the walls, inhabiting a settlement of ragged tents boundaried by the earthworks Var's men had thrown up. Talle had hexed some few, and twice ordered Spelt's redcoats out to clear the camp, but still the penurious and the homeless crept back like beaten dogs seeking the only refuge they knew. Finally, Talle had given up his efforts to drive them away, settling for the promulgation of new laws that forbade the donation of food to the refugees and forbidding vagrants within the city walls. Neither edict worked very well, save to fuel discontent and resentment of the Inquisitor and his new regime, of which Var was considered a part. There were folk legally inside the walls sympathetic to the beggars, and they contrived to circumvent Talle's measures. Save the Inquisitor risk igniting a civil war, he could not punish all those who succored the hungry.

Grostheim, Var thought as he trudged the frosty streets, was a powder keg ready to blow. And he was no longer sure where his own sympathies lay. As he had told Jaymes, he had his orders, his duty to obey, but when he saw folk stripped of hope, their faces planed stark by hunger, he found it hard to accept Talle's diktats. But still he was committed by duty, by his orders to support the Inquisitor. He was an officer of the God's Militia, dedicated to that service. It was a dilemma he could not resolve as he strode on, unhappy.

He remembered a town of lights and laughter, and glanced around at shuttered windows and silent people. They seemed—the silent, unsmiling folk he passed, the steaming windows, the smoking braziers, the skulking dogs—all hostile, as if he were not come as a savior, but as another threat. It was as if his blue marine's greatcoat marked him as Talle's man, and set his hand on the gallows' spring, and that the forts bounding the wilderness edge meant nothing. It seemed, as he looked toward faces that turned from him, as if the inhabitants of Grostheim had sooner faced the hostiles than welcome the Inquisitor and his lieutenant.

He passed an alley mouth where a dull fire burned, small and shrouded by what scanty shelter the occupants of the rude shack he saw had built there: mostly random planks and timbers charred from the last hostile attack and discarded, and lengths of torn tarpaulin. A man sat there, huddled close beside a woman, a child between them whose sex he could not determine. It happened that the moon struck down there so that he saw their faces clear, cheeked hollow and dark-eyed. Accusing, he thought, as he hesitated and met their gaze. He fumbled in his pockets for some coin—Talle be damned!—and then saw what he thought was the most amazing and inexplicable thing.

A tavern flanked the alley, and from its back a man came out with a wrapped bundle clutched in his hands. In the moonlight Var saw the *E* branded on his cheek. The man looked warily around and Var pretended to walk on—halted and doubled back, so that he might watch.

He saw the branded man deliver the bundle to the refugees, stripping off the cloth to reveal a loaf of bread and a part-eaten joint of meat. The indentured man glanced around and beckoned at the shadows, and a woman came out—a tavern girl, Var guessed, and that she'd wear a brand on her shoulder—who carried a pitcher and three clay cups. He could not tell what the pitcher contained; only that the refugees drank eagerly as they ate, and he watched in amazement.

He slid back into the wall's shadow, embarrassed and surprised; mightily disturbed.

The branded folk fed freemen? Servants fed those who had once been masters? Their *owners*?

Why?

The starvelings in the alley wore no marks of indenture, so they were surely free settlers who had likely possessed such folk as now gave them sustenance—in defiance of Inquisitor Talle's laws.

Var wondered why, and why—he knew—he would not report it.

He walked on, into the square where the gallows stood before the church.

The gibbet occupied the center of the square. It was built well—the carpenters would not argue with Inquisitor Talle—of solid oak, a platform raised up a full man's height above the ground, the scaffold over that, so that it dominated the center of Grostheim. Var was reminded of his childhood, of gamekeepers who hung ravens and crows and foxes in warning to others: it seemed to him like that as the sorry body dangled limp, the wood beneath its feet stained with its last, sad effluences. Its boots were gone, doubtless taken by the hangman, and that seemed to Var most sad, a last indignity.

He looked at the blank-eyed face as he came closer, wondering what hopes the corpse had brought to Salvation, what wife or children the man might leave behind. Unthinking, he crossed his fingers and spat.

"He'll do you no harm, Major. Not now."

Var cursed his squeamishness. Four of Spelt's Militiamen stood guard around the scaffold, bored and cold, a corporal grinning at his own sally. There was no need for a guard— Talle's hexes decorated the platform and the gibbet—and the presence of the redcoats was only a further ceremonial reminder of authority. Almost, Var answered sharply, but caught himself—these fellows did no more than he, only obeying orders—and softened his tone. "No, I doubt he will."

Save, he thought, every body Talle hangs there is like another small spark heating this dismal city, and how many shall it take before the fire burns hot enough to ignite it? He paused, wanting to say something to the soldiers and not knowing quite what.

He settled for, "A cold night, eh?"

"Chilly, sir." The corporal shrugged. "But you wait until winter. It gets truly cold then."

Var nodded. "Snow?"

"Usually." The corporal took a pace toward Var, thought better of such presumption, and halted. "Gets real deep outside the walls, but the branded folk keep our streets clear."

Var said, "Of course," and then: "How long does the snow last?"

"In a bad winter," the corporal shrugged again, "from around the midpart of Novembre right through to Marche, maybe."

"And in a good winter?" Var asked.

"Decembre to Februire," the corporal answered. "The roads are hard going for some while after, of course. The mud, you know?"

"I know." Var thought of winter campaigns, of cold and snow drifts that must be dug through, of roads so thick with mud the guncarts and supply wagons bogged down. "How long have you served here?"

"Nine years, seven months, and nineteen days." The corporal grinned, deciding this marine major was not so bad a fellow, even was he the Inquisitor's right hand. "Next year I get my Choice."

Var smiled. Service in the God's Militia was reckoned in decades, and when the corporal's tenure was up he would have his choice to make. The rankers capitalized the word: The Choice. In this case, it meant that the corporal could reenlist or quit the service. Did he choose the former, then he could look forward to promotion, to a sergeancy; the latter meant another choosing: either to return to Evander or to remain in Salvation. The one would mean taking the Militia pension—which was scarce enough to live on—and believing there was something or someone in Evander worth going back for, whilst the other would entitle the man to a piece of land in Salvation and two indentured exiles for his servants.

"Which shall you take?" Var asked.

The corporal scratched a cheek Var noticed for the first time was pock-marked, hesitating before he replied. "Well, that depends . . ."

Var made his smile more friendly. "On what, eh?"

"Well, sir." The corporal grimaced, embarrassed. "On you, I suppose, sir. On you and the Inquisitor."

"How so?" Var made his voice casual.

"Well." The corporal fidgeted with his musket, adjusting the strap so that moonlight flickered off the polished steel of the bayonet. "On what you do about the demons."

"How so?" Var asked again. He saw the corporal's indecision and looked to draw the man out. So far he had echoed Abram Jaymes, but Jaymes was committed to Salvation by choice, whilst this red-coated and suddenly uncomfortable Militiaman was in the New World by order of the Autarchy alone. "This shall go no farther," he said, "you've my word on that. Listen—I'll not even ask your name."

"It's Gerry, sir. Corporal Robyn Gerry."

And straightened, coming to attention, musket upright against his shoulder, hand to stock and muzzle, eyes fixed on the brim of Var's tricorne.

Var recognized the stance. It was not uncommon, if an officer asked you awkward questions, to come to attention and refuse to meet his eyes—but Gerry had initiated the conversation and seemed quite at ease then, and Var did not think he was so terrifying an officer as to induce this sudden reluctance in the man. Save he *was* considered Talle's right hand. He smiled in friendly fashion and said, "I'd appreciate your opinion, Corporal. And as I said, you've my word it shall go no farther."

"*Your* word?"

Var nodded solemnly. "My word as an officer and a gentleman; as a fellow soldier."

Gerry laughed, which surprised Var. Not so much that the chuckling was laden with contempt—hatred even—but that a humble corporal would dare laugh at all into the face of an officer. He stared at the man and found himself looking into eyes that were curiously blank.

"Your word," Gerry said in a voice that was no longer his own, but suddenly guttural, "means nothing to me. Your word is smoke in the storm wind. I spit on your word."

Var stared at the corporal, said—knowing it even then for foolishness—"Gerry, are you well?"

"Well?" It seemed that fire burned inside the staring eyes, behind them. And the voice was harsh thunder. "How should I be well when you come to take our land? *Ours!*"

Var said "Gerry?" and stepped back a pace, wishing his greatcoat were not buttoned over his pistol and that he wore his sword. But why wear a blade in a peaceful city? Save suddenly you be attacked by a man who seemed one moment friendly and the next possessed. He looked at Gerry's eyes and saw madness there: he began to unbutton his coat, to reach for the pistol.

And Gerry said, "No," in the same harsh voice, and slung his musket down, cocking the hammer. "You think to own our land, but you'll not."

Var reacted entirely on instinct. He flung himself to the side as the musket dropped, rolling away as the muzzle flashed flame and the lead ball gouged a furrow in the frozen mud of the square. Mud and ice plastered his face as he clambered to his feet, still fumbling at the buttons of his coat as Gerry lowered the musket and charged him, intent on thrusting the long bayonet into his belly.

The three other Militiamen guarding the gallows came—at

last, Var thought—to see what transpired. In that instant he condemned them all for idiots, for they stood gaping as Gerry looked to drive the bayonet into his guts as he danced away, shouting, "Shoot him! For God's sake, shoot him!"

Gerry laughed in a voice that was not his own: *"Our land! Never yours!"* And stabbed again at Var's belly.

Var lurched sideways. Damn the long coat! Damn the protocol that denied him wearing a sword inside Grostheim's peaceful walls! And danced another step away from Gerry's probing bayonet.

"Not yours," Gerry said, thrusting. "Never yours! Ours!"

Var backed away, seeking the opportunity to gain ground enough he might open his coat and draw his pistol. Shoot this madman who looked to stick him as the three other redcoats stared gape-mouthed at the impossible spectacle of a corporal in the God's Militia attempting to drive a bayonet into the belly of a major.

Gerry thrust again, and Var gasped as his greatcoat was pierced, lurched back. He felt his hand scored, like cold fire over the skin, and resisted the impulse to check the wound, springing clear of another darting attack.

Why did those fools not fire?

Then: If they do, they'll shoot me. Aloud, he shouted, "Use your bayonets! Stick the bastard before he kills me!"

The three Militiamen still gaped, numbed by that vision of the impossible.

Var felt cold steel prick his stomach and lurched backward, turning so that he began to circumnavigate the scaffold. The corpse there dangled in dead-eyed witness of the drama, indifferent as the moon.

Gerry thrust again and Var fell back against the wood of the scaffold's platform. The bayonet drove into the timber and stuck an instant. Not long—Robyn Gerry was a strong man, and accustomed to bayonet-work—but enough Var had time to haul clear and open the last buttons of his coat, drag out the pistol.

Not enough to cock the hammer or drop the strikerplate, but at least he held a weapon now. He darted back as Gerry came wild-eyed toward him, the bloodied bayonet a precursor of his advance.

Var stumbled against a soldier, cursing the gaping man as he shouldered him aside and dragged back the pistol's hammer.

"Stick him, damn you!"

He saw the Militiaman staring goggle-eyed as he dropped the strikerplate into position. Leveled the pistol at Gerry's chest and paced back along the edge of the scaffold as Gerry screamed an inarticulate cry and charged forward.

Var squeezed the trigger. A bloom of darker crimson blossomed on the scarlet of Gerry's tunic. The bayonet thrust toward Var, and he deflected the blade with the emptied pistol. Gerry stared at him, still moving forward. Var elbowed the musket aside as the dying body collided with him and the mouth opened to spit out hatred.

"Never your land! Ours! We shall destroy you!"

And at last the Militiamen acted: they came together to drive three bayonets into the body of Robyn Gerry, so that blood splashed over Tomas Var and stained his tunic even as he wondered what strange new magic was brought against Salvation.

A Certain Power

Hadduth sat naked and sweating, staring into the flames that lit the interior of the wa'tenhya with flickerings of red and shadow, blaze and darkness alternating in dancing patterns intricate as his thoughts. The pahé tasted bitter on his tongue, in his throat, and he felt it trace its delicate path through his body even as he turned to stare at the owh'jika whose eyes belled huge and terrified as the thing gazed at the Tachyn wakanisha.

Hadduth chuckled sourly. Did Chakthi frighten him, why should he not frighten the owh'jika? Besides, the sorry creature was necessary to his task. He *would* satisfy his akaman—else likely, he thought, he should die when next the rage took hold of Chakthi. He was not yet ready to die; perhaps to sell his soul, if that was not already bought, but not to die. So he stretched his lips and said, "Take more."

The owh'jika moaned and shook its head, shuddering against its bonds. Chakthi coughed laughter into the scented dream smoke and reached across the fire to spill more pahé into its mouth, forcing it to drink. Then he watched as the thing's eyes grew unfocused and closed, wondering idly if so much of the sacred root would kill the uninitiated. No matter: he could already feel the channels of the creature's being as if they were his own, look into its mind at all the secrets and the fears locked there. He sighed and felt his smile draw wider as his own eyes closed and he went away into the land beyond . . .

. . . Where he stood on a grisaille plain, the earth gray and ashy and wreathed with tendrils of dull smoke that rose like despairing fingers to falter against a colorless sky. No sun shone there, neither any moon, and were there stars they were lost behind and within the encompassing gray. He felt abruptly afraid and looked about him at a landscape that was devoid of feature—flat and stretching out in ashen parody of Ket-Ta-Witko's prairies in all directions. Save for the sorrily rising smoke, there was no movement, nor any sign of life.

And he realized he stood naked as a newborn babe: he moaned and cupped his hands about his groin, embarrassed and terrified.

And then, from far away across the featureless gray plain, he heard the pounding of hooves, like distant thunder rolling remorselessly closer, and saw off in the distance the sparks of fire struck from the ashen earth.

In moments the pounding filled up all the air and he dropped to his knees, hands pressed against his ears that he might block out that terrible thunder, but could not draw his eyes from what approached.

It was like the sun rising between the gates of hell, like the Storm Wolf charging the Grass Boy, save he was not the Grass Boy and had turned his face from the Maker and so could not anticipate divine favor.

And yet he could not close his eyes or turn his gaze away, for all the terrible splendor seared the orbs. He could only watch, submitted, as the dread horse galloped toward him, and see the night-dark skin, the blazing eyes, the horns and awful trappings of magnificent gold and obscene skulls, clattering bones. And on its awful back a worse rider: a man armored all in shining gold, whose hair spread loose as fire from beneath a concealing helm that revealed only eyes red as the ghastly mount's, and locked forever firm on Hadduth.

The wakanisha cowered, staring up as the rider reined in his mount and set it to prancing, sharp hooves sparking great flurries of flame from the dull soil. Hadduth thought his skull must be shattered and he bleed out his life in the dream land and never return to Ket-Ta-Thanne; and could not be sure that not be better than facing this creature, this majesty, he had at last summoned.

But the rider took off his helm and shook out his flame-red mane and fixed Hadduth with those eyes that were all fire, gestured with a gauntlet that was taloned cruel as any wolverine's paw, and said, "So, at last."

Hadduth ducked his head and said, "Master."

"Not Master but Akratil, the Master's servant as you are mine."

Hadduth said, "As you will . . . Akratil."

The flame-haired man danced his terrible horse in a circle around the crouching Tachyn, his words matched to the rhythmic pounding. "I am Akratil, worm, and greater than you as is a hawk to a ground-burrowing grub. But I am not the Master. He is greater even than I. He is death and destruction. He is the dark face of that mewling god you call the Maker. *Understand that!*"

"Yes," said Hadduth from where he huddled, feeling the sparks the horse's hooves struck up, the fire of its breath, burn his naked skin. "Yes, Akratil."

Akratil smiled as if a point were won—which, in truth, it was—and said, "And are you my servant, worm?"

Hadduth said, "I am."

"And those sad creatures with you?"

"They wait on your guidance."

"Good." Akratil reined his horrid mount to a halt, looking down at the Tachyn. "I have waited long for this."

"I called on you," Hadduth dared say, "before. But . . ."

"I was not ready." A golden gauntlet angled at Hadduth's face and the wakanisha lurched back for fear the talons rip out his eyes. "Nor you. Now I sense you are, and so I come."

Hadduth ventured a nervous smile. "To conquer this new land?"

"Not yet." Akratil shook his head and it seemed that fire flashed from his hair. "I am yet in that other land. Why did you call on me?"

Hadduth frowned, suddenly confused. "You know our fate?"

"Your fate is nothing to me," Akratil replied. "Save you serve me and do my bidding."

"I would," Hadduth said. "Only that."

Akratil laughed. It was the sound of lightning dancing on the earth, the sound of bones rubbing together, a storm wind shaking naked trees.

"Yet you failed me, worm."

"I did," Hadduth moaned, "all you bade me. Was there failure, then surely it was Chakthi's."

"Who is not here," Akratil said, and leant from the golden, skull-bedecked saddle to put his face closer to the wakanisha's, "whilst you are."

Hadduth felt the heat of those burning eyes, the mingled odors of rotted meat and sulfur that came from Akratil's mouth, and cringed.

"So why," Akratil asked, "should I not slay you?"

"Morrhyn opened the gate," Hadduth cried. "And closed it behind the People. I could not prevent that!"

"And it left my Breakers shut out." Akratil snatched at the reins, setting the blood-eyed horse to prancing again. "Locked from our prey. And now you'd ask a favor?"

"I'd bring you here," Hadduth screamed, feeling the gray earth shudder all around him, aware of the horns and fangs that darted close. "I'd give you this world and all those escaped you."

Akratil reined back the midnight horse; Hadduth ventured an upward glance.

"Think you that's possible, worm?"

"Within your power, surely." Hadduth unlocked his arms from his head. "With my help."

Akratil snorted scornful laughter. "*You* help *me*?"

"This is a strange land," Hadduth said, "it is not like Ket-Ta-Witko. The People are not alone here: there are others, and they have strange powers."

Akratil nodded thoughtfully: "Tell me, worm, and I shall decide whether you live or die."

Hadduth began to speak, urgently.

The owh'jika was drained close unto death by what Akratil took from it, but that was of small concern to Hadduth. The thing had served its purpose and that was sufficient—it was not, after all, a true human being, not even one of the People, far less a Tachyn, and it had little use now other than as a recipient of Chakthi's wrath. Hadduth wondered if it might not welcome death as he dragged it from the confines of the wa'tenhya and left it shivering and naked in the forest chill. It was still bound and he supposed that he would—did he remember—send someone to free it and feed it, but that was not important. He smiled hugely as he dressed, anticipating his akaman's pleasure when he told Chakthi of Akratil's gift, and how it might be used against the enemy. That should surely please Chakthi; and it was but the first step along the road to absolute victory. Yes, he thought, Chakthi would be mightily pleased, and the Tachyn raised high.

17 Strangely, in the Night

Celinda Wyme screamed when Var burst into the dining room, the glass she held dropping to the table to spread wine across the linen cloth like a great bloodstain. Her husband stared gape-mouthed at the disheveled officer, a frown forming on his pudgy face. Alyx Spelt's was disdainful, as if he considered Var's dramatic entrance in poor taste. Only Jared Talle exhibited no emotion, simply setting down his knife and fork and looking at Var with darkly questioning eyes.

"Forgive me." Var offered Celinda a brief bow. He supposed he did look somewhat disreputable: Gerry's blood stained his coat and tunic, and likely his face. "Inquisitor, I must speak with you."

Talle motioned that he continue, but Wyme raised a hand that still clutched a napkin and said, "Surely not here, Inquisitor. My wife . . ." He gestured at Celinda, who slumped back in her chair, ample bosom heaving as a servant flapped an ineffectual hand before her face. "Nathanial—smelling salts!"

Var said, "It were better told privately," glancing at the servants, and Talle nodded, rising.

"The study, gentlemen."

The Inquisitor led the way as if he owned the mansion, Wyme hobbling on his crutches behind, and it was Talle ordered the servant to stoke the fire and light the lamps, who bade the man leave. Wyme only slumped in an armchair, mumbling his thanks as Spelt brought him a glass of brandy.

"So, Major, what is it? You've the look of a street brawler."

Talle settled his spindly frame behind Wyme's desk. Var

shed his coat and faced the sallow man, relating the evening's events.

"And the body?" Talle's head was cocked like a crow's; he seemed not much disturbed.

"I ordered it carried to the church," Var said. "I thought . . ."

Talle husked laughter, cutting the explanation short. "You thought that were it possessed the holy ground of the church would hold it, no?"

Var shrugged and nodded; Talle laughed again.

"And the other sentries?"

"Ordered to remain by the body. To keep the doors locked and speak with no one."

"Good." Talle offered Var a thin-lipped smile. "That was wise. What else?"

"I told them," Var said, "that I would return with you. They're frightened, Inquisitor."

"Who'd not be?" Talle murmured, and glanced around the room. "Look at Major Spelt—does he not look frightened? And the governor?" His voice was dry enough it almost hid his contempt. Then the dark carrion eyes turned to Var. "Are you afraid, Major?"

Var felt embarrassed. For all he'd no great liking for Spelt or Wyme, still he saw no reason why Talle should humiliate them so. He licked his lips and said, "I am concerned, Inquisitor. A fellow soldier tried to kill me—for no reason I could discern—and that . . . Yes, frightens me."

"Then we'd best do something about it, eh?" Talle rose. "Let us observe this thing."

Var picked up his ruined coat and settled his tricorne in place. Talle waved Spelt back to his seat. "Stay here, Major; you and the governor. I'll send for you, do I need you."

Spelt's face flushed bright red, but he offered no objection; Wyme looked only grateful. Talle strode thin-shanked from the study, shouting for a servant to bring his coat and hat. Var followed him. Like a faithful hound? he wondered. Like the Inquisitor's right hand?

What else could he do? Evander, the Autarchy, vested command in Talle and gave Var orders to obey. And was he not a faithful soldier of the Autarchy? Save . . . He pushed the doubts aside. Time enough later to consider them; for now it was imperative that he know what agency had possessed Corporal Gerry to attempt his murder, and Talle was likely the only man in Grostheim could begin to uncover that mystery. So he matched his stride to the Inquisitor's as they trod the empty streets back to the square, and the church where Gerry lay.

The body still dangled from the gibbet; Var was vaguely surprised. Almost, he'd anticipated the corpse flinging free of the gallows and come dancing out to meet them, but there was only a waiting crowd, summoned by the commotion and wondering if some new demonic attack came against Grostheim. The square was noisy until Talle appeared, and then abruptly silent as the Inquisitor came through the crowd.

He heard Talle chuckle and realized the Inquisitor had caught his look toward the scaffold, his nervousness, as the man said, "That one shall do no more harm. His neck's well broken, and he's hexed besides."

"Could he," Var heard himself asking, "do otherwise?"

"Oh yes." Talle chuckled as if it were an enormous joke. "Were his neck not properly broken, was he not well hexed . . . Why, Major, he might well jump down from the gallows to bid you the day's greeting and take you with him to hell."

Var looked back at the corpse and felt his skin go colder than the night allowed. "I didn't know," he said. "Not that . . ."

"I honor you." Talle parodied a courtly bow. "Few are granted such knowledge. But I trust you, Major Var; and so I allow you insights to the arcane I'd not grant another man."

"And Corporal Gerry?" Var asked.

"We shall see," Talle said, and hammered a fist against the door of the church as he shouted, "The Inquisitor Talle demands entry."

"How do I know?" asked a nervous voice from the other side.

Var could not help grinning as he motioned Talle aside and called through the big door, "This is Major Tomas Var, do you recognize my voice?"

"Major? That's you?"

"Yes," Var shouted. "Open the door."

The metal-bound panels swung inward and three cocked muskets faced them. Before Talle could complain, Var said, "Well done, lads. You guard this place well." The Inquisitor only pushed past them, ignoring the bayonets and the threat of the musket balls.

"Where's the body?"

"On the altar," the oldest redcoat said. "Where the major told us to put it."

Talle chuckled and swung around in a swirl of black coat-tails. Like a crow dancing, Var thought.

"And what did you see? Out there in the square, where your corporal went mad."

The redcoats hesitated, looking nervously from the Inquisitor to Var. Talle's eyes narrowed irritably and Var motioned that the soldiers speak. The elder said, "Nothing, Inquisitor. We were all around the other side of the gallows."

"And did not go to look when you heard your corporal speaking with the major?"

Var caught the soldier's eye and nodded encouragingly, so that the man said, "No, Inquisitor. Officers' talk's not for us. We just did our duty."

"And when you heard your corporal's musket discharge?" Talle asked. "What then?"

The redcoat looked at Var. Talle barked, "Look at me!"

"We came a-running, Inquisitor. I saw Corporal Gerry try-ing to stick the major and I couldn't hardly believe it, but then the major shot him, and we all put our bayonets into him like the major ordered and he died. And then we brought him here like the major ordered, and . . ."

"Enough." Talle smiled and waved a dismissive hand. The three redcoats looked confused and relieved.

Var said, "Go. And keep your mouths shut about this."

From along the aisle, Talle added, "Else I'll hex you. I'll deliver you to silence forever, and pox besides."

The redcoats hurried from the church, dispelled on the echoes of Talle's laughter.

Var frowned, thinking to say something in argument of such bullying, but got no chance as Talle beckoned him along, down the aisle to where the body lay.

"They like you, Tomas; you are popular with them."

"Inquisitor?"

Talle chuckled, a dry whisper of only his own humor. "You're one of them, no?"

Var said, "I don't understand."

Talle said again, "They like you. They trust you, as they cannot trust me. They'd follow you, I think."

Var said, "*They?* Do you mean Salvation's soldiers? They'd follow me on order—under your command."

"And the settlers?" Talle spun his mad dance again, coattails raised and black-clad legs prancing their thin-shanked rhythm. "Would they?"

Var frowned, confused. "I think I'm no better liked than you," he said, "by the settlers."

"Are you not?" Talle ceased his capering dance; straightened his coattails. "Then good; and let's look at this body, eh?"

Var ducked his head and followed the Inquisitor to the altar.

He had no idea what signs Talle looked for, no idea what signs there might be to indicate possession, nor any great desire to see the dead man's face again, but he did his duty and stood close as the Inquisitor set to his examination. To him, Gerry seemed no different to a great many other corpses. Blood had drained from the face, leaving it—he stifled an almost hysterical chuckle at the unintended pun—deathly pale; the eyes were opened wide and staring sightlessly at the shadowy roof of the church; the mouth was open in the rictal snarl that had been the man's last expression. And if Talle saw aught else there, he made no comment, only said, "Help me undress him."

Var hesitated; the Inquisitor snapped imperious fingers, and with great reluctance Var set to removing the dead man's greatcoat and the uniform beneath.

When the body lay naked on the altar—that colored now with the gore that oozed sluggishly from the bayonet wounds—Talle leant close, examining every inch of skin. Then he had Var turn the corpse over so that he might repeat his minute search, even to the study of the dead man's ears and hair and private parts, the soles of his feet and between his toes. Var watched, disgusted and intrigued in equal measure.

"Fascinating." Talle stepped back, absently wiping his hands down the frontage of his black coat. "There's not a hex sign on him."

"Did you . . ." Var felt his voice failing him, cleared his throat and spoke again in firmer tones. "Did you anticipate hex signs, Inquisitor?"

Talle shrugged, which seemed to Var neither confirmation or negation. "Do you suppose he attacked you from choice, Major?"

"No." Var shook his head. "It was as I told you—we spoke equably enough until . . ." He shrugged in turn. "It was as if another spoke out of Gerry's mouth."

"Yes," Talle said, and suddenly smiled, which seemed to Var most odd. "Listen, and you shall learn more of my . . . art." He glanced at the corpse and then again at Var. "I might control a man—force him to attempt your murder, speak through him—but only with the use of the hexes. I'd need to hold him awhile, long enough I could put the marks on his body, and then he'd be mine. But the hex signs would remain after death. Do you understand?"

Var swallowed even as he nodded. "I think so, Inquisitor. Were Gerry hexed, then you'd have found the signs."

"Quite." Talle folded his hands as if about to pray, but instead tapped stained fingernails against his pursed lips, his dark eyes moving from Var back to the corpse. "And there are no marks on this. Yet, he was—clearly!—possessed. You say he spoke of owning Salvation?"

"Yes." Var licked his lips, reliving those horrifying moments. "He spoke of the land as 'ours'; he said, 'We shall destroy you.' "

"Which would seem to be," Talle declared in a thoughtful tone, "much what was said to . . . what was his name? That drunkard who first met the enemy and survived?"

"Corm," Var supplied. "Captain Danyael Corm."

"Yes, him." Talle nodded. Then was abruptly brisk again. "Do we find him, Major? This Captain Corm?"

"Now?" Var asked, confused by the Inquisitor's dramatic mood changes.

Talle said, "Now," and began to walk away.

"What of . . ." Var indicated the corpse with a sidelong shifting of his head.

"That?" Talle's voice was disinterested. "Have it burned."

"Inquisitor!" Var came down the aisle before Talle reached the door. "Whatever has transpired this night, the man was still a soldier in the God's Militia. Surely he deserves honest burial?"

Talle halted just inside the door. The smile came back to his face as he turned to Var. "Such niceties, Major; such delicacy. Burn it!"

Var swallowed his objections and nodded, following Talle out into the night. The crowd remained, curious in the square, held back from church and gallows by Militiamen. Lieutenant Minns saluted as the two emerged.

"Major Var; Inquisitor Talle—I am officer of the watch tonight. Do you have orders for me?"

Talle ignored him. Var said, "There's a body on the altar, Lieutenant. Corporal Gerry. See that he's burned immediately."

Minns's eyes expressed concern. "Burned, sir?"

"Yes." Var heard his voice come out harsh. "Burned."

Over his shoulder, Talle said, "And then bury what's left in quicklime, outside the walls. Tonight!"

Var said, softer, "Do it, Lieutenant, eh?" And then: "Had he any family? A woman?"

Minns nodded. "A common-law wife, sir; no children."

"Tell her she'll receive his pension," Var said. "And tell me where Captain Corm quarters."

Minns looked bewildered, but he gave directions and Var went to join the Inquisitor. Talle was staring at the crowd, which stared back in such silence as throbbed with hostility.

"They've little liking for me, eh?" The notion appeared to amuse him.

Var said cautiously, "I think they cannot understand what you do. Nor do they like me better."

"I'm God's hound." Talle chuckled and Var thought of a cold wind rattling withered branches. "And you're mine, did you know? That's what they name you—the Inquisitor's dog."

"I didn't," Var said, and thought of his conversation with Abram Jaymes. He added stiffly, "I do my duty."

"Indeed." Talle nodded affably. "So now have that young lieutenant clear the square and take me to Corm."

Var gave the orders and led the black-clad man away. Redcoats cleared a path for them, though it was unnecessary—folk stepped automatically out of Talle's way—and all the time Var heard the words echoing inside his head: *the Inquisitor's dog*. He liked that appellation not at all.

Captain Danyael Corm was quartered, like most of Grostheim's officers, outside the barracks. That latter accommodation was left to common soldiers, who could not afford better. Corm was a captain and had some small private income, which allowed him to rent rooms at an inn. The indentured man who served him was a perquisite of his rank.

The inn was called the Sailing Ship, located toward Grostheim's eastern wall, where mostly sailors and fishermen lodged. Corm occupied three rooms—one not much larger than a cupboard, where his servant slept—with a dismal view of blank timber walls and a filthy alley. The servant, whose name was Jon, was drinking in the common room.

"Sieur Corm gave me the money," he said, staring in open terror at Talle. "By God, I swear he did! A whole crown he gave me, and told me to spend it as I would. He said he'd not need me this night."

The Sailing Ship had fallen very quiet when Talle and Var entered, and Jon's voice rang out loud and frightened. His hand shook on the tankard he held, ale trembling over the rim to wet his hand unnoticed. The branded men who drank with him seemed to Var intent on melding themselves with the wooden walls, like those lizards he'd seen in Tarrabon that could assume the color of their surroundings and thus become invisible to predators. He smiled at the man—and was ignored, because Jon's gaze was fixed entirely on the Inquisitor. Talle only grinned and shook his head.

"You've naught to fear from me . . . Jon, is it?"

Jon nodded. Var felt embarrassed; it seemed to him that the man's undisguised panic was directed as much at him as at Talle. He said, "Where is Captain Corm?"

And was silenced by a wave of Talle's hand.

"First," Talle said, "tell me about your master's dreams."

"His dreams?" Jon's voice quavered between octaves. "Sieur Corm doesn't tell me about his dreams."

"But you know whether he dreams or not, eh?" Talle said. He put his dirty hands on the table, leaning closer to Jon's face. "Surely you hear him?"

Jon nodded. Var thought he might weep.

"And?" Talle prompted.

The branded man looked at the Inquisitor's eyes like a mouse transfixed by a falcon's gaze.

"He screams in the night, Inquisitor. Sometimes . . ." Jon spoke softer, ashamed for his master. "Sometimes, he wets the bed."

"And lately?" Talle asked in a tone that was so natural as to be quite unnormal.

"Lately?" Jon's whole head trembled, but his eyes did not leave Talle's. Could not, Var thought. "Lately he's cried out in a strange voice that I don't recognize."

Talle nodded and smiled and said, "Thank you; is he here now?"

Jon nodded.

"Direct us to him," Talle said; and when the terrified servant had done that, again: "Thank you."

Var followed him up the stairs, aware of the silence they left behind.

Corm's rooms were on the topmost level of the three-story building, close under the roof, so that he lived in solitary squalor, what other rooms were there given over to storage. The stairs creaked as Talle and Var ascended, and the boards of the attic chambers not much less. Dust gathered gray in cracks and corners, and spiderwebs decorated the beams above. It was dark up there, and musty, but through the odor of dereliction Var caught another scent that was to him familiar.

He said, "Powder smoke."

Talle said, "What?"

"I smell powder smoke," Var explained. He sniffed the air. "Not much, but it's here—as if a pistol's been discharged."

"Perhaps," Talle glanced around, "Corm has been hunting rats."

Var shrugged and set a hand to his own pistol, now reloaded. Talle pointed at a bar of faint light shining from under a door. "That must be his." He hammered on the wood. There was no response and he flicked the latch, stepping inside.

The room was dismally bright, the lantern suspended from the low ceiling wicked high and augmented by more that hung from nails hammered into walls and beams so that all the dust and ragged carpets, the cheap furniture, were illuminated. Jon was a poor servant, Var thought, or Corm a careless master. Shutters in dire need of paint were bolted closed over the window, the bolt wound round with string that held faded hawthorn flowers. The smell of powder smoke was stronger; Var drew his pistol.

Talle chuckled and said, "Too late for that, I think; nor any use." And louder: "Corm?"

There was no answer.

Two doors opened off the room, one standing ajar to reveal the narrow bed where obviously Jon slept. The other was closed: they went to it and Talle shoved it wide without further ado.

Var gasped. This was Corm's bedroom, and it was lit even brighter than the chamber beyond. Lanterns hung from the ceiling and candles stood on chairs and trunks, shelves, the floor. Wax pooled on unpolished boards and flames trailed upward, threatening to set the Sailing Ship ablaze. The single window was shuttered and bolted like the other, and also hung with hawthorn. Var noticed that the door latch was similarly draped, and that the smell of powder smoke was stronger.

It came from the wide bed, where Captain Danyael Corm, freshly shaved and dressed in full uniform, lay with a pistol in his still right hand. The heated muzzle had scorched the sheets. The discharge had exploded most of Corm's skull so that the dirty wall and the pillows behind his head were obscenely decorated with red, and sticky patches of grayish white that Var recognized as brain matter.

Talle said, "So, a suicide," and clicked his tongue against his teeth briskly. "And one who hangs his portals with hawthorn. Do you know what that means, Major?"

Var said, "Witchcraft?" surprised his voice came out so steady.

"That's the old belief," Talle replied. "That hawthorn protects against evil spirits. What do you think?"

He seemed to Var less appalled than intrigued. Var said, "I don't know, Inquisitor."

Talle chuckled. Var wondered if the candle flames truly shifted, or if that was only his imagination. Through the powder stink he could now smell Corm's blood. He stared at Talle.

Who said, "Perhaps it did once. But no longer, eh? Look at him."

Var had rather not. He was not squeamish—could not be, an officer of marines—but there was something horribly pathetic about Corm's demise, as if a fellow officer had given up to fear. Of what? he wondered.

"The servant spoke of dreams," Talle said, "and voices that were not his own. And now we find his master in sorry rooms lit like some cathedral, hawthorn hung around, with a pistol in his hand and his brains . . . Well." He gestured at the painted wall.

Var said, "What does it mean?"

"That we must examine him," Talle answered. "Like your Corporal Gerry."

To himself, Var said, Oh, dear God, no. And to Talle: "As you will, Inquisitor."

Talle said, "Quite. So, do you get his boots?"

Var sighed, not caring if Talle heard, and obeyed.

"They truly go mad?" Chakthi stared at his Dreamer, his smile ugly with pleasurable anticipation. "They slay themselves?"

"It is as Akratil promised," Hadduth confirmed.

"Through the owh'jika we've a pathway to their minds, and Akratil uses that."

Chakthi nodded. The firelight planed his face harsh, the lines there entirely predatory. "It was good to take the owh'jika," he murmured. "The thing is useful."

Hadduth hoped his akaman remembered whose idea that had been, but held his tongue. Chakthi was gone a long way into madness and his reactions were no longer at all predictable. He waited on Chakthi's next question.

The Tachyn leader stared awhile at the flames, then asked, "How long before our allies come?"

Hadduth shrugged. "I cannot say yet. I use that gift Akratil gave me to weaken the strangers, but when he will come I cannot say."

Chakthi glanced at him, frowning, and the wakanisha added hurriedly, "The Breakers are a law unto themselves. I cannot command them—only ask their aid. But that's promised, and surely proven by what Akratil does now."

"Valuable allies," Chakthi agreed, his eyes fastening on the Dreamer's like a stoat's on a frightened rabbit. "But I'd not wait overlong on their arrival."

"No," Hadduth agreed, "but meanwhile our enemies destroy themselves. Think on it, my akaman! That they turn their weapons against one another? Is that not a great gift?"

"Yes," Chakthi allowed. "But still I'd blood my own steel."

"And shall," Hadduth promised, "as soon as Akratil is ready."

There were no hex signs on Corm's body—save they'd been painted on that missing section of his skull—and Talle declared himself satisfied. Var wondered if he should dress the body, but the Inquisitor called him away.

"Send men," he ordered. "This one must be burned, too; and dropped in quicklime."

Var frowned. "Is that truly necessary?"

"Oh, yes." Talle paused at the bedroom door, fixing the marine with a wickedly mischievous smile. "Unless you'd chance the dead walking."

Var felt a chill run down his spine. He glanced back to where Corm lay, and on the floor beside the bed, where a decanter and an overturned brandy glass stood, saw a scrap of paper.

"What is it?" Talle sounded irritated as Var turned back.

"This." Var retrieved the paper. It was stained with spilled brandy and in one corner speckled with blood. The hand that had inscribed its message was remarkably firm, as if in the final hours of his life Corm had found calm. He read aloud: " 'I had believed them gone, left behind. I believed the Inquisitor had driven them out, but he has not. I do not think he can, for they are too strong. They have haunted me these past weeks, and bid me to murder, and I am too weak to resist them longer. I have seen disgrace enough and cannot countenance further ignominy. Therefore I elect to take my own life, which course shall, I trust, leave me with some little honor. Pray for my soul.' Signed, Danyael Corm, Lieutenant GM."

Talle grunted, lips pursed and eyes narrowed.

Var asked, "What does it mean?"

"That he took his life because he was haunted." Talle favored the body with a speculative gaze. "Brave man or coward? I wonder which."

His tone was dry, as if he pondered some academic problem. Var said, "Haunted by what?"

"His meeting with what he thought were demons?" Talle shrugged.

"And they returned to urge him to murder?" Var said. "Like the corporal?"

Talle smiled at him, as if pleased with his acuity. "We did well to promote you, Var; you've a sharp mind."

Var was not sure whether he should feel flattered or patronized. He asked, "There's a link?"

"All's linked," Talle replied, giving no clear answer. "Let's find some friends of our dead corporal, eh?"

Thoroughly confused and more than a little disturbed, Var followed the Inquisitor back through Grostheim's dark and chilly streets to the Militia barracks. There a Captain Mylle confirmed that Lieutenant Minns had taken Corporal Gerry's body outside the walls to burn and detailed six men to collect Corm. Before the squad left, Talle had it from each of them that they were not close friends of Gerry, and slept in a different part of the barracks. Then Mylle routed out the corporal's friends and bunkmates. There were some dozen of them, in varying states of undress, and all agreed that of late poor Robyn had been plagued with dreams, crying out in his sleep in a strange voice that seemed quite unlike his own.

"And you?" Talle fixed the nervous soldiers with his bird-bright eyes. He smiled, which seemed akin to the greeting of an executioner his victims.

Amidst a vigorous shaking of heads and a loud murmur of denial, eyes turned toward a single man.

"Your name?" Talle locked his gaze on the soldier.

"Eban Stour, Inquisitor." He came instinctively to full attention. "Militiaman in the God's service, sir."

"Are you?" Talle asked mildly. "Truly?"

"I am!" Stour barked, as if on the parade ground. "Devoted to the service, Inquisitor."

Mylle said, "He's a ten-year man, Inquisitor. Says he wants to sign for another ten."

"As he would," Talle murmured, "were he . . . infected."

"Sir!" Stour shifted his eyes far enough sideways to see Mylle; back to Talle. "Inquisitor! Permission to speak, sirs."

Mylle glanced at Talle, who nodded, so that the captain gestured that Stour proceed.

"We all dream, sir. I'm perhaps a little noisier than most, but that's all there is to it."

"What do you dream?" Talle asked in the same gentle voice that Var distrusted so much. "Tell me, eh?"

"I dream of conquest," Stour said, and his voice shifted down several octaves to become a harsh, guttural grunting such as Var had heard emerging from Gerry's mouth. "I dream of taking this land from you, who have no right to be here. I dream of slaying you all."

And suddenly as Gerry had launched himself at Var, Stour sprang forward to fasten his hands on Talle's throat.

The Inquisitor fell in a swirl of black coattails, borne down by the impact of the attack. So abrupt was it, none moved for long moments, but only stared aghast and unbelieving at the impossible assault. Var saw Talle raise his hands and move them—presumably to work some Inquisitor's hex magic—and Stour's hands trap Talle's wrists and pin them even as the soldier drove his teeth like some rabid dog's at the Inquisitor's throat. Talle screamed—which Var must reluctantly admit he enjoyed—and wriggled like a pinned black worm against the floor.

Stour fastened his teeth hard in the Inquisitor's neck and Var felt the fascination of the spell break. He drew his pistol, cocked the hammer, and snapped down the strikerplate. Set the muzzle to Stour's head and squeezed the trigger.

Powder discharge blackened Talle's face as Stour's head was blown clear of his throat. Var saw red wounds there as the soldier jerked out his death throes, and remembered Corm's ravaged skull as he stared at his immediate handiwork. The Inquisitor's dog?

Galvanized by the explosion of Var's pistol, Mylle and the others captured Stour's body. Var helped Talle to his feet.

The Inquisitor fingered his windpipe and coughed; examined his bloodied fingers and looked at Var.

"Thank you, Major Var. I owe you my life." His voice was hoarse.

"It was no more than my duty," Var said. "And surely you'd have slain him with your magic."

For a surprising instant Talle's eyes wavered, as if he were not certain of that outcome. Then he said, "Surely; but still I thank you."

Var ducked his head in acknowledgment and set to reloading his pistol. Talle touched his throat and muttered, and the wounds began to heal. When he spoke again, his voice was sound: "Take him out and burn him with the others."

Captain Mylle looked back in confusion: "The others?"

"Yes! And quickly, lest I lose my temper."

Mylle summoned the gaping soldiers to pick up Stour's body.

Talle said, "After the fire, quicklime. You understand?"

Mylle ducked his head and did as he was ordered.

They carried the corpse away and Var asked, "Inquisitor, what's happening here?"

Talle fingered his throat, the teeth marks not all gone yet, and said, "New magic. A different magic for a new world."

18   Rescue

The smoke was faded long before the three
horsemen reached the wood, but the drifting
smudge had hung long enough against the blue
that they were able to guess its source—not least because
Tekah recalled showing Davyd the hurst.

The young Commacht cursed and heeled his mount to a
gallop as the oaks came into sight. Rannach brought his big
stallion alongside, Arcole matching his pace so that they
flanked the anxious warrior. Rannach reached out to touch
Tekah's shoulder, slow him.

"Easy, brother. Best we approach cautious, eh?"

"And is he hurt?" Tekah flung his akaman a troubled
glance, turned it on Arcole. "Or dead?"

Rannach said, "Even so we go in wary. Is he there
still . . ."

"Where else *can* he be?" Tekah's voice was grown strident
with concern. "In the Maker's name, Rannach, we've sought
him every other place since Taza found his horse."

"Yes." Rannach nodded, his aquiline features thoughtful.
"Since Taza found his horse."

Tekah said, "I'll have an accounting of Taza for that."

And Rannach answered somberly, "Do we find him there,
I shall have answers of Taza. But not until Davyd tells us his
side. Until then . . ."

He couched his lance and set the stallion to a canter, his
eyes all the while scanning the ground ahead, the wood, as if
he momentarily anticipated ambush.

Arcole held his musket across his thighs, finger loose on
the trigger, thumb set ready against the hammer. Rannach's

wariness, Tekah's concern, invested him with a mixture of emotions, not least the fear they'd find Davyd dead.

God, it had been long enough since Taza brought the buckskin in from the north, and the People had spent time searching there. Yazte still had his Lakanti out looking—and had Tekah not remembered . . . God—Maker!—whatever You call Yourself, he thought, only let Davyd be alive. Let us find him. Please! It was hard to hold the gray horse down to Rannach's canter. Like Tekah, he'd sooner have gone charging in, save he knew Rannach was wise in this. Had aught happened to Davyd, then the Maker alone knew what lurked inside the wood.

He was vaguely surprised to find himself praying; the more that he prayed to the deity of this new land, not the god of his lost home.

They came to the edgewood and saw the remnants of a fire, long burned out and doused by the rain that had fallen that morning. Sodden ashes lay scattered over charred grass beside a stream that wound inward through overhanging trees, tracks beside that Arcole could not read.

But the two Commacht could. Rannach said, "Is it him, he built this fire as a marker. See?"

Tekah nodded as the lance angled down, inward, and said, "And those others?"

He nocked an arrow as he spoke, and Rannach answered, "Yes: wolverine."

Arcole felt a chill run down his spine, like iced talons scraping his backbone. He brought the musket's hammer to full cock: he had heard stories of wolverines.

"So, do we see?" Rannach settled his lance firm between elbow and ribs, not waiting on an answer—not needing to— as he heeled his horse onward and into the wood.

The day was warm, but Arcole felt cold as they rode the chuckling streambed. Light clambered down through the overhanging branches, dappling the water with intricate patterns of harlequin brightness and shadow that were disrupted and swirled by the hooves as if the three riders shattered some delicate balance. The wood seemed very still; there seemed an absence of birdsong, of squirrel's chattering, as if the hurst waited. Arcole felt sweat run down his face and back and did not notice it ran there cold.

Then they came to a clearing and Rannach was off his horse in a single bound, Tekah not much slower behind. Arcole eased off the musket's hammer and followed them, his eyes wide as he stared at Davyd.

The boy—no, he told himself, the man—lay naked beside the scattered ashes of another long-dead fire. He clutched a length of broken branch in his hands, the shorter end all splintered and chewed. Not far from him lay the owner of the farther end—jammed hard between the jaws of the wolverine, the sharpened tip extending from the beast's neck.

Arcole started as Tekah's arrow thudded into the predator. Rannach said, "It's dead. The Maker alone knows how, but he slew it." His voice was filled with awe.

Arcole dropped to his knees, setting his musket aside as he cradled Davyd's head, close to weeping at sight of the wounds decorating the starveling body.

Deep gouges all clotted with dried blood scored Davyd's chest and belly; parallel lines of old crimson sliced one cheek, and his hair was gone white as Morrhyn's. Arcole thought him dead until he heard the faint—God, so very faint!—exhalation of breath coming from the mouth, and saw the slight rise and fall of the thin ribs. He thought, Thank You, Maker. Now let him live, eh?

And started again as Rannach said, "Hold him. Those wounds need cleansing."

The Commacht spilled water over Davyd's chest and set to cleaning the terrible gouges, speaking the while.

"Tekah, find moss, then get a fire started. He'll need food, broth. And a shelter. We need to keep him warm. Maker, but I don't know how he's survived."

Tekah said, "He slew the wolverine," in a voice no less awed than Rannach's, and got back the answer: "Yes! And now we must do our part. Go!"

Arcole held his comrade and watched as Rannach bathed the wounds and set the healing moss over the incisions.

"Shall he live?"

"The Maker willing." Rannach did not look up from his

work. "He's near starved, and sore hurt. But . . . yes, I believe he'll live. I believe the Maker's set His mark on him, and
so he *must* live."

"Like Morrhyn?" Arcole stared at Davyd's hair, the bright
red all gone now, like a poppy field lost under snow.

Rannach said, "Yes, like Morrhyn. I think the Maker's
bound them both to His purpose."

Arcole stroked Davyd's new-white hair and felt a pang of
terrible sorrow.

It was strange, he thought, to be dead, but far better than the
agony. He had not often wondered about the afterlife, or
even if there was one, but when he felt the wolverine's talons
clutch out his life and smelled the animal's breath in his nostrils, he had been anxious of the pain. And there had been
none, or only briefly: only a descent into a comfortable darkness that smothered and took away the suffering.

He wanted to stay there, in the darkness, and could not
understand what raised him from it, or why. He did not want
to suffer any more, and so he cried out in protest.

He felt liquid spill down his chest that he supposed must
be his blood, and thought that it was not over and that he still
fought the beast, so he struggled, thinking that the Maker
tested him past endurance. He wished it be not so, but Morrhyn had explained to him something of the Maker's ways
and so he rose to the fight, not wishing to let down Morrhyn
or the Maker or himself.

And heard a voice he remembered from some other time
when he had lived say, "Davyd! In God's name, boy!"

He said inside his darkness, "Arcole? Are you dead, too?"

And got back, "No! Nor you. You live; now drink this
damn broth."

It was hard to open his eyes. Harder still to turn his head
because that movement stretched out cords of pain that ran
from his face to his chest and beyond, all through him. But he
did, and consequently saw the glow of a dim fire that outlined
the familiar visage.

He said "Arcole?" again.

And Arcole said, "Yes! And you live. Rannach and Tekah wait outside."

"Where am I?"

"In the wood, damn you. Where else?"

Arcole sounded very happy, and at the same time very concerned.

"The wolverine?"

"You slew it. They—Rannach and Tekah—say no man has faced a wolverine alone before and lived."

Davyd said, "I don't think I did. I think the Maker was with me." And began to laugh, which set him to coughing—which hurt so horribly that he began to choke. Arcole held him tight and slapped his back—gently—and then the light grew brighter because a lodgeflap was opened and Rannach and Tekah came inside the shelter and began to laugh and express their wonder at what he had done.

To which he replied, as he had told Arcole, "It was not me, I think, but the Maker."

Which for some reason set them to laughing the more, so that he could not help but join in, which hurt him and tired him, and he was pleased when they announced he had best sleep again and left him to sink into the easy darkness with only Arcole at his side.

"He should be dead." Rannach's voice was somber and awed at the same time. "The Maker knows, but he was starving before the fight. And to face a wolverine with but a sharpened branch . . ."

Tekah nodded, the fire's light dancing over his features, settling planes of shadow across his cheeks, beneath his troubled eyes. "And his hair? Like Morrhyn's . . ."

Rannach nodded in turn. "Yes; after he came down from the mountain."

"There's no mountain here." Tekah stared into the flames.

"Even so, the Maker has surely touched him." Rannach shrugged. "Morrhyn can likely explain it when we get him back."

"When shall that be," Tekah asked, "with such wounds?"

Rannach shrugged again. "Surely not soon, save the Maker heals him faster than mortal man."

Tekah said, "He did Morrhyn," and Rannach ducked his head in solemn agreement.

Fire played over his skin even as ice water filled his veins. It seemed that flames danced under his shuttered eyelids, and when he forced them open there was the same intricacy of light and shadow, transfiguring the faces that leant toward him and spilled warm broth between his lips, so that he could not discern between Arcole and Rannach and Tekah, not even when they spoke, for their voices seemed to come from far away, echoing down great distances as if they spoke from out of some land other than the territory he inhabited. He wondered if this was a last temptation: that he was shown the chance of survival, distant, that he know fully what he lost.

And then, without sense of time or place, his eyes opened clear and he saw that he lay within the confines of his rebuilt sweat lodge, and that a fire burned in the makeshift hearth and Rannach sat beside him, chin on chest, dozing.

He said "Rannach?" and the Commacht akaman started upright and was instantly alert, bringing a clay mug filled with cool stream water to Davyd's lips.

Davyd drank deep and looked around, seeing sunlight filtering past the edges of the lodgeflap. He said, "I'd go outside."

Rannach frowned. "You're weak yet."

"I'd go outside," he repeated. "I want the sunshine on my face. And then I must go home to speak with Morrhyn of my dreams."

He did not wait on Rannach's answer, but rather pushed up to a sitting position and thrust the blankets that covered him aside, so that Rannach had no choice save to support him and help him stumble out from the lodge.

The light was very bright after the shadowy interior, and he narrowed his eyes against the glare that dizzied him and set his head to spinning. Nor could he deny his weakness as his legs faltered, and he must lean on the strength of Rannach's arm lest he pitch over. He saw Arcole and Tekah rise from where they sat beside a fire and come toward him with amazement on their faces, joy in their eyes, and he was surprised that the smell of the fish baking over the flames made him hungry.

They brought him to the fire like an old man—an ancient tottery with years, or a weakling babe, one of the Defenseless Ones—and set him gently down. Tekah laid a blanket about his shoulders, and Rannach produced a knife and set to flaking a fish as Arcole held him upright.

"I'm stronger," he said, "and I must go home."

They exchanged glances. Rannach said, "Yes; soon."

He said, "I must speak with Morrhyn," and turned his head to study them each in turn. "There were dreams."

"Listen, Davyd." Arcole still held him and he thought that he might not be able to remain upright save for that arm about his shoulders. "You've taken sore wounds. You need to rest."

"I must go home," he repeated. "I must speak with Morrhyn."

Arcole said, "You'd not last a day horseback. God, boy! Those wounds would split and you'd bleed to death, or . . ."

He shook his head in frustration as Davyd raised a weakly hand, motioning him to silence. "I *dreamed,* Arcole. Do you not understand that?" He looked to Rannach and Tekah. "Morrhyn was right—I've the talent; and I've *dreamed*! Now, must you bring me back on a travois, then so be it. *But I must go home!*"

Arcole began to speak, to argue, but Rannach set a hand on his arm, staring firm at Davyd. "Morrhyn survived because the Maker kindled his life," he said. "So that he might bring back word of the Breakers and offer the People salvation. Do you claim the same?"

Davyd hesitated. Then: "I don't know; I am not Morrhyn, but . . ." He nodded slowly, conviction growing. "Perhaps; and be it so, then the Maker shall keep me alive, no? And do I die, then . . ." He shrugged.

Rannach looked at Arcole. "I say we build a travois and take him home."

Tekah nodded. "And I."

Arcole frowned, sighed, then said, "Tomorrow. Let him, for God's sake, have this day at least to regain his strength."

Rannach turned to Davyd, his dark eyes framing a question that for a moment Davyd could not understand. Then he realized the akaman waited on his decision as he might have waited on Morrhyn's—which was startling. He said, "Tomorrow, yes."

They came back to the valley in slow procession, Davyd blanket-swathed on the travois, the fever still on him so that the journey was a thing of jigsawed patterns, of passing in and out of consciousness until familiar voices rang loud all about and familiar faces stared down at him. He recognized Flysse and Arrhyna, Lhyn; then Morrhyn.

Who said, "Quick, bring him to my lodge."

Davyd said, "I've much to tell you."

And Morrhyn nodded as if he understood it all, and said, "Yes. But first, those wounds must be dressed."

"I dreamed," Davyd said.

And Morrhyn answered, "I know; and in a while you shall tell me."

19   Accusations

Taza experienced a moment of utter panic as he recognized what the People shouted. Mostly it was only Davyd's name, but in amongst the joyful din were such snatches as told him the outlander had survived and was brought home, which he had not believed possible. He wormed through the throng, not close, but near enough that he might catch a glimpse of Davyd's face and marvel at the snow-white hair, and feel the panic mount fresh heights.

The Maker knew but he'd been careful. Davyd's gear he'd scattered through the wood and beyond, trusting that were it ever found the scattering be assumed the work of the wolverine. The buckskin horse he'd led away on a wide circle a full three days before "finding" it and sending the bulk of the search parties off to the north and west, opposite to the wood's direction. He had been confident the raw meat and bloodspoor he'd trailed to Davyd's sweat lodge would bring the wolverine to his rival—nor any less that the beast would kill Davyd.

But now Tekah brandished the skin like a battle trophy and the upstart outlander was back in camp, alive, and Taza could not help but wonder how long it might be before the print was fitted to the hoof and he have questions to answer that must surely condemn him. He wondered if it were not best he find his horse and ride away now, save to where? Were he blamed, then surely the People would come looking for him, find him and bring him back to face judgment. He did not relish facing the circle of the Council, but . . . He looked again at Davyd's face, the wounds, and made a sudden decision: he'd bluff it out.

He eased back, standing amongst the throng, one small figure in a multitude, and watched as Davyd was taken to Morrhyn's lodge.

Lhyn was foremost amongst those surrounding Davyd. Rannach and Tekah carried the travois, and Arcole walked beside. Flysse took station on the farther side, clutching Davyd's hand and marveling at his gaunt features, the changed color of his hair. She spoke his name, softly, as might a mother murmur the name of a hurt child.

And he smiled at her and said, "Flysse? Don't worry, I can't die now. At least . . ." He coughed a laugh that clearly pained him. ". . . not yet."

Over his shoulder, Morrhyn said, "He'll live. Were he to die, I'd have dreamed it. But even so . . ." He raised his voice, addressing himself to Arrhyna and Lhyn, who came concerned with Flysse. "Hot water, eh? And clean cloth; needles and thread."

The two Commacht women strode briskly away and Flysse accompanied the travois to Morrhyn's lodge, where the wakanisha ordered it be set down and Davyd carried inside.

There was insufficient space for all who'd enter and Morrhyn asked that Rannach and Tekah stand sentry outside, hold back the anxious crowd, while only Flysse and Arcole accompany the wounded man into the rawhide shelter. Arrhyna was already there, busy about the fire, a pot set to boiling, her dark eyes flashing anxiously from Davyd's face to Morrhyn's. Then Lhyn came back with needles and gut thread, calm in the face of catastrophe: long used to binding wounds.

Hers were the hands that plied the needles, delicate as they were firm, stitching the ugly gaps the wolverine had imparted even as Morrhyn fed Davyd some palliative that lent his eyes a dreamy look and left him sighing as the bone pierced his skin.

"He'll sleep now." Morrhyn set compresses of herbs over Lhyn's handiwork, fixing them in place with lengths of cut cloth. "He'll feel no pain. Save . . ." He looked at the young man's face and grimaced. ". . . perhaps when he wakes and sees himself."

Arcole said, "He'll be no pretty sight," his voice grim, "and I'd know who stranded him there."

"Come tell me." Morrhyn gestured that they quit the lodge, pausing to glance at the waiting women. "Shall you stay with him? One, perhaps?"

Lhyn ducked her head. "I'll see to it."

Morrhyn smiled at her, and Arcole saw flash between them a lifetime of possibilities now burned down like the ashes of an old fire to friendly embers. He felt Flysse's hand in his and clutched it tight. God, but it was as if his own son were wounded: he had not properly realized until now how much he cared for Davyd.

Outside the lodge the People waited in the afternoon sunlight, silent as Morrhyn emerged. The wakanisha raised his hands and said loud, "He'll live. He sleeps now, but he'll live and there is no more you can do save thank the Maker for his survival."

There came from the crowd a murmur of gratitude, of relief, and it began to drift away.

Taza went with it, cursing the news even as he parodied a smile and his mind raced. Davyd could not have named him, nor Morrhyn dreamed his guilt, else he'd surely be taken. Why not? More, *how* not? His smile grew more genuine as he thought on the possibility that his deeds were somehow concealed, as if some power protected him. Yes, he decided, he would bluff it out. Bluff it out and win.

"There were tracks," Tekah said, "another camp. Who built that, watched Davyd."

Rannach glanced at Morrhyn, anticipating the wakanisha speak, but Morrhyn only nodded and held his own council, so that Rannach felt impelled to say, "We cannot be sure it was Taza."

Yazte said, "He was gone from camp. By all accounts, for all the time Davyd was missing."

"And he brought Davyd's horse back," Tekah said. "The horse would not have strayed far from the wood."

"Save it scented the wolverine," Rannach said, "and was panicked."

"Then it would surely have run for home," Tekah said. "Not gone away to the northwest."

Rannach nodded, his face thoughtful. He looked to Morrhyn, who in turn looked to Kahteney.

"What do you think, brother?"

The Lakanti Dreamer shrugged, his eyes troubled. "I wonder what to think. I think that we should have dreamed of this—foreseen the danger. But we did not! And is Davyd all you believe him to be, then surely we should have dreamed warning."

Morrhyn said, "Perhaps," and stared into the fire.

The rest—Rannach and Tekah, Yazte and Kahteney, Arcole—waited on him, on his response. He was, no matter his protestations, the Prophet, and they hesitated to foreguess him.

There was a long silence before he spoke again, and when he did his words were somber: "What you say, brother, is right—we *should* have dreamed the danger."

It was a warm night—the climate here in Ket-Ta-Thanne kinder than the lost homeland, the Moon of the Turning Year delivering soft promise—save it seemed a wintry gust blew over them all. And when Kahteney spoke it was as if the wind grew colder still.

"But we did not, and Davyd might have died. How can that be?"

Morrhyn sighed. Why was it always him to whom they looked for answers? He was only the Maker's tool, not some oracle. He knew only so much as the Maker allowed him, and in this matter, he knew nothing: he could understand it no better than Kahteney. But they looked to him and imposed on him a duty he could not refuse, and so he said, "Perhaps our dreams were clouded."

He had sooner not said that, not least for the widening of the eyes studying his face, the trepidation there. He had sooner given some easy answer, but he could not: only speak the truth that had gnawed at his mind since first Davyd was too long away.

Kahteney said "The Breakers?" in a voice that barely succeeded in rising above the fire's crackling.

Morrhyn shrugged and told the truth: "I've not dreamed of them; but . . ."

"Here?" Kahteney's voice was urgent. "Surely not. How might they find us here?"

Morrhyn saw Rannach's eyes dart wide, his hand lock instinctively around the hilt of his knife. Yazte made a sign of warding; Tekah whistled between his teeth and stared at the night as if he expected those creatures to come howling out of the shadows.

Morrhyn said, "The Maker willing, they'll not; cannot."

Kahteney said, slowly, "But you wonder?"

Morrhyn shrugged again. "Our dreams were clouded, no?"

Kahteney nodded; none others spoke.

"I do not say this is the Breakers' doing," Morrhyn said. "Only that we failed to dream of Davyd's danger. Which is not a thing I can properly understand."

Tekah said, "Taza!" And then lowered his angry face, abashed to have spoken out of turn.

Kahteney nodded slowly, carefully, looking the while through sidelong eyes at Morrhyn. "It might well be. Surely he's somewhat of the gift; save . . ."

"As we've agreed," Yazte declared loudly, "Taza's the gift, but not the sight of it. Could he cloud *your* dreaming?"

Morrhyn said, "Likely not; save he was aided."

"Maker!" Yazte's voice was suddenly no longer fueled with tiswin, but only solemn. "What do you say, Prophet?"

They waited on him in uneasy silence. All around, the great camp went about its nocturnal business; fires painted patterns of shadow and light over the massed lodges; cookfires scented the air; children called to one another, and dogs barked, horses whickered. Folk came to inquire after Davyd, answered by Lhyn or Arrhyna or Flysse, who waited tenderly patient on the wounded man. Those who saw the faces of the akamans and wakanishas assumed they discussed Davyd's condition and politely avoided that solemn circle. It seemed to Morrhyn that they sat within a vortex of cold, as if some great battle approached.

Then Morrhyn said, "I suspect this is a thing of importance, and we should not discuss it alone. Rannach . . . ?"

The Commacht akaman nodded. "Yes. Kanseah should be here; and Dohnse, I think." He looked to Tekah. "Do you ask them attend?"

The young Commacht sprang to his feet and was gone. Silence fell, and Morrhyn wondered what might be unleashed here. He stared into the flames, uneasiness growing.

Then Tekah came with Kanseah and Dohnse, the Naiche and the Tachyn somber as their escort, their faces grave as they took places about the fire.

"Welcome," Rannach said, and grinned dourly, "though I think what you'll hear might not be so welcome."

Dohnse, the older of the two, shrugged and took the cup Arrhyna offered him. Kanseah smiled nervously, his eyes downcast.

Rannach said, "We deemed it best you hear all this, that you speak on behalf of your clans."

Kanseah nodded. Dohnse said, "My clan is the Commacht."

"Even so," Morrhyn said, his voice gentle, as if he'd avoid the risk of hurt or insult, "you were once Tachyn, and they may have something to do with this."

"The Tachyn are no longer." Dohnse made a dismissive, chopping gesture. "Those people who went across the mountains with Chakthi are Tachyn. There are no Tachyn in Ket-Ta-Thanne."

His voice was flat as a knife's blade and no less edged. He faced Morrhyn as he spoke, and his eyes held steady on the wakanisha's. In them Morrhyn saw pain, old suffering held in careful check.

He smiled and reached out to touch Dohnse's wrist. "You are Commacht, brother, and the clan honored by that choice. But even so, best you hear this."

Dohnse nodded and Morrhyn turned to Rannach, motioning that the akaman speak.

Rannach outlined what they had already discussed, Morrhyn and Kahteney adding their pieces. Then Rannach asked that each present speak his mind.

Yazte was the first. He said, "I do not understand this

clouding of your dreams, but the rest seems obvious to me—Taza followed Davyd and stole the horse, wrecked the camp."

"We cannot know that," Kahteney said. "Not for sure."

"We can question him," Yazte said.

"Perhaps that might decide the one thing," Morrhyn said. "But the other? This obfuscation frightens me."

Morrhyn saw Kanseah glance up at that, the Naiche's face stark-planed, as if some supporting rock were snatched from under him. But he said nothing, only waited on the others.

Rannach said, "Did Taza look to slay Davyd, then he must answer for that crime; but I am not a Dreamer and I cannot speak on the other matter."

Morrhyn nodded. "Perhaps it were best we leave that aside for now. When Davyd's recovered, Kahteney and I shall speak with him. Do we, all three, dream together, then perhaps we can find an answer."

"And Taza?" Rannach asked. "Until we hear Davyd's side, can we properly accuse Taza?"

Past the circle of the fire's light, where close-packed lodges spread darkness over the ground, Taza stroked the neck of the yellow dog that lay beside him in the shadows. It was easy to eavesdrop on folk who assumed customary privacy; they did not anticipate anyone would intrude so. That was the way of the People: to live close but grant personal freedom through application of discretion. Because, he thought—not stopping to wonder if that voice was his or some other's—they are fools.

He felt his confidence, his strength grow, like sap rising from the ground in the New Grass Moon to fill the withered limbs of winter's trees, rendering them strong again, mighty and spreading.

Fools to think they might talk about him and he not think to listen. And the wakanishas' dreams were clouded? He chuckled into the yellow dog's hair. He'd show them! He'd show them he *was* a Dreamer, powerful as any of them; mightier than that weakling outcomer Davyd. And was there some other power lent him strength, then he'd take it all, and . . .

He eased back as he saw Tekah rise, Dohnse with him. Tekah would kill him on suspicion alone—the fool was besotted with Davyd—and Dohnse was a turncoat Tachyn who'd surely slay his own mother to please Rannach and Morrhyn.

Inside his head the voice he did not know was not his own urged caution, and so he slid loose from the yellow dog and crawled away, back to his bed, where he feigned sleep until they found him.

"I'll not pretend I like Davyd," he said. "That should be a lie, and I know I cannot lie to you."

Save I am protected and you are fools.

"Where were you?" Rannach asked. "By all accounts, you quit camp not long after Davyd. And you brought his horse back."

"I went out hunting. I thought to bring some game in—to ease the burden of my people."

And you cannot gainsay me.

"And the horse?" asked Yazte. "How do you explain that?"

"I found it. I found it wandering loose and frightened and I brought it back."

"Save Davyd lost it in the wood, and you found it—you say—far from there."

Prove me wrong, my fat akaman. If you can.

"I found it where I found it. I do not know how it got there: only that I found it there."

"There were tracks," Rannach said slowly. "In the wood. Someone followed Davyd there, and stole his horse to leave him stranded with a wolverine."

Taza nodded gravely. "I had heard that, and I thank the Maker he lived. He must be blessed to have survived."

Morrhyn said, "Yes: I believe he is."

Taza said, "The Maker be praised."

You cannot see me, eh? You are the Prophet, but you cannot see me. He felt the power grow in him, still unaware—uncaring—of where it came from; knowing only that it was there and hid him as if he were one of the Shadow People. He held his eyes firm on Morrhyn's, challenging the wakanisha to deny him, to doubt him.

Morrhyn said, "I think the Maker holds Davyd for a special duty."

Taza shrugged.

"Does that offend you?" Kahteney asked, and Taza heard scarce-hidden animosity in the Lakanti's voice.

He said—honestly—"I believe I might be a great Dreamer if you would only agree. . . . Give me the pahé and . . ."

Kahteney cut him short. "You are not ready. You've lessons to learn yet."

It was hard to stifle the gust of naked rage that flared at that, but the newcome power invested him and taught him caution, dissimulation, and so he beat down the flames and answered as calmly as he might, "Perhaps, and it is your decision. I can only obey."

Until I own power greater than yours and teach you the lesson of denying me.

"And you did not steal Davyd's horse?" Yazte asked.

Taza shook his head: "No."

Fat fool. You and all these others.

Morrhyn said, "This proves nothing; it gets us nowhere."

"Save we question Davyd," Kahteney said.

Who never saw me or knew I was there, new-come fool that he is.

Aloud, he said, wrapping hypocritical dignity around himself like a concealing blanket, "It is not for me to say this, but . . . you accuse me of things I have not done. I am innocent, but you presume me guilty. So, I say to you—let Davyd be full healed and he accuse me. And then let the Matakwa decide."

Yazte said, "We are like the Matakwa. We are all here."

Taza said, "Not the Grannach," wondering the while just why he spoke the words—as if they were not entirely his own, but set on his tongue by that other voice, that power that filled him. "Am I to be judged before all the People, then let it be in the old way; properly." He stared at Rannach. "As was the akaman of the Commacht. Would you deny me that right?"

Rannach met his gaze and said, "No. Do you wish this? You'd stand before the Matakwa?"

The voice inside Taza's head said, *Yes!* So Taza nodded and voiced an affirmative: "I would. I have done nothing to deserve your blame. Save, perhaps . . ." He lowered his head in parody of embarrassment. ". . . wished to become a Dreamer. I shall not deny that I envy Davyd; but that I sought to slay him—no!"

They studied him; *as if,* he thought, *they studied a trapped wolf, wondering whether to leave it go or slay it.* And he felt confident: the voice inside him spoke congratulations, that he had done well, and that they believed him, or at least owned sufficient doubts they could not on the spot condemn him.

Then Rannach said, "So be it, eh? Let there be no more accusations made until Davyd is recovered. And are they, the Matakwa shall judge."

Taza said, "That is fair," and Rannach glanced at Morrhyn, who shrugged and motioned that Taza be dismissed.

It was strange to own such power that he might look a wakanisha—the Prophet, even!—in the eye and speak untruths: and a heady seduction. He thought he must own a power greater than Davyd's, and could not properly understand why Kahteney denied his right to become a Dreamer, why Morrhyn would name the upstart his successor. How could they be so wrong, so misguided?

Because, the voice said, *they do not understand. They are blind to the real power, which is not the Maker but what lives inside of you, inside of all men. Take what you want! That, or be a worm crawling through the grass. Would you be a worm?*

Taza said, "No!"

Then be what I can make you.

Taza said, "Yes!" And felt the heat of ambition fill him, and knew that some great destiny came to him.

Only wait, said the voice, *until Matakwa. Then you shall become great. Far greater than Davyd or Morrhyn, so that all shall hail the mighty Taza.*

∎   ∎   ∎

Yazte said, "He lied."

Kahteney said, "We cannot know that; not for sure," and looked to Morrhyn.

"I do not know." Morrhyn shrugged helplessly. "I sensed nothing. He spoke . . . honestly? But if . . ."

Tekah said, bluntly, "Kill him."

"We cannot," Rannach said. "Not without proper judgment, proper evidence. And that cannot emerge until we speak with Davyd."

"Who likely cannot say," said Tekah, angrily.

"Perhaps." Rannach shrugged. "But I'll not judge a man on hearsay and suspicion alone." He turned to Morrhyn: "How think you?"

"That," Morrhyn replied, "you grow wise."

Rannach shrugged again, irritable now. "Wise? The Maker knows, but I fumble in the dark for answers. Must I decide everything? Advise me, eh? Like you did my father."

"Your father," Morrhyn said, "made his own decisions."

"With your guidance!" Rannach chopped air. "I am not my father: I am myself, and imperfect."

Yazte's big hand reached out to grasp his wrist. "Racharran was not perfect," the Lakanti akaman said. "Surely wise, surely sensible; but not perfect. He only did the best he could, thinking always of the Commacht and past that—to the good of the People. As you do! Like it or not."

"Ach!" Rannach took up the flask and spilled tiswin into his cup; drank deep. "Must I make all the decisions?"

Yazte said slowly, "Perhaps; here in Ket-Ta-Thanne."

"Without," Rannach grunted, "even the advice of my wakanisha?"

Morrhyn said, "With all the advice I can give you. Save in this matter of Taza I can give you none. He is a mystery."

Kahteney nodded silent agreement, and Rannach found himself facing a ring of watching faces that waited on his decision. He said, after a while, "Then we wait. Let Davyd recover his strength and tell us what he can; then we go to Matakwa—the decision shall be made there, before all the People."

I   I   I

Even after so long amongst them Arcole found these things hard to understand. All circumstantial evidence pointed to Taza, and clearly—he had seen the faces about the fire's circle—most there agreed. But none would voice condemnation or appoint trial until all the People be present, the Matawaye and the Grannach both. He stared around, wondering anew at these people who trusted so well in their god to judge, and would condemn no one before all have a voice. It was not at all like Evander.

Then Yazte nudged him and offered him the flask again, and he shook his head, and said, "Thank you, brother, but no. My wife is over there, and I'd . . ."

What he might have said was lost under the Lakanti's roar of laughter, and he blushed as he heard the words that trailed his parting heels.

"A man in love, no? There she sits, and he runs to her."

Arcole paused long enough to make a rude gesture that elicited fresh gales of humor from Yazte. He smiled at Arrhyna and put his hand against Flysse's cheek.

"How is he?"

Flysse said, "Mending faster than any mortal man. His wounds knit up like streams in the Moon of Ripe Berries. He'll be well enough to ride to Matakwa, I think, save his face shall be always marked. And his hair."

It came to Arcole that they spoke the language of the People, not their own. Save, he wondered, was it not now their own—the tongue of their adopted land, their savior people? He asked, "Can I see him?"

And Arrhyna answered, "Best leave it, eh? He sleeps now, and I think you'd wake him. Lhyn is with him."

"Then can I," he asked, "take my wife away for a while?"

Arrhyna shrugged and smiled at Flysse: a shared glance that was full of promised hope. "I think that Lhyn and I might well care for Davyd awhile," she said. "So yes."

Arcole took Flysse's hand and lifted her upright. She smiled as she came into his arms and put hers around him. Then said to Arrhyna, "Does he wake you'll call me, eh?"

Arrhyna smiled and nodded. "Save we both be otherwise engaged, sister."

Arcole could not understand why he blushed; nor care.

20   To the Hills

Davyd sat the buckskin uncomfortably, the steady movement of the horse seeming to tug at the healing stitches decorating his body so that each one became a dull, fiery talon sunk in his skin and he felt as awkward as the first time he'd sat a horse. He did his best to ignore the pain, fixing his face in what he hoped was a calm and stoic smile, acknowledging the greetings of the riders who passed, telling himself it should not be long before they halted; wishing he believed himself.

The People spread out in a great, magnificent column behind, and it was a strange sensation to ride at the head of such a multitude, as if he no less than Morrhyn and Rannach and the others led them. They moved slow—which was a blessing—even did they carry the lodges on the carts Rannach had designed. Still, the rough-hewn wheels handled the ground swifter and smoother than the poles of the travois—which Davyd could not help somewhat regretting.

They told him he healed faster than any mortal man had right, and that must be the Maker's blessing, but still the wounds pained him and he wished the Maker heal him swifter. Then felt guilty at that thought: he should be dead. No man had survived a wolverine's attack alone and naked. He touched, unthinking, the skin Tekah had brought him, wondering. It was somewhat of an embarrassment, that skin, and also . . . He was not sure, could not define it properly. He wore it because Tekah had skinned the beast and cured the hide and given it to him with pride, and now it sat across his shoulders, the still-fanged skull surmounting his head. Where, he thought with yet another spurt of amazement, his hair was all white, like Morrhyn's.

That had been the hardest thing to accept. The wounds, yes—he must admit he was somewhat proud of those for all they hurt him, for they were battle scars, and he had, after all, defeated the beast. But to find his hair gone pale as snow was . . . He could not define it. Did it mark him, as the Matawaye believed, touched by the Maker? Like Morrhyn, holy? He did not feel holy. He had dreamed and believed that the Maker had sent him those dreams, but he also believed that Taza had ambushed him, and for that felt a great resentment that he must struggle to conceal. . . .

Morrhyn and Kahteney had come to him when the women allowed he was fit enough to stand questioning, and spoken at length. Then Rannach and Tekah, Arcole and Yazte, had come to say their pieces. And he had told all he could remember past the hunger and the fear and the fever and the fight, and wondered if Taza *had* truly sought to kill him. And when he thought on it longer, he had decided it must have been so—and wondered what to say, to do, about his enemy.

But he could not be sure. What evidence there was, was only circumstantial, and he could not give them—Tekah especially—what they wanted: the yea or nay of it, not firmly and without doubt. And he had realized that he could not condemn a man on only hearsay, and so told them only the truth: that he had seen no one in the wood.

That had seemed to please Morrhyn, Kahteney less so, though both wakanishas still showed doubt that Davyd had not understood until Morrhyn explained.

"Listen," the Prophet had said, "it is possible—I say only that! no more, eh?—that some power cloaks Taza."

Davyd had felt a terrible fear then and started up from his bed so that the stitches threatened to split asunder. Morrhyn had pushed him gently back and urged him to calm and said, "When you're better mended I'd give you pahé again, that we all dream on this."

"I did!" Davyd had cried. "I dreamed in the wood, Morrhyn! There are things I must tell you."

And Morrhyn had said, "Later, eh? First, let those wounds

heal and then we'll dream. Do you and I and Kahteney take the pahé, then you can share those wood dreams with us."

And it had been so, though none could properly interpret the meanings, and surely there had been nothing in any of their shared dreams that might convincingly condemn Taza. He remained an enigma.

"But these other things," Morrhyn had said, "seem to me significant. I wonder if the Breakers do not trail us somehow."

"In Ket-Ta-Thanne?" Kahteney had asked nervously. "Another world?"

"They inhabit no world," Morrhyn had answered, "and all the worlds, I think. They are . . ."

Davyd had never thought to see Morrhyn look afraid. It made him afraid, as if some solid platform had been snatched from under him.

"What does it mean?" he had asked. "What do my dreams mean?"

Kahteney said, low and slow, "I thought the Maker gave us this world. I thought we were safe here."

Morrhyn had chuckled then, humorlessly. "Do you not remember the story of the Green Turtle and the Grass Boy?"

Kahteney had nodded and looked lost. Davyd had asked, "What is that story?"

"An old one," Morrhyn had replied, "from the first days in Ket-Ta-Witko. Listen: The Grass Boy was fat from all the grass he'd made—and comfortable, because there was no one else there to eat it. But then the Green Turtle came and ate it, and the Grass Boy made himself a spear—which was the first in the world—and threw it at the Green Turtle. It bounced off the turtle's shell and the turtle laughed and said, 'That cannot hurt me, but if you go across the river the Water Daughters made, I'll eat only the grass on this side.' So the Grass Boy went across the river on the backs of the Daughters and seeded the land there with his spit so that the grass grew and he could eat again. But then the Green Turtle ate all the grass on his side of the river and got hungry.

"The Grass Boy laughed at him, because he had plains full

of grass and the Green Turtle had nothing now, and the Grass Boy did not believe the Water Daughters would allow the turtle to cross the sacred river. But the turtle could swim, and he plunged into the water and snapped at the Daughters when they tried to stop him, and crawled out on the Grass Boy's side and set to eating the grass there. And when the Grass Boy asked him why he had broken his word, the Green Turtle said, 'That's my nature. I like to eat everyone's grass.' Do you understand?"

Kahteney and Davyd had both nodded. Then Kahteney asked, "You say they come against us again?"

"I say only," Morrhyn had returned, "that we should not trust the Green Turtle; nor think the river holds him off."

Davyd had said, "And my dreams? Are they not of invasion? Tell me what they mean."

"I cannot," Morrhyn had said. "I think we had best leave all this until the Matakwa. I'd hear what the Grannach have to say."

And so they rode, the vast, splendid column of all the People, the Commacht and the Lakanti, the remnants of the Naiche and the Aparhaso, those Tachyn who remained loyal to Dohnse—or to the concept of the People Chakthi had forgotten. All of them—the survivors of Ket-Ta-Witko, that the Breakers had denied them and taken from them—going to Matakwa in a new world, in Ket-Ta-Thanne.

And Davyd rode, headily, at the front of the great mass. Rannach rode to his left, Tekah a little way behind, Morrhyn on the farther side. Fat Yazte was there, and Kahteney; Arcole on his right. He wondered where Flysse was, and supposed she went with Arrhyna and Lhyn, farther down the column.

He turned in his saddle, looking back, and folk caught his eye and smiled, or raised lances in salute, which filled him with a guilty pride so that he turned again to the fore. The movement tugged at his wounds and he winced, which brought Arcole's head around, the older man's eyes filled with concern.

I I I

"Are you . . ." Arcole hesitated. Davyd was become something more than the scareling thief he'd taken under his unwilling wing on the *Pride of the Lord.*

Davyd tightened his smile and said, "Yes," understanding. "Don't worry."

Arcole shrugged—God, but it was hard to understand him since the wood—and shifted the musket to a more comfortable position across his thighs. "We could halt soon."

"No." Davyd shook his newly white head. "Best we find the Meeting Ground soon as we can, no?"

"As you say." Arcole smiled to hide his confusion and turned his horse away in search of Flysse.

He found her down the column and reined in beside her. The roan and the gray snapped at one another and then decided to make friends. Flysse asked, "How is he?"

"Hurting, though he'll not admit it." Arcole shrugged. "It's as if he *needs* to ignore the pain. I think he'd get to the Meeting Ground without delay."

Flysse smiled and took his hand. "And would you not be the same, husband? Were you hurt, but felt a need to tell your story?"

"It's not the same." Arcole shook his head. "He's old before his time. That hair . . ."

"Marks him," Flysse interrupted. "The Maker's mark."

"Do you believe that?" Arcole asked. "Truly?"

"Yes." Flysse nodded slowly, solemnly. "Was it not Davyd guided us out of Grostheim, and saw us safe along the river, through to here?"

Arcole ducked his head in agreement.

"And was it not Davyd's dreams brought us to the Grannach?" Flysse asked.

Again, Arcole nodded: "Yes."

"Then why doubt him now?" Flysse wondered. "Trust him."

"He speaks," Arcole said, "of war. Of things I cannot believe can be. Alliance between Salvation and Ket-Ta-Thanne? How?"

Flysse said, "I don't know, only that I trust him."

"As do I," Arcole said, "though I cannot understand how."

"Then trust me," Flysse said.

And Arcole nodded and held her hand tight and said, "Yes."

Fools, all of them. Fools piled on fools, all trust and honor, none of it counting for aught save the sorrow they deserve for denying you. They'll pay the price of their foolishness, believe me. Oh, yes; and a heavy price, a steep toll on their stupidity. At Matakwa: I'll show you then, and they'll all tremble in fear of you and know that they should have listened to you before, because you are great as any of them—Morrhyn or Kahteney, or the upstart Davyd. Yes, I'll show you how to best them all at the Matakwa.

Taza no longer cared whether the voice was his own or some other, only that it promised him what he wanted. Neither could he any longer decide between what it and he truly desired: there was no longer any difference between his ambition and the voice's, and he was seduced.

He smiled as he rode, all docile, knowing he was watched, and held his own council—his and the power's—and wondered what the voice's promise should deliver.

Scouts rode out ahead, not for fear of attack—Morrhyn had suggested, and so it had been agreed, that nothing be said of Davyd's dreams before Matakwa—but to check the land and alert the Grannach to the People's coming. Davyd had tentatively suggested that Tekah be one, but the young Commacht had instantly rejected the notion, insisting that his place was at Davyd's side, and so he rode attendant on his self-selected ward.

Davyd found it somewhat embarrassing: he could hardly shift in his saddle without Tekah asking was he well, did he need rest; and nights, Tekah stationed himself guardian outside Davyd's lodge, armed against further betrayal for all Taza was himself well guarded. It was not said, not aloud, but word had spread swift amongst the Matawaye that at Matakwa Taza would be accused of attempting Davyd's murder, and so it was as if Davyd were protected by all of the

People, for they looked on him now as Morrhyn's proven acolyte. Had he not the Prophet's hair? Had the Maker not blessed him with dreams and given him the strength to slay the wolverine?

At night, free of Tekah's vigilance, Davyd would yank off the skin and fling it irritably across his lodge.

"It is a mark of honor," Morrhyn said. "Of courage."

"It's a skin," Davyd returned. "The skin of an animal I don't even remember killing."

"Perhaps because it was the Maker slew it," Morrhyn said.

Davyd shrugged. "I'd sooner He'd slain it before it clawed me."

"You hurt? Shall I ask the women attend you?" Morrhyn asked.

And Davyd shook his head. "Thank you, no. I'd sooner speak of my dreams."

"You have," Morrhyn said, "and you know that neither I nor Kahteney have answers."

"Even so." Davyd lay back on furs that came—praise the Maker!—from buffalo and bear, not wolverines, and said, "I dreamed I fought. I dreamed I was a wakanisha and a warrior, both. But you say that cannot be; does that mean my dreams were false?"

"I cannot say." Morrhyn shrugged, reaching to the kettle heating over the fire. "Tea?"

"I'd sooner tiswin," Davyd said.

Morrhyn smiled and went to the lodgeflap, speaking with the waiting Tekah. In moments a flask of tiswin was brought—Tekah inquiring, again, if aught else was needed.

"I wish," Davyd muttered when the flap was closed on the warrior's earnest face, "that he'd not mother me so."

"He blames himself for what happened," Morrhyn said. "Since that first day he feels a debt, it's a thing of honor."

"I know," Davyd grunted. "But still . . . Ach, Morrhyn, please fill me a cup."

The Prophet nodded and spilled the liquor into the clay mug, passed it to Davyd. "I think," he said, "that we must wait before we can understand your dreams properly. Best wait until we speak with the Grannach."

Davyd drank deep of the tiswin and sighed. "I'd know now," he said.

"Be patient," Morrhyn urged. "Perhaps the Grannach shall have news of events beyond the mountains."

"And is it like before?" Davyd scowled impatient at the flames. "Shall the Breakers creep up on us?"

"We cannot know, but we can be ready," Morrhyn answered. "For now, we can only wait."

And Davyd must be content with that, which chafed him sore as his wounds.

Taza lay on poorer furs than the upstart, but won by his own skills—not gifted!—and pondered the wonders to come. He was, he knew, become a pariah amongst the People. His foster parents no longer welcomed him to their lodge and he had set up his own, which he knew was watched for fear he make another attempt on Davyd's life. Such was unfair without proof, but even so the solitude suited him, allowed him the privacy to commune with the newfound power.

That came stronger in the night when he lay alone, the voice clearer, filling him with confidence and purpose so that he knew what he must do. What he would do, and teach all these fools the lesson they deserved.

He hoped the upstart stranger's wounds fester and poison him; if not . . .

Then he shall die anyway, the voice said. *We'll slay him together, you and I. I'll give him to you for a plaything. Him and all the others who laugh at you and condemn you.*

Taza closed his eyes and slept, warmed by his hatred.

The mountains bulked ahead, like vast walls erected against the land beyond, great bastions that must surely hold out Salvation, hold the People free from Evander and the Autarchy. They rose up from the oceanic swell of the grass-girdled foothills, climbing higher than the timber could reach, to vaunt themselves indomitably against the hazy heavens. Arcole could not see the topmost peaks, only the cloud that masked them, as if stone and sky met and blended in impassable barricade, but still he touched absently at the scar branded on his cheek and thought of that country beyond, of all it meant, and of Davyd's confusing dreams.

"They cannot reach us here." Flysse's voice intruded on his musings and he smiled, not quite cheerfully.

"No? Are you sure?"

Flysse gestured at the bulwarks ahead. "How could they? Think you the Grannach would grant Evander passage?"

"No." Arcole shook his head. "Not likely. But even so . . ."

"Leave off," she urged. "Doubtless we'll learn the import of Davyd's dreams in time, but meanwhile we've Matakwa to attend. You know what that shall mean?"

"That we become . . ." Arcole assumed a dignified expression, a portentous tone. ". . . *adopted* Commacht?"

"That, yes; which is no small thing," Flysse replied, more serious. Then more serious still: "And Davyd . . ."

"Shall become what he becomes," Arcole said, and felt his doubts return. "Which shall be what, eh? Are his dreams true, then . . ."

"We shall find out in time," Flysse finished for him, "but until then, do we enjoy what we have now?"

Arcole nodded, but still the doubts lingered. He put on a cheerful face and studied the mountains ahead, wondering what lay beyond them now, in Salvation and in all the unknown worlds.

21 Matakwa

The site chosen for the new Meeting Ground was similar in many ways to the old, and did it lack the overseeing mass of the Maker's Mountain, still it was hill-ringed and woody, with a narrow stream meandering across the lush grass that covered the floor of the bowl. One pass granted ingress from the west, another to the east, showing a rocky trail that wound away upward to lose itself amongst the peaks. That was the direction from which the Grannach would come, and the People waited on them. Lodges covered the grass now, fewer than in Ket-Ta-Witko, but nonetheless an impressive number, with the owners' favorite horses tethered close by, the rest herded to the south, tended by youths.

Morrhyn looked out across the camp and felt a mingling of pride and sadness. The People had survived the Breakers, but so many had been lost. And were Davyd's dreams true . . . Rannach caught his eye and he shrugged and said, "We can only wait," guessing the nature of his akaman's unspoken question.

"And there are other matters," Yazte said. "Not least, Taza."

"Not least," Kahteney corrected, "the adoption ceremonies."

"Ach!" Yazte shook his large head. "Those are surely no more than formalities. They're Matawaye now in the eyes of the People."

"Not in Taza's," Kahteney murmured, and looked to where the twist-footed young man had pitched his tent.

The lodge was new, and newly painted with the eagle emblem of the Lakanti, as if Taza challenged his clan to deny him. It was set on the fringe of the Lakanti grouping, a little way apart from the rest, with Taza's horse on a grazing string and the youth himself squatting in the sun, industriously stitching a torn shirt. Was he aware of being observed, he gave no sign, but seemed entirely content.

Morrhyn frowned, thinking the malcontent near great an enigma as Davyd. He surely owned the dreaming talent, but all wound up with the pride and ambition that persuaded both Morrhyn and Kahteney he should not be named wakanisha. It was hard, for all he told himself he should not judge until both sides were heard in council, to doubt that Taza had sought to slay Davyd. But how to prove that? His dreams told him nothing, and neither had Davyd or Kahteney dreamed of Taza. So was it as he feared, that somehow the youth clouded the talent? And were that so, what unrecognized power did he own?

Morrhyn sighed unthinking, and Rannach looked to him, giving him back his own words: "We can only wait."

"Yes." Morrhyn forced a smile and ducked his head in agreement, letting his eyes rove on to where Davyd's lodge was pitched.

That stood beside his own, the shared lodge of Flysse and Arcole close by, Tekah's—inevitably—near. It should be hard, Morrhyn thought, for anyone to get close to Davyd with that watchdog alert.

Then a shout from the eastern edge of the bowl caught his attention and Rannach's hand clasped his shoulder.

"They come! See?"

A column wound down the rocky trail, its leaders already within the shadow of the pass, bellowing greetings that echoed magnified off the stone walls, so that the Grannach arrived as if heralded by roiling thunder. At such a distance they looked like animated, hairy boulders, all small and round and hard, drawing their little handcarts piled high with trade goods.

Rannach said, "I'd greet them properly," and was gone running to his horse.

"And I," Yazte added, though his run was more of lumber akin to a bear's charge.

Morrhyn turned to Kahteney. "Best prepare, eh, brother?"

Kahteney nodded and they walked at a dignified pace to their lodges.

Davyd lay near naked and totally embarrassed in the shade of his lodgeflap. Flysse and Lhyn tended his wounds, and for all he denied they pained him and he had no need of such ministrations, they ignored him, applying womanly wisdom to damage and protests alike. Those wounds *would* be dressed, and he accept it else they summon Arrhyna from where she nursed Debo and ask she hold him down. He had no choice save to acquiesce, even when he heard the shouting and endeavored to rise.

"Easy, easy." Lhyn set a hand against his chest and pushed him gently back. "This first, eh? Then you can greet Colun. Let him and Marjia come to you, eh?"

"I'm . . ." Davyd began to say, and then shrugged, sinking back: as well argue as try to wrestle the Grannach.

Even so, it was difficult to lie supine and impatient as all around the Meeting Ground exploded tumultuous. But wait he must until Lhyn was satisfied and declared that he might now dress, and Flysse added her consent, and he was left alone to tug on his clothes himself—which was a mercy for which he thanked the Maker, thinking it quite likely the two women insist they perform that office for him.

He emerged from his lodge to find Flysse and Arcole outside, Morrhyn and Kahteney there, Arrhyna holding Debo's hand, and Tekah hovering behind. Briefly Davyd wondered if the Commacht feared the Grannach might attack him. Then Colun and Marjia came striding over the grass, Rannach and Yazte walking their horses alongside in honor guard, and Davyd forgot Tekah as he smiled at his friends.

"It's good to see you," he said. "The Maker bless you."

"The Maker damn whoever did that to you." Colun was blunt as ever. He halted staring up at Davyd with a mixture of sympathy and anger in his gray eyes. "Is he not already dead, name him and I'll slay him."

Davyd had no doubt but that each word was sincerely meant. He said, quickly lest any other—especially Tekah—answer on his behalf, "It was a wolverine, Colun."

It was strange to see stark surprise on the face of a rock. Almost, Davyd chuckled as Colun gaped, then turned to Marjia, whose big blue eyes showed only concern. "Tell me." Colun returned his gaze to Davyd. "No, wait! Clearly there's a great tale here, and great tales are best told over a flask of tiswin, no?"

From where she stood with Rannach, his arm around her, Arrhyna said innocently, "I thought you made your own now, Colun."

"We do." Colun beamed. "Thanks to you, we've a goodly supply. Save . . . Ugh!" He broke off as his wife's elbow dug his ribs.

"The thought of Matakwa was celebrated," Marjia continued, "and then our departure. The more as this is the first we women have attended. And, of course, fortification was needed on the journey here." She glanced archly at her husband. "Some things do not change, and consequently our stocks are depleted."

"Near gone," Colun agreed, his face solemn, "and me with a thirst. And," he looked again at Davyd, "a great tale to hear. Which surely cannot be told without . . ." He groaned again as his wife's elbow once more collided with his ribs.

"Tiswin," Marjia said, smiling. "So—why do you men not go tell your tales and drink your tiswin while I go with my friends, who shall likely have a different story. Save," she encompassed both Davyd and Arcole in her look, "I am glad to see you both alive and . . ." She fixed Davyd with an almost accusing glance. "Reasonably healthy."

Davyd shrugged, not knowing what to say.

"And I, sweet Marjia, am pleasured by the sight of you." Arcole flourished a bow that might have graced some Levanite dowager. "Your loveliness is unchanged."

Davyd wondered if Marjia blushed at that. It was hard to tell, but surely she smiled and patted Arcole's cheek, which rocked his head sideways and left him a moment blinking. He wondered if he should attempt some equally florid compliment, and decided he could not; the gutter was a poor schoolground for such matters. So he only smiled and watched the women gathered up by Marjia as if by some flaxen-haired avalanche that carried them away and left the men alone.

"So?" Colun demanded. "Tiswin?"

Rannach laughed loud. "The Maker knows, old friend, but you've not changed."

"Should I?" Colun asked. "Should you like me better?"

"No." Rannach shook his head, then studied Colun as if appraising a likely horse. "I doubt I could like you better."

"Ach!" Colun made a dismissive fist. "Leave the soft words for your pretty wife, eh? Only give me . . ."

Before he could complete the sentence, Rannach and Yazte, Arcole and Davyd, even Morrhyn and Kahteney, said in unison, "Tiswin!"

The flask went around the circle and the People stayed distant, aware that such matters were discussed as should come before the Full Council, when all might have their say. For now, it was a thing of akamans and wakanishas and the creddan of the Grannach. And did Tekah hover in the background, then Tekah was Tekah, and blood-sworn to defend and guard Davyd—whom all acknowledged was to be Morrhyn's successor. And what matter that Arcole sat with them, for was he not one of them and favored of both Rannach and the Prophet, Morrhyn? None would argue that: not Morrhyn's wish, nor much Rannach's. The People had come to depend on those two, who had come down from the mountains of Ket-Ta-Witko to bring word of the Breakers and save them from annihilation.

And so the People enjoyed this first night of true Matakwa, when the Grannach were come again amongst them, and entertained their Stone Folk friends and drank much tiswin, and roasted the best meat, thinking that on the morrow the trading would begin—Grannach metalware for skins and clay pots; sound blades for beadwork and decorated shirts; furs for arrowheads and lance points. Matakwa as it had been in Ket-Ta-Witko!

And did any think of Taza, they set the thought aside: he would be judged, and were he guilty then surely the Council

must know it and decide his sentence. But that was for the
morrow: this night was for celebration.

For most.

It shall be soon now. Are you strong?

Taza said, inside his head, safe inside his lodge, Yes: are
you with me I am strong.

*It shall not be easy, but the reward shall be great. Are you
sure?*

Yes. What shall be my reward?

*All that you want: Davyd's death; Morrhyn's. Respect. That
the People lower their heads before you and shudder at your
words.*

Truly? So much?

*Truly. You shall be as thunder over the earth, mightier than
the buffalo herds when they migrate. You shall have dominion
over them all.*

And I need only do what you ask?

What I tell you, yes. Shall you do that?

Yes!

Then only wait and I shall show you the way.

I shall!

Good, we are agreed.

"I've seen nothing," Colun said, reaching for the flask. "The
Tachyn—the Maker damn them!—seem to have given up
their assaults. The forests that side are quiet."

"And you've seen naught of the . . ." Morrhyn hesitated
at the unfamiliar word, "Evanderans?"

"No." Colun shook his head. "Nothing at all. Do they
build these fort things, then it must be far away. Not where
we can see them—which means a long way away."

"And yet . . ." Morrhyn hesitated, glancing at Davyd.
"The dreams . . ."

Colun shrugged. "I can only tell you what I know—that
Chakthi no longer brings his Maker-forsaken Tachyn against
our hills, and I have seen none of these . . . Evanderans?

Neither the ones marked like our friends, nor the . . . soldiers?"

Kahteney looked at Davyd and frowned a question.

Davyd said, "I know only what I dreamed. I do not understand it."

"I think," Morrhyn said, "that it were best we conduct the ceremonies and then build a wa'tenhya. Perhaps if you are formally named . . ."

Davyd said, "Perhaps," feeling unsure.

Colun said, "Is there any more tiswin?"

Those rites adopting the newcomers into the People were conducted the next day. While the sun yet trembled on the edge of the encircling hills, Arrhyna came for Flysse, Rannach for Arcole, and Morrhyn for Davyd, and they were led in silence to the center of the Meeting Ground, where all the Matawaye and the visiting Grannach waited. The previous night's feast fire was built up again, and the three were led three times around the flames. Then each in turn, their sponsors asked their wishes, and they answered as they had been tutored: "I would be one with the People in the eyes of the Maker." Then each sponsor walked the circle, asking did any present object, and when there came only a great shout of agreement, returned to the waiting adoptee and intoned formally: "The People accept you as one with them."

Then Morrhyn and Kahteney shook rattles over the heads of the new Matawaye, and gave them each the feather of an eagle, and spoke the ritual words: "Praise the Maker, and may He welcome these folk amongst us. May they become as one with us and be named as us—Matawaye."

The three lowered their heads as the sun came up over the peaks and struck full into the bowl. It illumined the grass and the lodges, light streaming radiant over the camp as if in blessing, and then all the akamans and both wakanishas cried out, and all the People came from where they waited to gather round in a great milling throng that threatened to overwhelm them with good wishes and hearty backslaps, and invitations to feast—though those were scarce necessary, for already meat was roasting on the fire and the chill dawn air filled with the succulent odor of venison and buffalo. Colun and Marjia came laughing, he with a flask and she with cups, and toasts were drunk and the celebratory feasting began.

It was chaotic. For all they'd lived long amongst the People, they were now truly Matawaye and therefore welcomed anew. Arcole had no sooner settled beside Flysse, a buffalo rib dripping fat over his hand, than he was beckoned away by Dohnse, who'd offer him tiswin while Flysse was carried off by laughing women, and Kahteney came shyly, but nonetheless beaming, to invite Davyd to share quail's eggs. The day, it seemed, was to be spent in celebration.

"Your naming shall come later," Morrhyn told Davyd when the young man found his way back to the central fire. "Tomorrow, perhaps; or the next day."

"And the dreaming?" Davyd asked, wiping grease from his chin. "You and I and Kahteney?"

Morrhyn hesitated.

Davyd belched—the Maker knew, but he'd eaten more than enough—and could not help a slight frown as he recognized a curious reluctance in the wakanisha. "That first, no?" he asked. "Surely it must be so—I tell you, Morrhyn, I dreamed that I was wakanisha and warrior, both; but you say that cannot be." Now he hesitated, troubled by his own thoughts and the clouding of Morrhyn's pale blue eyes. "So— were my dreams true, how can you name me?"

Morrhyn had sooner this not come up: he elected to put his faith in the Maker and trust in those answers, but Davyd forced him to commitment. "I do not know," he said honestly.

"Then best put off my naming," Davyd said. "At least, until you've dreamed."

Morrhyn nodded slowly. There was such wisdom in this young man as must surely make him a great wakanisha; and the Maker knew but Morrhyn *would* name him his successor, confident that could only be for the good of all the People. But it was as Davyd said, and that Morrhyn could not understand at all.

"Perhaps best," he allowed, hearing his own reluctance. "Do you and I and Kahteney dream, and then we shall decide."

∎   ∎   ∎

*Only sleep and I shall show you the way to all your dreams.
Forget what they said, for I shall make you strong enough that
they cringe before your wrath and eat their laughter like bitter
ashes.*

Taza curled on his furs, comforted by the promises. The
Maker knew, but they'd laughed at him when he made his
rightful claim to naming, and that—for all the voice's assur-
ance—had hurt. They'd laugh at him? Not at Davyd, but at
him; and soon look to see him tried before the Council. He
had scant doubt of the outcome: all faces were turned from
him, smiling toward the upstart Davyd.

But they do not understand, the voice said. *They do not
understand what you are. Heed me and they shall know.*

Into his furs, Taza murmured, "Yes."

Good, said the voice, gentle now as a mother's caress. *So
listen, learn; and all shall be yours.*

Taza slept and dreamed and knew in his dreaming what he
must do: what must be done, and how.

Colun turned restlessly, shifting from side to side so that his
snores gusted like some loud and veering wind. Marjia retrieved her share of the sleeping furs and sighed, thinking that
her husband had drunk somewhat too deep of the tiswin, and
eaten too well—even for a Grannach—and therefore found
sleep hard. She lifted up and gently stroked his craggy brow,
and for a while Colun lay still, his breathing even, but then,
when she thought him sound asleep, he began to stir again,
snoring and mumbling.

Finally Marjia prodded him—there were limits even to
Grannach patience—and was startled when he lurched upright, reaching for his ax and crying out as if afraid.

"What, what?" she murmured, clutching at the hand that
quested after the moon-bladed ax. "There's nothing, eh?
Only dreams."

For an instant she did not recognize her husband's face as
he stared around, and held him tight for fear he strike out
sleeping.

Then Colun shook himself like a small bear emerging from a stream and shuddered and returned her grip.

"Maker!" His voice was dry and harsh. "I thought . . ."

"What?" Marjia looked into his blurred eyes and felt herself afraid. "Only dreams, my husband."

Colun rubbed at his face as if to wipe away some horrid taint. "I thought," he said in a slow and hollow voice, "that I opened the tunnels to the Breakers."

"A dream, no more than that." Marjia held him tighter. "Only a dream."

"It was as if," he said hoarsely, "they came inside my head and turned me withershins."

"Old memories." She clutched him firm as he trembled feverishly. The Maker knew, but she'd never known her husband like this. She'd seen him face the Breakers in battle and strike them down. She knew him brave, but as she held him and felt him shake in her arms like a youngling new-woke from nightmare, she felt a great dread rise in her.

"Old memories?" Colun released himself from her grip that he find the water jug. "I've not had such before."

"You've not attended Matakwa," she said, "not since . . ."

"No." Colun drank, splashed more water over his face. "Not since that last." He chuckled humorlessly. "Shall this be the same?"

"How so?" Marjia demanded. "Surely we are safe in Ket-Ta-Thanne."

"The Maker grant it so." Colun relaxed a little, sighing near noisily as he'd snored. "But even so, it was as if some vile worm crawled through my mind, seeking answers I'd not give it. It . . ."

"Hush, hush." Marjia stroked his brow as if he were a babe. "Only dreams, eh?"

"Perhaps," he allowed. "I trust so."

"Surely so," she told him. "Dreams born of too much tiswin and rich meat. Now sleep, eh?"

Colun nodded and lowered his stocky body back amongst the furs. Marjia held him until he began to snore again, and this time she did not prod him but only watched, a sentinel in the lonely night.

∎ ∎ ∎

The herbs were easy to find. None watched him save when he walked amongst the People, and they were busy with their feasting, their welcoming of the newcomers—when he went away from the camp he went alone, easily able to find those plants the voice told him were needed.

It was not much harder to place them where the voice urged—in water jugs and tiswin flasks, for he was a pariah and therefore like a shadow or an invisible thing. Even Tekah was occupied with the celebrations; never far from Davyd's side or back, but less vigilant. Doubtless, Taza thought, anticipating the outcome of the trial.

Save—he laughed silently, enjoying the thought of the disappointment he'd deliver, the anguish; most of all, the sweet taste of revenge for all his slights—there would be no trial did all go well. And it should: he no longer doubted any of the voice's promises.

He sprinkled the last of his herbs and stole a rib of buffalo, a chunk of meaty venison, and returned to his lodge to wait.

The Moon of the Turning Year stood high and full over the Meeting Ground, bathing the sleeping camp in silver light. A night breeze rustled through the trees, like a reply to the soft laughter of the stream. An owl hooted from the timber and a nightjar called; in the high hills a gray wolf howled and was answered from afar. A dog barked briefly and was hushed by a sleepy man; the horses shuffled a moment and were quiet—they were safe here, amongst so many of the two-legs who rode them and fed them.

And the People were safe. They slept comfortable in this new land, at this new Matakwa, and all was well.

Taza came from his lodge shadow-decked and silent as a Night Walker. He *was* a Night Walker: the voice had promised him that—that he'd not be seen or halted, but only achieve his purpose and prove himself and own his vengeance in full measure. Taza smiled wolfishly and obeyed the dictates of his heart and the voice.

Rannach's lodge stood close on the center of the Meeting

Ground. The big fire there was burned down now, banked against the night and spitting somewhat, its dulled glow out-washed by the moon so that the bodies sprawled around, all wrapped in furs and blankets, were like snow-covered corpses, unseeing. And Taza the Night Walker went invisible amongst them.

Rannach's stallion nickered softly as he approached, but the herbs he'd fed the horse dulled its senses and it gave no loud warning. Nor did the dogs bark: fed well on this feast day, they knew Taza—the Maker knew but he'd spent enough time in their company when the People ignored him—and watched him pass with sleepy, indifferent eyes.

The lodgeflap was, of course, laced, but his knife was sharp and cut the cords easily. Taza slipped inside on his belly and stared around.

The dung fire at the center afforded him a degree of red light that suited his purpose. He saw Rannach and Arrhyna in one another's arms beneath the sleeping furs, little Debo in his cradle across the width of the lodge. All slept soundly as the voice had promised, lulled by the secreted herbs. Taza smiled and wormed his way to the cradle. He lifted Debo gently, and when the child stirred, stroked a fat cheek, the thatch of red hair. It was tempting to slide his blade between the ribs of the sleepers, across their throats, but he resisted that, knowing their dying cries might give him away and lose him everything the voice had promised. So he only took Debo and slithered out.

He hugged the child to him as he made his way back toward his own lodge, where his horse waited, saddled ready.

Then Tekah appeared, adjusting his breeches, sleepy-eyed.

He stared a moment at Taza, blinking in the moon's light like a day-woken owl.

"What are you doing?" His voice was thick with slumber and tiswin.

Taza said, "Chasing my destiny," and held Debo in his left arm as he slid his knife into his right hand.

Tekah said, "What's that you've got?" And then gasped as he recognized the child Taza held.

Taza said, "Shout and I'll kill him."

Tekah said, "I'll kill you," and stepped forward with up-raised hands.

Taza moved to meet him, Debo a shield between them, and as Tekah hesitated, danced a farther step onward and slid his blade hard up into the soft flesh beneath the warrior's ribs.

Tekah gasped, his eyes starting wide. Taza twisted the blade and stabbed again, still holding Debo before him so that Tekah, even in his pain, dare not risk the baby's life. Tekah's mouth opened and Taza slashed the blade across his throat, cutting off the burgeoning cry, smiling as he watched Tekah's eyes go dull and the man fall down onto his knees with one hand pressed to his belly, the other against his severed windpipe.

He said something that Taza could not understand through the whistling of the blood coming from his throat and lowered his head as if weary. Taza stabbed him once more, in the neck, at the joindure with the backbone, and Tekah grunted and fell onto his face.

Taza smiled and carried Debo off to where his horse waited.

22 The Chase

Arrhyna stirred within the compass of Rannach's arms, not full awake but seeking consciousness against the tug of drugged slumber. There was a wrongness she could not define, but only sensed—and knew, within the deepest parts of her being, that she must awake else all be lost. She forced her eyes open and looked around. The fire was a dull glow at the center of the lodge and Rannach slept on oblivious. Pale dawnlight entered through the laced lodgeflap. Too much light: with a start, she realized the cords were cut. Her eyes swung to Debo's cradle and her shout woke her husband.

"What?" Rannach blinked as he pushed up from the sleeping furs. "Arrhyna?"

He saw his wife on her knees beside the cradle and assumed Debo suffered some illness. Groggily—in the Maker's name, had he really drunk so much tiswin?—he clambered from the furs and moved toward her. And Arrhyna turned and on her face Rannach saw stark fear, utter panic.

"He's gone!" Her voice was strident. "Debo's gone!"

Shock sobered Rannach and dispelled the effects of Taza's potion. He shivered as he saw the empty cradle, myriad possibilities flooding his mind, not one an explanation. He looked around the lodge—hopelessly, for the child could not hide there—and saw the cut lacings of the lodgeflap.

"Maker, no!"

He snatched on his breechclout and was gone from the lodge into the dawn chill, shouting. Arrhyna followed him, tugging on a robe with no thought of modesty as sleepy-eyed warriors and wondering women gathered.

"Debo's taken! Search the camp!"

Morrhyn came up, wrapped in a bearskin, followed close by Davyd, Flysse, and Arcole not far behind. "When?" he asked.

"This night." Rannach stared helplessly at the Dreamer. "Whilst we slept."

"Search Taza's lodge!" Morrhyn wondered why his tongue was so furred, his head pounded so, and felt a terrible suspicion. But that must wait—for now the finding of Debo was paramount.

Led by Rannach, they hurried toward Taza's lodge, and found Tekah's body. Briefly, guilty that he could not concern himself more with the man's death, Rannach touched the corpse, dabbled his fingers in the blood pooled beneath and around.

"He cools. He's been dead for perhaps four hours."

They went on to Taza's lodge and found it deserted, the crook-footed youth's horse gone; and as warriors returned, that three other mounts were stolen, all fleet and sturdy.

"Maker, but he planned this well." Morrhyn spoke his thoughts aloud. Then clutched at Rannach's arm as the akaman shouted for his horse. "No! Rannach, heed me—we cannot know where he takes Debo. Send men to find his tracks first, then go out. Until then, wait here."

"Where he goes?" Rannach took the wakanisha's hand from his arm. "He goes there, no?"

He stabbed an angry finger at the shadowy bulk of the distant mountains. Morrhyn felt a sudden chill that Rannach was so sure, and glanced swiftly at Arrhyna. Her eyes were wide, staring at her husband.

"Why there?" she asked in a hollow voice.

"Why, because he'd curry favor with Chakthi." Rannach turned tortured eyes on them all, on Arrhyna and Lhyn, who stood beside her, on Morrhyn. "He'd bring Chakthi a grand-child."

"You knew?" Morrhyn asked.

Rannach nodded. "I guessed. Vachyr raped my wife, no? And surely Debo bears a marked resemblance to the

Tachyn." He laughed a moment, bitterly, then warmer as he put an arm around his wife's shoulders. "It was nothing to me—Debo was my son, and I love my wife."

"I was not sure." Arrhyna clutched him, wetting his chest with her tears. "I only knew I loved my baby."

"Our son!" Rannach held her tighter. "I loved him no less. And I'll bring him back to you."

"He'll fetch up against the hills." Colun ran fingers through his beard. "He'll not pass them."

"He'll not reach them," Rannach vowed. "I'll run him down ere then."

"Save . . ." Morrhyn trawled his thoughts, seeking those hidden notions, those half-formed suspicions that might clarify the dreadful doubt he felt growing. "Does he take Debo to Chakthi, then he must believe he can cross the mountains."

"He cannot!" Colun promised. "And even does he find his way into the tunnels underhill, then my Grannach will hold him."

"Nor let harm come to Debo," Marjia added.

"Even so, he must *believe* he can reach Chakthi." Morrhyn frowned. "Why would he believe that? Unless he's guidance of some sort."

"No Grannach would stoop so low," Colun barked, his outrage halted by a wave of Morrhyn's hand.

"Not Grannach," the Dreamer said, "but some other." Across the anxious circle he saw Kahteney staring at him, the Lakanti wakanisha's eyes narrowed as he caught the drift of Morrhyn's thoughts. "Our dreams were clouded, no?"

Kahteney nodded silently.

"And there were Davyd's dreams," Morrhyn continued.

"I'd no dreams of this," Davyd said. Then gasped as he, in turn, understood where Morrhyn's thoughts went. "You say the Breakers guide him?"

Almost, he wished he'd not spoken aloud as he saw Arrhyna's face pale, and heard Lhyn's strangled cry, saw Rannach's hands clench tight. But he had dreamed of the invaders, and of soldiers, and of meetings between the People and the Evanderans—and surely, did Taza look to take Debo beyond the mountains, it was a tangible step toward the realization of his dreams. He felt a strange excitement, as if matters moved toward conclusion, leaving no further room for doubt, but only action; and at the same time he felt very cold and afraid. He looked at Rannach and said, "Must you go into Salvation, you'll need a guide."

"I go!" Arcole stepped forward. "I know the forests of Salvation as well as Davyd."

"But you cannot dream of danger, eh?" Davyd smiled forlornly: the Maker knew, but he'd no wish at all to return to Salvation. "And we both bear the exile's brand, so must we go beyond the forests. . . ." He shrugged. It should be ironic were they to fall back into the hands of the Autarchy.

"You're hurt," Flysse reminded him. "Your wounds are not full-healed."

"And it shall be a hard, fast chase," Arcole echoed. "Can you stay in the saddle? Can you not, then best you remain here."

Davyd said again what he did not wish to say: "Does this chase continue into Salvation, then shall you not need my guidance?"

Arcole looked to Morrhyn for support, thinking Davyd in poor shape for a desperate pursuit, but the Commacht Dreamer only sighed and shrugged, and said, "Must you go across the mountains, you'll surely need such help as Davyd can give."

"And do his wounds open," Arcole demanded, "and he begin to bleed?"

"Then he must turn back," Morrhyn said. He looked Davyd square in the eyes. "Does that happen, I'd have your word you'll halt."

Rannach said, impatient, "I'll send men back with him."

Morrhyn said again, still looking at Davyd, "I'd have your word."

Davyd had never thought to argue with Morrhyn, but now he said, "And do I not give it?"

A tight smile thinned the wakanisha's lips, perhaps in approval of his protégé's determination. "Then I'll not give you those herbs and medicines that shall sustain you."

Davyd chuckled bitterly. "Then you've my word."

"Good," Morrhyn said, and grasped the young man's wrist. "Listen, I think perhaps it's the Maker's will you go—

but not to your death! Do what you can, but no more, eh? Do those wounds open, then you return here."

Davyd nodded slowly. "I gave my word, no?"

"Yes, you did," Morrhyn answered, "and when you come back, we'll conduct those ceremonies that shall make you a true Dreamer."

"Perhaps." Davyd met the pale blue gaze unfaltering. "But do I fight? What if I become a warrior?"

"I don't know," Morrhyn answered honestly. "Had we the time to dream, we might find the answer to that."

Rannach interrupted. "But we've no time, eh? Davyd, do you come with us, then let's ride. Are all these fears aright, then I'd take Taza before he reaches the mountains."

"He'll not pass the tunnels," Colun insisted. "Even does he enter, how shall he escape my Grannach?"

"Is he guided by the Breakers . . ." Morrhyn shrugged. ". . . who knows their power?"

"How could they find us?" Kahteney's voice was hoarse, harsh as the planes of his horrified face.

"Perhaps they've not yet; not in Ket-Ta-Thanne, but . . ." Morrhyn hesitated, looking toward the mountains, a vast, dark bulk against the still-dull sky. "But Chakthi's folk dwell there, and was it the Breakers turned the Tachyn mad, then perhaps there's some communication between them now."

"Surely not even Chakthi . . ." Fat Yazte shook a bearlike head. "Surely not even Hadduth . . ."

"Whether or not, it means nothing!" Rannach turned his head, glowering at each in turn, his patience all run out. "My son is taken and I ride after him."

Beyond the western egress of the Meeting Ground the terrain rose in a series of thickly wooded ridges and sweeping mountain meadows. None were difficult to negotiate—the hard part would come later, when the true mountains were reached—and Taza made good time, even must he wind his horse. He had three others, after all, and for now it was imperative he stay ahead of the search parties Rannach would doubtless send after him. He sneered at the thought—even did the Matawaye catch him, still he had Debo as a shield, and all the promises of the voice inside his head. The child gurgled now, settled in a pannier behind Taza's saddle. His initial outrage on waking to find himself carried off on horse-back was replaced with pleasure at this unusual turn of events, and he napped and woke and settled down to watch the countryside go by. Taza—guided by the voice—had brought food and drink for the child, and when Debo complained he'd pass him juicy buffalo meat and let the young-ling suck on the waterskin he'd filled with milk. It seemed enough, and he was able to feed the boy from the saddle, without stopping: he dared not halt, not with Rannach doubt-less blood-raged behind him.

And so, when the paint horse foundered on the rim of a meadow where a steep trail climbed up winding through stands of new-leafed aspen, and stumbled as it reached the grass, its head downhung and lather white all down its chest and legs, he dismounted. Took off his saddle and the pannier holding Debo, and slung them on a white pony taken from Tekah's string. Then he set off again, at the same desperate pace, trusting in the voice to bring him safely through and show him the way past the hills ahead. He had no other choice now.

The paint horse watched him go and made no move to follow.

All the warriors would have gone out with Rannach had he not forbade it, but he elected only fifteen to that pursuit. The rest he urged to patrol the Meeting Ground a day's ride out, and did they find Taza's trail, to bring both Taza and Debo—most definitely Debo—back alive.

Morrhyn was proud of him, for the constraint he showed and the calm he forced on himself as he organized both the hunt and the running of the camp in his absence, more when he counseled Yazte to remain, charged with holding the People in order and to prepare against the possibility of the Breakers.

That word had spread fast, and Morrhyn was largely occu-pied with assuring the Matawaye that he'd not dreamed of attack, nor was any likely, as Rannach prepared to leave.

Davyd and Arcole rode with him—the assumption tacit between them all that they must perhaps return into Salvation.

"The Maker grant it not be so," Flysse whispered into Arcole's chest, "but must you—take care, eh?"

"I've you to come back to." He stroked her hair, wishing he'd no need to go. "So, yes: I'll take care. I'd not lose you, my love."

Davyd watched as they embraced, and could not help wondering how it should feel to have Flysse's lips on his, to see that look in her eyes. And then she was looking at him, and hugging him, and admonishing him to caution, and he felt only embarrassment and was grateful when Rannach shouted for them to mount and be gone. He climbed limber astride his horse, gritting his teeth as the stitches in his wounds tugged, promising himself he would not succumb, but ignore the pain and go on to whatever lay ahead.

They rode out at a gallop, each man leading two extra mounts. They went as if on a raiding party, save they wore no paint, kitted for hard travel with little food to weigh them down and only their blankets to sleep in. The Matawaye carried bows, knives, and hatchets; Arcole and Davyd brought with them their muskets and a pistol apiece, all the powder and shot they had left. Colun and his Grannach would have come with them, had Morrhyn not pointed out that even the Stone Folk's pace could not match that of a running horse, nor horses easily carry both a warrior's and a Grannach's weight. So the creddan promised to abide awhile on the Meeting Ground and only when all seemed secure return to his mountains.

"But he'll not pass through," he shouted after them. "Not past my Grannach."

None heard him: all were intent on the chase.

Night fell, colder on the high ground than in the valley, and Debo set to wailing. Taza halted long enough to wrap a blanket about the child and feed him—chew on a strip of jerky himself—but still the boy complained as they pressed on. The novelty of the ride was gone and he longed now for his mother, his father, and familiar surroundings. It was a great temptation to abandon him: his cries split the darkness like the howling of a hungry wolf, but the voice had made Taza understand his importance, and so the crippled youth endeavored to block his ears to the screaming and continued his ascent of the foothills.

It seemed he no longer needed to sleep, as if some vast and undeniable energy filled him and drove him on, or he were a chip of metal drawn to a lodestone. He could not—would not!—deny it, but only go where the voice told him, which was onward and upward to his just ascension. He felt no cold as the night grew older and a wind came down off the peaks, but only heated by his ambition, his desire, warmed and comforted by the promises. Neither did he wonder why he no longer heard the voice. He supposed it came in sleep—for which he had no time or need—and would come again when he achieved his goal. He entertained no doubts, but only certainty, and forced his stolen horses on through the darkness and the chill, uncaring.

The searchers found the paint horse around the midpoint of the day. The animal watched them with weary eyes, torn between curiosity and the temptation of the grass. It followed them a little way as they rode off, but then gave up and returned to its cropping.

"He came this way." Rannach pointed at the tracks. "And he's only three horses now."

"And killing them," Dohnse said. "Can he hope to reach the mountains?"

Rannach looked at the crags, bright in the noonday sun, light sparking off granite and snow, and set to transferring his saddle from the wearied black to a fresher roan. "Does he kill them, likely he can."

"And then go where?" Dohnse asked. "Surely it must be as Colun says—the Grannach shall halt him and hold him."

"Save it's as Morrhyn fears," Rannach answered, his voice bleak.

"Think you so? Truly?" Dohnse shaped a sign of warding. "The Breakers come again?"

Rannach sighed. "I'm no Dreamer, brother; and all I know now is that my son is taken—and I'd have him safe back."

He swung astride the roan and cantered off. The black stallion snorted its protest at the interruption of its grazing and tugged awhile on the rope, then fell into pace behind, drawing a piebald gelding with it.

"Shall we catch him?" Arcole held his musket cradled across his hips. "Have we a chance?"

Davyd answered honestly: "I don't know."

"But your dreams . . ." It was difficult to talk, the pace Rannach set, climbing swift as horses and men were able up steep and winding trails that seemed mostly bare stone, galloping wild when the plateaus came, ducking under branches as they charged through stands of timber.

"They told me nothing of this," Davyd called back. "Only what I've said."

He was grateful that a dense swath of pine fronted their path and they must fall into single file and duck low to avoid the overhanging branches: Arcole's questions were too hard to answer, too heavy with obligation. He had dreamed, yes—but not of this, nor of where it might lead. He feared all Morrhyn's wonderings were true—surely they appeared commensurate with his dreams—and that Taza *was* somehow in communication with the Breakers, or at the least with the Tachyn beyond the hills.

Save, he thought, the Tachyn could not own such power, and so—he forced himself to contemplate the likelihood of it—it *was* the Breakers' hand in this, somehow reaching out across the worlds to guide Taza.

But to what purpose? That he bring Debo to Chakthi, present the Tachyn akaman with the fruit of his son's assault? Why?

He cursed as a branch struck his face and he swung in the saddle, almost losing his musket. He was not so good a rider as he'd thought, and he was afraid.

The Maker knew, but he was afraid.

There grew in him the certainty that Taza *was* guided, and would find a way through the Grannach tunnels, and would take Debo to Chakthi. And then he—his branded cheek seemed to burn at the prospect—must go back into Salvation, back into that land of indentured folk and the Autarchy. For a moment fire flashed before his eyes, like the flames consuming a condemned Dreamer. Then he saw it was only the ending of the pine wood, where the trail came out onto a rising slope of green grass struck vivid by the sun, and he laughed for sheer relief.

"You're cheerful." Arcole came up alongside. Their pace did not slow—neither Rannach nor any others there would allow that. "So tell me, what of your dreams?"

Davyd did not feel cheerful, but he put on a smile and said, "I think the Maker moves us. I think that perhaps all this is somehow a part of my dreaming. To what end, though . . ."

Arcole saw his comrade's face grow solemn and felt somewhat of that dread Davyd experienced. "To Salvation?" he asked. And when Davyd nodded: "Then it shall be the Maker's will, no? And He'll protect us. God knows, I've already promised Rannach I'll go back."

"Yes, and I," Davyd returned, and voiced a silent prayer to the Maker that it not be so, that they catch Taza—at least, rescue Debo—before the mountains.

He would not admit it, but his wounds pained him. The hard riding jarred his ribs where the wolverine's claws had scored him, and he feared the stitches should burst loose and he begin to bleed. The two horses he led behind dragged on his arm and threatened to turn him in the saddle, which dragged the more on his wounds. He thought this as hard or worse a ride as that first terrifying arrival in Ket-Ta-Thanne. And then of how he had mastered horsemanship, and learned the ways of the People, and of Morrhyn's teachings and all they promised, and of how much he loved his life amongst the Matawaye.

And then—for the first time, he realized—he thought of Tekah's body, all cut and bled out, lying alone in the cold gray light of yesterday's dawn, and he felt a great resentment of whatever power or madness of ambition had driven Taza to murder his friend, to kidnap Debo, and he felt suddenly strong. It was as if righteous anger filled him and dulled the pain of his wounds, lending him strength, and he knew that he *would* go on, would not succumb to weakness.

He clenched his teeth and urged his horse onward, aware of Arcole's eyes on him, troubled. Finally, as they slowed their pace to accommodate a narrow trail that wound tortuously up between high walls of naked blue-black stone topped with solitary pines, Arcole asked, "Can you do this? Might you not better return?"

"No." Davyd fixed his comrade with a blazing gaze and shook his head. "I go on."

Arcole shrugged and fell silent. Davyd wished he had given his friend some better response than that look, but he could not: only go on, aware of the anger burning through him, spreading as if feverish. It went past the kidnap of Debo, the murder of Tekah, to encompass all those things might mean, all Morrhyn's reluctantly voiced fears, the warnings of his own dreams in the oak wood. Suddenly he knew beyond doubting that if Taza were guided by the Breakers, then he would stop at nothing to defy and deny and resist whatever foul intentions the invaders had. He would go back into Salvation without demur to fight the greater enemy. He would risk burning for the sake of the People—*his* People now—and perhaps no less for all those other unfortunates beyond the mountains who carried the brand of exile on their bodies. He saw again—as his horse labored up the steep incline and the two spare mounts labored behind—the content of his dreams, and knew with a sudden and frightening certainty that he rode to meet them.

If only, he thought, I knew the outcome.

Save that, as Morrhyn had ofttimes told him, was uncertain. Must be: the Maker did not lay out the paths of men in sure and guided lines, but left the trails open and branching, that men might choose their own way.

Taza, he thought, had chosen his way, just as Chakthi and Hadduth had chosen theirs. And theirs had led to disaster—would Taza's? He vowed that were it in his power, it should not. He would do what he could to prevent that, even unto his own death.

He turned again in the saddle as he topped the rise and came out onto a flat shelf ringed with windblown pines all bent and angled like old, withered men sat talking in a circle, and smiled genuinely at Arcole.

"I'll survive," he said, hoping it be true. "Morrhyn's potions ease me, and I *can* ride."

Arcole nodded, still disturbed by that look, and then looked away as Dohnse shouted.

A white horse he recognized as one of dead Tekah's string lay at the center of the shelf. Crows rose in protest of their arrival, and wolves and foxes, and likely other feeders, had ravaged the corpse, and from its flank a sizable chunk of meat had been cut. There was no sign of a fire, but cold droppings littered the grass, and when Rannach broke one open, he announced Taza a full day or more ahead.

"How can he travel so swift?" Dohnse asked of no one in particular, only voicing what they all wondered. "Does he not sleep, nor stop to eat?"

Davyd answered out of the surety that grew in him: "No. He does not sleep, but only rides. He eats in the saddle and feels nothing."

They stared at him, all of them, and he abruptly knew how Morrhyn must feel when folk named him the Prophet and looked to him for answers he did not know he owned.

Then Rannach ducked his head as if in acknowledgment of Davyd's power, and said, "Still, he's my son with him, and must I ride all night and not eat, so be it. So—ride!"

They mounted and went on up through the foothills, Taza ever ahead, the slopes growing steeper, decked with only pine now, and that bleeding out as the heights rose, until only naked stone lay before them.

And still no sign of Taza.

23

Taza's last horse gave up before a great blank wall of gray stone that rose sheer to meet the twilight sky and lose itself in shadow. The animal snorted and went down on its knees, pitching Taza over its head so that he cried out as he struck the hard, cold ground and must stumble to his feet and limp back to retrieve Debo before the horse rolled and crushed the complaining child. He snatched the youngster loose, listening to his wails reverberate off the cliff and the surrounding crags, wondering if Grannach listened, or if the cries carried down the mountains to Rannach. The horse fell on its side and lay heaving; Taza ignored its discomfort as he worked his saddlebags loose and dragged the pannier clear. He soothed Debo's protests and found a piece of jerky that he handed the child, who took the dried meat with a reluctant scowl. Taza took his hand and led him up the trail.

"Where are we going?" Debo asked around the mouthful of jerky.

"There." Taza pointed upward. "To the high hills."

"Why?"

"It's our quest," Taza extemporized. "You know how Morrhyn went on his quest, and then Davyd on his?"

Debo nodded.

"We do the same."

"For the sake of the People?"

Taza nodded enthusiastically. "Yes, for the sake of the People."

Debo grinned and asked, "Shall I be a warrior then?"

"Yes," Taza promised. "A great warrior."

The path he followed—by courtesy of Colun's dreams, invaded by the force that guided him—went on past the cliff, climbing steep toward two jutting crags, their tips lit red by the setting sun. Eastward, the moon was up, its light not yet strong enough to illuminate his way, so that he must go slowly, burdened by Debo's slight weight and the bulk of the saddlebags. Both were necessary: the one that he find a welcome beyond the mountains, the other that he own the sustenance to bring him and Debo safely through. He did not anticipate a welcome from the Grannach and knew that he must avoid them; nor less that he could: the voice had told him that, and shown him how. So he clambered wearily up the trail toward the crags, knowing that he must find a safe place to rest. He had gone four days now without sleep, and eaten little enough, but the voice had told him that once he gained the mountains he might halt and rest awhile—and he trusted the voice.

He climbed until the path gave out on a wide ledge like a shelf between the peaks. They bulked overhead, moon-washed now, all silver and black, with a cold wind blowing from between them as if in warning. He laughed at that and defied the wind or any other force to halt him, and found an overhang where he could build a hidden fire from the gnarly shrubs that grew here. He ate a little then, and gave Debo some milk, wrapped the child in a blanket, and himself settled cold to sleep, trusting the voice would come and show him clear the next step.

"He cannot travel so swift!" Rannach stared at the mountains as if he'd force his sight out through the darkness to where Taza hid. "Even killing the horses, he cannot."

Davyd sighed, huddling closer to the fire. He ached now, his wounds throbbing in the high mountain cold, and he had absolutely no doubt but that Taza should reach Salvation—save he die in the high passes, and Debo with him. It was as if, he thought, Debo were a piece in some incomprehensible jigsaw, or the lure in some inexplicable game, his kidnap designed to draw Davyd back to Salvation; and did he go, then surely Arcole would follow, and doubtless Rannach. He thought on his dreams and wished there'd been the time to take the pahé with Morrhyn and Kahteney, and perhaps find answers. He surely had none, save what he gave Rannach back.

"He can; he does."

"Because of what you fear, you and Morrhyn?" Rannach hesitated to speak the Breakers' name aloud.

Davyd shrugged, not speaking. He wanted sleep; more, he wanted to understand. Had Taza not taken Debo, then perhaps this day Morrhyn would have named Davyd a wakanisha, and he begun the full initiation. Now, however, he seemed caught at some midpoint betwixt Dreamer and warrior—which Morrhyn had said could not be, and the dreams said could. Surely, he carried a musket he'd not hesitate to use were he threatened—the thought of returning branded to Grostheim was anathema—and at the same time relied on his talent to bring them safe through the forests. Rannach and the others deferred to him as they did to Morrhyn, as if he were already a wakanisha, and that made for a heavy burden.

"Perhaps," he said at last. "I don't know."

"Do you not dream?" Rannach fidgeted impatiently as he stood. "You're a . . ."

"No." Davyd shook his head. "I'm not a wakanisha; neither a warrior. I don't know what I am."

"Davyd Furth," Arcole said, "of the Commacht, who are of the Matawaye."

Davyd nodded. "But am I not also a branded man, an escaped exile?"

"That, too," Arcole allowed. "As am I."

"Perhaps we're no one thing," Davyd said, "but different in different places."

It was Arcole's turn to shrug. "Surely we're different in the eyes of Evander," he said, "but I'd sooner live amongst the People."

"Yes." Davyd nodded. "But we're going back to Salvation."

He thought he understood then the burden Morrhyn carried, and Kahteney, and knew why they were so careful in choosing their successors. Taza, he knew, would be a Dreamer like the legendary Hadduth. And should he be any better, even were he eventually named? He let himself fall back, tugging his blanket tight. The Maker knew, but they'd surely start out again ere long, and until then he'd snatch a little sleep.

It was a strange dream, reality and revelation so intertwined that he must struggle to discern them.

Davyd rode a weary horse ever higher into the mountains, with Rannach and Arcole straggling behind. From a peak, Taza jeered, holding Debo above his head like a trophy, or in threat of murder. And behind Taza, vague as dawn mist, loomed a dreadful figure Davyd recognized from the dreams in the wood. Spiked golden armor glistened dreamy in the moonlight, matched by the trappings of the obscene horse the Breaker rode. The horse reared, pawing the night, its fanged mouth snarling. Then the rider fought the creature still and animal and man, both, stared at Davyd with fiery red eyes. Then the rider unlatched his winged helm and shook out a mane of fire-bright hair, and raised a taloned gauntlet to stab a finger at Davyd in . . . Davyd was unsure . . . condemnation? Or challenge? Perhaps contempt.

Surely the weirdling figure laughed, and for all there was no sound, still Davyd knew that laughter contemptuous. He raised a fisted hand, but the figure was gone—and Taza and Debo—and he saw them hurrying afoot through the underhill passages, the golden-armored Breaker and the great, dread horse trotting ethereal ahead.

And then he saw the forests beyond the hills and Taza was there, carrying Debo to an encampment of the People, save it was all tree-girt and not on the open grass. Folk came toward them, applauding them, and Taza handed Debo to a man Davyd knew must be Chakthi. The child stirred in fitful sleep, crying out at the disappointment.

And then the camp was ringed with folk in rainbow armor, all mounted on such beasts as he'd heard described and seen in his oak-wood dreams. The golden-armored man led them and it seemed to Davyd that he looked out from the dream at the reality and sneered in triumph. Then raised a hand and took the horde away, the Breakers and the Tachyn both, and went out onto the plains of Salvation leaving fire and destruction in his wake. And soldiers in red coats, and others in blue, came out to meet the horde and a great battle commenced, muskets and cannon filling the air with sound and fury. . . .

And Davyd woke to the rattle of thunder, lightning dancing atop the mountains, and found Arcole shaking him.

"We ride." Arcole knelt at his side, passing him a horn cup of tea that was thankfully still warm. "Rannach will wait no longer."

Davyd swallowed the tea in a gulp. "I must speak with him." He rose, wincing as his wounds tugged tight.

Arcole nodded, and went with Davyd to where Rannach stood, ready beside his horse.

"Taza will reach Salvation," Davyd said without preamble. "Our only chance is to beat him there."

"You know this?" Rannach's face was planed hard by the lightning, his dark eyes anguished.

"I dreamed it," Davyd said. "I dreamed he brought Debo to Chakthi, and the Breakers were there."

Rannach's lips stretched in a feral snarl. Almost, Davyd stepped back from the accusation he saw in the Commacht's eyes, but he stood his ground, pained for the hurt in his friend.

"There's no chance we can catch him this side of the mountains?"

"No." Davyd shook his head, filled with a terrible certainty. "He's guided by the Breakers."

"The Maker damn his soul," Rannach snarled, then sighed and shivered, as if accepting some awful judgment. "What do we do?"

A part of Davyd's mind found it odd that the akaman of the Commacht should ask of him their next step; another part was full of dream-born certainty, *knowing* what he must say.

"We must find an entrance to the Grannach tunnels and look to take him on the other side."

Rannach nodded. "Then we shall do that." He turned, shouting into the night. "We ride! We find the Grannach!"

It seemed to Taza as he rose and took Debo's hand that they were not alone. The voice had come to him again in sleep, and shown him the knowledge stolen from Colun, but now it seemed the voice took on magnificent form and he blinked and struggled to discern it through the lightning-pocked night. It was hard—like trying to pin down the images of a dream—but he thought he saw a splendid figure kitted in gold armor, riding such a horse as had never trod the plains of Ket-Ta-Thanne before him, and the figure turned in his skull-hung saddle and beckoned Taza on, pointing to a trail that ran between the twin peaks, and Taza knew a way through the mountains waited there to receive him. So he smiled and all his weariness was gone as he followed.

He found an entrance to the Grannach tunnels that he opened with dream-stolen knowledge, and took Debo inside.

The storm grew stronger, the mountains lit all stark black and silver by the lightning bolts that crashed down as if determined to contest the mastery of the skies with the vast uprising hills. Thunder roiled, echoing off the peaks, and though no rain fell as yet, the threat hung pungent in the air. Davyd gritted his teeth, urging his mount up the trail after Rannach. It seemed the thunder dinned against his wounds, and he felt afraid and terribly weary, and longed for rest, knowing he should find none until their purpose was accomplished or they be slain.

And are we slain, he thought, what shall happen then? Shall the Breakers flood through Salvation and then come against Ket-Ta-Thanne? Shall the indentured folk die for Chakthi's ambition and the Breakers' lust? Shall the People?

Inside him, a voice said, *No,* and he felt righteous anger fill him and warm him so that he forgot his aching body and his desire for sleep and urged his mount on until Rannach's stallion snorted a protest and Rannach turned in the saddle to look back.

"Soon," Davyd called. "We'll find an entrance soon."

Rannach looked at him with anguished eyes and ducked his head. "Do you take the lead? You'll know it better than I."

Davyd did not know how he should, only that he would,

and so he heeled his horse past Rannach's stallion and led
them on.

The tunnels smelled of stone and moss, and as Taza pro-
gressed deeper underhill light shone from the walls before
him, fading behind like dying witchfire. None opposed his
passage, and Debo was entranced with the journey, staring around and sometimes asking Taza where the Grannach
were.

"Asleep," Taza told him, "and we must go quietly that we
do not disturb them." Which Debo accepted, and only complained when his short legs grew weary, so that Taza lifted
him up and set him in the pannier and carried him on
through the silent passageway.

He supposed this was some tunnel the Grannach seldom
used. Surely it was unwatched, nor was there much sense of
use to it. There was no dust, but neither were there any signs
of other passersby; only the strange light that glowed ahead
and faded away behind. It was an eerie sensation, akin to his
journey through the Matakwa camp, when he'd sprinkled his
herbs unnoticed, all the time wondering if some fool such as
Tekah might happen on him. And did he finger the knife he
carried, still he felt a vast and certain confidence that he must
succeed and claim his rightful destiny.

He came to a branching of the way and halted. Two tunnels went off to the left, and three more to the right. He stood
within a circular chamber that appeared to be some kind of
way station. A well stood at the center, flanked by stone-
shaped benches, and around the cavity niches were cut into
the walls with shelves inset that might accommodate a sleeping Grannach. More niches held food, which he raided, halting just long enough to satisfy his and Debo's hunger, and
allow the child to dabble his fingers in the well water.

"What is this place?" Debo asked. "Where are the Grannach?"

He had not thought Debo would talk so much, but as the
child chattered on he answered the myriad questions, knowing that it were best he keep the boy happy: he did not know

how far a voice might carry along the branching ways, and he must be careful.

After a while he rose and told Debo they must go on, not knowing which path to take, looking from one to the other, unsure. Then he saw the rider again, standing his dread horse within the ingress of a tunnel, and knew he was still guided and went that way, confident.

The trail curved around an outcrop of vertical cliff that thrust out from the mountains like the prow of some great ship sailing into the night. It reminded Davyd of the *Pride of the Lord,* and he felt a moment's hesitation as he shouted for the column to halt. This, he thought as he studied the lightning-lit cliff, was not so different from boarding that other vessel: surely a journey to another new land.

"It's here," he said, not knowing how he knew, only that he did. "The entrance is here."

There was no room on the trail for more than two other riders, and Rannach and Arcole brought their horses alongside, both staring at the blank rock and Davyd with a mixture of confidence and bewilderment.

Davyd dismounted, pain forcing out a grunt as his feet struck the ground, and went to the cliff. He placed his hands flat against the slick surface and, still not knowing what he did, shouted, "I am Davyd of the Commacht—I am Colun's friend—and I'd ask entry."

Light sparked across the sky as if in acknowledgment, and an area of imponderable stone became an opening in which a quartet of Grannach stood. They wore armor—mostly breastplates and helms, but one with grieves and pauldrons—and all carried spears and axes, wide-bladed swords sheathed on broad belts. One stepped forward and said, "I am Vitran. What do you flatlanders want?"

Davyd said, "Passage underhill; and swiftly."

Vitran studied him awhile, the spear he held cradled across his chest as if he'd as soon use it as grant entry. Then he shrugged and stood back.

"Enter and we'll talk."

∎   ∎   ∎

The cavern was large enough that it encompassed all the horses and the men. Ale was brought, and food, and discussion of the passage began in the slow and patient Grannach way.

It chafed on Davyd—far worse on Rannach—as Vitran insisted he hear a full explanation of all that had transpired: of Davyd's dreams and Debo's kidnap, the People's opinion of Taza, of Colun's thoughts and Morrhyn's—all of it, at great length.

Finally he said, "And you'd ask us to bring you underhill to the Tachyn country?" And laughed. "Do you truly believe this . . . Taza? . . . can pass unnoticed through our mountains?"

Davyd said, "Yes: he's guided by the Breakers."

And felt a measure of guilty satisfaction as he saw Vitran's swarthy stone face pale, and the gesture of warding the Grannach made.

Rannach said, impatient, "Davyd is a true Dreamer. Morrhyn would name him his successor."

Vitran frowned and said, "But he carries a thunder-stick. You name him wakanisha, but he's the look of a warrior. Does the Ahsa-tye-Patiko not deny that?"

"He is different," Rannach said. "He guides us where we must go, and it does not matter to me. Only that I get my son back."

"And you are akaman of the Commacht." Vitran nodded ponderously. "I wonder what Colun would decide."

"To bring us through," Davyd said, "and swift."

Vitran looked at him awhile, then nodded again. "You've Morrhyn's look about you, boy, so I shall trust you. Swift passage underhill, eh?"

Davyd said, urgently, "Yes."

"Into the land beyond?" Vitran said. And when Davyd voiced his agreement: "And your horses? We cannot drop them down our cliffs."

Before Davyd had chance to answer, Rannach said, "Then we leave them. We'll go afoot."

"So be it," Vitran declared. "And shall you all go?"

Arcole spoke then. "Can we beat Taza, it were better only a few go."

Rannach said, "Why?"

"Because," Arcole replied, "you shall all be demons to the Evanderans, and are Davyd's dreams all true then Salvation is likely alert, and any of the People shot on sight. Better only a few men, who can slip unnoticed through the forests and onward."

"How few?" Rannach demanded.

"You," Arcole said. "Me and Davyd. No more."

Rannach nodded. Dohnse and others protested, but Rannach voiced them down: "It shall be so—as Arcole says. I go with him and Davyd, and you go back. Dohnse, I name you leader, eh? Tell Arrhyna and Morrhyn what we do."

Dohnse scowled but offered no further protest, and it was decided. Vitran said, "Is all you've told me true, then best we go now."

Davyd looked at Arcole, exchanged a smile, and laughed as Arcole rubbed the brand on his cheek, knowing his comrade felt his own fears.

Then they rose and began the journey back to Salvation.

24 To the Old Land

Rannach had seen little of the Grannach's underhill world, and nothing to compare with the
marvels he observed as Vitran brought them
through the passages at a steady trot. Light glowed from un-
knowable sources and intricate carvings wound about the
walls and roofs. Time seemed immaterial here, a concept
without place in the Grannach's subterranean world, and
when they reached the great cavern, Rannach had no idea
whether he had trotted behind Vitran through all the night or
only jogged a few hours.

Vitran halted on an ornately carved balcony overlooking
the cave, allowing his guests a moment's breathing space in
which to survey the vast hollow. Rannach stared about with
wide eyes, then turned to Vitran.

"How much farther?"

"A ways yet," the Grannach returned. "We'll rest here
awhile and then go on."

"My son is taken," Rannach said. "I'll not rest."

Arcole set a hand on the Commacht's shoulder. "We need
to rest," he said. "The Maker knows, but we've ridden hard,
and we shall need our strength to descend the farther slopes."

"While Taza has Debo?" Rannach shook off the placatory
hand. "No; I'll not rest till I've my son back safe."

"Do you not," Vitran remarked, "I doubt you'll get him
back. You need sleep and food—heed your friend. Besides, I
must speak with my fellows and send out search parties. If it's
as you believe and this child thief has found a way into our
tunnels, then we'll likely find him, and you shall eat breakfast
with your son."

Rannach would have argued, but the Grannach allowed

him no opportunity, starting down the broad stairway that descended from one side of the balcony to the distant cavern floor at such a pace that none had time to speak. Rannach could only follow, each jarring step—for the stairs were designed for the length of Grannach legs, not a Matawaye's—reminding him that he was, indeed, mightily weary. Nor, he thought, would Vitran do other than what he said. Did the Grannach insist he rest, then rest he must—or attempt the tunnels alone, which he knew must be impossible.

Save Taza did it, and were Davyd's dreams true, then Taza would reach Salvation guided by the Breakers.

The akaman of the Commacht felt remorse then, for all his thoughts were with his son and he had given few to the plight of the People, who likely stood in jeopardy were the Breakers come again. He wished Morrhyn were with him, to advise him, and glanced back at Davyd, wondering at the talent in the strange young man.

Davyd came down the stairway with the look of a man suffering and refusing to admit the pain. His teeth were gritted, his hands locked tight about the musket he carried, as if he feared to drop the weapon. In the cavern's strange light, his hair shone silver as moonlit snow and his eyes held the same expression Rannach had seen in Morrhyn's. Then he caught Rannach's look and smiled, and Rannach felt a great and sudden confidence. Had Morrhyn not chosen this man to be his successor? How then could Rannach doubt his ability?

They reached the foot of the stairway and Vitran led them across an arching bridge that spanned a swift-running stream, connecting with another rising arc that brought them to an avenue where pillars of stone were shaped to resemble trees, dendrous branches all hung with stony leaves intertwining overhead. They went on to a steep stair that brought them to a house jutting from the cavern wall, and Vitran beckoned them inside.

A woman, her brown hair straight and fastened with silver brooches, came bustling out, two curious children peering from around her full skirts. Vitran said, "This is my wife, Greta. The younglings are Tobah and Eryan. Greta, we've guests."

"That," Greta replied, as if the arrival of three flatland strangers in her home were the most common thing, "I can see. And weary guests, by their look. Come, come."

Within moments, they were ensconced on cushions, mugs of ale in their hands, Greta bustling about her kitchen as she readied food. Tobah and Eryan peered from a doorway, their eyes wide and wondering, remarking in whispers on the strange height of the newcomers until Greta called them away. Rannach watched them go, his eyes filled with pain. Vitran left them there, announcing his intention of organizing the search parties and vowing that Debo should be returned ere long.

"Shall he be?" Rannach asked Davyd.

Who could only shrug and answer, "The Maker willing."

"And if he's not?" Rannach's hand gripped the clay mug so tight he feared it might shatter. "If Vitran cannot find him?"

"Then," Davyd said wearily, "we go into Salvation. Rannach, listen—I am not a wakanisha, not Morrhyn, that I can tell you sure what shall or shall not be. I can only tell you what I dream, and we do our best."

Rannach nodded slowly, his grip on the mug easing. He raised the cup and drank deep and said softly, "The Maker be with us, eh?"

Davyd said, fervently, "Yes!"

He was the Night Walker again, traversing the tunnels unseen, unheard. Debo trotted beside him or was carried in the pannier, and Taza felt no weariness or fatigue, but only the strength that filled him as he followed the ethereal figure in the golden armor. When he faltered, the figure would look back and beckon him on and his strength was renewed, so that he went on, remorseless, his body become an automatic thing that walked and ran and moved oblivious of weakness. He was, he thought, become power incarnate thanks to the gift of the voice that came from the golden-armored warrior, who must surely be powerful as the Maker Himself.

Several times the dreamlike figure ahead halted and gestured that he hide, in side tunnels or niches—which he did, seeing the figure evaporate like dawn mist struck by the sun as swift-moving Grannach came by, all armed and armored so that he knew they hunted him but could not find him. He was the Night Walker, and possessed of such power as defeated all his enemies.

He went on, oblivious of time as he was of hunger or fatigue. At way stations he took food and water, and once the figure allowed him a little rest, which he took in an unfinished tunnel where golan-shaped stone bled out against naked rock, and then went on again, toward his goal.

How long he traversed the tunnels he neither knew nor cared—only that he moved toward his promised destiny—but in a while he came to a wall of blank stone and his confidence faltered until the golden figure laughed and rode his night-dark horse through the stone, and Taza followed and found himself looking out at a wide slope of shale-strewn rock that went down to a great swath of green pine that seemed to run on forever. The sun shone bright there, and from its angle in the sky he calculated it was early morning.

He laughed and raised Debo in his arms and called out, "Chakthi, I bring your grandson to you."

Rannach chafed at the enforced delay, anxious to be gone. He ate the meal Greta provided and drank a second mug of ale, swiftly took the bath their hostess offered, but scowled when she suggested they sleep.

"Where is Vitran?" he demanded. "Is there no word?"

"Not yet," she answered calmly, "but likely soon."

Rannach paced the chamber, his head ducked beneath the low roof, his hands fisting and unclenching, his lips drawn tight.

"Heed me," Greta said in the same voice she'd used when ordering her children to bed; Rannach ceased his restless per-ambulation and stared at her. He topped her by some spans, but the Grannach woman set hands on her stout hips and faced him square, as if he were a recalcitrant child. Abruptly, he nodded and found a bench, thus bringing his eyes level with hers. "My husband does all he can—if this Makerbedamned kidnapper is in our tunnels, then he shall be found."

"And if not?" Rannach asked, his voice soft as a child's pleading. "What then?"

"Then you shall have all the help we Grannach can give," Greta promised. "You know that, eh?"

"Yes, I know that." Rannach smiled as if muscles moved unwilling in his cheeks and jaw. "But my son is taken, Greta!"

"I know; do you not think I understand your pain?" The Grannach woman nodded solemnly and opened her arms, pacing a step forward to stand face-to-face with Rannach. "I am a mother, no?"

She put her arms around him and with a helpless cry he leant forward, his arms encircling her ample waist, his head drawn down to her shoulder. She stroked his plaited hair, murmuring softly as she might to a troubled child, and Rannach wept against her blouse.

It was strange to see that proud man weep, and Arcole felt a curious mixture of sympathy and embarrassment. How should it be, he wondered, if Flysse and I had a child stolen from us? He touched Davyd's shoulder and whispered, "I'll take that bath, I think."

Davyd nodded unspeaking, staring at the strange spectacle of Rannach weeping on Greta's shoulder. Does Arrhyna weep? he wondered. Does she pace the night thinking of her son? Does Flysse shed tears for Arcole? And then: Who cries for me? Shall I go back to Salvation to die at Chakthi's hands, or under the musket fire of the God's Militia, on the pyre of an Inquisitor's witch-burning? And do I perish, who shall cry for me?

And into his head came a voice that asked him, Does it matter? Are you not become more than you were?

Am I? he thought. I dream now, and I am not afraid—no! I *was* not afraid, until now—when I must go back to where they burn Dreamers.

But you've a duty, no? the voice asked. Morrhyn would name you his successor, and you shall lead the People in the dreaming ways. Surely the People would weep for you, were you to die.

I don't want to die, he said.

And the voice answered, Few men do, but would you live forever?

No, Davyd replied, only my natural span—but not yet.

Perhaps you shan't, the voice said, sounding somewhat amused. Perhaps you'll live; survive and be the greatest wakanisha the People have known.

That should be vanity, Davyd answered. Morrhyn is the Prophet, and I cannot be greater than he.

Morrhyn doubted, the voice gave back. He was afraid—is, still—but he goes on, because he is what he is and knows his path in life.

I don't, Davyd returned. Am I warrior or wakanisha? Morrhyn says I cannot be both, but . . .

Morrhyn does his duty, the voice said. His duty to the People and to himself, for the way he chose. Yours might be different.

But the Ahsa-tye-Patiko explains this clear, Davyd said. That a man cannot be wakanisha and warrior, both.

In Ket-Ta-Witko, yes, said the voice. It was so there; but you are in Ket-Ta-Thanne now, and soon shall go into that other land you name Salvation. Things change; perhaps it is time a new order was established. The Ahsa-tye-Patiko is not inviolable: it shifts and alters with men's will . . . and other things.

Tell me, Davyd pleaded.

And the voice said, I cannot: you must decide for yourself. Choose your path!

He said, "No; tell me. Show me!"

And looked up at Arcole, who knelt above him and said, "God, but you were in the grip of nightmare. Are you awake now?"

Davyd groaned and nodded: "Yes."

He sat up, realizing he lay on cushions, furs and blankets spread over him, in the outer chamber of the Grannach house.

"Where am I?"

"You fell asleep," Arcole explained. "Can you go on?"

Davyd said, "Yes." And: "What's happened?"

"Taza's gone," Arcole explained. "He crossed through the tunnels with Debo and is gone into Salvation."

Davyd sighed. "Tea?"

Arcole passed him a cup, said, "Rannach's outside now, and anxious to go. Shall we?"

Davyd sipped the tea. It was hot and strong and cleared his head so that he knew what he must do. The echoes of the dreaming voice still reverberated inside his skull, his ears, and he knew he took a path that should change all the differing worlds; nor less that he could do no other thing—save give up and die. Which he could not do, for that would be a denial of friendship and trust, and leave all the worlds open to the depredations of the Breakers.

"Then we go back to Salvation," he said. "But give me a while, eh?"

"Rannach's impatient to go," Arcole said. "And all well, we might catch Taza before he reaches Chakthi's camp."

"Even so." Davyd pushed the blankets aside. "A moment, eh?"

Arcole nodded and left him.

Davyd rose and straightened his clothes. Found the bathing chamber and splashed water on his face. Then looked at his scarred image in the polished silver mirror and dragged unsteady fingers through his lengthened hair. A comb of delicate filigree stood in a clay pot and he took it out and worked it through his hair, unscrambling the long tangles until he was able to draw it all out loose around his shoulders.

Like a wakanisha's: like Morrhyn's.

Then he took the strands and worked them into braids that hung to either side of his face, like Rannach's or any other warrior's. Then he went back to the main chamber and picked up his musket and his bag, and went out onto the balcony to join Rannach and Arcole, who waited with Vitran.

They stared at him, seeing the braids, and he smiled and said, "I had a dream." And when Rannach started: "Not of Debo—forgive me—but only of what I must do."

Soft, Rannach asked, "What are you, Davyd?"

And he answered the only way he could: "I do not know. Shall we go to Salvation?"

"I've no answers." Morrhyn looked helplessly at the anxious faces awaiting his response. Arrhyna's was haggard, lined with concern for her husband and her son; nor less Lhyn's, or Kahteney's, or Yazte's. Colun remained stone-faced. "I've no dreams, save they've reached the hills. Beyond that . . . nothing. Forgive me."

Kahteney said, "We've eaten pahé and learned nothing. It's as if something blocks our dreaming, beyond the mountains."

"The Breakers?" Yazte asked, eliciting a cry from Arrhyna, a gasp from Lhyn.

Morrhyn said, "Perhaps. Surely I doubt Taza acted alone in this."

"I can see no other way," Kahteney offered. "Who else owns such power?"

Yazte said, "Do I alert the camp? Shall they attack us?"

"No." Morrhyn shook his head. The Maker knew, but he felt weary and afraid and confused. It was as if malign power clouded his dreams—as once it had before—save this was different: he did not feel the threat he'd known when he climbed the Maker's Mount; only sensed the same threat rested now with Davyd, in another country he could not enter, neither in dreams or physically. Somehow he *knew* that Davyd held the answer, but Davyd was gone beyond his dream-calling into the unknown land, all he could do was wait on the outcome.

"I think," he said, "that there shall be no attack. Not here, or yet. Perhaps later . . ." He glanced at Kahteney, who shrugged and ducked his head. "Perhaps across the mountains. I cannot say."

"I'll take my people back," Colun declared. "Do they come again, we shall be ready. They'll not enter Ket-Ta-Thanne so easy."

"The Maker willing," Morrhyn said, "they'll not at all. I think this shall be decided on the other side of the mountains."

"So what shall we do?" Yazte asked.

"I think," Morrhyn said, hoping he said the right thing, "that the People had best remain here. Do we extend Matakwa, perhaps we'll get word ere long."

Colun said, "Are the Breakers come again, I shall take my people home and ready the tunnels for war."

Morrhyn sighed and said, "That might be best, old friend. I pray it not be, but . . ."

"We leave come morning," Colun declared. "The ways shall be scoured and guarded, and none come through; on my life."

Morrhyn nodded and looked to where Lhyn sat with her arm around Arrhyna, who wept silently, and wished he understood more and could offer comfort. But could not—only voice the truth of his doubts, which were stark and unpalatable.

Did the Breakers truly come again? Had those horrific destroyers of worlds somehow found the People down the trails of time and space? Followed them from Ket-Ta-Witko to Ket-Ta-Thanne like scented hounds, blood-struck with lust for destruction?

How?

Had someone called them? Was Hadduth so depraved he'd bring destruction down on all the scattered People, all this new world, or was Chakthi so bent on vengeance that he'd summon annihilation? Did they not understand that the Breakers were destruction incarnate? That they be only tools in the destroyers' hands, discarded and ruined when the horrid purpose of the Breakers was accomplished?

Morrhyn sensed no answers: only a terrible fear that folk he loved went into a strange land he did not understand, and his only hope for their survival was Davyd.

"We'll guard the Meeting Ground," Yazte said. "Save the Prophet orders different."

The Prophet? Almost, Morrhyn laughed at that: what could he prophesy, save confusion and doubt? But he must put on a brave face and so he said, "Yes, let the People remain here ready. Extend the Matakwa, and does worse come to worst, then . . ."

He prayed it not be: Yazte put it in blunt words. "Do the

Breakers come again, we shall be ready and fight them as we did before."

Morrhyn said, knowing they all waited on his word, "Yes; but pray it shall not be."

And wondered at his own doubt.

Rannach carried a bow slung in a quiver of goose-fletched arrows, and a hatchet and a long knife. Davyd and Arcole had a pistol and a musket each—bags of powder and others of what shot they had left on their belts—and knives.

Vitran brought them to an opening of the secret Grannach ways and bade them farewell.

"I am sorry," he said, looking up into Rannach's angry downcast eyes, "that I could not find Taza sooner; but . . ."

"He's guided," Rannach said, glancing at Davyd. "He's the Breakers to show him the way."

"It might," Vitran said, "be wiser that you wait. Let Colun come back and we'll send warriors out with you."

"No!" Rannach shook his head, echoed by Davyd and Arcole. "We go now, and find my son."

Vitran shrugged, which was like a rock shaking its shoulders, and said, "I cannot send men with you, not without the creddan's word."

Rannach said, "I'd not expect it. Only show us the way."

"So be it," Vitran said, and moved his hands over the blank stone that stood before them, so that it shimmered and shifted and became an opening that shone out on a wide landscape of tumbling rock and wind-twisted pine that ran down the rock like old sad dreams to meet some unforeseen conclusion.

Rannach stepped out first, his bow slung and an arrow nocked. Arcole came after, his musket cocked ready to fire. Then Davyd, slower, knowing no danger threatened—yet.

He breathed in the pine-scented air and turned to wave farewell to Vitran.

"Tell Colun, eh?"

Vitran nodded solemnly as if bidding his goodbyes to men condemned to die. Davyd smiled, watching the opening in the rock close, wondering if he should come back from this venture, or die a branded man, condemned by fate or the scar burned forever into his cheek.

"So," he said, "do we go find Debo and bring him back?"

They started down the slope.

25 Dangerous Journey

Debo considered it all a great adventure—far more exciting even than the grandeur of Matakwa, which he did not properly understand save that it was an occasion important to his father and mother. But Matakwa seemed not so different to daily life, whereas with Taza he had embarked on a wild ride up into the hills and then gone underhill, which he knew vaguely was something not even his brave father had done. He had not seen the ethereal figure that guided Taza—that vision belonged to the traitor alone—and so could only marvel at his friend's wondrous powers: that Taza could go where none of the People went, into strange unknown places. It was, indeed, a marvelous adventure, and Debo thought that when they returned he would have so much to tell Rannach and Arrhyna. It did not occur to him, as Taza lifted him down from a shelf onto the rock below, that he might not return to Ket-Ta-Thanne. Taza was his friend and Debo trusted him.

"Where are we going now?" he asked.

Taza stabbed a finger downslope, in the direction of the great green timber-sea. "There. Down into the forest, to meet your grandfather."

"My grandfather is dead." Debo halted, frowning. "He was killed fighting the Breakers. My other grandfather is in camp."

"You are luckier than other children," Taza answered with a sigh. "You have *another* grandfather, who lives in these forests and will be very glad to see you."

"How can I?" Debo demanded. "No one has more than two grandfathers."

"You do." Taza bit back his irritation as Debo went on

frowning, contemplating the impossible likelihood of having three grandfathers, and again demanded, "How can I?"

Taza shrugged, squinting into the sunlight that poured over the trees to bathe the slopes in golden light. "You are very lucky," he said. "Most boys have only two, but you have three because you are very special."

"How many do you have?" Debo asked.

"None," Taza answered with ill-concealed impatience. "All my people were killed in the fighting."

Debo nodded solemnly and said, "I'm sorry. Are you lonely?"

"No." Taza forced a smile. "I'm going to meet friends. And you're my friend, no?"

"Yes." Debo smiled back. "Tell me about my other grandfather."

"As we walk," Taza suggested. "He is an akaman—like your father—and he leads a clan that lives on this side of the mountains."

"I thought only the bad people lived here," Debo said, hesitating.

Taza said, "That's not true. Listen—walk with me and I'll tell you all about them."

Debo said, "All right," and went willingly with his kidnapper down the slope toward the timber.

"They are coming." Hadduth blinked and rubbed at his tired eyes: so much pahé, so much dreaming, took a toll. Perhaps there was a greater toll exacted for what he did, who he dealt with, but he elected not to think on that. "They are through the mountains now."

Chakthi smiled. "I'll send men to find them. And the others?"

"I think Rannach follows." Hadduth shrugged. "I cannot be sure, but . . ." He broke off as Chakthi's smile became a snarl.

"You cannot be sure? Do you not have . . . *their* . . . help?"

Owan Thirsk, the owh'jika, stirred nervously on his filthy blanket, crawling to the limit of his tether that he be as far as possible from Chakthi. The Tachyn akaman wore a familiar expression: such as came on him with anger. Chakthi noticed his movement and sneered, throwing the bone he gnawed at the sorry, nameless creature. Owan Thirsk winced as the bone struck his face and then snatched it up and began to tear at what little meat was left.

"I do," Hadduth said, struggling to ignore his throbbing head. He had sooner found his lodge and crawled beneath his furs than chance his akaman's intemperate rage, but Chakthi allowed him no choice—save to suffer that fury, which might well, Hadduth knew, end in his death. So he spoke swiftly, and with far more confidence than he truly felt. "They have guided me through all of this. They led me to the boy, Taza, and let me into his dreams. They showed me how I might bring Taza into Colun's head, to learn the way through the mountains. They . . ."

"Yes!" Chakthi chopped a hand, dismissive. "I know all this. But what of Rannach? I'd see his head hung in my lodge."

"And shall," Hadduth promised. "His head, and—when we go back across the mountains—Morrhyn's and any others' who oppose you."

"That shall be good." Chakthi's smile grew a fraction warmer; then froze and became a snarl again. "But when?"

Hadduth gulped tea. His throat and mouth were dry and his head ached abominably. He sensed he trod a knife's edge: not only with Chakthi, but with powers he scarcely understood. He had found the leader of the Breakers in his dreams—and wondered if Akratil sought him out. A compact of some kind had, after all, been made in Ket-Ta-Witko, and Hadduth recognized that now his lot lay with the Breakers rather than the Maker. He doubted even the Maker would forgive him what he'd done; but neither could he entirely trust Akratil. He scarcely understood that weirdling creature, whose purposes and motivations seemed so alien, save they be entirely directed toward destruction. But no matter: he had cast his dice and the way was chosen now beyond changing. He only hoped he lived to see his plans reach fruition, and even then wondered if Akratil not renege on his promises and bring down the Tachyn with all the others.

But that was not what Chakthi wanted to hear, and Chakthi sat before him, fingers toying with the hilt of his knife. So Hadduth said: "Soon. I cannot say exactly when—they've not vouchsafed me that knowledge—but it shall be. Such is their promise."

"And Rannach?" Chakthi snapped.

Were he honest, Hadduth would have told his akaman that he did not know, had no idea at all—his dreams extended only so far as Akratil's influence allowed, which was so far as men's corruption ran. But honesty was not always a sound ploy around Chakthi, and so he said, "Rannach's son is taken—shall he not come seeking the child?"

"Shall he?" Chakthi asked. "You promise me that?"

"Send men to find Taza and the boy," Hadduth replied, "and others to scour the forests for Rannach—he'll not be far behind."

It was what Chakthi wanted to hear and so he nodded and shouted orders that sent warriors running into the woodlands, then turned again to his wakanisha.

"And when I've Vachyr's child and Rannach's head? What then?"

Hadduth had hoped the interrogation was over; surely he had done enough for now? "They will tell me," he said. And quickly, as Chakthi's face darkened, "With the knowledge Taza brings, we can find a way through the mountains into Ket-Ta-Thanne. And do we go with the Breakers . . ."

"There's this land first!" Chakthi gestured angrily. "I'd have this land first!"

"You shall," Hadduth promised, wondering if he spoke true or false; knowing it too late now to go back. "Akratil has said as much."

Chakthi nodded sullenly. "I'd speak with this Akratil myself."

"Save you've the talent for dreaming," Hadduth answered carefully, "you cannot. As yet he and all his folk remain in Ket-Ta-Witko, and until we open the way. . . ."

"He cannot fulfill his promises," Chakthi said.

"Does he not already?" asked Hadduth. "Does he not send dreams against the strangers here? Taza brings you the boy, and Rannach after him, no? The rest shall come—my word on it."

"Your life on it," Chakthi said.

The day was warm, but still Hadduth felt a chill run down his spine as if some malign crawling thing investigated his backbone. He no longer doubted but that his akaman was mad, nor that he had any other choice save do what Chakthi ordered. "It shall be as you wish," he promised. "Only wait, and it shall all come to you."

"Best it does," Chakthi said. "On your life. I'd know Akratil's plans, and when he'd implement them. Dream me that, eh? And tell him in your dreams that I'd speak with him myself, chieftain to chieftain."

"I shall do my best," Hadduth agreed, thinking: You are not so great a chieftain, my akaman. I doubt you truly understand the power Akratil wields. But I think also that you shall learn it—and that frightens me.

Chakthi said, "Good; and soon, eh?"

Hadduth nodded and walked away.

"They came this way." Rannach knelt, staring intently at the faint tracks left in the shale. "Two sets of footprints going into the trees."

Arcole stared at the shattered stone, trying hard to discern the marks the Commacht indicated. He could not, but he trusted Rannach and so said, "Then we follow, no?"

Rannach nodded, rising, and glanced at Davyd, a question on his handsome face.

It was strange to find Rannach waiting on the youth, as if Davyd were truly a wakanisha like Morrhyn. But Davyd only turned away from the intent eyes and looked down the slope and said slowly, "I have not dreamed of danger yet."

Rannach said, "That's enough for me. Come!" He started down the shale.

Davyd hesitated and Arcole waited with him, studying that scarred face. Davyd was no longer the boy who had escaped indenture in Grostheim, nor the young man who studied with Morrhyn: he was become something other. It was as if, Arcole thought, his sojourn in the oak wood, his fight with the wolverine, had changed him forever. Surely he was changed physically—the Maker knew, but he came to resemble Morrhyn now, with that snow-white hair and the oddly distant look in his eyes, as if he gazed on sights unknown to ordinary mortals—but there was more. He seemed both more confident and more afraid. He seemed, Arcole supposed, committed, as if he had perceived a dangerous path he had sooner avoided, but took anyway, for fear of some greater loss than his life.

Arcole touched his shoulder, said, "Do we go?"

"Why not?" Davyd shrugged and essayed a smile lacking in humor.

Arcole stared a moment at the brand on his cheek, pale against the tan, paler than the long scar, and stroked absently at his own. "All well," he said, unsure whether he sought to reassure Davyd or himself, "we shall catch up with Taza, and not come close to any Evanderans."

Davyd paused an instant in his negotiation of the shale and smiled wanly at his comrade. "Yes, all well."

His tone suggested he could not believe all should be well, and Arcole would have spoken again save a foot slipped on the treacherous ground and he must fight to hold his balance, and when he was recovered Davyd was already downslope, closing on the hurrying Rannach.

They went on across the shale to where it washed up against naked rock that jutted like the fangs of some vast buried dragon drowned by the stone. Beyond that more stone stretched out, smooth and slick, to the beginnings of the upper timberline. The trees were sparse here, but past that first thin line, the hills dropped away and became all tree-clad, dense with pine and maple. Gullies and ravines cut through, white water tumbling in iridescent sprays over tumbled boulders, streams disappearing into the forest. Hawks wheeled overhead, and flights of raucous crows; behind them, bighorn sheep watched from ledges as if marveling at the audacity of the trio, and once as they continued downward, a mountain lion snarled protestingly from the shelter of a branch.

Rannach did not hesitate. It was as if he read the land easily as Arcole might read a book. Arcole had learned somewhat of the tracker's art in his time with the People—and had hunted in the Levan—but the signs Rannach spotted were invisible to him. Here was a stone disturbed by a small foot, another disturbed by a larger; here a minuscule thread recognized instantly as coming from Debo's breeches; here a twig broken by hurried passage. It was as if the Commacht saw a world beyond Arcole's ken, just as he believed Davyd did, and Arcole felt almost inadequate—as if he were a mere passenger on this dangerous journey.

"We're catching up." Rannach examined the ashes of a hastily buried fire. "They're a day ahead; perhaps less. Taza will have to halt to sleep—surely Debo will need to."

"Save he carries the boy," Arcole said. "And does he need sleep?"

He flinched as Rannach turned eyes both angry and filled with pain on him.

"I only . . ." He shrugged helplessly. "Forgive me, brother."

Rannach nodded and looked to Davyd.

"Do we go on, until sunset at least? Can you trail them in the dark?"

Reluctantly, Rannach shook his head.

"Then best we make camp," Davyd said. "There might be Tachyn scouting the forest—and can I sleep, perhaps I'll dream."

Rannach's expression suggested he had sooner go on through the night, but he nodded agreement and went on through the trees.

The sun was close on the western mountains now, bathing the peaks in red-gold radiance that outlined the flights of roostward-winging birds like markers against the darkening sky. In the east, the New Grass Moon shone indifferent. Squirrels chattered overhead and a wolf howled, answered by others. Under the pines the light faded fast, the great forest ceiling closing down on the three lonely men. Soon all was darkness, and they elected to make their camp.

They found a place where the hills folded, narrowing down into a gulch where a stream ran noisy, the walls close enough that their fire should not be seen. Even so, they deemed it wise to mount a guard—this was, after all,

Chakthi's domain, and were Davyd's fears correct, warriors might well be out seeking them.

"We'll split the watch," Rannach said, looking at Arcole, "that Davyd be able to sleep."

Davyd said, "I'll take my turn," and both older men answered him back: "No; sleep."

"Best that," Arcole said. "That you be able to dream. Besides . . ." He gestured at Davyd's body, the wounds. "You need to rest."

He saw that Davyd would have protested—surely the old Davyd would, filled with pride—but now he only shrugged and ducked his head in acquiescence. Arcole watched as he opened his pack and measured out portions of the herbs Morrhyn had given him.

"I'll take the first turn." Rannach glanced at the moon, now close overhead. "Perhaps I can find . . ."

Arcole nodded, understanding. "If not tonight, brother, then tomorrow, eh?"

Rannach smiled like a man tortured and took his bow and faded into the night. Arcole settled himself beside Davyd, watching as the younger man spilled herbs into a cup and drank deep.

"Are you in much pain?"

"I hurt somewhat." Davyd's eyes belied his smile. "Not much; and a night's sleep . . ."

"Shall not help much," Arcole declared. "God, Davyd, are you truly fit enough for this?"

Davyd's smile grew genuine. "Does that matter, my friend? We do what we must do, no?"

"Not," Arcole said, "if it shall kill you."

Davyd swallowed the last of the herbs. "It might kill us all," he said. "And what else can we do? Shall we leave Rannach here alone; shall I go back? Who'd dream for you then?"

"Listen," Arcole said earnestly. "I'd not see you die of those wounds—can you not go on, then say so. Honestly, eh? And I'll bring you home to Ket-Ta-Thanne, no matter what Rannach wants."

Davyd said, using the language of the People, "Thank you, brother, but I've things to do here; things I must, else there be no Ket-Ta-Thanne. I cannot explain it—only *know*!—so do not talk to me of going back, eh? We go on!"

Arcole nodded silently, thinking that he no longer knew Davyd at all.

Taza crouched within the shadow of a wide-branched pine, studying the slope ahead. The timber grew so thick here the light of the waning moon was filtered in tricksy patterns that denied clear definition of the ground. He had thought something moved in the shadows and tugged Debo into the first hiding place available, not wishing to stumble on some hunting bear or other predator. He motioned the child to silence and Debo, thinking this all a great game, complied. Taza cocked his head, listening intently.

Surely something did move ahead, coming up the slope toward them, and instinctively Taza drew his knife. He thought for a moment of lifting Debo up into the branches, telling the boy to climb, then discarded the notion. If he were to die here, then Debo would surely starve. He grinned cynically, wondering if he grew fond of the youngster, and gripped his knife tighter as the sound grew louder, peering out through the overhang.

Shapes moved through the shadows and Taza thought of questing wolves. But there were none of the sounds wolves made, and soon he identified the shapes as men. They made little effort to conceal their approach, save they moved with the silent efficiency natural to the People. And when one passed through a pool of moonlight he saw plaited hair and buckskin shirt, breeches, the bow in the man's hand.

Tachyn! They had to be Tachyn, for surely none others of the People dwelt in these dense woods, and he was confident he remained ahead of any pursuit. Even so, caution seemed advisable: it should be ironic were he to be slain now, by some wary scout. So he waited until he saw five men halt atop the low ridge and confer, as if debating whether or not to continue their search. Then he heard the name Chakthi spoken and could contain himself no longer.

"I am Taza," he called, "and I bring Chakthi his grandson."

Five faces swung toward his hiding place, bows rising, strung with nocked arrows.

"Don't shoot!" Taza called. "I've Chakthi's grandson here."

"Come out," a warrior called.

Taza answered, "Let down your bows then."

The spokesman nodded to the others and they lowered their bows, waiting as Taza emerged from the shade of the pine, Debo on his heels. He took the boy's hand and walked slowly toward the waiting men. He held his head erect, proud of himself and determined to show no fear.

When he was within a few paces of the group he halted and said again, "I am Taza. I have come from beyond the mountains to bring Chakthi his grandson."

The man who had spoken before nodded as if this were nothing unusual and said, "I am Besdan; we have been looking for you. Hadduth said you were coming."

Taza smiled, hiding his surprise. Did the wakanisha of the Tachyn know of his arrival, then surely Hadduth must communicate with the golden-armored figure—and be a most powerful Dreamer. "Then take me to him," he declared.

Besdan grinned and said, "We take you to Chakthi. Hadduth answers to him."

"No!" Debo recognized the name of his grandfather now and tugged on Taza's hand, shaking his head. That name was spoken seldom in Ket-Ta-Thanne, and always with loathing. Debo did not wish to encounter so detested a person, and began to cry. "No!"

Taza said, "It's all right. We're safe now; there'll be food and a proper fire."

Debo went on tugging at Taza's hand, trying to drag him away from the unknown warriors. "Take me home!" he wailed. "I want to go home."

Taza said, "You are home."

"No!" Debo shrieked. "I don't want to meet Chakthi. I want to go home!"

He broke free of Taza's grip and began to run back the way they had come. Besdan chuckled and went after him, snatching the boy up across his shoulders, where Debo beat his small fists in futile protest against the man's broad back.

"Be quiet," Besdan commanded, "else I shall whip you."

Debo was so startled by the threat he ceased his struggling and lay inert over Besdan's shoulder as the Tachyn started down the slope.

"Come," he said to Taza. "Chakthi awaits you."

"We must walk wary," Davyd said, smiling his thanks for the tea Arcole passed him. Dawn light fell on his face and the air was warm with morning's promise, easing his aches somewhat. "These forests are full of Tachyn."

"We knew that," Rannach grunted, disturbed by the notion of delay. "What of Debo?"

"He's alive," Davyd said. "At least, as best I know. . . . My dreams were strange, as if there's a power here that clouds them."

"Chakthi's here, and Hadduth." Rannach spat. "As is my son!"

"And are we slain, what chance has Debo then?" Arcole demanded. "Listen to Davyd, Rannach."

The Commacht sighed and made an apologetic gesture. Davyd said, "Warriors seek us, that much I know for sure. Haste shall be our enemy now; lest we go careful, we shall all die."

"Then lead us," Rannach said. "Show us the way."

Davyd nodded and drank his tea, then clambered wearily to his feet. He felt not at all rested, for his sleep had been filled with strange dreams that he could not understand. Save that danger threatened—such as might well see the three of them slain, but also a far greater hazard that might well engulf all Ket-Ta-Thanne and Salvation, both.

26

Grostheim ran out of quicklime that winter, and for every bonfire warming the streets it seemed there were three pyres beyond the walls consuming the corpses of the possessed. Folk lived in fear again: at first of the rumors, then of the reality—or its fantastic counterpart.

At first it was only soldiers of the God's Militia—possessed by the dreams, by the voices—who attacked their officers. Var suffered five assaults, two of which left him with cuts that pained him in the growing cold; Jared Talle cloaked himself in magic and defeated no less than nine attackers; Alyx Spelt was attacked four times; after one assault, Wyme refused to leave his mansion without an escort of twenty men.

Fear filled the garrison, breeding dissent. Officers took to wearing pistols at all times, and kept their swords ready. They trusted no one, and the garrison troops resented the mistrust that spread and wondered if the madness might not affect them. When old friends turned mad, no one knew who should be slain next, who next succumb to this strange madness, and often civilians became the targets. Once a squad of Militiamen guarding a well-stocked granary turned their muskets on a growing crowd and slew thirteen men and seventeen women. Another time, nine soldiers entered a tavern with drawn bayonets and slaughtered six men, seriously wounding eleven more before they were overwhelmed—four of them beaten to death by angry citizens before the remaining five were shot by Var's marines.

In all of Grostheim, it seemed that only Var's marines were unaffected. They remained true to their duty. Until, at least, the snow grew deeper and the full weight of Salvation's cruel winter settled over the city.

The Restitution froze. Ice settled solid over the water a half-mile beyond the rebuilt docks. Floes drifted angry as winter's teeth against the incoming tides that raged storm-driven against the harbor, and all the land beyond the walls was cloaked in white, snow layering deep as a tall man's waist. It was a hard winter. Indentured folk were set to clearing the streets, scraping clean the rooftops, setting braziers to burning in the streets while outside the pyres blazed on Talle's order, consuming the slain possessed.

Food grew short, and then settlers—mostly those come into the city to escape the harsh winter—began to attack the soldiers. It was, Var thought, a pattern similar to that first seen. Questioning these people—too often under Talle's cruel supervision—revealed that those suffering the madness had encountered the "demons" and spoke as Danyael Corm had, in voices of guttural protest. They spoke of driving the new-comers from "their" land, of the inhabitants of Grostheim and all Salvation fleeing before they were slain for their ef-frontery.

Then it got worse.

Ghosts were seen in the streets: dread riders on horrid mounts whose clawed hooves left burning imprints in the snow. Folk ran crazed from the apparitions, screaming that devils—even worse than the demons of the last year—were come amongst them. Talle went out, escorted by soldiers he did not trust, to assure the citizens that all should be well, that his magic and the might of the Autarchy must surely overcome this strange new invasion, and was not believed. Folk turned their backs on him; once he was pelted with snowballs, another time with mud and harder missiles. Riot threatened. Talle and the Autarchy were held responsible for the citizens' dire plight, and when answers were demanded of the Inquisitor, he had none to give. For he did not properly understand what happened here, Var knew, and closeted himself away, dissecting bodies and seeking answers to a magic he could barely comprehend.

He forgot his plans for a winter campaign. Indeed, it seemed to Var that he forgot the far-flung forts guarding the forest edge, for when carrier pigeons came in with word of similar apparitions seen about and inside the forts, Talle offered no response save that each garrison must hold firm and wait on his occult investigations. Var thought the man consumed by his inquiries—as if his delving into this weirdling mystery preoccupied him and rendered him forgetful of his first duty, which was, Var felt, to the people of Salvation who suffered under this strange new onslaught.

And did Var speak with the man, Talle only bade him wait and trust—that answers should come in time and the demonic assaults be ended. And Alyx Spelt hid within his quarters, or ventured out only under escort of trusted men who had not faced the demons, and that only seldom. And the governor shut himself inside his mansion with his plump wife and advised anyone who dared ask that the Inquisitor Jared Talle must answer their questions and accept responsibility for what befell Grostheim.

Var saw the ghosts twice.

The first time he was come out of a tavern where he had been drinking with Abram Jaymes and stepped down into the snowbound street with one hand on the butt of his pistol and the other on his saber, glancing around for fear there be some red-coated Militiaman maddened to kill him, and saw a creature he could scarce describe, save it bore resemblance to an amalgamation of lion and lizard charging at him. He saw, atop the horrid thing, a figure dressed in antique armor, shining under the cold starlight in rainbow hues, a great curve-headed ax raised high and swinging down to take off his head.

It was dream and reality combined. Beast and rider were ethereal: he could see the flames of a brazier flickering through them, the houses beyond, lit windows, but even so . . . They were possessed of such immediate presence that he drew his pistol and fired even as he snatched his sword from the scabbard—and saw his shot go through the lion-creature's snarling skull as he swung his blade against the rider's down-swinging steel.

There should have been the sound of metal on metal—the

clash and the jarring of arms—but there was nothing: only confusion as the beast and its rider passed by, phantasmic smoke trailing in their wake.

Var heard a shot, and turned to see Abram Jaymes spitting a fresh ball into his Hawkins rifle, trailing the apparition that was already gone into the winter night like wind-drifted snow. None others had ventured out from the inn.

Var sheathed his sword, somewhat embarrassed, and set to reloading his pistol. He looked at the draggle-haired frontiersman.

The scout shrugged, and said, "I saw it, so I guess you ain't mad. Less'n maybe I am, too."

Var said, "Perhaps we both are."

"Well then, we ain't alone," Jaymes said. "You want some company?"

Var nodded: he felt no wish to walk alone this night.

"What are they?" he asked as they trod the silent, snow-bound streets. Overhead, the sky was a sullen gray, snow-laden cloud obscuring the stars and whatever moon might have risen. "I don't understand this."

Jaymes laughed and spat a stream of tobacco onto the snow. "Nor me," he said cheerfully. "I never seen anythin' like them afore."

"Don't they frighten you?" Var asked. "By God, they make me wonder."

"Wondering ain't the same," Jaymes said. "There's a difference between being frightened an' wondering."

"Yes." Var ducked his head in agreement. "But even so . . ."

"It cross your mind," Jaymes asked, "that there's been nothin' like this until you an' the Inquisitor arrived here?"

Var shook his head. "What are you saying?"

Jaymes shrugged. "I don't rightly know, save that last time we got hit by livin' creatures—demons if you like, but they could be killed—an' now it seems like we're attacked by ghosts. Only they can't hurt anyone, only scare folks." He spat a stream of tobacco. "Me, I'm more concerned with what *can* do me harm."

∎   ∎   ∎

Var put that argument to Jared Talle, after the second time he saw an apparition.

He had inspected his men and made his way to the governor's mansion, and halted at the gate when out of nowhere a fanged horse with skin the color of darkest midnight and eyes burning the same fire that gusted from its mouth reared above him. It seemed more solid than the other beast. Surely, he believed the clawed hooves that struck at his head might easily crush his skull. Instinctively, he ducked below the creature's pounding hooves, instinctive, snatching out his pistol and saber at the same time, slashing, the pistol blasting.

On a saddle of gold, hung with gilded skulls, a rider in golden armor laughed at him from under a golden helmet and pointed a wide-bladed golden sword at his throat.

You'd defy me? You pride yourself, man. You are nothing! You are a worm, crawling in the dirt to be crushed and severed. Do you understand?

Var rolled away from the pounding hooves that trampled fire out of the cleared ground and sparked like blazing moonshine on the piled snow. The horse—a horse? He had seen no horse like this before, not with horns and tusks—trod him down, clawed hooves tramping him. He screamed in anticipation of the pain that did not come, and flung his emptied pistol at the thing's face as it snarled at him and ducked its head on the rider's command to drive its horns down into his chest.

He screamed again as the golden-armored rider pointed his sword and leaned out of his magnificent saddle to drive his blade into Var's skull.

Var felt a terrible cold invade his body, and at the same time a feverish heat. Then all was gone and he felt only embarrassed as servants and soldiers came running to the commotion of his shouting, where there was nothing save the Inquisitor's right-hand man—the Inquisitor's dog—rolling in the empty street, his saber slashing empty air.

"So you saw a ghost." Talle took the decanter from Nathanial's hand and waved the branded man away. "Tell me—exactly—what you saw."

Var drank the brandy, warming his chest where the hooves had struck, easing his head where the golden blade had gone in. He felt cold, as if ice were placed inside him, and told the Inquisitor everything.

"Like the rest," Talle said. He rubbed his hands, and it seemed to Var that sparks of darkness fell from his fingers, matches to his lank hair and crow clothes. "Like all of them."

"I saw," Var said, reaching uninvited for the decanter, "what I saw."

"Which," the Inquisitor said, "were only ghosts. Phantasms; images."

"I thought," Var said, slowly, his voice clogging in his throat, "that I was dead. They seemed most real to me."

Talle said, "They would," calmly. "They've powerful magic, these folk who oppose us. It confirms my belief that we must mount a campaign against them."

Var said, sipping more brandy, not liking at all what Talle was saying, "In this winter? I thought you'd given up on that notion."

Talle shook his head, and said, "Not a military campaign, my friend. Only a small expedition—you and I, and your frontier scout friend; perhaps a few others."

"Against . . ." Var shrugged, helping himself to a fresh measure of brandy. "Whatever these things are?"

"Would you grant them sway?" Talle sat behind Governor Wyme's ornate desk, his fingers steepled. Var saw blood ingrained beneath his nails, in the ridges of his knuckles, and wondered at his practices. "They bring this new magic against us, and I—*we!*—must fight it, no?"

Var nodded, reluctantly.

"And what magic they bring," Talle said, "they deliver from out of their forests, no?"

Again, Var had no choice but to duck his head in agreement.

"And we are only servants of the Autarchy," Talle said. "We are sent here to resolve such . . . problems. . . . So, do you go find your scout and bring him to me?"

Var hesitated; Talle cocked his head, again reminding Var of a carrion crow anticipating a feast.

"What?"

Var mustered his thoughts. "You and I and Abram Jaymes?" he asked. "Perhaps a few others? How many, Inquisitor? And to do what?"

"A . . . sortie, wouldn't you put it? A small venture to identify our enemy; not so many men as shall make us noticeable, but enough to find their weaknesses."

"And how shall we do that?" Var asked.

"Why," Talle said with disturbing calm, "we shall go out to the border forts and find us a savage. Take it alive, learn what it knows. I can do that, Major Var, have I one living to question."

Var felt no doubt but that the Inquisitor could. He ducked his head a third time and went to seek out Abram Jaymes.

They made an odd trio, Jaymes thought, the Inquisitor and the marine major and the scout. They sat ensconced in the governor's study, the fire burning merrily, logs crackling sparks up the chimney and over Wyme's carpet, a decanter passing between them—used mostly and lustily by Jaymes. The windows were shuttered against the Candlemas night and the door locked against intrusion. Talle sat still behind the desk, clad all in black. Var sat erect in his blue marine's tunic, sword and pistol at his side. Jaymes lounged, legs stretched and wide, in dirty leathers, his shirt unbuttoned against the heat.

"An' you want me take you into the woods," he said, cradling a goblet of imported glass loose against his chest. "Take you into the—what do you call them now? Demons, territory?"

"Savages," said Talle. "They are only savages."

Jaymes shrugged, seemingly careless of the Inquisitor's black-eyed gaze. "Savages, demons—call them what you want, they can still kill you."

Talle said, "I'm hard to kill."

"Yes: I seen that." Jaymes emptied his glass and looked to Var for another measure. "But still . . . I reckon they could kill you if they want. I reckon they got magic big as yours."

He looked Talle in the eyes. "How else they been making such trouble here?"

Talle smiled. "That's what I need to know; that's why I need you."

"An' if I refuse?" Jaymes asked.

Talle's smile grew broader, thin lips stretching back over stained teeth like a rabid dog's. "I could hex you," he said.

"Sure." Jaymes nodded easy agreement. "But could I scout like you want then?"

Talle shrugged, acceding the point: "Or I could have you hanged."

"An' I be no good to you at all," Jaymes said.

"Quite," Talle allowed. "So what do you say?"

Jaymes glanced at Var and asked, "Who else comes?"

Var looked at Talle and said, "I am commanded by the Inquisitor."

"So?" Jaymes asked again, this time directing his glance at the black-clad man.

Talle said, "Perhaps only we three. What do you suggest?"

"Three," Jaymes said, "could slip in easier than any of your Militiamen. God knows, but they move noisy, an' the . . . whatever you want to call them . . . are likely to hear 'em coming long afore they arrive. Hear them an' slay them."

Talle looked at Var, a question in his eyes.

Var was surprised the Inquisitor bowed to his knowledge. He shrugged and ducked his head and said, "In this, I'd be governed by Abram."

Jaymes chuckled as Talle said, "Then so be it. Only we three."

Governor Wyme was no less pleased to be left again in command of Grostheim than was Alyx Spelt. Neither man had thought to see his command returned him, but when the Inquisitor announced his imminent departure, accompanied by his dog, who left his marine contingent under Spelt's orders, both men were delighted. Not least to see the usurpers of their power gone out to what they believed must be certain death.

That they must face the problems of a dissenting populace, of dwindling food and ghosts in the streets, did not occur.

They both believed the Inquisitor and his dog must die out in the forest snows and welcomed that demise, anxious to show Evander and the Autarchy that they could prevail.

They were wrong, but that should be learned later.

27

Strange Meetings

The Restitution was frozen too hard to carry any river traffic, so they rode out shrouded in furs against the bone-numbing cold, Abram Jaymes leading a pack mule behind his own lop-eared animal. Each man wore a furred coat, hooded and well padded, and Var carried a new Hawkins rifle—requisitioned, like all their gear, from Rupyrt Gahame.

It was, inevitably, slow going. Jaymes's mule handled it best, plunging lustily through the deep snow as Var's and Talle's horses ducked and struggled complaining through the drifts. Var had thought perhaps the Inquisitor might clear them a way. He had seen, in the War of Restitution, magic-wielders open tracks through snow to allow attacks, assaults. But Talle made no such offer—neither explained why not—and they could only move at such pace as the animals allowed until they reached the harder inland snow, unaffected by the salty wind blowing in from Deliverance Bay, where hooves did not break through nor drifts deny them passage.

That was a full day clear of Grostheim; two more at least before they reached the closest holding where they might find honest lodgings under a sound roof, with a fire burning in the hearth. Var longed for such shelter, and wondered if he grew soft, for he knew they must make camp that night under the sullen sky, in the snow. He gave thanks to God that Abram Jaymes was knowledgeable of Salvation's winters—there were none such in Evander or any other land he'd visited—and had procured from Trader Gahame thick furs and sound canvas tents, charcoal to light fires, and had thought to bring kindling and dried meat.

It was all very different from a military campaign: three

men alone, he thought, as they halted on Jaymes's advice to pitch their tents. The wind got up and sent snow skirling against the canvas as if winter sought to blow down their refuge.

They were camped under a bluff where knobby pines grew wind-twisted and gnarled, scrubby brush coming down to the ice-edged river, which was all one great expanse of dimly shining silver, hard as lost hope. Jaymes gathered brushwood and built a fire that sparked and crackled in the blustering wind, trailing sparks horizontally across the darkness. The scout brewed tea that he fortified from a bottle of trader's brandy, and Var was surprised to see Talle drink deep and ask for more before they ate. Overhead, the sky hung sullen, empty of anything save threat. It began to snow as they ended their meal and retreated to their tents: Var wondered if that might not be some portent.

The next day the sun shone cold: an unforgiving eye that stared at the three travelers from out of a colorless sky that blew a harsh wind into their faces as they moved westward. The landscape around them was bleak, snow-clad and desolate, and they moved unspeaking, the wind tearing conversation from their lips before the words might be heard. Frost coated the manes of the animals and the furs of the riders; snow crunched crisp under the hooves, and their breath gusted thick billows of steam into the freezing air.

A day later they reached the closest homestead. It was inhabited—close enough to Grostheim that the holder and his wife felt safe—and they put up their wearied animals in a warm barn and saw them fed by indentured folk, and accepted the comfort of the hearthfire and the food.

The holder's name was Anton Groell, a man in his middle years, not yet either old or young, though strands of gray stretched through his beard, and his eyes hung nervous on Jared Talle.

"I'm not quitting," he said. "I kept this holding going through the troubles, and I'll not let it go now."

"Why should you?" Talle asked amiably. "Have you problems now?"

Groell shook his head.

Talle said, swinging his dark eyes from Groell to the man's wife, "You've not seen ghosts? Riders in the snow?"

"No. Nothing like that." Groell stared at the Inquisitor as if he were mad, but made no further comment.

Talle nodded and said, "Excellent. Come morning, I'll hex your steading against attack, and you'll be safe."

"Thank you, Inquisitor." Groell tapped his head in obeisance.

Talle smiled his thin-lipped smile and nodded benignly, which Var found most unusual. He caught Jaymes's eyes on him and shrugged in answer to the unspoken question he read there.

Nor did the Inquisitor grant any answers when they were escorted by the grateful homesteader to the small room usually occupied by the house servants—the branded folk were turned out into the barn—and settled to sleep. Var found it awkward. He'd speak with Talle of what, exactly, the Inquisitor thought to do, and why, and could not for Jaymes's presence—he yet felt the weight of his duty to the Autarchy. No less, he'd speak with Jaymes and discover the scout's opinion of their mission and Talle's curiously pleasant attitude.

But he could do neither, for the room was small—sufficient only for the indentured husband and wife who would usually sleep there. Talle, claiming precedence, took the bed, leaving Var and Jaymes to spread their blankets on the floor so that any discussion became impossible—especially when the Inquisitor's loud snores filled the room.

The next day Talle was affable as ever, even gracious in his thanks for the breakfast Liesli Groell provided, and the supplies offered by her husband. He hexed the house and all its outbuildings and fences, watched by the holders and their branded folk alike, all marveling at his magic, convinced they should be safe from any attack.

The sun was already close on its zenith before he was done, shining bleakly out of a sky the color of polished steel. Breath gusted great gouts of steam and the waiting horses stamped impatient hooves on hard-frozen snow. Var and

Jaymes stood watching Talle at work, mugs of hot tea fortified with homemade brandy in their hands.

"What's he up to?" Jaymes asked with his customary bluntness. "Around Grostheim he was a real bastard, but now he's actin' nice as apple pie with hot custard."

Var said, unthinking, "I don't know. I don't understand it either," before he realized he spoke with the grizzled scout as with an equal. And then that he *did* regard Jaymes as an equal: he felt abruptly confused, and hid his face in his cup.

Then Talle called: "So, it's done. Shall we ride on?"

Groell and his wife were profuse in their thanks as the trio mounted, the man even clutching Talle's hand as he voiced his gratitude.

Var had never seen the Inquisitor allow another to touch him, but Talle only smiled down and nodded like the Autarch granting a blessing.

And it remained so at every holding they encountered: Talle was a fur-clad crow come with help and blessing, hexing farms and vineyards and mills with smiling visage and only kind words for the holders; even for the few indentured folk who dared approach him.

"Why not?" he answered when, at last, Var broached him. "Am I such a tyrant?"

Var was mightily tempted to answer yes, but forbore that response, settling instead for equivocation, saying, "This hexing of farms and such delays us." He gestured at the bleak landscape. "The snow delays us, when I'd thought we hurried to the wilderness."

"Did I say we hurried?" Talle asked. "Should I ignore the plight of these far-flung holdings?"

Var shrugged, thinking that all this hexing might well have been done the previous summer—when Talle had looked only to get the borderline forts built and seemed to give little, if any, thought to the homesteaders—and said, "There are a great many holdings along our way, Inquisitor; and a great many more beyond."

Talle nodded. "True, Major," and said no more, but only urged his horse after Jaymes's mules.

Var sighed, accepting he should get no clear answer, and followed in the tracks.

■ ■ ■

"What's he up to?" Jaymes let his mule slow enough that Var came alongside. His voice was a low murmur, conspiratorial. "He's not behavin' like his usual unpleasant self."

Var frowned, glancing back, fearing Talle might overhear. But the Inquisitor only sat his mount, the reins loose in his hands, allowing the horse to follow the two animals in front. He seemed lost in thought, unaware of the muted conversation.

Var said, "I don't know; only that whatever it is slows us."

"It surely does," Jaymes nodded. "An' I thought he was in a hurry."

Var shrugged, unable to offer any other answer.

"It's almost like he wants to spread as much of his magic as he can around Salvation," Jaymes murmured. Then frowned himself. "It's almost like he's settin' up a trail of some kind. Like he's deliberately leavin' signs for the ghosts to find."

Var stared at the scout and wondered if he was right.

They were two days out from the first fort when the ghosts appeared.

It was close on twilight, the landscape painted by the settling sun, all gold and blue, the shadows of the copse that sheltered them thrown long across the unending whiteness, the night wind starting up to prick scatters of snow from the branches of the trees. A flight of crows winged overhead, raucous in its protest of the cold and the poor pickings. Jaymes had built a fire and seen the animals fed; Var helped him with the pitching of the three tents as Talle sat warming his hands.

Then out of nowhere appeared a group of riders.

It was as if the sun flickered in its setting behind the distant mountains and blinked the dread group into existence. Or as if, Var thought as he felt his blood run cold and reached instinctively for his new Hawkins rifle, old memories came back to haunt him. He cocked the long gun, aware of

Jaymes's hammer clicking into position, and glanced sidelong at the scout.

Jaymes stood with squinted eyes and readied rifle. Var thought he saw sweat on the man's dirty face. He turned a little and saw Talle rising from his place beside the fire, coat-tails swirling as the Inquisitor's arms spread as wide as the smile on his narrow face.

The riders came across the snow. God! Var recognized those things they rode: lizards and lions combined, with great padded feet that sprouted claws soft as honed steel, scales and fur combined, the eyes slit and red above jaws that gaped eager to rend and gnaw, exposing fangs like blades. Nor any easier to behold the creatures that sat the ornate saddles, for they were dressed in such armor as seemed to fold into the sunset and the shadows, flickering rainbow-hued to defy clear vision and trick the eye.

Only the leader could be clearly seen, and Var knew him from before—and felt the terror he'd known when the clawed hooves of that midnight horse had fallen ethereal on his body, and that ghastly horned head descended to pierce his chest.

He did not know he'd fired his rifle until, in the aftermath of its discharge, he heard the boom of the heavy-caliber cartridge echo off the trees, and saw the powder smoke swirl before him.

And heard the laughter that exploded from beneath the golden helmet even as the great curved sword angled at his chest, glittering in the fire's light as the rider urged his dread mount closer.

We've met before, have we not? The voice was simultaneously musical, deep and resonant, and at the same time like a cold wind whispering through a graveyard. Var shivered, struggling with numb fingers to reload the unfamiliar Hawkins rifle. *And you were frightened then. Did you think I'd slain you; did you think you were dead? Do you oppose me now, you shall be. Dare you that?*

"Perhaps he'll not, but I shall!"

Jared Talle stepped away from the fire, trudging over the snow to confront the golden-armored rider. He seemed not at all afraid or perturbed, but rather pleased, as if this weird meeting gratified him.

Ah, the one who spreads magic.

Var felt the awful chill depart as the magnificently armored figure turned its attention to the Inquisitor, who said, "I wield magic, yes. Does that frighten you?"

Fresh gusts of laughter came from under the golden helm. *Your magic frighten* me? *No, it does not.*

"Then why," Talle asked calmly, "are you come to shout at me? At me and my companions, like some schoolyard bully?"

The red eyes beneath the golden helm flared in outrage. The sword rose. Var heard Abram Jaymes's rifle go off, and Talle laugh and shout into the night, "Leave off, my friends. Shots cannot harm these phantasms; nor they harm us."

No?

The leader raised his blade anew, drove heels against his dread mount's flanks and brought the awful beast charging forward. Var forced himself to concentrate, to prime the flashpan and aim the rifle, even knowing it useless: it was all he had against such creatures.

Talle only stood, hands shifting as he muttered words too low to be heard. The golden blade cleaved through his skull, through his lank hair and the narrow face beneath—and still he did not move. Hooves rose above him and pounded down, claws descending to the snow, through his furs and his black suit—and he only smiled. The snarling head dipped and drove its unicorn horn through his chest—and he laughed and waved his hands and shouted, "Begone! You are nothing. You are no more than snow on the wind; shadows! You cannot harm me or frighten me, because I am stronger than you."

Are you? The golden-armored man reined back his horrid horse. *Who are you?*

"I am Jared Talle, the Inquisitor."

And I am Akratil, who shall drive you away and destroy you.

Talle said calmly, "I think not. I think *I* shall destroy *you.*"

The fantastic shape that was Akratil brought its awful mount swirling around in a circle. Behind, the others sat uneasy, their lizard mounts pawing snow Var vaguely noticed was not at all disturbed by their movements.

Akratil said, *We shall see, man. We shall see who destroys whom,* and was gone.

Talle said, "Yes, so we shall."

The fire spread sparks into the gusty night. A lonely owl hooted.

Abram Jaymes said, in a hushed voice, "What was that?"

"Our enemy," Talle said. "Not yet in this world, but growing ever stronger."

Var asked, "What are they?"

"I don't know," Talle answered. "Not for sure, but they empower the hostiles, I think. They are, if you like, the demons."

Var steadied his hands and his breathing; lowered the Hawkins rifle. "Is that why you've lingered, Inquisitor? Is that why you've hexed every holding we've come across?" He wiped sweat from his brow. "Is that why we're out here alone?"

Talle beamed and said, "Absolutely, Tomas. I'd let them know who they face." His smile faded into a chill equal to the land around, the night. "And I'd know just what they are—to which end we must capture a hostile."

Abram Jaymes said, "I don't rightly understand any o' this."

"How should you?" Talle insulted the scout. "The dreams that drive men crazy in Grostheim? You thought the hostiles sent them? No—that was the creature you saw. Doubtless it works with the savages, but the savages have no power of their own, save what these creatures give them."

"They was real enough when they attacked the city," Jaymes said.

"Of course." Talle shrugged. "And were defeated, no? But now they've new strength—got from the true demons."

"Are they part of this land," Var asked, "the true demons?"

"I think not." Talle shook his head. "Were they, they'd have physical form. But, as you saw"—he drew a line from his skull to his abdomen—"I was no worse cut than you, Major, when you saw them first."

Var nodded, shuddering at the memory. Jaymes asked, "An' the crazy folk in Grostheim, what about them?"

"All had encountered the savages," Talle said. "Every one—I ascertained that before we left. Don't you understand?"

Var and Jaymes said in unison, "No."

"The savages and the demons work together," Talle said. "One has summoned the other, or followed the other: it matters little. What does matter is that we destroy them—all of them!—so that Salvation is saved for the Autarchy."

Abram Jaymes produced a plug of tobacco and cut a wad that he stuck in his mouth and began to chew as he asked Talle, "An' what about the branded folk?"

"What," Talle returned, "about them?"

"None had dreams," Jaymes said. "Not one o' them went crazy; only freemen."

The Inquisitor shrugged. "Branded people are not my concern. Why should they be, save they look to escape?"

"They get killed too," Jaymes said.

"And more come," the Inquisitor replied. "Evander's prisons are full of potential exiles. God knows, we can fill this land with indentured folk once we've rid it of the savages and the demons. We can make it a paradise for Evander, for the Autarchy."

He turned away. Jaymes caught Var's eye and spat a stream of liquid tobacco across the snow. Despite the cold, despite the residue of his fear, Var felt his cheeks flush, warming as he thought on Talle's casual dismissal of the Autarchy's slaves.

Perhaps, he thought, I do become a dissident, a secessionist.

Nathanial opened the door to Major Spelt and took the officer's greatcoat and tricorne hat. He noticed that the major wore his ceremonial shortsword and a brace of pistols, which was not unusual in such troubled times—save that when he offered to relieve the major of such burden his request was irritably denied.

"Where's the governor?" Spelt demanded.

"The dining room," Nathanial replied. "The lady Celinda is with him."

Spelt nodded and stalked away. Nathanial glanced out across the yard, pleased to see that the pickets still stood on watch and that Spelt's escort—he had no doubt but that the major had come with an escort—had dutifully presented itself at the rear door, as befitted common soldiers.

He carried the coat and hat to the cloakroom and ducked his head into the kitchen along his way, calling that Major Spelt was come and cook had best lay on more dinner, set the table for three.

Then, precisely as he spoke the words, as if in punctuation of his sentence, two shots rang out.

"Alyx!" Andru Wyme levered his bulk a little upward from the chair. "It's good to see you. Is it not, my love?" He turned to Celinda. "See, an old friend come visiting in troubled times. You'll dine with us, won't you, Alyx? No matter, eh? I'll not let you say no."

Celinda smiled and gestured that Spelt take a chair; the major bowed elegantly. The governor of Grostheim laughed. Major Alyx Spelt, commander by the grace of God of the God's Militia in the Grostheim garrison, drew both his pistols and shot Governor Andru Wyme and his wife, Celinda, in the heart. Then he drew his sword and set to carving them apart.

When Nathanial appeared with worried soldiers on his heels, both the governor and his wife were reduced to bloody rags.

Alyx Spelt laughed as his own soldiers shot him dead.

28 Chaos

The first fort had been named for a hero of the War of Restitution—Jonathon Harvie, who had led the assault on Trebond's most impressive citadel and had taken the great fortress before succumbing to his wounds. Var had met the man and thought him cold and calculating, empty of anything save ruthless ambition: Fort Harvie seemed a fitting monument.

It sat beside the Restitution River like some squat guardian of the Autarchy's possessions, a wooden emblem of power. The engineers had done a fine job. The walls stood twenty feet high, massive boles settled deep in the ground beneath, carved and fire-hardened to points at their tips, cut away at intervals to allow for embrasures from which jutted the mouths of cannon and swivel guns. Talle's hex signs sat dulled by wind and weather on the timbers. A glacis had been set up before the walls, rising to drop into an outer ditch some fifteen feet across before the counterscarp was reached. Any attackers would come under the fire of the cannon, the swivel guns, and the muskets of the infantry long before they reached the sheer facings of the final defenses.

Var checked such details automatically as they approached, and wondered why no sound came from Fort Harvie: neither shouts nor bugle blasts, only a silence that seemed to fill up the bleak day as if with clarions of alarm. He studied the walls ahead and urged his mount alongside Talle's.

"There's something wrong here."

The Inquisitor scowled at Var and then at the fort: "I know."

Abram Jaymes reined in his mule and swung around in the saddle, letting loose a stream of black liquid before he spoke.

"Save they all gone blind, they must've seen us comin', no? An' where are the sentries?" He gestured with his rifle at the high walls. "You see anyone?"

Var shook his head. It came to him that they had last heard from Fort Harvie some time before they quit Grostheim, the messenger pigeon advising the garrison that all was well. They had been traveling for weeks now—God knew, but winter was approaching its end—and perhaps some news had been sent as they rode the snow. Or not: he felt a chill that had nothing to do with the cold run down his back and eased the Hawkins rifle from its protective sheath.

"I doubt that gun shall aid us," Talle said, and heeled his horse forward.

Var said "Wait!" but the Inquisitor ignored him, riding up to the cutback running through the glacis, shouting, "The Inquisitor Jared Talle comes! Open the gates!"

There was no answer. Jaymes said, "He ain't afraid o' much, is he?"

And Var shook his head again and followed his nominated master down the cutback.

Jaymes said, "Goddammit," and spat more tobacco and followed behind.

They rode up to the gates and found them open; rode inside and found Fort Harvie was empty of anything save bodies. They lay frozen where they had fallen, picked over by crows and foxes and rats—or even the dogs and cats that inhabited any fort, though these latter were gone now, as if scared off by the terrible emptiness filling the desolate bastion. Var was glad of the cold: the place should otherwise have stunk like a midden.

Jaymes climbed down from his mule and stared around and said, "By God, what happened here?"

Talle said, "Magic; madness. See?" He gestured at the corpses.

Var fought a desire to vomit. He had seen slain men before—done his own share of killing—but never anything like this. These were men of the God's Militia, hardened troopers, engineers, artillerymen seasoned in war: comrades. Yet they lay entangled, slain not by any external enemy but by one another. He looked around and saw a Militiaman near-beheaded by an engineer's shovel; an engineer with a bayonet pinning him to the frozen ground; artillerymen bloody with musket fire, and the redcoats who had fired all bludgeoned and bayoneted by their fellows.

"What happened?"

"As I said: magic." Talle shrugged, seeming quite unperturbed by the carnage. "These demons are, perhaps, stronger than I thought."

"Strong enough to do all this?" Var wondered if his voice truly rang so loud as he thought. "To turn an entire garrison on itself?"

"It would seem so," Talle replied, and rubbed his hands busily together. "Now do you go find us quarters, Tomas?"

Var said, aghast, "We're staying here?"

"Where else?" Talle asked cheerfully. "Shall we camp out again, or sleep comfortable behind these solid walls?"

Var had almost done the former; Fort Harvie had about it an air of menace now. He remembered Jaymes bringing in Matieu Fallyn's body, and the presentiment he'd known then that this land seemed to offer little in the way of salvation. It seemed to him that sleeping here was akin to settling in a graveyard. He crossed his fingers and spat, wondering if the specters of men he'd known might not walk the yards come nightfall.

But he was an officer in the God's Militia and Jared Talle was his commander, so he ducked his head and strode away in search of rooms he hoped should not be filled with corpses.

Talle looked to Jaymes. "And you—bring me him and him." The Inquisitor angled stained fingers at the selected bodies.

Jaymes frowned. "You want me to carry corpses for you?"

"Yes." Talle smiled. "I want you to bring them to the kitchens. There should be knives there, no?"

Jaymes swallowed tobacco, coughing. "What you plannin' to do with them?"

"I intend," Talle said with horrid calm, emphasizing each word, "to cut them up and seek for the magic that brought them to this."

Jaymes spat out more tobacco and nodded and did as he was ordered.

Jolyon Minns wiped his mouth and took a deep breath, wondering if he was up to the task of commanding Grostheim's troops even as he recognized he had no other choice.

Major Spelt was dead; the governor was dead; every officer above the rank of lieutenant was dead. And Grostheim was in chaos. It was as if someone died for every snowflake that fell: soldiers turned on one another; settlers seeking shelter from the harsh winter slew one another; Trader Andyrt had shot Trader Gahame; innkeepers slew their customers, and the drinkers slew each other. Horrid riders on ghastly mounts stalked the streets by night and day, and Lieutenant Minns had no idea what was going on—save that did it continue, Evander's foothold in the new world must fall down and be consumed.

"Tea, 'sieur? Or something stronger?"

Minns looked up as the indentured man appeared at his elbow. What was the fellow's name? Jacque or Jayke, something like that. He smiled wan thanks and said, "Tea, if you will. And a tot of brandy, I think."

The servant nodded, the movement of his head plucking light from the scar on his cheek, and quit the room.

Officers, Minns thought, and troopers. Traders and innkeepers. Housewives and businesswomen. But never branded folk! Why not?

When the servant came back, bearing a tray that held a pot of tea and a decanter, Minns gestured that he sit.

"Forgive me," he asked, "but I forget your name."

"It's Jayke, 'sieur." The man looked uncomfortable.

"Drink with me." Minns wondered if he asked or ordered. "I'd speak with you."

Jayke looked startled. He hesitated, then said warily, "I'd be honoured, 'sieur."

Minns filled the glass with brandy and passed the receptacle to the servant. "You've seen the ghosts?" he asked.

Jayke nodded and said, "Who's not, 'sieur? Horrible, they are." He shuddered and drank deep, crossing his fingers. It was clear that were he not in the presence of a freeman, he'd have spat.

"And do you dream?" Minns wondered.

Relaxed by the brandy, Jayke chuckled. "I've not the time, 'sieur. I just fall into my bed and go to sleep."

"And your fellows?" Minns asked. "The other . . ." He touched his cheek, feeling himself embarrassed now, and wondering why, save that this indentured servant was old enough to be his father. "The other . . ."

"Branded folk?" Jayke finished for him. "God, no, 'sieur. We don't dream."

Minns nodded, essaying what he hoped was an encouraging smile. "And did you see the savages when they attacked us?" he asked. "Did you come close to any of them?"

Jayke emptied his glass. "God, 'sieur, that I did! I saw them close as I am to you—three of them!—and they'd have killed me if your Militiamen hadn't shot them down. In God's name, one of them had an arrow pointed right at my face!"

"But you don't dream of them?" Minns asked, reaching across the desk that had once been the property of Major Alyx Spelt to fill the servant's glass again. "Not at all?"

"The odd nightmare." Jayke shrugged, lifting the glass. "No more than that."

"Nor any of your fellows?" Minns asked again.

Jayke shook his head.

Minns said, "Thank you."

Jayke said " 'Sieur?" and the lieutenant smiled, wondering why none of the branded folk dreamed and went mad. Why that insanity applied, it seemed, to only Evanderans—to only freemen. He waved the man away unthinking and did not know he was gone until he looked up and found the room empty.

He was still sitting deep in thought when two Militiamen whose names he'd never known burst into the room and stabbed him before turning their bayonets on one another.

Then there was no order at all in Grostheim, only chaos.

■   ■   ■

"Can he really figure out magic by cuttin' up dead men?"

Jaymes spilled the rough trade brandy into his cup and passed the bottle to Var. The major shrugged as he filled his own tin cup. They sat in a room cleared of bodies, the fire they'd built releasing the sour-sweet odor of blood from the floorboards. But at least it was warm.

Var said, "I suppose so. I don't know."

"Maybe," Jaymes swallowed brandy and spat tobacco, "he just enjoys it."

And perhaps, Var thought, you're right. I don't understand any of this. He looked across the corpse-littered yard at the brightly lit windows of the kitchen, where Talle went about his grisly work. The sky was cloud-scudded this night, a waning moon glancing from between the wrack long enough to illuminate the bodies. Aloud, he said, "He's an Inquisitor, Abram—he must know what he's doing."

Jaymes decided his wad was finished and sent it tumbling into the hearth, where it sizzled horribly. At least the smell covered the odor of the blood. "You reckon so?"

Var looked at the scout and sighed. "Honestly? I don't know. But he *is* an Inquisitor, and the highest power in this land. So . . ." He shrugged again, helplessly.

"You obey his orders, eh?" Jaymes grinned wickedly.

"What else can I do?" Var asked.

Jaymes offered no answer.

Var said, "We've gone through this before, no? I am an officer in the God's Militia and the Inquisitor is my commander—I have no choice but to trust him." He drank brandy. "God, man! Do you know what's going on here? I don't!"

Jaymes nodded. "Has it occurred to you," he asked, "that the same thing might be goin' on in Grostheim?"

Var set down his cup. It seemed that cold fingers scratched each knobby ridge of his backbone. It had not, and the notion was horrifying. He shook his head in mute denial.

"Might be," Jaymes said dourly. "Might be these demons are havin' the same effect there as they done here. Might be the whole o' Salvation is fallin' apart."

Var said, softly, "God!"

Then Jaymes ducked his head at the window. "He's comin' back."

Moments later the door flung open and Jared Talle stalked in. He was smiling as he shucked off his fur coat and went to the fire. As he extended his hands to the warmth, Var saw that his arms were bloody to the elbows, and that gore splattered his shirt and black coat.

"There's hot water?" the Inquisitor asked cheerfully. "And food?"

Var rose to indicate the pot boiling on the stove. "There's no food here," he said.

"Ah, no; of course not." Talle set to scrubbing his bloodied hands. "That will be in the kitchens. Do you see to it, Tomas?"

Var nodded. "Now, Inquisitor?"

"I'm hungry," Talle said. "It's fatiguing work, necromancy."

Newer, colder fingers trailed down Var's spine. "And was your work . . . successful?"

"Absolutely." Talle turned from the stove. "A towel, if you will?"

Var handed him a towel and stood waiting. Talle said, "The food, Tomas? I've truly a great hunger on me."

Var nodded again and went—like some indentured exile, he thought—to the kitchens.

The slaughter wreaked within the confines of Fort Harvie was bad enough, but when he stepped into the kitchens and saw what the Inquisitor had done to the bodies he felt his stomach clench. He hurried past the carnage to the pantries, snatching meat and loaves he hoped remained fresh: the makings of dinner.

Back in the room, he found Talle lounging at the table, a cup of Jaymes's brandy in his stained hand. He appeared entirely at ease; Jaymes seemed unusually discomfited. The scout rose and set to helping with the preparation of the meal for which Var felt little appetite. He forced himself to eat as Talle spoke.

"These were much better than the affected ones of Grostheim," he said. His tone was conversational. "I wonder if proximity to the wilderness does not render both the magic and its traces stronger."

Var forced down a mouthful of salted beef, grunting his thanks as Jaymes pushed a filled cup toward him.

"It would seem," Talle continued, "that a similar affliction applied—the garrison here dreamed and went mad, and set to slaying itself. But of course," he chuckled, "you've seen that."

Var nodded silently; even Jaymes appeared disconcerted by the Inquisitor's casual assessment of so many dead.

"It's the demons, of course," Talle said. "Not the savages—who are really no more than that, save perhaps they own some crude form of magic. But this was done by the true demons."

"Who are?" Var gasped.

"Demons." Talle shrugged as if the answer were obvious. "They oppose the will of our God, no? The will of the Autarchy. So what else should they be?"

Var asked, "How? We've seen only ghosts."

"Oh, they've no sure form yet." Talle shrugged, smiling his thin-lipped smile, and reached across the table to help himself to more beef. "They seek that through communion with the savages—who are, of course, quite real. They have corporeal form in this land, and through them the demons would enter." He chuckled. "What the savages fail to realize is that the demons will destroy them as surely as they'd destroy us. The ignorant beasts believe they've found allies. In point of fact, they've brought down their own destruction."

"And ours?" Var asked, feeling himself massively out of his depth.

"Perhaps." Talle's smug smile disappeared an instant. "Save I defeat them."

"Can you?" Var asked.

Talle nodded solemnly, and then his smile came back. "Am I not an Inquisitor, Tomas? Chosen by God?"

"How'd you find all this out?"

Abram Jaymes's blunt question wiped the smile from the Inquisitor's face. "I raised the dead," he answered equably, "and they told me."

Jaymes swallowed, his grizzled face rigid. "An' what do we do now?" he asked tightly.

"What I said," Talle replied. "We must capture a savage."

"That," Jaymes said succinctly, "will not be easy."

"I understood," Talle said with horridly reasonable menace, "that you know the wilderness. You are the scout, no? So lead us to them, and leave the rest to me."

"Why d'you want one?" Jaymes pushed his plate away as if, like Var, he lost his appetite in Talle's presence, in the Inquisitor's bland acceptance of horrid and arcane practices. "Don't you know all you need to? Why d'you want another body to chop up?"

Talle mopped greasy gravy with a hunk of old bread, and for a moment did not speak. Then he looked at Jaymes as might, Var thought, watching, a cat observe a cornered mouse.

"Do you argue my command?"

Jaymes shrugged, and suddenly Var became aware that the scout wore a brace of pistols on his belt and that his hands fell toward them. No less Talle, whose smile grew wide and ugly.

"Those shall not harm me. But I can do you great hurt."

Jaymes's hands returned to the table, toying with a crust. "I don't doubt you can, Inquisitor." He managed to invest the title with insult. "But what if you do? You and the major go ridin' off into the wilderness woods all on your own? You think you can find your way through the trees? You think you can find the savages you're lookin' for without me? You think you'd last long in the snow and the forests?" He paused, holding Talle's suddenly outraged gaze long enough to cut a plug of tobacco and insert it in his mouth, begin to chew. Var admired his courage. "I'd reckon you'd both be dead inside a week. From the cold or arrows, whichever, or maybe starve to death. I surely to God don't believe you'd find any savages. But they'd find you."

For long moments Var feared the Inquisitor should work his magic on the scout, thought that Talle should raise his hands and hex Jaymes as he'd done the recalcitrant settlers. He wondered, aghast at his conflicted loyalties, which he would support. But then Talle shrugged and said, "You say I need you?"

Jaymes nodded. "You want to survive out here, yes. You don't understand this land. You think you can come here an' tell folks what to do—jump this way an' just so high—but this isn't Evander. This is a whole new world, with new thinkin' an' a whole different set o' rules. God knows," suddenly he smiled, exposing tobacco-stained teeth, "that's what you just said, no? An' for that—to live in the wilderness—you need me."

"I could hex you," Talle said. "I could make you obey me."

"Sure you could." Jaymes leant away to direct a stream of black liquid into the fire. "But don't your magic attract the demons? So if you hex me, I'd likely be a real attraction, an' then the demons'd likely tell the savages where I am—which would be with you—an' then they'd all come lookin', no?"

Var could applaud the argument; Talle could only scowl and duck his head in agreement.

"So best," Jaymes said, "if you don't hex me, eh?"

"Perhaps," Talle allowed slowly, "it were better I don't. But . . ."

"I'll bring you safe as I can into the wilderness," Jaymes interrupted. "I'll do my best to find you a savage. But you don't ever threaten me again."

For long, slow moments the two men stared at one another, then Talle raised an agreeing hand. A lie, Var thought, that should be broken soon as Abram was no longer useful.

"An' when we leave this godforsaken fort," Jaymes said, "you'd best do what I say. You want to survive the wilderness, then you'd best agree to that."

Talle said, "Very well. You are, after all, the expert in such matters."

"Yes," Jaymes agreed, "I am. An' now I'm going to find me a place to sleep that don't stink. I'll see you in the morning. Major." He waved at Var and went away.

"The man is incorrigible." Talle reached for the bottle Jaymes had left on the table. "But we need him, so we shall use him."

"And when you've got what you want?" Var asked. "Does he find us a savage for you to . . ."

"Question," Talle supplied. "Why, then we shall need him to bring us back to Grostheim."

"And when we reach Grostheim?" Var asked.

Talle smiled and shrugged and gave no answer—which was all the answer Var needed.

Abram Jaymes lay wrapped in his bedroll, his seamed features impassive as Var spoke.

"He plans to hang you. He'll use you and then have his revenge."

The scout eased up just long enough to empty his mouth of tobacco. "I figured that," he said amiably, "but there's been folk looked to kill me afore, an' I'm still alive."

"He's an *Inquisitor*," Var said.

"Sure." Jaymes rearranged his blankets. "But he don't know the wilderness, nor much about Salvation."

"He owns magic." Var set out his bedding. "He can hex you and hang you, and no one will argue his right."

Jaymes chuckled. "You thought he was about to do just that, no? An' you was wondering whether you'd go with him or with me."

"Damn you," Var said, "you know where my loyalties are."

"Maybe," Jaymes answered. "But do you?"

Var asked, "What do you mean?"

"Work it out" was all the answer Jaymes gave.

They set out the next day, not to the forts Var had sooner checked—though he assumed them likely in the same disarray as Fort Harvie—but directly into the wilderness. It was a high, clear day, with no threat of snow and the sun burning bright out of a steely sky. Crows rode the air currents above, and a lonely hawk. They passed the fort's cemetery, where Matieu Fallyn's body lay with the others slain in that first attack. Var thought they likely rode to their deaths, but could not argue against Talle's decision—for was the Inquisitor correct in his necromantic prognostications then all Salvation stood in dreadful jeopardy and he could see no alternative save to trust the man, and pray he was right.

The forest stood threatening before them, a vast swath of darkness stretching across the western horizon, cut as if wounded by the wagon road, the great mountains beyond no more than a cloudy line under the hard sky.

Somewhere in there, Var thought, are the savages. And their demonic allies? What if those creatures achieve physical form? He thought on what he'd seen—the golden-armored rider on his awful horse, and those other warriors on their indescribable beasts—and stroked the hammer of his rifle for the comfort of honest steel, a thing he could understand. It should serve him well against the savages, he thought. But the others? Even did they become corporeal, could powder and shot slay them? He wished he had his marine company with him.

Nor less was he concerned for the fate of Abram Jaymes. He had no doubt but that Talle would look to extract his revenge once the scout's usefulness was ended, and had no wish to see Jaymes die. He felt a great fondness for the grizzled, foul-smelling scout, and none at all for the Inquisitor. But Jared Talle was his commanding officer and he was sworn to support and defend Evander and the Autarchy, and did it come to that line he hoped he might avoid, he could not help but wonder which side he'd take.

He raised his eyes to a sky that offered him no answers and followed Jared Talle down the forest trail that Matieu Fallyn had taken to his death.

29 Out of the Woods and . . .

"We leave the animals here."

Abram Jaymes indicated the clearing he'd chosen. A stream ran through, swift enough to disrupt the ice, flanked by sufficient tall pines that the deep bowl might remain invisible to passersby not seeking three intruders. Scrub grew between the trees, holly and other bushes that served to conceal the depression, and he'd flanked it with rope that the beasts not stray. There was forage under the snow and sufficient fodder packed on the second mule that the animals could survive for some days at least. Five, he calculated, wondering if he should be still alive in that time, or the horses and mules still there. He felt a terrible fear that he would die on this mad venture. But even so, he had given his word—less to that dark raven bastard Talle than to Tomas Var—and he'd keep it, even were his life forfeit.

Nor less Salvation, he thought, was Talle correct in his assumptions of demonic interference. Almost, he laughed, thinking that Talle's interference was not much different. Was there much difference between one form of demon and another? He didn't know. He had little experience of hell's minions, save in the form of the Autarchy he despised, and the Inquisitor surely seemed as evil as any savage or ghost Jaymes had encountered. But Var—Major of Marines Tomas Var was a bird of different hue, and Jaymes could not but help feeling hopeful that the major understood.

And live: he checked the last of his camouflagings and brought the Hawkins rifle to his shoulder.

"Let's go hunting, gentlemen."

"Where?" Talle asked, gesturing irritably at the surrounding mass of the forest, all shadowy under the pale winter sun.

"This way." Jaymes beckoned, bringing the Inquisitor and the major up through the stream to where tumbled rocks afforded footing that might not be seen; from there to a patch of wind-bared ground where only pine needles lay. "This is a game trail, see?"

Talle shook his head, strands of lank black hair flapping about his face; Var, more knowledgeable, nodded.

"We follow this," Jaymes explained with exaggerated patience, "so that our tracks get lost amongst the others. Then we find an ambush site an' wait."

"For what?" Talle demanded irritably.

"For your savages," Jaymes answered. "What else?"

"I can use magic," Talle said, "to bring them to us."

"Sure you could. But how many? An' what about the demons? Listen, *Inquisitor,* I'd like to get out of here alive." Jaymes smiled sweetly as he could. "An' bring at least the major with me. So you best do what I say now—this is my country we're in."

Talle scowled and said nothing; Jaymes suppressed a chuckle as he followed the black-clad figure up the slope.

They walked for half a day before Jaymes decided on a suitable location, and then settled his company beside the trail. Var could see that it was heavy with tracks, and he wondered if the scout could truly discern the shapes of men's feet from the marks of the animals. Talle complained as Jaymes ordered him to lie down and covered him with a square of tarpaulin, over which the scout shoveled snow until only the Inquisitor's angry dark eyes showed from beneath the covering. Across the way, Jaymes took position beside Var.

"Was that necessary?" the officer of marines asked as they crouched behind a thicket. "Covering him like that?"

"It keeps him quiet, don't it?" Jaymes returned, and grinned. "Wouldn't you sooner he was quiet?"

Var resisted answering in the affirmative for all he smiled back at the scout. Instead he asked, "How long shall we wait?"

Jaymes shrugged. "No knowin', Major. They might come sooner or later. Maybe tonight; maybe not for days. But they use this trail, so . . ."

Var nodded and hoped it be soon; he'd have this thing done and over with. The more he saw of the Inquisitor Talle's practices, the less he liked them. He hoped it be soon and they return to Grostheim with the knowledge that might defend Salvation. Save then Jared Talle would undoubtedly look to hang Abram Jaymes. . . .

But they came that night: first a deer that trod the path wary, many-pronged antlers ducking and weaving in the filtered moonlight as the animal tested the wintry air; then three savages, clad all in furs and rawhide, with nocked bows in their hands and eyes downturned to the trail they followed.

The ambuscaders did as Jaymes had ordered.

Var confronted the first man, springing out from cover to drive his saber clean through the savage's belly. Jaymes came not far behind, swinging his rifle to slam the stock against the face of the third man as Talle sprang up and flung himself on the second.

Var's target was slain in the instant, carved through by the saber that pierced his heart. Jaymes's was smashed unconscious. Talle muffled his in the tarpaulin and struggled with the burden until Jaymes tapped, almost gently, on the upraised head and the savage fell silent.

"Bring them." Talle again assumed control. "I need the two alive."

"Best cover our tracks first." Jaymes faced the Inquisitor with obstinacy writ hard on his dirty face. "Lest you want their brothers trailin' us back."

Talle snarled a curse, then ducked his head. "Your country, old man."

"You better believe it," Jaymes said, and hauled the slain savage off the trail to hide the corpse amongst the snowy undergrowth. He came back and set to scuffing up the snow. "Who's carryin' them?" he asked, looking at the Inquisitor.

Talle appeared outraged at the suggestion.

Jaymes said, "You an' me, then, Major. Inquisitor—why don't you use that tarpaulin to sweep our backtrail?"

Talle looked further outraged, but he took the canvas sheet and set to wiping out their tracks as Var and Jaymes each shouldered a supine body and began to move, as fast as they could under their burdens, back to the hollow where the horses were hid.

"They'll be missed come mornin' at the earliest," Jaymes said, "an' if God's on our side, later—so we got a little time to get out of here before their friends come looking. So let's ride!"

Without further preamble, he heaved one unconscious savage onto the pack mule, lashing hands and feet in place across the crosstree saddle, then set the other on his own mount. The mule snorted irritably and Jaymes slapped it across the muzzle.

"You'll go afoot?" Var asked. "Can you keep up?"

"I reckon," Jaymes answered. "Can you keep the mules on the line?"

Var nodded; Talle only sat his horse, impatient to depart.

"Then ride out," Jaymes said. "I'll cover your backtrail an' I'll see you at the fort." He chuckled. "Maybe I'll be waitin' for you."

Talle needed no further bidding: he beckoned that Var follow him and drove harsh heels against his horse's flanks. Var hesitated a moment, looking back at Jaymes, wanting to say something but unable to find the words. He settled on a nod and a smile and went after Talle.

Jaymes watched them go, thinking that it would be easy to put a rifle ball into the Inquisitor's back, and at the same time wondering if the bullet would—could—kill the man. And then what Var's reaction would be: he wanted the major on his side. Talle's throat he'd cheerfully slit, and not feel a grain of remorse . . . save he wondered if the Inquisitor was necessary now, to help defeat the wilderness folk and their demonic allies.

He hid the tracks as best he could—knowing the while that the savages would find them if they came looking—and took after the horses. He supposed Talle would perform his filthy magic back at Fort Harvie, and did not look much forward to that witnessing, save that it appeared the future of Salvation was at stake, and therefore—perhaps—the Inquisitor was necessary.

Do the ends justify the means? he wondered as he went after them. If Talle can defeat the demons, then do I go along with him? Or will that just hand him command? God, but it would be so much easier if the demons slew Talle—unless I need him to make Salvation free. Abram Jaymes amused himself, as he loped long-legged through the snow, with musings on which threat was worse: Jared Talle and the Autarchy he'd see the New World freed from, or the demons he knew too little about . . . until Talle gave him that knowledge.

Best, he decided, to let the Inquisitor have his way for now and decide what to do when they got back to Grostheim. Snow fell on his face, dislodged by a bird that took flight at his passing, and he laughed softly, wondering how Major Tomas Var should take the news that he led what little resistance existed in Salvation. He liked Var; it would be a pity if he must kill the major.

Reluctantly, Var did as the Inquisitor ordered, hauling each savage from the mules and manhandling them—awake now—into the kitchens. Still obeying, he secured them each on a table, arms and legs lashed firmly in place before he slit their crude leather clothing so that they lay naked, screaming imprecations.

"What now?"

"Build up the fire, eh?" Talle smiled. "It's cold in here."

Var thought the man's smile colder and did as he was bade.

"Now leave us," Talle said. "This is not for your eyes."

Var hesitated. Talle studied him a moment, as if he looked upon another specimen suitable for necromantic dissection, and Var quit the room, busying himself with the animals and wondering on the fate of Abram Jaymes. He saw the horses and the mules bedded and fed and went to the barracks, stoking up the fire there, setting water to boiling as he examined what supplies were left.

It was near dark when the first scream exploded across the yard. Var stiffened, almost dropping the cup he held. He had heard men screaming before—men shot or bayoneted, men struck by cannonballs, men struck by sabers or trampled down by charging cavalry horses—but he had never heard such a scream as that, and it chilled his blood. Almost, he went across the yard to . . . he was unsure . . . protest? To watch? Instead, he told himself he had a duty to obey, that Jared Talle was his commanding officer and dedicated to the Autarchy, doing what he did only to secure Salvation's future. But he could not, entirely, shake off the notion that Talle did what he did from sheer enjoyment.

Then the door flung open and Abram Jaymes came in, snow-sheeted and shivering.

"Dear God, it's cold out there." The scout glanced back, through the still-open door. "What's he doin'?"

"Whatever"—Var shrugged miserably—"Inquisitors do."

Jaymes kicked the door shut and crossed to the stove. "Sounds like it's not much fun, except maybe for him."

Var shrugged again. The screaming echoed off the fort's walls. "The savages take heads, no?" he asked dully. "Don't they torture prisoners?"

"Sure, but they're savages." Jaymes shrugged out of his furs and turned his back to the heat. "Aren't we supposed to be civilized?"

All Var could think of by way of response was to ask, "Is there any brandy left?"

They emptied the bottle as the screaming went on. One man died—both Var and Jaymes recognized the sounds of dying—and then the other began. Jaymes tossed meat and vegetables into a pot, constructing a stew that neither man ate, their appetites quite lost. The moon rose over the fort's walls and spilled cold silver light across the yard, the frozen bodies lying there, and the screaming went on. Then ceased abruptly.

Jared Talle came out, shrugging into the fur coat that seemed to dwarf his frame. In the moon's light shadows stretched dark across his face that, as he came through the door, Var saw were great splashes of blood. He carried his jacket and shirt in his hands, and his bare chest was boltered worse than his face. He was smiling.

"Hot water, excellent." He tossed his clothes aside, gesturing at his chest and face. "I need to wash, no?"

It was Jaymes who asked him, "What did you find out?" Var felt too benumbed to speak.

"Much." Talle set to splashing water over the blood, sluicing it carelessly off, so that slews spread over his breeches and through his hair. He seemed not to notice, or to care, as he pulled on his shirt and jacket and found a place at the table, waiting as Jaymes handed him a bowl; then eating with hearty appetite. "Listen . . ."

He spooned up stew before he spoke again. Then: "These savages call themselves Tachyn. They came here from across the mountains, but before that they dwelt in another place, another world." His predatory face grew animated. "They came here by magic! Not by land, or boats, but by magic! Think on that, eh? If we could learn such skills, then the Autarchy might go anywhere . . . conquer all the worlds there are!"

"You'd like that?" Jaymes asked.

Talle looked at the scout as if he were mad. "Of course! To own such power?"

"Why?"

"Because we can," Talle said. "Because with such magic we might cross the mountains and own all the land beyond. Past that—all the worlds."

"Ain't that," Jaymes asked, "somewhat like what the demons want to do? An' what are you planning to do about them?"

"The savages are Dreamers," Talle said. "Some of them, at least. The demons enter their dreams and show them how to influence us—that's how"—he flung a careless hand at the window, indicating the bodies—"they achieved this; what they did in Grostheim. They can make men dream and go mad."

"Then surely we must defeat them," Var said. "Face them

with this knowledge and drive them—savages and demons, both—out."

"Save we can gain their knowledge." Talle's thin face was animated. "I'd have that knowledge for the Autarchy. Think on it! Could I only learn how they transport themselves across the worlds, what might we not conquer?"

Jaymes said, "Who knows?" and looked at Var.

Var held his expression carefully bland. "What do we do next?"

"Return to Grostheim," Talle declared. "We must go back with this news and send it home. Then more Inquisitors shall be sent, to plumb all the depths of this land. After that? Why, we shall mount a great expedition that shall capture savages and demons and learn everything they know."

"I thought," Var said, "that the demons are not physically in this world. How then, shall we capture any?"

Talle laughed. "They're coming! There's a sacrifice the savages intend to make that shall deliver them here. And then . . ." He went on laughing.

Var asked, "What sacrifice?"

"I'm not sure," Talle said. "A child? Some link with that world they came from. My . . . subjects . . . were not entirely clear. But when the sacrifice is made, the demons shall take form here, and we can capture them and learn from them."

"What," Var asked, "are they planning to do here?"

"Conquer," Talle said, beaming as if he entirely approved of such ambitions. "They're dedicated to conquest."

Like you and the Autarchy, Var thought.

"And can we not defeat them?" Var asked. "What then?"

Talle stared at him as if he were mad. "We are the Autarchy," he said. "*The Autarchy!* We rule the known world—how can we be defeated?"

In that instant, had he not known it before, Tomas Var recognized that the Inquisitor Jared Talle was entirely insane. He did not know, in that instant, that he threw in his lot with Abram Jaymes; only that the Inquisitor was crazed, and likely as great a threat to Salvation as any demonic invasion.

He nodded politely and said, "Of course," and looked at

Jaymes, who raised an eyebrow, then back at Talle to ask, "What next?"

"We leave for Grostheim in the morning," Talle said. "We must mount an expedition in the spring. That's when the demons shall come."

"Likely there'll be savages before that." Jaymes studied the exhilarated Talle with calm, cold eyes. "We left tracks they'll be followin' soon as they find out about your . . . subjects."

Talle frowned; Var, his military training to the foreground, asked, "How soon?"

"Can't rightly say," Jaymes answered cheerfully. "It'll depend on when they find our tracks an' work out what's been done. But I tell you this—they can travel a lot faster than us, so we might have a fight on our hands, 'less we can lose them."

"Can we?" Var asked.

Jaymes shrugged. "Maybe; maybe not."

Talle said, "I can use magic. I can set hexes around this fort."

"An' we sit here," Jaymes returned, "like chickens in a coop, waitin' on the foxes?"

"No!" Talle shook his head irritably. "We must get back to Grostheim."

"Then we best ride fast," Jaymes said.

Var thought the man enjoyed the situation, the Inquisitor's discomfort, and asked, "How can we escape them?" He glanced at Talle. "Without the use of magic?"

"I can bespell our trail," Talle snarled. "I can confuse them."

"Does your magic not attract the demons?" Var said. "I thought it brought them to us."

Talle's sallow face darkened in a furious scowl. Jaymes asked innocently, "Ain't that right, Inquisitor?"

Talle's scowl grew deeper, his cheeks darker as he nodded.

"Then best we only ride," Jaymes said. "An' you do exactly what I tell you."

Talle seemed ready to argue: Var stepped into the breach. "So tell us how we escape."

"It won't be easy," Jaymes said, "not if they pick up our tracks an' decide to come after us. But . . ."

"I'd thought you our scout and guide," Talle interrupted. "I'd thought you entrusted with our survival in this wilderness. Was that not your promise?"

"Sure." Jaymes was not at all daunted. "An' if you shut up an' listen, I'll tell you how we might get away safe."

Var watched Talle frown and knew the balance of power was subtly shifted. He did not recognize quite how, save in terms of simple survival, and at the same time knew it ran deeper than that. He could not define it, save that Abram Jaymes had slighted the Inquisitor and forced the man to recognize a greater authority—that he knew Talle must resent and seek to revenge. Don't get yourself hanged, Abram, he thought.

Jaymes said, "Listen . . ."

They quit Fort Harvie in the still, cold hour before dawn, when the sky hung gray above and no birds sang. The air, for all winter ended, was chill, breath steaming and frost riming the walls and all the unburied corpses between. They went out down the cutroad through the glacis and headed straight for the Restitution. Var liked Jaymes's plan not at all, but could think of no better alternative. Talle made no comment, and Var wondered if the Inquisitor sulked as he sat his horse, for he was slumped in the saddle and only followed.

The river stretched wide before them, a gray-sheeted barrier flanked with drifts of snow and frozen floes that bulked in great icy splinters against the north bank like the bulwarks of some primeval fortress. The far bank was lost behind gray and misty air. Var studied the width and could not help but doubt the wisdom of Jaymes's plan. Winter was ending and spring approaching: the ice they'd crossed to reach this side looser now, beginning to split and break up.

"Can we do it?" he asked.

"We don't have much other choice," Jaymes replied. "Look back, eh?"

He gestured at the wilderness edge, beyond the fort. Riders showed there, coming out of the trees—upward of twenty men, Var estimated—mounted on hairy horses that plunged eagerly forward through the snow, urged on by their riders.

Var wondered if he truly heard the whoops of triumph, or if that was only his imagination.

"No; let's go."

Jaymes laughed and took his mule down the bank.

He led the way, Var behind and Talle in the rear, to where the tumbled floes ended and the breaking crust of the river began. The ice was thicker along the bank and for a while they traveled safely, even did hooves skid and slide on the uncertain surface and the animals nicker protest. Then the ice broke up and they must take different paths, not follow Jaymes but seek separate ways across the splitting crust.

Var saw Jaymes's mule go through the surface and come up with a great snort, Jaymes shaking his head and shouting the animal on. Then Var's own mount stumbled and he was lost in dark and icy water that took away his breath and numbed his whole body, so that when the beast fought its way out he was trembling with the chill that seemed to pervade his entire being and could not imagine ever being warm again. He forgot anything other than survival then, until he realized his horse stood shuddering on a wide slab of ice that shifted beneath them and that he must drive it on again or freeze to death—or fall to the savages now closing on the north bank.

"I'll get a fire built. Warm you, eh?"

Jaymes's shout came back to him like a promise and he drove heels hard against the ribs of the trembling horse and forced the animal to jump the floe, to the next, to the one after that, ofttimes swimming between, convinced the cold must kill him.

But he reached the south bank and was hauled to his feet by Abram Jaymes. His teeth chattered uncontrollably and he could not stop shivering. He looked back to see Talle emerging from the river, and knew the Inquisitor had used magic to keep himself warm.

Jaymes said, "I'll build a fire. Can you use that rifle?"

Var nodded, quite unable to speak, not sure he could use the long gun; knowing that he likely must. Their pursuers were closing fast on the river.

The scout said, "Shoot anyone who tries to cross, eh?"

Var pulled off his soaking gloves and took the Hawkins

rifle from its protective casing. He replaced the priming and the shot and tried hard not to shudder as he set the barrel across a fallen branch and endeavored to focus his eyes on the farther bank.

"Let them get about halfway over," Jaymes said. "Only fire when you're sure of your target."

Var did his best to say "Yes," but only managed a stuttering answer.

Talle, miraculously dry, said, "I can destroy them."

Jaymes said, "Sure you can, but then we got demons on our trail, so leave this to us, Inquisitor—that, or help me build a fire."

Var was surprised at Talle's agreement. He leveled his rifle and did his best to fight the numbing cold.

The savages—what had Talle said they were called, Tachyn?—reached the far bank. Var had forgotten time in his chilly misery, and consequently not noticed that the sun had risen and driven off the mist. The north bank of the Restitution was still little more than a gray-white blur, but on it he could see horsemen urging their animals out onto the ice. He waited.

Three ventured out. He waited until they were in midstream before he squeezed the trigger of the Hawkins, and as the drift of occluding smoke got blown away, saw a man was down. He was reloading by then, the action automatic—a reflex born of training and war. His second shot took the horse out from under the second man, and the rider slid between the breaking floes, screaming as he was sucked under. Var wondered why that had not happened to him as he set to priming the Hawkins again.

Then a third shot rang out and a Tachyn was plucked from his saddle.

"I've not lost my touch," Jaymes said over Var's shoulder. "An' there's a fire built: go warm yourself. The Inquisitor should have some food ready before long."

Var was too cold, too numb, to argue. He only nodded and stumbled away through the snow as Jaymes recharged his own Hawkins and set to picking off the venturesome Tachyn daring enough to attempt the river under such horribly accurate fire.

■　　■　　■

"I must go back." Var had drunk tea and taken food; in a while, he thought that he might even feel warm again. "I can't leave Abram to fight them alone."

"Why not?" Talle asked. "It appears he can handle the savages, so leave him."

Var stared at the Inquisitor and asked, "To what? To face them alone?"

"To your duty," Talle said. "To your duty to Evander and the Autarchy."

"We need him," Var said, "to get back to Grostheim."

Talle waved a dismissive hand. "No; we can get back without him now. Leave him!"

Var said, "I can't," and went back to the river. It did not occur to him to do anything else: Abram Jaymes was his friend and might die without help. Jared Talle was . . . God! Jared Talle was a black crow who strutted over riven corpses, who enjoyed too much the exercising of his power. He no longer cared what Jared Talle thought of him or might do to him: he felt mightily relieved.

Tomas Var threw himself down beside Abram Jaymes and thumbed back the hammer of his Hawkins rifle.

"Not too many left," Jaymes said, "an' the ice is all broken, so they won't likely attempt crossing too much longer."

Var said, "No," and knocked a man off his horse.

"Nice shot," Jaymes said. "How's the Inquisitor?"

"Angry," Var replied. "He wanted me to leave you."

"But you didn't," Jaymes said as another Tachyn was dropped from his mount into the cold water.

Var said, "No, I didn't."

"Why not?" Jaymes asked.

"I don't know," Var answered. "Tell me."

Jaymes laughed and said, even as he sighted on a rider coming over the ice and smashed the man from his saddle with a single shot, "You work it out."

Var said, "I can't," as he took another rider down.

"You will," Jaymes said, priming his long rifle. "God willin', in time you will."

■   ■   ■

The Tachyn were defeated and could not cross the river, for fear of the deadly rifle fire and the killing ice: they gave up and let the three men go.

And the three returned to Grostheim to find chaos awaiting them.

30

Choices

Downstream, the breaking ice that cluttered the farther reaches of the Restitution relinquished its hold to the gray swell of the tidal current. The water churned surly and sullen as the sky above, nor was the snow much better as it, in turn, gave up its hold in acknowledgment of spring's approach, becoming a watery slush that clung to hooves and boots and threatened to transform the ground beneath to cloying mud. Random shafts of sunlight struck through the scudding gray cloud, lighting the river and the land with fleeting promises that disappointed in their brevity. A cold, wet wind blew in from the bay. Grostheim loomed ahead, alternately lit and shadowed as the cloud played games with the sun, squatting beside the river like . . . Var was no longer sure, save that when he looked at the walls he wondered why they were manned by so many of his own marines, not the red-coated Militia Alyx Spelt commanded. He shivered inside his furs, sensing a wrongness.

"Something has happened here." It was the first time Talle had spoken in hours. Indeed, for most of their return journey the Inquisitor had gone silent, clearly angered by Var's refusal to desert Abram Jaymes. "I sense the dimensions of magic."

"You would." Jaymes spat a stream of tobacco that got lost in the slush, and grinned. "You bein' an Inquisitor, of course."

Talle glowered. Var said nothing, only wished his friend might keep his mouth shut and not provoke Talle further.

Talle said, "Do we go see, then?" And heeled his mount on. Var and Jaymes followed.

As they came closer, Var saw muskets aimed in their direction and rose up in his stirrups to halloo the citadel.

"I am Major Tomas Var, and I ride with the Inquisitor Jared Talle! Do you hear me?"

From the walls came an answer: "Approach slowly, else we fire."

Var recognized the voice of Captain Jorge Kerik and shouted back, "Jorge, do you not know me?"

The response was cautious, torn between suspicion and hope: "Major Var? Is that truly you?"

"Who else?" Var shouted. "Don't you recognize me?"

"I recognize very little these days," Kerik returned. "Come on slowly, eh?"

"Enough of this." Talle mouthed a curse and drove his horse forward, his voice lifting to a magic-enhanced bellow: "I am Jared Talle, the Inquisitor, and do you oppose me I shall see you hexed and hanged, and hexed again so that your soul shall never rest."

The shout seemed to echo off the walls, dinning loud in the blustery air. Var saw its effect on his men: some lowered their muskets, accepting, whilst others took surer aim, as if quite untrusting of the three approaching riders. He wondered what had transpired during his absence.

Talle appeared unconcerned, bringing his mount plunging through the melting snow to confront the wide gates that remained closed.

"Do you open, damn you?"

From the wall above, Kerik shouted, "Are you truly the Inquisitor, you open them with your magic."

Talle mouthed a second, fouler curse and raised his hands. Var watched as they moved in the complexities of arcane knowledge, seeing Talle's lips move but quite unable to grasp the words the Inquisitor spoke.

Bolts slid back untouched by hands and the gates flew open. Talle rode through and halted as Captain Kerik came pounding down from the catwalk above.

"Forgive me, Inquisitor; Major." He cringed as he spoke. "You'll understand why I had to be sure when I tell you what's happened here. God knows, but it's all chaos."

■   ■   ■

God knew, but it was.

Var was horrified as he listened to Kerik's account of the winter: Governor Wyme slain by Alyx Spelt, the major shot in turn; then officers slaughtered, men of the God's Militia turning on one another, landholders fighting, traders fighting—until all Grostheim was reduced to anarchy and the only remaining authority was Var's own marines, whose hold was tenuous and resented by freemen and exiles alike.

"It was the ghosts," Kerik finished. "Them and their dreams, I believe. Most of the refugees have fled back to their holdings—these days they think they'll be safer there than here." He looked anxiously at Var. "I've got our men stationed in the Militia barracks, Major. Got the place fortified. God, but we were attacked by redcoats even then. I never thought that I'd fight our own kind."

"You didn't," Talle interjected. "You fought men possessed of demons. You slew them, I trust?"

Kerik nodded sorrowfully. "They left us no choice, Inquisitor."

"Good." Talle rubbed his hands before the fire. "Hold no regrets, Captain—you did the right thing."

"Shooting redcoats?" Kerik asked mournfully. "It didn't feel like the right thing."

"They had forsaken God," Talle declared. "They were possessed."

Abram Jaymes nudged Var in the ribs and murmured, "Like them soldiers in the fort, eh?"

Var nodded and asked of Kerik, "Any word from the border forts?"

"None." Kerik shook his head. "No pigeons have come in, nor riders. I've sent messages, but got no answers—the birds return with their pouches intact."

"The border forts are lost," Talle said. "At least, for now. Forget them."

"What's happening here?" Kerik asked.

"We're under siege," Talle answered. "Salvation faces a terrible threat, and Grostheim stands alone."

"What," Jaymes asked, "about the holdings? Are they under siege, too?"

Talle shrugged carelessly. "Perhaps; perhaps not. I don't care—only that we defeat the demons."

"How you goin' to do that?" Jaymes inspected his fingernails, using a knife to extract the dirt there.

Talle said, "I don't know yet—but I shall! The Autarchy will not give up this land easily."

Jaymes nodded and turned to Kerik. "The branded folk affected by all this?"

"No." Kerik shook his head. "It seems like only the free folk are."

Jaymes grinned as if holding secret knowledge to himself. Talle spun to face the scout, demanding, "What are you getting at?"

Jaymes shrugged. "It seems pretty obvious, don't it? You got folk goin' crazy from dreams—sent by the demons, you claim. But who goes crazy? Only folk with a vested interest, no? Folk who own land, or soldier for Evander to protect the landowners. No one else!

"You say the demons want to conquer Salvation; we all know the savages want to claim the land. So, what you got here seems to me like a fight for the territory—you want it an' the savages want it an' the demons want it. The demons an' the savages are workin' together an' they got the upper hand right now, it seems. God knows, but you lost your forts an' you got a real problem here. Listen!" He gestured at the window. Shouts came through the glass, voices raised in protest and outrage, punctuated by the rattle of musketry. "What's goin' on out there?"

It was Kerik who answered: "Likely another riot." He glanced helplessly at Talle, at Var. "There's little we can do to quell them: we've not enough men. Folk are mightily hungry, and the stores are already used up. Folk are starving, and with the governor dead . . ." He shrugged, unconsciously aping Jaymes. "I've had men killed on the streets. . . ."

"But now," Talle said, "I am back. Now order shall be restored." He looked to Var. "Tomas, your first duty is to organize your men and get this city settled."

Var nodded. Then felt his belly chill as Talle added casually, "But before that, a small matter of discipline." He gestured at Abram Jaymes. "Put this man in a cell, and once the square's cleared—hang him."

Var said, "I'm sorry, but what choice do I have?" as the door closed on Jaymes.

The older man said, "You always got choices; it's just that sometimes it takes awhile to see them."

"What does that mean?" Var asked.

And Jaymes grinned through the bars and said, "You'll work it out, I reckon."

"I warned you," Var said. "Why didn't you get away before we came back here?"

"Maybe I wanted to see what was goin' on." Jaymes shrugged and cut a plug of tobacco. "Maybe I wanted to see what you'd do."

"My duty, I trust," Var said.

"Sure." Jaymes stuck the black wad in his mouth and began to chew. "But what's your duty, Major?"

It was a question that troubled Var as he went about his appointed tasks.

Was it his duty to restore order to Grostheim with squads of marines that shot down looters and dissidents on Talle's orders?

His duty to defend Salvation against the incursions of the savages and—now, it would seem—their demonic allies?

His duty to obey Jared Talle, unquestioning?

He could no longer do that. He was full of questions, and could not help wondering if the Autarchy were not better abandoning Salvation, even setting free the branded exiles.

Dear God, but it was not easy to play the part of loyal officer in the God's Militia. Not when such doubts skirled like the freshening spring wind around his mind.

Nor could he stomach the notion of Abram Jaymes swinging from the gallows tree, no matter Talle's command.

He did his best to restore some semblance of order and found, as he did, that he resented Talle's methods the more:

the inhabitants of Grostheim were frightened, terrified by the ghost-ridden winter, afraid of hunger, wondering what was to come; and Talle quelled them with magic or the bayonets of Var's marines. It was, Var thought, a reign of terror, one greater fear imposing itself over another—Talle more frightening than any of the phantasmagoric demons that still stalked the streets—and he wondered again which was the worse.

But as winter ended and the first fresh breaths of spring wafted the air, order was restored. And Jared Talle commanded that Var delay no longer in hanging Abram Jaymes.

"I can't," he said through the bars. "God help me, but I can't."

Jaymes shrugged and spat a stream of tobacco over the straw of his cell, scattering cockroaches. "What else you goin' to do?" His voice was even, tinged with amusement. "You got your orders, no? The Inquisitor says you've got to hang me, so I guess you hang me."

"I could . . ." Var said.

"Do what?" Jaymes asked.

The Inquisitor's dog? Was that all he was? He told himself *No!* and said to the prisoner: "I could help you escape."

"How?" Jaymes asked bluntly. "You goin' to turn against Talle?"

Var shrugged and shook his head in confusion.

"You break me out," Jaymes said with such calm as embarrassed Var, "Talle's got to know about it. He's the *Inquisitor*—he'll know."

Var said, "Yes."

Jaymes said, "How'd you think to do it?"

Var said, "I don't know. Perhaps if I ordered my marines . . ."

"They'd go against the Inquisitor?" Jaymes asked.

Var shrugged again and shook his head again. "Some might; not all. Talle's . . ."

"Scary as all hell," Jaymes supplied. "An' got hex magic on his side, too."

Var said, "Yes." And then: "But if I acted alone . . ."

"We'd both be fugitives," Jaymes said. "We'd have to run a long way from Grostheim to escape Talle. Maybe as far as the wilderness, even."

Abruptly, as if the scout's words conjured up old memories, Var thought of Arcole Blayke. Had he not escaped indenture in Grostheim?

"Did you ever hear of a man called Arcole Blayke? An indentured man?"

"Sure." Jaymes nodded. "Old Wyme took him on, but he ran out when the savages attacked. Him an' his woman, an' a boy indentured to Rupyrt Gahame. Likely all dead now—if they got past the heathens attackin' the walls."

"But they got out," Var said, wondering even as he spoke if he went mad. *What am I doing? This is insanity: planning to free a man condemned by the Inquisitor?* "They *did* escape."

Jaymes said, "We'd need sound horses."

Var said, "What about your mule?"

Jaymes said, "I ain't in love with the beast, an' his absence'd be noticed. No—horses are better: two at least, an' good runners."

Var said, "And supplies?"

"Food for a few days," Jaymes said. "Rifles an' shot."

"Campaign gear," Var said.

Jaymes said, "Yes. We'd need to run fast—Talle's not likely to let you go easily."

Var said, "No," and realized that he was committed. That he was about to throw away a lifetime's dedication to the Autarchy, to his career, for the sake of a draggle-haired old man who chewed tobacco and stank of sour sweat. But he could think of no other honorable path to take.

"We can find shelter along the way," Jaymes said. "I've got friends."

"Who'd hide us?" Var asked.

Jaymes nodded. "Plenty."

Var swallowed, turning his tricorne hat between his hands. "If I do . . ." he said.

"I'll be grateful," Jaymes said, and grinned. "An' if you don't, I'll understand."

Var said, "I can't let you hang. You don't deserve that."

Jaymes said, "No; but nor do you."

Var shrugged and said, "I'll let you know when," and rose, quitting the cell block.

A slow and satisfied smile spread across Jaymes's weathered features as he watched Var depart.

By God but he'd had high hopes of the major since first they met. The man seemed different to most officers of the God's Militia—more amenable to reason, clearer-sighted— and now it looked like those hopes reached fruition. Jaymes had studied him carefully; cautiously at first, but with such increasing confidence as persuaded him to reveal more of Salvation's hidden depths. That Var had taken his side against the Inquisitor back there on the river had been the final confirmation, and now the scout knew that Var took his part; even at cost of the major's career. He nodded to himself, and settled on the narrow bunk chained against the inner wall.

Var had given his word, and Jaymes knew that was good: the major would do his best to effect an escape, and then he must surely be totally committed to the cause. Still smiling, Jaymes stretched his lanky frame on the bunk and consigned himself to waiting.

A false spring fell on Salvation's coast. The sun shone and the winds grew warm. Flowers, all yellow and blue, sprouted along the shoreline behind the rolling dunes and the pines began to bud. Grass grew around the citadel and the gulls that had been the only occupants of the sky were joined by swallows. Frozen ground grew muddy and then hardened— firm as Var's determination.

Order—at least, of a kind—was restored. The gallows that had carried those first to argue Jared Talle's rule had been occupied long enough that winter's crows were sated and dissidence quelled, so no others took the place of the dangling corpses. The ghosts had gone, as if blown away on the new wind, and Jared Talle was confident that he had reestablished order. And that it was now time to hang Abram Jaymes.

"Let it be ceremonial," he told Var. "I'd have him brought out by your marines and hung before all the populace. A warning, eh? A rite of spring!" He lifted the decanter that had once belonged to Andru Wyme and filled both their glasses. "I know you felt a certain fondness for him, Tomas, but the man was offensive, no? And we need, I think, one last example."

"One last?" Var asked.

"Absolutely." Talle sniffed the goblet, savoring the bouquet. The windows of Wyme's study were opened to the warm spring air and Var caught a waft of brandy and sweat, the sour odor that accompanied Talle. He wondered why he found that offensive and not Abram Jaymes's musky smell. "We must quell any doubts of our authority—of the Autarchy's power. The demons shall come against us soon, and I'd not have dissidents at our backs, eh? Better that all Grostheim—all Salvation—understand who's the power here."

"And if they resent his hanging?" Var asked.

"Who could?" Talle returned. "God, Tomas, the man insulted me, questioned my authority. Would you see him go free? Besides, what does it matter if they resent me—us—so long as they fear us and obey?"

For an instant, Var wondered if the Inquisitor played with him, but Talle's expression was entirely complacent, as if the man only enjoyed his contemplation of Jaymes's demise and Var's part in it, so Var smiled and ducked his head and said, dissembling, "I've a certain fondness for him, yes. He's surely a character."

"Undoubtedly." Talle chuckled. "But not so much as should jeopardize your standing here, eh?"

Var shook his head, not liking himself for the silent lie.

"So, then," Talle said, "do you organize it and see him hanged on . . . do we say, Sunday? When all the indentured folk may come see him swing. Let all of Grostheim see him, eh?"

Var nodded and emptied his glass. "I'll see to it," he promised.

It was Thursday: he had three days to organize the escape. He no longer doubted but that he should; and God help him for what he did.

Surely, he thought as he paced back to the barracks, it was a betrayal. But also an affirmation; though of what he could not be sure. . . . Friendship? New loyalties? He wished, sincerely, that he had never been granted this command, never met Jared Talle or Abram Jaymes, never seen Salvation. But he had, and the past could not be changed, only the future made better, and Tomas Var could not stand by to watch a man he deemed innocent hanged by the neck, no matter the cost to himself.

So . . .

. . . The horses were easy to arrange. It was not unusual that an officer requisition animals for riding beyond the city walls, and Var had a pair ready. The supplies—of trail food and blankets, such stuff as they'd need—he'd already organized. He had his own Hawkins rifle and had taken possession of Jaymes's. He had powder and shot to see them through to God-knew-where, so he need only stow the gear on the animals and break Jaymes free.

That, and wonder at his insanity—which he elected to ignore: Abram Jaymes was his friend and he could not retain his honor and watch the man die on Talle's gallows.

So . . .

He went into the barracks and announced that the Inquisitor would interview the prisoner. He was Major Tomas Var—the Inquisitor's dog—and none dared question him. Abram Jaymes was brought out from his cell in shackles, and when Var demanded the key it was given him. He pocketed the thing and gestured that Jaymes proceed him.

They quit the barracks and stepped out into the square beyond. Jaymes shuffled awkwardly, hampered by the chains connecting his ankles. It was close on dusk. The new-come swallows darted amongst the buildings, black shadows against a sky the color of drying blood; gulls mewed, but otherwise a sullen quiet pervaded Grostheim. The guards outside saluted Var and watched him go with his prisoner. He crossed the square, Jaymes stumbling ahead, and took the avenue leading to the governor's mansion, to where Talle sat ensconced.

Then Var caught up and turned Jaymes into a side street. Under the shadow of a porch he unlocked the shackles and beckoned the man to follow him.

Jaymes said, "About damn' time. Those chains were startin' to hurt me."

Var said, "Shut up." He felt very afraid that Talle would somehow sense what he did—or already had, and that all of this was part of the Inquisitor's malign game, and at any moment they be apprehended.

Jaymes grunted and went after him; in the burgeoning twilight Var could not see his smile.

"Here." The horses were saddled ready, tethered beneath the outcrop of a partially burned building, a legacy of the winter's riots. "Put these on." Var tugged a dead marine's greatcoat from the bundle stowed on Jaymes's mount, a tricorne hat.

"We playin' at soldiers?" Jaymes chuckled. He seemed far less concerned than Var with the dangers of their situation.

"Dammit, yes," Var replied. "How else do we get past the gates?"

Jaymes went on smiling as he pulled on the blue coat and settled the tricorne on his head. He seemed confident—far more so than Var, who waited nervously, wondering what madness possessed him that he throw away his life for this grinning old fool.

"Major?" Jaymes aped a salute. "Shall I do?"

"You'd best," Var gave him back, "or we're both dead."

"Well, let's see." Jaymes swung astride the patient horse. "I'm ready if you are."

Var nodded curtly, fear and irritation blending. "Then let's go."

He turned his own mount down the alley, Jaymes following behind, and they rode toward the gates.

The evening, for all of spring's promise, was chill, but Var felt sweat bead his brow and trickle anticipatory down his back. The sun was set now and the darting swallows replaced by bats that swept like dark omens through the shadows. The clopping of the hooves sounded unnaturally loud, and Var wondered if the faces that watched them pass knew of his subterfuge. Cold, sharp fingers seemed to run down his spine as he momentarily anticipated the appearance of Jared Talle, the Inquisitor's hands flung up in the arcane movements of hex magic. He was not sure which should be worse: sudden death at Talle's hands, or the ignominy of arrest.

But he was committed now and could not turn back: his path was chosen, for honor's sake, and friendship—he rode toward the gates.

Jorge Kerik was again on guard, and recognized Var.

"Major!" He saluted. "I'd not thought anyone would go out so late."

"The Inquisitor's business, Captain." Var returned the salute. "We're to scout the environs, for fear of demons."

Mention of those dread entities was enough. Kerik shouted that the gates be opened, Var and Jaymes rode through, followed by Kerik's shout: "God be with you both."

"Amen to that," Jaymes chuckled. And then: "Tidily done, Major."

All Var said was "Ride, damn you," as he dug his heels against his horse's flanks and lifted the bay to a gallop.

He wanted to get as far from Grostheim as he could before Talle realized what had happened and sent chasers after them. He wanted to ride wide and far, knowing that all his past was given up now, all his career and loyalties; knowing that the Autarchy must now deem him outlaw and he be no different to any branded man running from his master. He felt lost and afraid, alone, with all the width of Salvation spread before him—and likely, he thought, nowhere to hide.

31

The Fire, Far Away

Morrhyn woke sweat-sticky and shuddering, the dream still so vivid in his mind that it was awhile before he could control his limbs and stumble from the bed to splash welcome water on his heated face, and even then he must kneel and brace himself before he might rise to face the awful truth of revelation.

The Breakers came again! Or would, did all their filthy plans come to fulfillment—the which depended on . . . He shook his head, denying the horror of that knowledge. It was too gross, too far beyond the comprehension of any caring man. It was, to him, unthinkable . . . but to the Breakers, to Chakthi?

He tugged on shirt and breeches. His hands shook as he laced his boots, and when he pushed through the flap of his lodge it seemed the sun burned accusing on his face, the breeze that ruffled his hair a lash of condemnation for his lack of foresight.

They name me the Prophet, eh? What poor prophet that I failed to foresee this.

He paused only long enough to make brief obeisance to the Maker, raising his hands and face to the four corners of the world and the mountains beyond, praying the while that the dream did not come too late, and went at a run to where the Lakanti tents were pitched.

Lhyn called to him as he passed, asking if he'd take breakfast with her, but he did not hear her in his urgency, or even smell the biscuits and meat savory in the pan. Arrhyna and Flysse watched him go by and saw his face and turned to Lhyn for reassurance of what they saw there, for his expression frightened them.

"Wait," Lhyn urged when they'd go after him, to know what drove the wakanisha so swiftly—so urgently—on his way. "Has he dreamed of your husbands, he'll tell us in time. We can only wait."

Morrhyn found Kahteney's lodge and slapped his hand against the entry flap.

"Are you awake, brother? I'd speak with you."

The curtain was thrust aside on the instant, Kahteney beckoning Morrhyn inside, the lodge filled with the sweet smell of brewing tea. Kahteney's face was pale, his eyes stretched wide as any owl's.

"I'd have come to you. I dreamed . . ."

"Tell me," Morrhyn urged.

Their dreams coincided: a fire sweeping over the land, consuming everything; the Breakers come again, their resurgence dependent on the terrible sacrifice neither Dreamer cared much to discuss.

"If it happens," Morrhyn said, "then I think we are lost. It shall deliver them all the knowledge they need, and they shall find Ket-Ta-Thanne and Salvation, and destroy the People and the Grannach and those folk who live beyond the mountains. It shall give them dominion over this world and all the others."

Kahteney nodded, his angular face planed deeper by the horror as he asked, "What shall we do? What *can* we do?"

"All we may," Morrhyn said, "but it shall not be easy. Listen . . ."

Davyd woke struggling against the hand that clamped against his face. He tried to shout and could not for the pressure there, so he reached up to grasp the strangling wrist and force his attacker away. He reached for his knife, thinking to plant the blade between his assailant's ribs. . . .

Then heard Arcole say, "In God's name, be quiet! Would you bring all Chakthi's Tachyn down on us?"

Davyd's eyes opened and he saw Arcole straddling him, gagging him.

Arcole saw the awareness there and released his grip; Davyd let go the knife.

"God, I thought you'd kill me!" Arcole glanced at his shirt. A pinprick of blood showed on the dirty material. "You dreamed?"

Davyd nodded. His mouth was very dry and he gestured at the waterskin, waiting until Arcole passed it to him and he had swallowed sufficient to loosen his tongue before speaking.

"Where's Rannach?"

"On guard," Arcole said.

"Bring him. He must hear this."

There was such immediacy in his voice Arcole did not hesitate, but rose and went to where Rannach stood his early-morning watch.

When they returned to the banked fire it was to find Davyd crouched over the embers, his blanket drawn tight about his trembling shoulders, his face haunted.

He stared aghast at Rannach, who gasped, "Debo? He's dead?"

"Not yet." Davyd shook his head, weary and urgent at the same time. "But . . ." He paused, shaking. "Listen . . ."

Taza had not expected such a welcome. He had thought that the deliverance of Chakthi's grandson must bring him acclaim, a position of honor amongst the Tachyn, but it was as if he were no more than a messenger, a mere carrier, and he sulked as Debo was given to Chakthi and the Tachyn akaman raised the child high above his head.

"My grandson!" Chakthi shouted. "Vachyr's child is given back to me!"

Debo screamed, demanding that this strange man set him down. Chakthi ignored the boy's wailing, holding him aloft as he paraded the camp.

"You shall be praised in time." Taza felt a hand on his shoulder and turned to find Hadduth smiling at him. "Let Chakthi have his pleasure for now, and later he'll reward you."

Taza nodded sulkily. "It was not easy," he said, "bringing him here. I risked much."

"I know." Hadduth's hand grasped firmer. "But you were aided, no?"

"You?" Taza looked askance at the Tachyn Dreamer. "That was you?"

"Not alone." Hadduth's smile was enigmatic. "There are . . . others . . . who aided your dreaming."

"The golden warrior?" Taza looked about the camp and saw no sign of that strange figure. "He's here?"

Hadduth said, "Not yet. But now you've brought us Debo . . ."

"I thought . . ." Taza said, and shrugged.

"Thought what?" Hadduth asked pleasantly.

Taza shrugged again and said, "That Chakthi should welcome his grandson's savior."

"He does," Hadduth said. "He will—but for now he's only delighted that Vachyr's child is delivered him."

Taza said, "Shall I be adopted into the Tachyn, then? Shall you teach me to be a wakanisha?"

"Yes," Hadduth answered. "And more; far more."

Owan Thirsk knew he was close to death, and welcomed that promise of oblivion. He was drained in ways he could not previously have imagined, as if the pahé Hadduth fed him leached out all his spirit, so that he no longer cared to live but only looked forward to the ultimate calm of his life's ending.

Hadduth had used him badly. The wakanisha had got language from him—Evander's tongue—and knowledge of Salvation, of its geography and social structure and all Thirsk knew of Grostheim and the forts, of the soldiers and the people, both branded and free. And as the Tachyn sucked out his dreaming knowledge, there had come into Thirsk's mind a terrible figure—a dread warrior armored in gold, whose horse clattered with bleached skulls—and Thirsk had known that he was forced to commune with true devils. That the laughing figure whose eyes glowed red as furnace fires was, truly, the embodiment of all evil, of destruction rampant and unthinking, uncaring—save for annihilation. And Thirsk, the owh'jika, had aided that creature in its plans, and that likely Salvation should fall because of his aid.

He longed for death. It should, he hoped, be an atonement before God.

The ragged man tethered like some captive animal to the ground could barely open his eyes as he felt Hadduth's kick.

"This is the owh'jika," Hadduth said. "He taught me the language of this land, and how to enter the minds of its people so that I can send them dreams that drive them mad and set them to killing one another." The Tachyn Dreamer chuckled. "It is most satisfying to set them to slaying one another."

"You are a great wakanisha," Taza said, staring at the skeletal figure. It was a sorry sight: gaunt and filthy; near, he thought, to dying. "Morrhyn would not do that. He would not even give me pahé, or accept me as pupil."

"Morrhyn," Hadduth said, "is a fool. He fails to recognize the true source of power."

"Which is?" Taza asked.

Hadduth laughed. "Morrhyn believes the Maker is divine—and perhaps He is—but He is surely not alone. There is another source . . . that you've seen."

Taza said, "The golden warrior? The one who brought me through the Grannach caverns?"

"Akratil," Hadduth said approvingly, "who is powerful as the Maker."

"Surely he must be." Taza nodded. "Is he like the Gray Wolf, and the Maker like the Brown Doe?"

"Old stories from an old world." Hadduth set an arm around Taza's shoulders. "Ket-Ta-Witko is far away, and this is a new land, with new masters—new gods."

"Shall you teach me to understand them?" Taza asked eagerly. "Shall you teach me to dream and become a true wakanisha?"

Hadduth said, "Yes, I shall. But first you must prove yourself."

"Have I not already?" Taza protested, gesturing at the celebrating camp where Chakthi still paraded the screaming child. "I stole Debo, no? I brought him here, did I not? How else shall I prove myself?"

"Kill him." Hadduth kicked the owh'jika hard in the ribs.

"I slew a man already," Taza said. "I put my knife into Tekah when he tried to stop me taking Debo."

"Then it should be easy now," Hadduth said. "Prove yourself to Akratil."

Taza thought a moment, and then decided that he had come too far to turn back. Did Hadduth demand a sacrifice, then he should have it: what matter another life now? He drew his blade and knelt down and thrust it hard into the owh'jika's throat, twisting the good Grannach steel until he felt the point grate on bone.

He could not understand what Thirsk said to him as the blood fountained and the owh'jika died: "Thank you." But Hadduth was approving, and that pleased Taza.

"Now," Hadduth said, "you are one of us."

Debo screamed his protest as Chakthi carried him about the camp. He hated the dank forest and the sad lodges and the smell of the man who held him aloft. There was an odor of blood and sweat about the man that Debo had never known when Rannach carried him: an odor of decay the child could not define but only incognitively recognize and protest against. But he had no choice—Chakthi paraded him like a trophy, and his friend, Taza, only stood watching and smiling as if all his dreams were come true and the Green Grass Woman had touched him.

Debo wished he had never gone with Taza. It had seemed a great adventure at first, but now it became a terrifying thing and he longed for the comfort of his mother's arms, his father's presence. He beat his small hands against Chakthi's head and voiced what few curses he knew in condemnation of his traitorous friend. But Taza paid him no attention, and he knew he was lost.

And in Ket-Ta-Witko, in the blood-strewn valley of the old Meeting Ground, Akratil sat before a fire on which a man's body was spitted and knew that soon his dreams must become reality, and he lead the Horde onward in service of his dread master. Onward to the land his prey had fled to, where he should destroy them, and all the others, so that nothing remained save destruction. They would not, he vowed, escape. He was unaccustomed to defeat—it sullied his honor. More, he served a dark force that knew nothing of sympathy, and should he fail . . .

He shook his head, dismissing the thought. He would not fail! He looked to where Bemnida waited, a knife poised in her hand, ready to carve.

"I am hungry."

Instantly, the woman set to slicing the choicest cuts from the body, layering them on a silver platter that she carried to Akratil, kneeling as she served him.

He said, "My thanks," and stroked her hair, at which she smiled and made a sound akin to the purring of some great cat.

"Shall it be soon?" she ventured as Akratil selected a piece of bloody meat.

"Yes," he answered, pleased with her loyalty. "Soon, my pretty."

Bemnida stared at him with eyes filled with adoration.

The pahé filled Morrhyn with its comforting languor. The wa'tenhya seemed to shift and shimmer before his eyes, Kahteney becoming a blurred shape stretched out indistinct beyond the fire. The flames were far more interesting, for in their writhing he began to see the shape of futures possible and futures that might be, and even—he prayed as he felt his eyes droop shut—what he need do to deny the threatened terror. . . .

He woke thickheaded. The fire was gone down into embers, Kahteney slept on, and he could not tell what hour it was, night or day—only know the terrible urgency of the dreamt answers. He found the waterskin and drank deep, then crawled to where Kahteney lay and shook the Lakanti wakanisha awake.

Kahteney groaned, rubbing at his red-rimmed eyes, and said anxiously, "Must it be so?"

"I think," Morrhyn said, "that there is no other way."

"We might well lose Ket-Ta-Thanne," Kahteney moaned.

"Do we fail the Maker," Morrhyn returned him, "we shall surely lose Ket-Ta-Thanne. And more, besides."

Kahteney said, "Yes," in a tone that suggested he'd sooner reject the awful certitude of their shared dreaming.

"Then do we go tell them?" Morrhyn asked.

Kahteney gave him back, "Shall they listen? Even to the Prophet?"

Morrhyn shrugged. "Those who'll listen shall come with me. I only pray there be enough."

Kahteney swallowed water, spilled more over his face and naked chest, and said, "We've no other choice, eh?"

Morrhyn said, "No."

"Then do we go speak with Yazte and the others." Kahteney sat up, reaching for his shirt. "Ach, Morrhyn my brother, is there any end to this?"

"Perhaps." Morrhyn smiled wanly. "Perhaps, do we defeat them now. Can we defeat them now . . ."

Kahteney nodded and followed the Prophet from the dream lodge.

Lhyn felt her breath clog in her throat as she watched Morrhyn emerge, Kahteney on his heels. Both Dreamers wore the expressions of men who had seen more and worse than either would envisage, and at the same time seemed determined. She recognized that look: Morrhyn had worn it when he announced his intention of going to the Maker's Mountain, nor less when he returned with his awful news. She watched them hurry to Yazte's lodge, seeking to conceal her own fear as she felt Arrhyna's eyes on her, and Flysse's.

"Wait," she said. "They'd speak with Yazte, and when that's done doubtless we shall be told."

"What?" Yazte stared aghast at the Dreamers. "Do you know what you ask of the People?"

Morrhyn nodded. "Much." His eyes fixed the Lakanti akaman with a pale blue stare that forbade denial. "But do we not attempt it, then Ket-Ta-Thanne and all the worlds shall be lost. Would you see that happen?"

Yazte shook his head like a bear woken from hibernation and resentful of the disturbance, but he said, "No; how can I?" He sighed and studied the wakanishas each in turn. "Best call a Council, eh?"

Davyd shivered, unsure whether it was the knowledge of his dreaming or the effects of his wounds that set his body to trembling. The Maker knew, but the dreams were bad. And did worse come to worst . . . He pushed the thought aside: there was no path left save onward in hope, even could he scarce dare own that precious commodity. He pushed clear of his blankets and rose to squat beside the fire. Spring came late to Salvation, and the early-morning air was chill. He wished forlornly that he were back safe in Ket-Ta-Thanne—save Ket-Ta-Thanne was no longer safe. Nor was safety anywhere did Chakthi and Hadduth succeed in their horrid design.

Rannach stirred and was instantly awake.

"Debo?"

"Tonight," Davyd said. "They shall attempt it tonight."

"Then we'd best find them," Rannach said.

Davyd nodded. "I know the way now. It shall take us the better part of the day, but the Maker willing, we'll be in time."

Taza had thought only to earn Chakthi's approval by bringing the Tachyn his grandson, that the akaman should welcome the return of his dead son's child. He had believed it must earn him his dearest wish—to become a true Dreamer—and that was now promised him. Hadduth had given his word that Taza should become his named pupil, that he be given the pahé and taught the dreaming ways. He had thought that Debo would be raised as a Tachyn, likely to be named akaman after Chakthi.

He had never thought on such plans as the outcasts held for the little boy, and for all his hatred of Davyd, his resentment of Morrhyn, he found what was planned abhorrent.

"It's the only way," Hadduth explained, casual as if they

discussed the slaughtering of a deer. "Akratil and his Break-ers are trapped in Ket-Ta-Witko. When Morrhyn opened the Gate, it closed behind us and left the Breakers there—save we open a fresh pathway, they must remain."

"Is that so bad?" Taza asked, nervous now.

"Save they come here," Hadduth replied, "we must re-main like fugitives in these forests. Are we to own the grass of this land—and the grass of Ket-Ta-Thanne—we need their help. Akratil promises much! Did he not bring you safe through the Grannach caves? Do you doubt his power?"

"No." Taza shook his head, remembering the golden-armored warrior. "But even so . . ."

"The strangers of this land own strange powers," Hadduth said. "Without Akratil's aid we cannot hope to defeat them all. Surely we cannot hope to go back to Ket-Ta-Thanne."

"But Debo . . ." Taza said.

"Must be sacrificed," Hadduth replied. "He's the blood of both the Commacht and the Tachyn in his veins, and so links the two lands."

"But he's only a child," Taza said. "And Chakthi's grand-son! Shall Chakthi truly slay his grandson?"

"To own this land—yes," Hadduth answered. "To destroy Rannach and his Commacht—yes. So when the moon rises tonight, Debo shall be slain and his blood shape the gateway for the Breakers."

32 Sacrifice

Tomas Var learned more of Salvation's social structure as he rode outlaw from Grostheim with Abram Jaymes than he ever should have as an officer of the God's Militia.

Branded folk gave them shelter, hiding them in barns and outhouses, bringing them food unbeknownst to the masters, feeding their horses—even, when the animals grew too weary, supplying them with fresh mounts that they promised they'd claim had been stolen by savages.

"I don't understand," Var said. "God knows, I am— *was*—an officer of marines. The Inquisitor's dog, isn't that what they called me? So why do they help? Why not give me up?"

"Don't you understand yet?" Jaymes spat a stream of liquid tobacco as Var shook his head. "I told you how folk feel about the Autarchy—about Evander an' Jared Talle. Now you're one of us—no better than a branded exile—an' so folks'll help you. So long, of course, that you're with me."

"Who are you?" Var demanded. "Just *what* are you, Abram?"

Jaymes shrugged, gesturing at his dirty rawhides. "I'm just a scout, Tomas."

Var shook his head. "No: you're more than that. Do you tell me?"

Jaymes laughed. Overhead a rat scuttled across the barn's straw. "I guess I can," he said, "now that we're on the run together."

"So?" Var chewed the last of the gristly bacon.

Jaymes thought awhile. Then: "I guess I'm an observer . . . an' a messenger, I suppose. I get to talk with a lot o' folk, both high an' low." His tone and face grew serious. "I get to travel around a lot, so I see most of what's going on in this country. I see the holders living high on the labor of all those poor folk with branded cheeks or arms—folk with money living off . . . What would you call it? Slavery?"

Var shrugged, not knowing how to answer: not having thought much on it before.

Jaymes continued: "I see poor folk sent over from Evander with scars on their bodies that mark them down as nothings—no rights, save to do what their owners tell them. Some poor man steals a loaf to feed his starving family an' what happens? Evander brands him and sends him to Salvation to be a servant. A woman picks a pocket because her children are starving, an' she gets a brand an' gets sent to Salvation, where she's a servant. Her owner wants to fuck her? Why, he's got the right, and if she argues, she's in the wrong. Think about it, Tomas—would you like that?"

Var thought again about Arcole Blayke and the pretty woman on the boat, and shook his head.

"No."

"Then you know there's something wrong about this country," Jaymes said. "And that's a start."

Var nodded. "Yes." Then, unthinking: "But what can we do about it?"

Jaymes chuckled. "Right now, not a lot. Stay clear of the Inquisitor. Run for the wilderness."

"There's more." Var dislodged a chunk of fat from his teeth. "And are we outlawed together, I think I should know."

"I guess," Jaymes agreed. "There's a feelin' here that Evander don't have the right to govern us. That the Autarchy's too far off to tell the people of Salvation what to do. An' that sending branded exiles over is *wrong*! There's a feelin' that Salvation should govern herself—no Inquisitors or governors or shiploads of soldiers, but we just get on with our own affairs. You want trade agreements, fine. You want to buy from us, or us from you, fine—we'll trade with you. But don't *dictate* how we live. Don't send redcoats to keep us in line, neither—" He spat. "—damn Inquisitors. Work something out, eh?"

Var nodded. "And marines?"

"You're not a marine anymore," Jaymes said. "You're just a runaway now."

Var could only say, "Yes," because it was true, and he felt a sympathy for all Jaymes said, and the plight of the people he'd not before thought about. He had become, he supposed, a secessionist.

The moon rose thin above the trees, a slender crescent that Arcole supposed was the final remnant of the New Grass Moon, did Salvation's calendar turn to the same rhythm as that of Ket-Ta-Thanne. From where he crouched upslope of the Tachyn encampment he could see the lodges clear, lit bright by the fires burning there as the outcasts prepared for that horrid celebration Davyd had forecast: he shivered, wondering—praying—that their plan be successful. God knew, but it was hazardous, and were he honest with himself he could not envisage it working—could not believe he'd survive this night—but there was no other choice, save to foresake Debo and let the Breakers in, and that he could not do. He checked the priming of his musket yet again and thought of Flysse—which filled him with a terrible loneliness, for he could scarce credit he might see her again.

"It can work." Davyd's voice came in an urgent whisper from the shadows. "It *has* to work, else . . ."

Arcole nodded into the night, neither knowing nor caring if Davyd saw. He believed all Davyd had said, all the dread warnings, and in that balance his life was nothing. He looked up at the sky, stars glittering through the overlay of branches, and said, very softly, "Flysse, I love you."

"What?"

Davyd's voice came gentle as the night wind rustling the timber, and Arcole shook his head and whispered back, "Nothing." Then: "Shall Hadduth not dream of this?"

"Perhaps," Davyd answered, "and perhaps not. The dreaming is strange, Arcole; it does not tell you everything— only show you possibilities. As if the Maker opens ways for us to follow, but leaves us the choice of which path we take. If

Hadduth has dreamed of this, then we're lost; but if he's not . . ."

"Then we've a chance?" Arcole said.

"The Maker willing." Davyd laughed softly, and Arcole struggled to find resolution, belief.

Rannach crept through the trees. The Tachyn celebrated, dancing about their fires, flasks of what he supposed was tiswin passing around. It seemed to him like some obscene parody of Matakwa, save these outcasts would deliver this world and all the others into the hands of shadow and death. He could scarce believe that even Chakthi was sunk so deep in evil, yet Davyd had said it was so and he could not disbelieve the strange white-haired young man. Morrhyn claimed him, and Morrhyn was the Prophet, touched by the Maker, so Rannach could only believe and do his best to rescue his son. It mattered nothing to him that Vachyr's seed had shaped the child in Arrhyna's belly: Debo was *his* son, and even was the intended sacrifice of less portentous moment, he could not relinquish the child. He loved Debo, fierce as he loved Arrhyna, fierce as he loved the People—and must he give up his life for that love, then so be it; it should be worth the price.

So he slunk toward the Tachyn camp, intent on pursuing Davyd's desperate plan.

Debo sat sulking and afraid. He had been fed and set in the lodge, which was warm enough, but guarded, with the entry flaps laced tight, and he commanded to remain by the ugly man who claimed he was Debo's grandfather, and the other, whose eyes frightened Debo.

The child could not articulate his fear, but in the depths of those eyes he recognized a dreadful loss, as if the man had given up his soul to dark powers and was no longer entirely of this world. Neither had Taza visited him, for he walked with the one named Hadduth as if they were become great friends—of which Debo had none here. He wished he had not gone with Taza, but remained amongst the People. He missed his mother and his father: he began to cry softly.

Taza drank deep of the tiswin. It was not so good as that made in Ket-Ta-Thanne, but it was strong and dulled his doubts. He felt Hadduth's arm about his shoulders and laughed as the Dreamer murmured something he could not understand into his ear. It should be sad to see little Debo given to Chakthi's knife—and even now the notion that a grandfather might sacrifice his son's child stirred ugly feelings in his belly—but Hadduth had explained it was necessary, and promised so much that Taza must allow Debo's death necessary.

He drank more tiswin and watched the moon climb slowly up through the trees, thinking of the golden-armored warrior whose name was Akratil, and whose power would imbue him.

Hadduth had promised that.

Rannach got in amongst the first lodges and moved toward the tent holding Debo. A dog barked; unthinking, he swung his hatchet and split the animal's skull. The barking halted and none noticed: the Tachyn were too excited with their promised triumph.

Rannach moved on, cautious through the fire-lit shadows, dodging from lodge to lodge until he reached the one he'd seen from the vantage point where Arcole and Davyd waited with their muskets. He had little faith in muskets, but neither of his comrades was good enough with a bow that he'd trust them to cover his retreat, so muskets it was—and the Maker grant he bring his son out safe.

Like Arcole, he wondered if he should live out this night.

He found the lodge and paused. It was set back from the central area where the fire burned and no others close, as if Chakthi would hold Debo separate. The Tachyn buffalo symbols were painted on the hides, and other arcane designs that Rannach did not understand. Two warriors lounged outside, passing a flask between them. Rannach crouched, surveying the encampment, then drew his knife and began to slit the leather.

The hide cut easily enough, and as he parted the opening he saw the tearful face of his son. Debo stared at him, eyes widening in amazement and relief, and Rannach felt both a terrible sadness for Debo's plight and a great joy that they were reunited. Debo vented a wail of delight, and Rannach whispered for him to be silent. But too late: already the lacings of the entry flap were tugging loose.

Rannach beckoned, and Debo came running to the gap. Rannach dragged him through and turned as a guard came hurrying around the lodge's perimeter. Rannach pushed Debo aside, ignoring the child's shout of protest, and turned his blade on the Tachyn. He dimly recognized the man's face as the Grannach steel sank into the belly. He twisted the blade and the man screamed. Rannach cursed and drew his hatchet, smashing the ax down against the skull. The screaming ceased. Rannach prayed the sounds of celebration drowned out the noise, and looked for the second guard.

A head showed through the cut in the lodge and he swung his ax in a sideways motion that drove the steel head deep into the Tachyn's temple. The man jerked away on the impact, eyes wide as blood gouted, his head tossing from side to side between the opening. Rannach struck again, down hard into the apex of the skull, and saw the rising moon outline the dying of the light in the Tachyn's eyes.

He sheathed blade and ax and snatched Debo up in his arms, began to run as shouting sounded behind.

Then the crackle of musket fire.

Debo hung sturdy arms around his neck, crying and laughing at the same time. Rannach said, "Hold tight and we'll be safe, eh?"

Debo said, "Father," and buried his face in Rannach's shoulder.

A thrown hatchet sailed past them, and then a lance. Rannach sheltered his son with his body as Tachyn howled vengefully behind, and ran for the slope.

From above came the flashes of the exploding powder that propelled the musket balls down into his pursuers. He heard screams, and wondered how much shot his comrades had

left. Enough to see him—and Debo!—safe? An arrow cut air
beside his head.

He ran.

In the shelter of the overlooking timber, Davyd primed the
musket as Arcole had taught him. Set powder in the pan and
hiked the hammer back. He aimed down the barrel, trying
hard to remember the lessons—downslope requires angula-
tion, and a moving target is hard to hit. He squeezed the
trigger and saw a Tachyn jump backward, the ax the warrior
held flinging loose of his opened hand. He felt a savage satisfaction that—fleetingly—he doubted Morrhyn would approve of, and wondered what he became. Wakanisha and
warrior, both, as his dreams had suggested? Or some abbera-
tion, neither one thing nor the other? Too late to wonder
now; too late to hesitate. He reloaded and sighted again.

Rannach was coming up the slope, Debo clutched to his
chest and Tachyn shafts flying after them, the man dodging
from tree to tree, running fast as the gradient and his son's
weight allowed. Davyd fired and another Tachyn fell back;
Arcole had taught him well.

To his right, Arcole's musket blew flame and sound as if
some explosive metronome ticked out its rhythm. In the
twinned lights of moon and muzzle flash Davyd saw Arcole
smiling, and wondered if he wore the same expression of
grim delight.

Maker, forgive me, he thought, sighting on another man,
and saw his ball blow red from the chest.

Then Rannach was there, Debo hung like a talisman from
his neck, and Arcole shouted, "Withdraw! Fall back, or
they'll be on us!"

They went up the slope as Davyd had planned it, and then
skirted through the pines, along a bluff that ran southwest-
ward, down into a draw that took them full south. Hopefully
the overlay of pine needles and dead ground would hide their
tracks.

"They'll think we run for the mountains," Davyd had said.
"Think we look for Grannach help—so we don't. We circle

around and go down into Salvation. They'll inspect the hills and we'll be south of them. We can circle back later."

None had argued with him—he was the Dreamer—and so that was the way they went.

They found a stream and splashed through the chilly water, densely wooded banks to either side, with brush that hid them from sight. They could hear the Tachyns' howls ringing through the trees, and from that concatenation tell that their pursuers divided into separate groups. Davyd prayed they escape, that their trail not be found, nor their hunters guess they ran not west but east.

"Sounds like a war, don't it?" Abram Jaymes spat tobacco into the fire. "Might be we should kill them flames."

Without further ado he opened his pants and set to carrying out his own instructions. Var joined him, listening to the rattle of familiar sounds.

"What d'you think it is?"

"Who knows?" Jaymes shrugged. "Muskets in the wilderness ain't exactly usual. The savages don't have none, save what they've stole, an' no way to get powder or shot. . . . So." He shrugged again. "I don't rightly know what it might be. Best wait up here an' see, I reckon."

Var nodded, listening: two muskets, and a great deal of howling—as if folk were angry and in pursuit.

He said, "They're coming closer. They're coming down from the hills."

Jaymes said, "Yes," and checked his rifle.

Var picked up his own Hawkins, staring into the shining night where moon and stars played games with the trees. Light and shadow danced over the vast spread of pines, cold and lonely on the mountains beyond, which seemed to rise up to meet the heavens and meld land and earth into one solid firmament. None in Salvation knew what lay beyond. He felt very small and very alone, as if he were some jot cast loose into a world he did not properly understand or comprehend—and could not, properly, come to terms with—save he accept simple philosophies and forget all he'd known and accepted for all the years of his life. He still wore his tunic—

mark of the God's Militia—but now he was outlaw and wanderer, cast out by his own decision, his own instinctive choice: lost in a wilderness from which came musket fire and savage howls. He wondered what he had done, casting his lot with Abram Jaymes.

And Jaymes said, "They get much closer, we might likely need to do somethin'."

"Like what?" Var asked.

"Well," Jaymes stared at the dense timber, "folks with muskets is most likely to be on our side, no?"

Var shrugged: "I suppose so."

"So stand ready," Jaymes said, "just in case."

It had not all gone as Davyd hoped—the Tachyn had split into hunting groups and one had found their tracks where they came out of the stream. Fortunate for them, it was but a small group—eight or nine warriors—but still enough to slay them. Powder and shot ran short now, and Rannach labored panting under Debo's weight and Arcole gasped for breath. Davyd thought he could not go much farther; it seemed his lungs burned fiery as the pain that scorched his ribs, and his legs trembled with the effort. He feared his plan had failed. They had run all night, and dawn was not far off; none of them could run much farther. Davyd thought they must likely stand and fight, and then die as the Tachyn sent back word to the others and all the outcast clan come against them.

They came through trees with the Tachyn closing behind, running as if all the hounds of hell bayed at their heels. Davyd and Arcole turned to fire back, horribly aware of the dwindling stock of powder and lead shot. Arrows flew by them, the two outlanders shielding Rannach and Debo with their bodies. The Tachyn were closer now, screaming in anticipation of triumph.

Then Rannach stumbled, his weary legs tripped on a spreading root. Debo shouted as he was spilled from his father's arms. Rannach cursed and clambered to his feet.

"Enough!" He unsheathed his bow and nocked an arrow. "I can run no more. Debo!" He pointed at a massive pine. "Behind that, eh?"

Debo trotted toward the big tree. A shaft imbedded in the trunk and he crouched. And from the brightening shadows behind them a voice shouted: "Not the child! Chakthi wants him alive."

Davyd shuddered at thought of why and cocked his musket. A man showed and he fired: saw the warrior flung back, a shadow redder than the waning night's spread across his chest.

Another fell with one of Rannach's arrows in his throat; a third blown down by Arcole. But still there were too many, spreading like ravening wolves through the timber, closing on the three men.

"There are six of them left," Rannach said. "We must kill them all, else . . ."

He need say no more, nor had the time, for the Tachyn closed in, intent on their kill.

Two were braver than their fellows—they charged screaming, with raised hatchets and knives in their hands. Arcole shot one; Davyd missed the other, who ducked under Rannach's flighted arrow and came on shrieking his war cry, like some demonic shadow running out of the night.

Rannach dropped his bow and drew his own hatchet. Ducked under the Tachyn's swing to sink his ax hard and deep into the Tachyn's ribs, rising up to propel the warrior over his shoulder so that he thudded against the tree behind which Debo hid. Rannach turned, arm lofted, the Grannach blade spinning from his hand to descend into the Tachyn's skull, splitting bone so that blood and brain matter spread sticky across the tree.

The remaining Tachyn sent arrows flying. Then rifles barked from out of the night and pained screaming from behind the beleaguered defenders, and the arrows ceased. The rifles echoed again through the trees and a voice shouted in Evanderan, "This way, eh? Come in slow."

Rannach said, "What's this?"

"Friends, I think," Davyd said. "Perhaps the Maker favors us."

Rannach stared at him with doubtful eyes. "Here? In this strange land?"

"They've slain our enemies, no?"

There was no more sound from the Tachyn: perhaps he was right. Surely, he prayed it be so.

"I'll see. Wait here with Debo."

The Commacht akaman retrieved his hatchet and slipped away. Moments later he returned to announce that all the Tachyn were, indeed, dead. "I do not understand this," he said.

Davyd shrugged. "We can find out."

"You comin' in or not?" the voice asked.

Arcole said, "He's Evanderan, and there were two guns firing. They might be soldiers in the God's Militia."

Davyd shook his head, not quite sure why he did—only knowing that he felt safer now—and said, "What choice do we have?"

Arcole said, "You're our guide—what do you say?"

Davyd said, "Let's talk to them."

They went forward, and Arcole hesitated as he saw Tomas Var standing beside a long-haired man dressed in filthy rawhide, his mouth working disgustingly on what was obviously a wad of tobacco from the stains decorating his straggly beard. Both held long rifles cocked and aimed.

Var gasped. "God, is that Arcole Blayke?"

"Var?" Arcole returned. "Tomas Var?"

"What in God's name," Var asked, "are you doing here?"

And Arcole said, "I might ask the same question of you."

"You know him?" Abram Jaymes looked from Var to Arcole.

Var nodded; Arcole nodded, and both said, "Yes," together.

Jaymes said, "Well, make your reunion later, eh? The noise we made'll likely bring us some more hostiles, unless they got somethin' better to do. So we'd best get out o' here."

Var stared at Rannach, clearly suspicious, and Arcole said, "He's a friend, not one of them," stabbing a thumb back at the trees. "Rannach's his name, and he carries his son— Debo. You remember Davyd?" And when Var shook his head: "From the ship. He was with me and Flysse."

Var shook his head again, perplexed. Jaymes said, "Dammit, you plannin' to stand here talkin' until them hostiles arrive?"

"There's a fort nearby, no?" Davyd's question surprised them all. "We'd best go there."

"It's deserted," Var said. "Everyone slain."

Davyd said, "We shall be safe there. For a while, at least."

Arcole said, "Trust him—he's a Dreamer."

Debo was set astride Jaymes's horse and Davyd on Var's. The others went afoot, trotting beside the animals, urgent through the fading night until they came to a wide avenue of cut trees, the ground wagon-trammeled underfoot, and ahead bulked the lonely shape of Fort Harvie. They reached the gates and ran between them, Var and Jaymes pausing to shoulder the heavy timbers closed, Arcole slamming the great crossbar into place.

He stared around, eyes widening as dawn's early gray revealed the contents of the fort. Death hung fulsome in the air, redolent of what had transpired here.

He said, softly, "God!" and heard Davyd groan, and went to help his comrade down from the winded horse.

Davyd's eyes were wide as his own, and he felt the young man shudder as they both stared aghast at the relicts of carnage. He stared at the corpses littering the ground and felt the day press horrid omens on him.

Davyd seemed incapable of movement and he clasped the youth's shoulder, forcing his voice to a confidence he scarcely dared trust. "God knows it stinks, but it might hold them out." He chuckled cynically. "And we've nowhere else to go, eh?"

"No." Davyd shook his head and jabbed a finger at the bodies. "Save to join them."

Chakthi raged at the descending moon and the rising sun. His men had come back with nothing—neither news of Debo recaptured nor Rannach caught. He tore at his hair and ripped at his face until blood streamed his cheeks and tainted spittle flecked his mouth. He screamed his anger so that none dare approach him save Hadduth.

"There's another," the wakanisha said. "And it must be done this night."

"Another?" Chakthi rounded on his Dreamer, bloodied nails clawing at Hadduth's throat. "Did you not tell me it must be Vachyr's son? Did I agree to that sacrifice for nothing? The blood of my son's son, you said! That should deliver me all I want, you said!"

"It were better Debo," Hadduth said, lurching back, dodging a flailing fist, "but if not him, then another. *But tonight!* It must be on the waning of the New Grass Moon—when it happened before. Only now can Akratil come to us in body, with all his Horde."

Chakthi stared hard at the man who had promised him everything: revenge and dominion. He wiped blood from his cheeks and contemplated slaying his wakanisha. Save perhaps the man might still deliver him his goals: "Tell me."

"It depends," Hadduth said, "on coincidences—on the moon and the time—on things I cannot properly explain. We need one raised in Ket-Ta-Thanne, who's come through the Grannach ways. Debo was the choicest—mingling Tachyn and Commacht blood—but we've another."

Chakthi scowled and asked, "Who?"

"Taza," Hadduth said. "He's not Commacht, but Lakanti—but even so . . ." He shrugged. "He looked to slay the stranger, Davyd, and brought us Debo. He came through the Grannach tunnels with Akratil's aid: he'd do, I think."

"He could bring the Breakers here?" Chakthi asked.

"I think so," Hadduth said.

"Then do it," Chakthi commanded. "Now!"

Taza was drunk on the tiswin. His head swam so that the crescent of the moon shone trebled before his swimming eyes and the trees seemed to shift before his gaze as he lounged beside the fire. He could not feel entirely sorry that Debo was rescued—he felt a certain fondness for the child—but he wondered how that escape might affect his standing with his new clan.

He found out when Hadduth approached, Chakthi at his side and warriors in escort.

He opened his mouth to ask if Debo had been found and gasped as he was lifted up and hauled bodily to the center of the camp. Suddenly he felt very afraid; more so when Chakthi smiled.

There was a pole erected before the central fire, decorated with the symbols Hadduth had promised to explain to him: he was abruptly lashed to the post. He began to scream, protesting this indignity. Chakthi snarled and struck him across the face, the blow hard enough he was stunned. By the time he recovered his senses, he was bound by feet and hands, tight against the pole. He was tied naked, paint daubed on his chest and abdomen, his face. And Hadduth was studying the moon, a knife in his right hand, his mouth moving as he spoke.

Taza heard him say, "Akratil," and began to scream again, but then the blade slid down his chest, tracing the outlines of the sigils painted there. It went across his belly and his screaming shrilled. He wished he'd never come to this place, never betrayed the People. Then the blade landed across his throat and only a bubbling sound came out, washed away on the flow of blood.

Abruptly, as if ignited by the gore spilling from Taza's severed throat, he was consumed by flame. It began where his windpipe was cut, and spread swift as wildfire over his body. It burst from his eyes and his mouth, from out of his nostrils and his ears. He became a torch, flames rising incandescent into the night, a great swirling pyre that outshone the fire behind him as if that were a mere candle dimmed by the greater brilliance. In moments he was gone and where he had stood there was a great corona of flame out of which rode a dread warrior armored all in gold, with skulls hung from the saddle of his weirdling horned mount, whose eyes, like those of its master, seemed to shine with internal flame, as if they reflected the pits of hell.

Akratil looked down on the gaping Tachyn and smiled from under his golden helmet.

"You have done well."

He walked his dread mount forward. Hadduth and

Chakthi cringed as he loosed the helm and shook out his flame-red hair. Hadduth mumbled, "Master, welcome." Akratil laughed and paced the sable horse on, clear of the flames.

Trees scorched in that blaze, pine sap crackling as it burned, cones popping; lodges took flame and the Tachyn howled in awe and terror.

And then, as Akratil raised a beckoning gauntlet, the Horde came through the fire, out of Ket-Ta-Witko into Salvation.

33 The Terror Again

Jared Talle stirred in his sleep, disturbed by the images of his dreaming. Unpleasantly familiar figures stalked the avenues of his nocturnal imagination, prompting him to twist and turn in the unkempt bed, sweat starting on his sallow brow, his heart pounding arrhythmically. He was not a Dreamer, but deep within the confines of his soul he knew that what he dreamed now was true—that the ghostly figures that had wandered the streets of Grostheim were become fleshed: were come to Salvation.

Abruptly, he woke, wiping at his sweat-streamered face with a sheet that was no drier as he forced his mind to calm, demanded that the terror subside. Slowly, by sheer effort of will, he made his breathing and his heartbeat slow, and he rose, tugging on one of dead Andru Wyme's opulent dressing gowns. He snatched at the bell cord that would summon a servant, and when the indentured man appeared ordered that the fire in Wyme's study be built up and coffee brought him there. It was, he noticed when he glanced at the window, a little after midnight, and the moon was a narrow slash of curved light against a cloudless sky all filled with twinkling stars. Both the moon and its attendant satellites seemed to him fiery, as if some vast conflagration reflected against the sky. For a moment he thought he heard the pounding of clawed hooves vibrate the floor beneath his feet, and the howling of myriad savage voices; and then, as if the dreams were reborn, he saw again, vividly, the dread riders pouring out of fire, spilling like some awful bloody flood into the lands of the Autarchy. He shook his head and poured a glass of water, frowning irritably as the surface rippled in his trembling hand.

Dear God, he thought, grant me strength against whatever comes. I am Your servant and do Your will: be with me. Then he dressed and went to the study.

The nervous servant—Talle had never bothered to learn his name—had built the fire and lit the lamps. A woman came with a silver tray bearing a pot of coffee and a cup. Talle waved them both away and they scuttled out, glad to be dismissed. He knew he frightened them, and savored their fear: that was only just—he was, after all, an Inquisitor. But what disturbed him this night was the fact *he* felt afraid. He knew what came toward him—into Salvation and toward Grostheim—from his necromancy. The raised spirits of the dead Tachyn had told him what these creatures were and what they intended, and he had thought to harness that power to move between worlds to the Autarchy's yoke, to shape an alliance. But now . . .

He swallowed coffee and paced the chamber, thinking on his dreams and all he'd seen in them, *known* in them. The raised dead had talked of hope, of ambition, of revenge and dominion—but that was no more than fanciful dreaming. Those pitiful savages were doomed as any others the Breakers had conquered and destroyed. Talle *knew* this, surely as if it were writ in stone: the Breakers were destruction incarnate; they would use the Tachyn and turn against them sure as some farmer might raise a pig and slaughter the animal when it grew fat. And they would come against Grostheim, such dread warriors as could traverse the paths of time and space, dependent on man's perfidy.

Jared Talle paced the floor, contemplating such power. Could he but own it, place it in the hands of the Autarchy . . . why, all the universe might be delivered up, and he forever hailed as the greatest Inquisitor of all time. But how? Should he wait for them to come, or go to them? He drank coffee as the sky grew light and birds began to sing, his mind racing, formulating and discarding plans until he hit upon the one he thought might succeed.

Fire climbed the sky, dimming moon and stars as if all the wilderness took flame to ignite the heavens. There was no sound, but still it seemed the very earth trembled. It seemed to Davyd that a great thunderclap shook the world, and he cried out, staring at the blazing sky. The flames reminded him of all the old fears—forgotten since he'd come amongst the People in Ket-Ta-Thanne, but now returned manifold. He saw again the burnings in Bantar and felt the old terror: he began to shudder.

Abram Jaymes said, "What was that?"

Debo began to wail. Rannach held him close, stroking his hair as he looked to Davyd for answer.

Davyd said, hoarse, forcing himself to speak through the dryness in his throat, "They've brought the Breakers back." He repeated the statement in the tongue of Evander, that the others understand.

Rannach cursed and invoked the Maker's name; Arcole asked, "What do we do?"

Davyd shook his head, unable to say more.

Tomas Var said, "These are the ones Talle would communicate with?"

"Talle?" Arcole asked. "Who's Talle?"

"An Inquisitor." Var scanned the terrain beyond the walls. Their pursuers appeared to have gone, dissolved into the shadows or returned to the fire. "His name is Jared Talle. He's . . ."

"A sorry, miserable bastard," said Abram Jaymes, "who's made Salvation his province worse even than that fat cripple Wyme. He raised the dead here."

"He thought to . . ." Var shrugged, hesitating. "Communicate with the . . . Breakers? He thought to utilize their powers on behalf of the Autarchy—that together they might conquer worlds unknown."

Arcole said, "He's mad."

Davyd only shuddered, wondering what had come into this world and what he might do to halt it.

Rannach frowned and said, when their words were explained to him, "The Breakers kill everything! They slew the Whaztaye and half the Grannach, they would have slain us, had we not fought them and Morrhyn opened the gate to Ket-Ta-Thanne. They must be stopped, and if this Jared Talle believes he can deal with them, then he is corrupted as Chakthi and Hadduth."

"Likely he is." Arcole barked a cynical laugh. "He's an Inquisitor. But what can we do? The Maker knows, we're stranded here in this damn fort, and if Davyd's right, then they're come."

"Davyd *is* right," Rannach gave him back. "Davyd is a wakanisha such as we've never known, and he will find an answer. Morrhyn believes in him, no? Should we not?"

Davyd heard their words dimly through the tension that seemed to vibrate his body. His heart raced, and it was as if his bones shuddered so that every wound, each scar, throbbed with pain. The very air seemed to him to bear the taint of evil, washing acidic over his skin. He knew the night was cold, but his face burned. He felt old and weary and would have sooner curled up and gone away into death's sleep than face what he *knew* must lie ahead: it seemed too much, too many demands on his tired soul. He wished Morrhyn were there to advise him. He said, in both tongues, "I must sleep."

Abram Jaymes said, "I don't rightly understand much of this, but we should be safe here awhile, so why not? You surely look weary."

Arcole said, "Here, I'll help you," and took Davyd's musket away and put an arm around the snow-haired young man and led him down from the parapet to a room where he lit a fire and set Davyd to rest on blankets and makeshift pillows and left him there.

. . . Where Davyd dreamed.

. . . Of fire and blood and the Horde, and Var's blue-coated marines fighting alongside the People; and of a terrible fire that consumed the world, and all the worlds; and of branded folk striding alongside soldiers, and of himself lashed to a stake as the flames took hold and filled his nostrils with the stench of his own burning flesh . . .

. . . And of confrontation with a warrior armored all in gold, mounted on a dread horse, who brought a great, curved sword sweeping down against him . . .

. . . And finally of Morrhyn, who strode a familiar tunnel, lit by the Grannach's magic, his seamed face determined, as if he moved toward some terrible conclusion. It seemed to Davyd that the Prophet marched at the head of an army, as if all the warriors of the People followed behind. Davyd saw Yazte there, and Kanseah, and Dohnse; Colun and his sturdy Grannach fighters, and—dimly, this confusing—Flysse and Arrhyna, each dressed in warlike garb, with weapons that usually the women of the Matawaye did not carry. Then the images blurred, as if flame filled the tunnel and in their place was a vision of the Horde riding in such fire that consumed all else, as if worlds burned on their arrival.

He heard the roaring of their strangeling beasts, and the battle shouts of the Breakers; dying screams and the sound of breaking bones, of blades cutting into flesh. Then there was only fire and the roaring of flames, and he woke, sticky with sweat and panting, for he was filled with a terrible dread and could not properly understand the dream, only know that the future of Ket-Ta-Thanne and Salvation balanced on a knife edge, and the Horde was come.

He wiped a hand over his face and licked dry lips, clambered upright from the tumbled bed to find water that he gulped down before dousing his face. He thought he'd not the knowledge to interpret the dream correctly—it seemed all confusion and doubt—but that he must do *something*. Save he knew not what.

Morrhyn said, "We have no other choice. Save to see all we know destroyed. I'll not stand by to watch that—nor you, I think."

Yazte sighed. "You ask much of the People, Prophet."

Morrhyn said, "Yes: much is demanded of us."

Yazte drank tiswin and sighed again. "I cannot argue with you," he said, "so let us go."

Morrhyn smiled, then felt it falter as Flysse and Arrhyna approached. They wore the apparel of warriors and determined expressions—rawhide breeches and linen shirts, their hair tied back in approximation of the braids. Flysse wore a pistol on her belt and carried a musket; Arrhyna had knife and hatchet sheathed, a quivered bow slung across her back.

Worse, to Morrhyn, was that Lhyn was with them and looked no less determined.

"We go soon," he said, nervously. "What do you want?"

Flysse glanced at Arrhyna; Arrhyna glanced at Flysse. And together they said, "We are coming with you."

Morrhyn said, "No! That cannot be—we go to war, and women do not fight."

"You're going, no?" Lhyn asked. "And Dreamers don't fight."

Morrhyn said, "It's different. I cannot dream beyond these mountains any longer—there's a Breakers' spell on them—so I have to go."

"As do I," Arrhyna said. "My husband and my son are somewhere beyond those mountains, and I must go to them." She made a gesture of respect. "Nor shall you stop me, Morrhyn. Even are you the Prophet, I *shall* go."

"And my husband is there," Flysse said, "and I'd go to him. I'll not be stopped, Morrhyn. Do you try, then I shall find a way across."

Lhyn said, "Best allow it, eh?" And smiled.

Morrhyn looked into her eyes and knew he was defeated by the power of women. Almost, he laughed—he was the Prophet, no? The People looked to him for guidance, yet he could no more argue with these determined women than halt an avalanche with his hands. So he shrugged and gestured that they join the column of the People winding up the mountain to where Colun had opened the Grannach's secret ways that would allow the Matawaye into Salvation to seek loved ones, and—they hoped—defeat the Breakers. But he was not sure. There was such power in the Breakers as made him doubt, and he wished that the women were not with the party. But he could not argue with them, only smile at Lhyn and wonder at all the things that might have been had she not chosen Racharran—and lead the war party on.

He'd no taste for this duty—he was a wakanisha, a Dreamer, not a warrior, and surely the Ahsa-tye-Patiko denied the wakanisha's right to fight in battle. But who else could lead the People? Yazte looked to him for guidance and Kanseah followed blind. Did he not take the Matawaye warriors through the mountains then none should go, and then

. . . He'd sooner not think of that, for surely it must mean the Breakers conquer and all be destroyed, nothing left save ashes and dead bones. But did he deny the Will in taking arms?

He felt a hand upon his shoulder and turned to find Kahteney grim-faced at his side.

"I do not understand this," the Lakanti Dreamer said, "but I know we must do it. Even does it fly in the face of the Will."

Morrhyn said, "I no longer understand," and shook his head.

Kahteney said, "Nor I, brother. Save that we *must.*"

Morrhyn nodded and looked to where Colun waited. "Do you bring us through to the other side?"

Colun nodded grimly. He was battle-decked, all in leather and metal, with his ax slung across his back and a wide blade sheathed on his belt. "My folk shall come with you," he said. "Are we to fight them again, then the Grannach shall play their part."

"We shall move fast," Morrhyn warned. "We must."

Colun laughed. "We can run swift, my friend; and your horses shall move slow through the forest. Needs be, we can ride double, eh? Nor would I miss this battle."

"Then come." Morrhyn smiled, sadly and proudly. "Are we to die, it shall be in good company. Nor less, do we triumph."

"So, swift," Colun said, and turned to shout that the ways be opened that the warriors of the Matawaye come through. Then faltered as he caught sight of Flysse and Arrhyna. "What are they doing?"

"They come with us," Morrhyn said.

"Women?" Colun's voice rang with disbelief. "You allow this?"

Lhyn spoke before any other: "He's scant choice; and the Maker knows, I'd go were I not needed here. They've menfolk lost beyond your mountains."

Colun opened his mouth to argue, but from behind him Marjia said, "As would I, husband. Save there must be some left behind to tend the young and the sick and the old."

Colun looked at Morrhyn, who shrugged; then at Yazte,

who raised thick brows in helpless acceptance; Kanseah only averted his eyes. So Colun raised his arms and said, "The Maker forfend I argue with women, for that's an argument lost from the beginning. So—do we go?"

Morrhyn nodded and Colun shouted again that the ways be opened and the Grannach golans weaved spells that the face of the mountain part, and the men of the People—Flysse and Arrhyna with them—went under the hill to whatever fate awaited them beyond.

Morrhyn prayed as he led them in: Maker, be with us. Grant us strength, that we prevail. May Rannach and Arcole and Davyd and Debo be safe. Grant that we come timely and save them, and all the worlds. Grant that we defeat the Breakers.

He wondered if his prayer was heard, or if the Breakers now commanded the world.

Were that so, he thought dismally, then the account lay at men's feet. Was it not Vachyr's betrayal of the Will that had first set these dreadful events in motion? And after that, Rannach's—when he, in turn, broke the Ahsa-tye-Patiko? But surely Rannach had atoned for that sin. And were not sufficient slain to atone in death and blood for wrongs?

I no longer understand, he thought. You showed me how to bring the People to this new land, and now we leave it to fight in a strange country, which I do not properly understand. They scar men and women there, and use them as slaves, and I do not understand that, but I am going to fight with them. And I do not know if I should fight, but I know that if I fail to lead the People to this battle they shall all die, and that I cannot bear.

Please . . . guide me.

Flysse wondered if Arcole survived. She felt a terrible fear that he was dead, which should leave a part of her lost forever. She thought on all she'd heard of Racharran, and wondered at Lhyn's loss: how could she bear it? She thought she could not bear the burden of Arcole's death, and in her turn prayed to the Maker that he be alive and return to her, or she

die with him. The thought that they not be together was too
hard to bear.

She took Arrhyna's hand, and the dark-haired woman
smiled at her wanly. Flysse thought that she had so much
more to lose: not just a husband, but also a child. She said,
"We'll find them, eh? We'll find them and bring them back
safe."

Arrhyna said, "The Maker willing."

Flysse said, "Yes, the Maker willing," and walked along
the oddly lit tunnel, holding Arrhyna's hand and praying it be
so.

Hadduth crouched fawning like an eager dog at Akratil's elbow. Chakthi faced the leader of the Horde, attempting to
retain some measure of authority, of dignity, even as his eyes
shifted nervous under the pressure of the Breaker's unswerv-
ing red stare. All around, the forest rang with the sounds of
weirdling beasts. Far off, as if driven away and mourning, a
wolf howled. Those Tachyn dogs not already eaten by the
Breakers' animals skulked and hid, and children wailed, silenced by mothers simultaneously terrified and proud. The
men of the Tachyn sat or stood, intent on the central fire,
endeavoring—like their akaman and his wakanisha—to maintain some semblance of calm, of resolve. Chakthi had promised them conquest with this alliance, but now that the
rainbow-armored Breakers were here, mingling with them, it
was hard not to show the fear they felt.

These strange folk were destruction incarnate. They followed paths none of the People—not even outcast Tachyn—
understood properly, as if destruction were their only goal. It
was as if blood filled their nostrils and all they'd do was kill,
like a wolverine or a dog gone mad.

On the edge of the gathering a warrior called Chappo
asked one whose name was Goso, "Was this wise? Has
Chakthi done the right thing, bringing them here?"

Goso had rather not been asked that question. He considered it most unwise to speak of these strange warriors where
answers might be overheard. But Chappo nudged him in the

ribs and so he said, "Chakthi deems it so, and Hadduth. So . . ." He shrugged.

"They smell of blood," Chappo said. "They smell of death."

And started as a soft voice said, "Because we kill; because that is what we do."

Goso turned to find a tall figure at his back. It was a woman, her hair a mane of moonlit blond, her features fine, her eyes alive with laughter. She wore pale green armor that shone like the shell of a snapping turtle basking in the sun. She wore a long sword at her side and an ax was strapped across her back. She asked, mildly, "Do you object to that?"

Chappo said, "No . . . I . . . I only . . ."

The woman said, "I cannot believe you are truly with us," and drew a knife that she plunged between Chappo's ribs.

As Chappo died, Goso heard her say, "We'll eat well this night."

The Breakers with her laughed; the Tachyn who had seen the slaying cringed and gasped. Ripples of alarm spread, and doubt. The watching crowd separated and the discussion at the center paused.

Goso stepped a pace back, Chappo's blood on his shirt. He clutched at his belt knife, then looked at the woman's challenging smile and loosed his grip, hands raised in gesture of acceptance. He heard her say, as if from a distance, "I am Bemnida, and I serve my master, Akratil. Do you argue with us, you know your fate."

Goso saw her eyes travel to Chappo's body and nodded, swallowing the bile that rose in his throat. He feared his belly should empty, for it was hard to see a friend slain so casually—harder still to hear it announced that friend be eaten. He wondered what manner of allies Chakthi had found.

From where he sat with Akratil, Chakthi watched uncaring.

Akratil said, "Not all your folk are with us, it seems." He gestured to where the woman dragged Chappo's body away.

Chakthi said, "So? They'll follow me, do you give us this land."

"Is that all you want?" Akratil chuckled. "That's no large thing."

"This land," Chakthi said, his eyes shifting away, back, "and revenge for our banishment. Vengeance on Rannach—I'd have his head. And Morrhyn's; and I'd take Ket-Ta-Thanne for my clan alone."

Firelight shifted over ornate armor as Akratil shrugged. "Easily done. Which first?"

Chakthi glanced at Hadduth, and for all his own awe and—were he to admit it—fear of the Breaker, could not contain the contempt he felt at his wakanisha's fawning. Hadduth was entranced: he stared at Akratil as if the man were a god whose every word was holy law. Chakthi felt anger stir and said, "Hadduth promised me Rannach. He said that Debo's taking would bring me my son's murderer."

"It has," Akratil said. "You know where they are."

Chakthi snarled. "Yes! But they hide behind the magic walls of the fort! I cannot reach them there—the magic defeats us."

"You, perhaps," Akratil returned. "But us?"

"Give me Rannach," Chakthi said. "The rest later."

"The one," Akratil said, "leads to the other. But Rannach—yes; and soon. Your grandson?"

Chakthi shrugged. "I promised you his life, no? Do you still want it, then it is yours."

"It matters nothing now," Akratil replied. "A sacrifice was required, and that we got. But perhaps he'd make good eating."

Chakthi shrugged.

Akratil said, "So, we go first against this fort," and laughed. "I'll give you Rannach's head, and those of any with him. My word on it."

34

Downstream

The sun shone bright and warm out of a sky devoid of all save a few wind-shepherded flocks of rolling white cloud; swallows and martins swept the heavens, and Fort Harvie stank of corruption. Crows and magpies sat the walls, waiting for the living inhabitants to depart, and rats scuttled boldly to the corpses. They went ignored by the five men who watched the wilderness forest from the ramparts, where the breeze blew stronger and somewhat took away the stink of death.

Rannach asked, "You're sure?"

"Yes." Davyd nodded miserably, wishing he were not. "Chakthi would have his revenge, and so they'll come here first—to take your head, and all those with you."

"And then?"

Davyd shrugged. "I dreamed no more than that. Salvation or Ket-Ta-Thanne? They might turn either way. But they are coming!"

"And the People?" Rannach asked. "Do they come?"

"I don't know." Davyd shook his head. "Perhaps. The Maker help me, Rannach, but I cannot know for sure."

"You dreamed it," Rannach said.

"And much else," Davyd replied. Maker, but with this warm sun on him, why did he feel so cold? Save it be presentiment of his own death. "I am not Morrhyn, that I can give you the clear yea or nay of it. I only know that the People *might* come—or not—and the only thing I can tell you for sure is that the Breakers come here in search of you."

Rannach grunted. Debo found missiles to hurl at the carrion birds so that they rose in skirling flocks above the fort—

and then came back to settle anticipatory along the walls. Arcole translated for Var and Jaymes.

Var said, "Are these folk bad as you describe, then we'd best be gone, no?"

Jaymes said, "To where?"

Arcole said, "I don't know. Can we get past them, through the wilderness? Perhaps reach the hills and find the Grannach?" He glanced at Davyd. "Or the People coming to our aid?"

In turn, Davyd translated for Rannach, who said bluntly, "Were I Chakthi, I'd put men all through the woods, so that none might pass unnoticed. I think it should be very difficult to go back."

Var said, "If all this is true, then all Salvation stands in peril."

Jaymes said, "You doubt it? You saw the ghosts, no? You know what they did in Grostheim an' here. You know the other forts are likely the same, no?" He gestured at Davyd. "You think he's wrong?"

Var shook his head reluctantly: "No."

"Then we have to decide what we do," Jaymes said. "Folk'll need warnin' of this, else it'll be nothin' but slaughter."

"But what," Var asked, "can we do?"

They looked to Davyd. As if, he thought, I were the Prophet; as if I need only dream and give them answers. *Maker help me!* He stared at the bright sky, watching the birds dart and swoop, and shook his head. "If we stay here," he said at last, "I think we shall all be slain. I doubt the hexes on this fort can hold the Breakers out. And even can they, we shall starve. So we must go."

"Where?" Arcole asked.

Davyd shrugged again. "I don't know."

"Well," said Abram Jaymes, "if Rannach here thinks we can't make it through the wilderness, there's not too much other choice, eh?"

They looked at him and he sniffed, spat tobacco, and said, "We need to leave, else we're all dead, no? We don't have enough horses to carry everyone—so we go by the river."

Arcole said, "How?"

"We build us a raft," Jaymes said, "an' float downstream. We get away from this place."

"To where?" Arcole demanded, touching the scar of exile that decorated his cheek. "Back to Grostheim and the gallows? I'd not welcome that. Remember that Davyd and I are branded exiles."

"An' I was sentenced to hang," Jaymes said. "An' Tomas here deserted his post to save my life, so likely he's proscribed outlaw an' renegade, too. An' Rannach's a savage Jared Talle an' more'n a few landholders would shoot on sight. But what other choice we got? They need to know what's coming at them."

Arcole said, "I'll not go back to Grostheim. What does it matter to me if that place dies? Let the Breakers have it, and damn the Autarchy. Let the God's Militia fight the Breakers and the Tachyn—and may they slay each other."

Davyd said softly, "They won't: the Breakers will conquer. Save . . ." He broke off, shaking his head.

Var said, "Most of the garrison is dead. The madness took them and they slew one another. Andru Wyme's dead, and Alyx Spelt. I think that only marines defend the city now."

"An' there's another thing," Jaymes said. "Grostheim's full o' folk like you—the ones with the brand on their cheek. You think they should die?"

"Not them," Arcole replied. And looked to Var. "But why should I help your marines, or any other Evanderans? You brought us here, no?"

Var nodded. "Yes, I did. I served the Autarchy and obeyed my orders. But now . . . ?"

"Can we not learn from one another?" Davyd asked. "Look at us! The Maker knows but we're different, no? Rannach's Matawaye and I'm a branded exile like you, Arcole. Major Var's an officer in the God's Militia, but he's standing with us alongside Abram and talking of fighting the Breakers. And if we don't fight them, then all is lost—Salvation and Ket-Ta-Thanne, both. You and Var fought the sea serpent together, no? Why not fight together now?"

Arcole said, "And if we do bring word? What then?"

Abram Jaymes answered: "A new order, a different world. Not Evander's rule, but Salvation's. No more branded folk—

only free men an' women. Nor any Inquisitors or the God's Militia or governors—only folk who live here; free."

Arcole looked at Var, who ducked his head in agreement and said, "I find I've come to agree with Abram. Evander's no more right to claim this land than these Breakers, or Chakthi. Salvation should have the right to govern itself, free of the Autarchy."

"And shall the Inquisitor agree this?" Arcole smiled dubiously. "Or the soldiers of the God's Militia? Shall the landholders agree to free their branded servants? Shall all those folk who came here to make their fortunes agree to sever ties with Evander?"

"They might just agree to be independent," Jaymes said. "Talle's not exactly popular, nor the Autarchy. An' remember—there's more branded folk in Salvation than free men."

Davyd said, "Are the Breakers not defeated here, they'll conquer and go on." He frowned at the blue sky. "Likely to Ket-Ta-Thanne first, but then across this whole world. That should be a dreadful slaughter, Arcole."

"My marines will fight," Var said. "But they're not so many; and are they unready. . . ."

"You ask me to aid that which put this on my face." Arcole touched the scar on his cheek. "I committed no crime, save to kill a man in a duel of his own choosing—and for that, Evander branded me and made me exile." His voice grew bitter. "I was sent indentured to this land for that, and now you'd ask me to aid the ones who did that to me. Why should I?"

"I'd ask you to help the branded folk," Jaymes said.

"And I'd see the Breakers defeated," said Davyd.

Arcole said, "I'd go back to Ket-Ta-Thanne. Let the Breakers have Salvation."

"It cannot be that way." Davyd shook his head. "Do the Breakers conquer Salvation, then they'll next come to Ket-Ta-Thanne, against the People."

"Then let us warn the People," Arcole said. "Let's go back to the mountains."

"No, we cannot." Davyd shook his head again. "It's as Rannach says—those paths are too well guarded."

He turned to the Commacht akaman, translating what was said, and Rannach stared hard at Arcole.

In the tongue of the People he said, "Do you remember when you first came to us? I saw that mark on your face and could not believe men could do that to one another. I said then that I'd aid all like you—I say it again! We must warn these folk of what comes against them."

"Even do they slay us?" Arcole demanded.

"Even so," Rannach answered. "We've a duty to the Maker, no?"

Defeated, Arcole shrugged: "So let's build that raft."

They gathered wood as the sun stalked fast across the sky—lengths of timber and barrels for buoyancy; ropes to lash the makeshift structure together. It seemed barely large enough to hold them all, and surely not the horses that they turned loose. They gathered up what supplies they could find and stowed them ready to mount on the raft. At least Arcole and Davyd had ammunition for their muskets, powder and shot in ready supply from the fort's armory.

The day lengthened, shadows spilling deep beyond the walls as the sun closed on the wilderness forest and began to decorate the timber with dancing light and shadow in harlequin patterns that tricked the eye and hid the shapes that came out from the trees. . . .

For they were hard to discern. Their armor seemed to take in light and throw it back all tricksy, so that they rode as if between day's light and night's, and could not be clearly seen but only came on astride slavering beasts that defied imagination in their ghastly delineaments.

Davyd *felt* them coming and shouted for the others to hurry with the raft, but even forewarned he was horrified by what he saw. Tekah had described them to him, and Rannach and Morrhyn, but . . . what were they, that they sat such creatures? That they wore such armor; that from them emanated so awful a sense of wanton destruction? He felt his belly cramp and his hands shudder as he leveled his musket and squeezed the trigger.

He could do no more: he felt a great calm possess him, and

something go away from him and something else open before, perhaps better. He had wanted—so badly, so much—to be a wakanisha, as was Morrhyn. To follow the Ahsa-tye-Patiko, which denied the Dreamer warrior's rights—the right to kill. But as he saw the Breaker slung from the saddle to tumble backward over the strangeling beast's hindquarters and dropped fresh powder into his musket, spat a ball into the muzzle, tamped it down and sighted again, he felt only the savage satisfaction he'd known as he slew Chakthi's warriors.

He sighted on the animal—what was it: lizard or lion?—that still charged roaring at the walls and put a ball between its eyes. The thing dropped, an obstacle that tripped those behind, and he shouted—needlessly, for all the others could surely hear the roaring—"Make haste!"

The rifles of Var and Jaymes cracked, Arcole's musket a deeper sound. Then they were clambering aboard the raft, Rannach and Arcole and Var pushing the fragile craft out from the bank, hauling themselves onto the planks as the current took hold and they began to drift downstream. Debo stared at the approaching riders and wailed in terror. Rannach thrust him down, unshipping his bow. Davyd reloaded his musket and thought better of firing—he was not so good a shot that he might find a kill from the swaying platform, but surely he felt a great desire to slay such abominations as charged to the river's bank.

He stared at them as arrows cut the air and splashed into the water. The sun was far westered now, the light translucent as it faded, drifting over their rainbow armor so that they seemed to dance in light and shadow, the Tachyn who rode with them drab figures, mundane in comparison for all their war paint. The Breakers were beautiful as tempting sin, and that contrast of beauty and evil was such as spun his mind. He thought he understood Hadduth's seduction, and Chakthi's, and wondered how the People had fought such beings—his musket stood forgotten in his hands as he stared, awed. It was as if the terrible grandeur of the strangeling folk entranced him.

Then powder blasts evaporated his reverie and he saw Jaymes and Var turning their rifles on the Breakers as Arcole and Rannach dug makeshift paddles into the river, propelling them away, farther out toward midstream. The Breakers and the Tachyn, both, howled in frustration and set their mounts to running alongside the Restitution. Shafts flew, but the raft rode the current now and moved swift through the burgeoning twilight. The sun settled behind the distant mountains and the waning moon spread the river with silver ripples. In time, the arrows ceased, and the howling, and then they only drifted eastward, toward Grostheim.

Morrhyn stared at the great spread of forest, wondering if he did the right thing in bringing the People here. There lay before him a vast wilderness, all high timber and steep stone that seemed to stretch on forever as if all the world was become forested and there was no grass left. It was not a place for horses, not at all like the clean plains of Ket-Ta-Thanne, but rather, he thought, all dark and gloomy—a fitting place for Chakthi's Tachyn. He felt troubled: it was as if the very air became redolent of evil.

"I do not like this," Kahteney said, glancing about as if he anticipated momentary attack. "This place is . . ."

He shrugged, and Morrhyn said, "Yes, my brother; I know. But still . . ."

Yazte asked, "Do we camp here or go on?"

Morrhyn looked to Colun, who said: "A little farther and there's a good place. I'll send scouts out, but I think there are none of Chakthi's folk close."

"Are there," Yazte said, "let's slay them and get on. I do not like these woods."

None did: the People were plainsfolk, accustomed to open spaces, not the confines of the wilderness forest. Their horses found the steep slopes difficult to negotiate, the tangled roots of the great trees a constant danger; the thick brush and low branches a constant nuisance as they came down from the high hills to where Colun suggested they camp.

"There are no Tachyn close," he told the war leaders when his scouts came back, "nor Breakers, I think."

"Then we halt here this night," Morrhyn said, "and tomorrow go out in search of Rannach and the others."

"And the Breakers," Yazte grunted. "And Chakthi's Tachyn; and whatever else faces us here."

Morrhyn said, "Yes. What else can we do?"

Yazte only shrugged and asked Colun if the Grannach had any tiswin with him.

"You promised me his head!" Chakthi gestured furiously at the moon-shadowed river. "His head, you said! Your word, you said! And now? See? They're gone, and we cannot pace them—they escape us!"

"You lack patience. Do you doubt my word?"

Akratil turned his horned mount away from the Tachyn's. The smaller animal was frightened of the sable creature, and in his rage Chakthi swung it hither and yon, prompting it to dance. He clutched the ax he'd anticipated swinging against Rannach's neck and glowered at the leader of the Breakers.

"His head!" he repeated. Spittle flecked his lips and his eyes stood wide with rage. "You promised me his head and now he's escaped us."

"You doubt my word?" Akratil asked again.

And Chakthi answered: *"Yes!"*

Akratil said, "Fool," and swung the golden reins over so that the sable, nightmare horse came shrilling against the lesser animal and ducked its horrid head and drove its central horn deep into the chest of the Tachyn animal.

Chakthi's mount screamed and struggled to free itself of the impaling horn. Blood spurted from its mouth and nostrils as the Breaker's dread beast gouged deeper. Then it faltered and fell, pitching Chakthi from the pad saddle. The sable creature snorted and shook its head free.

The Tachyn akaman landed on his face. Rose to his knees with an expression of mingled outrage and amazement, and swung his hatchet.

Akratil laughed and swung his terrible sword.

The head of Chakthi's ax was severed from the pole. It dropped to the grass and Chakthi, propelled by the momentum of his attack, followed it down. Once more he pitched full length as Breakers laughed and Tachyn watched in nervous apprehension. He spat and pushed to his knees, but as

he began to rise Akratil's blade touched his throat and
Chakthi found himself looking up into the red-lit orbs that
shone from the carapace of the golden helmet. A bead of
blood escaped his neck as Akratil leant from the saddle.

Chakthi froze. Slowly, he shifted backward from the
sword, still on his knees, and Akratil heeled the dread horse
forward, so that the blade remained firm against the Tachyn's
throat.

"Shall I take your head? Or shall you apologize?"

Breakers pressed in close, ringing them round, and
Chakthi swallowed. Blood trickled down his neck now, disappearing beneath his shirt. He stared at Akratil with maddened
eyes. For all the snorting of the Breakers' beasts and the nervous wickering of the Tachyn's horses, the night was suddenly
very quiet.

"Well?"

Akratil's voice was soft, amused as if it were nothing to
him to slay his ally. Chakthi swallowed again, his eyes flickering from side to side, finding no support, only the fear of his
warriors that they'd brought something greater to their aid
than they could know, or fight. He saw their reluctance, and
Hadduth nodding that he should do as the Breaker said, and
spat again.

"I . . . apologize."

The words were hard to find, harder to say, and Chakthi
realized that he hated Akratil no less than Rannach and his
cursed Commacht, or the outlanders who claimed the land he
thought his own. He felt a terrible frustration. Was he to
obtain his goals, then he needed the Breakers; but he was
akaman of the Tachyn and to be forced to this groveling was a
dire hurt that seared his twisted soul.

"Good." Akratil's sword came away from Chakthi's
throat. "I do not appreciate those who doubt my word."

He sheathed the blade, motioning that Chakthi rise, and
when the Tachyn did, brought the horned horse sideways,
slipping an armored foot from the stirrup. He smiled as he
kicked Chakthi in the face, sending the Tachyn tumbling
backward to fall again onto the grass.

"Never question me." His voice rang through the night,
commanding. "Doubt me again and I shall slay you and wear

your miserable skull like these others." He set the sable animal to prancing so that the skulls hung from the saddle rattled and shook. "Do you understand?"

Chakthi wiped blood from his mouth and ducked his
head.

"Good." Akratil chuckled. "You hate me, eh? That's
good—hatred is good: it fuels us."

Humiliated, Chakthi could only stand and glower at the
Breaker. Akratil laughed again and said, "But I'll make good
my word—you shall have that head you want so badly, and
more besides."

35

Fire and Water

The night grew older and the screaming of their pursuers faded into the darkness. The moonlit glittering of the Breakers' armor disappeared behind, whilst ahead the Restitution stretched wide and silvery, running to the sea, the raft carried swift on the current, twisting and turning as eddies swirled. None spoke for a while as muskets and rifles were reloaded, then Abram Jaymes said, "We lost them for now."

"To find Grostheim?" Arcole grunted. "That's to jump out of the frying pan into the fire."

"We'll find a holding first," Jaymes said confidently, "an' rest up awhile. Put the word out."

"And the owner shall accept us?" Arcole demanded.

"Likely," Jaymes replied, "he'll not have much choice."

Arcole stared frowning at the grizzled man. Var said enigmatically, "Abram has many friends, I discovered. I think you'll be surprised."

Arcole was, when a little before dawn Jaymes steered the raft in to the north bank, where a jetty thrust into the river, the shadowy bulk of a cluster of buildings showing beyond, squat and dim in the gray light. They beached the craft and made their way up the sloping bank, Jaymes in the lead. Rannach carried the sleeping Debo in his arms. A dog began to bark and Jaymes halted them with an upraised hand.

"Wait here."

He went forward and the dog stopped its barking, and a while later he returned.

"Come on."

They went to the lesser house, where branded folk were already rising, preparing to go about their duties. There were six men and six women, and a cluster of children who stared in goggle-eyed amazement at the visitors.

"This is Bryn." Jaymes indicated a hulking man whose long hair almost hid the scar on his cheek. "He's a friend."

"Welcome," Bryn said. "Abram's told us about you." He gestured at the table, which the women were setting with breakfast. "You'll eat with us?"

Rannach was nervous, glancing around as if anticipating some trick, an ambush. Then a smiling woman came to him and said, "Ach, but the wee one's sleepy, no? Give him here and I'll set him abed."

She reached for Debo and Rannach jerked away; Debo stirred in his arms, opening sleepy eyes. Davyd translated and Rannach allowed his son to be taken and set down on a bed recently vacated by one of the indentured children.

"Why do they help us?" he asked.

"Why wouldn't they?" Jaymes answered through Davyd. "I told them you're not one o' Chakthi's clan, an' they know what we're trying to do." He grinned. "Besides, they trust me."

"You risk much," Var observed to the table at large. "What if your . . . owner . . . discovers us?"

Bryn shrugged massive shoulders. "Abram told us what you done for him." He spooned porridge into his mouth and spoke past the mush. "That was a decent thing, I reckon—we all reckon. And things are changing in this land. Does Sieur Vitale object, then . . ." He chuckled. "We'll object back, I reckon."

He glanced around, his eyes met with nods of agreement, murmurings of assent.

"Do you speak of insurrection?" Var asked. "You'd over-turn your master?"

"Didn't you?" Jaymes asked quietly.

Var thought a moment, then nodded.

"He'll have a choice," Jaymes said. "To join us, or not. That's fair, no?"

Again, Var thought awhile and then ducked his head in agreement. "So what's our plan?" he asked. And grinned: "Or, rather, *your* plan?"

"Bryn here'll stock us with food," Jaymes said, "an' carry word to the next holding about what's coming. . . ."

"You'll run away?" Surprised, Var addressed himself to Bryn. "You'd risk that?"

"In light of what Abram's told me," Bryn said, "yes. Wouldn't you?"

Var shrugged. "You chance much."

"There's much at stake," Bryn said. "And I can reach the Freynche holding in a day and be back the next. And they'll send word on to the Stottyr farm—and they'll send it on until all the holdings know what's coming. So at least the branded folk'll be ready."

Var nodded. "And us?"

Jaymes had no chance to answer, because the door flung open and a short, red-featured man strode in. He wore the marks of a heavy drinker on his nose and in his eyes, and a brace of pistols on his belt. He looked angry; then amazed as he saw his indentured folk's strange visitors.

"What in God's name is this?" he cried, gaping at Rannach. "A God-cursed savage on my land?"

He drew both pistols and leveled them at the table.

"Who are you?" He answered his own question: "By God, that's Abram Jaymes, no? And you are the turncoat." He glared at Var. "Sworn to God's duty, eh? And you took this scum from prison. What are you doing here?" His angry eyes took in Arcole and Davyd. "And these with brands on their cheeks? Runaways, eh? Bryn, take them! We'll deliver them all back to the Inquisitor in Grostheim."

Bryn said, "No," and rose ponderously from the table.

"What?" Sieur Vitale cocked his guns. "You argue with me?"

Bryn said, "Yes. Listen—these men bring dire warning of . . ."

"Quiet!" Vitale shouted. "Take them now! Else your life be forfeit!"

"Sieur," Bryn said, "only hear me out."

Vitale said, "No, damn you," and aimed a pistol at Bryn's chest. "You'll do as I order, or I'll shoot you. And you'll do it now—take them!"

Bryn said again, "No," and his owner shot him in the chest.

Bryn pitched back, blood spreading over his shirt as porridge sprayed from his mouth. He hit the wall behind and bounced off, falling down across the table, bowls and plates and cups tumbling under his weight. A woman screamed and children began to wail. Vitale snarled, pointing the second gun as Rannach's hatchet spun through the dawn light to imbed in his chest, and at the same time Var's pistol blasted, so that the landowner was thrown back through the open door and fell down on his back in the yard beyond.

Davyd and Arcole reached for their muskets. Abram Jaymes sat still, spooning porridge.

"I'd say," he remarked, "that you're committed now."

"What else could I do?" Var looked startled by his own actions. "God, but the man shot Bryn on no more than a whim."

"Bryn was a branded man," Jaymes said calmly, "and that is how the Autarchy works." He pointed a spoon at Rannach, who worked his hatchet from Vitale's chest, wiped the blade on the dead man's shirt, and returned to the table. "He understands it better than you."

Davyd translated and Rannach shrugged: "Bryn was a friend," he said, "and the red-faced man killed him. What else should I do?"

"You see?" Jaymes said to Var.

Var nodded. "I think I do."

Morrhyn swallowed the pahé and settled himself beside the fire. Kahteney lounged across from the flames, his eyes already wide and blurring as the dream root took hold. Morrhyn smiled and mouthed a silent prayer that the Maker show them what to do, where to go. And dreamed . . .

Of Davyd and Arcole and Rannach, two strangers with them, floating down a great river that washed out into a vaster expanse of water he supposed was the ocean of which the outlanders had spoken. It went past a great, walled place that he knew must be the city they'd told him of, and from behind the walls he felt a disturbing presence, as if something evil as the Breakers lurked there.

Then he saw the Horde moving over this strange land, and Chakthi's Tachyn with them, allied, as if a prairie fire raged, sweeping over the grass, consuming all before it. He saw the flames encroach upon the river, threatening to burn up Rannach and the others, and they come to land, where folk with the scar on their cheeks gave shelter before they went on, toward the city.

He did not understand why they went toward the city, and in his dreaming reached out to Davyd, seeking communion.

It was hard to establish contact. The Breakers' presence clouded the aetheral ways, their innate magic obfuscating the dreaming paths so that even when he found Davyd it was difficult to express himself clearly, or to understand Davyd's responses.

We are come to Salvation, he said. *I dreamed we should.*

The Breakers are here, Davyd replied, *allied with Chakthi and his Tachyn.*

Yes, I know. That's why I brought the People here—to fight them.

They hunt Rannach. Chakthi would have his head.

Chakthi shall lose his own: he's a fool.

Yes, but the Breakers use him. They follow us down. . . .

Where are you? Morrhyn asked, and got back only the image of the river lit by fire and a golden-armored warrior he recognized prancing a horrid horse, laughing out of the flames. Then all was confusion, images and impressions—of awful peril and battle, factions he did not properly comprehend vying for supremacy. The river blazed, and the walled place, and out of the walled place came men who fought, though he could not, in the confusion, tell whom—the People or the Breakers, or both. He felt an urgent *summoning,* such calling as he had known when Davyd first approached Ket-Ta-Thanne, but could not properly define it for the intervention of the flames and the sound of thunder. He knew only that he must take the People toward that calling, and pray to the Maker that they come timely.

He woke sweaty, groaning as he shifted, his head throbbing. He found water and splashed his face, then looked to Kahteney.

The Lakanti Dreamer opened frightened eyes and said, "I dreamed of fire, of battle; but I could not understand it. Save that the Breakers threaten again."

"We knew that," Morrhyn said, and swallowed water that his voice not croak. "Now we must find them, and fight them."

Kahteney said, "Yes, I know. But shall we survive this battle?"

"That," Morrhyn remarked, "is in the hands of the Maker, and in ours, but we must attempt it, no? We cannot ignore them—we've a duty."

Kahteney ducked his head: "Yes." He seemed unhappy with that duty, and Morrhyn could understand his reluctance. The Maker knew, but the Breakers had almost destroyed the People in Ket-Ta-Witko, and now the Matawaye went out to war in a strange land filled with potential enemies. He wished it were not so, but could see no other path to take—not save the People run like panicked animals from the Breakers' fire, and lose themselves and die. He tugged on shirt and breeches and ran fingers through his unbound hair and smiled at Kahteney with what he hoped was a brave expression.

"So come, brother, and let's to our duty."

Kahteney groaned and rose, dressed, and followed Morrhyn from the tent.

Outside, the camp was awake. Yazte and Kanseah and Dohnse sat with Colun about a fire on which Arrhyna and Flysse cooked. All their faces turned toward the two wakanishas as they approached, and Morrhyn caught the tail of a conversation from which he judged the two women advised the chieftains that they were not servants to fetch and carry, and did the chieftains wish to eat, in future they could cook their own meals. It ended as the Dreamers came up, and Morrhyn nodded greetings.

Flysse thrust a plate into his hands as Arrhyna served Kahteney, and in both their eyes Morrhyn saw questions.

"They are alive," he said, "but somewhere east of here. They go down a great river toward a walled place."

Flysse said, "The Restitution, and the place must be Grostheim." She frowned. "Why would they go there?"

Morrhyn shrugged. "I don't know. Perhaps to warn the people there? The Breakers go after them, with Chakthi and his Tachyn."

"That whoreson allies with the Breakers?" Yazte spat into the fire. "I'd see my lance in his chest."

"Not," Colun said, stroking his ax, "do I reach him first."

"You're sure?" Arrhyna's hands shook, tea spilling from the cup she held. "They are truly come again?"

Morrhyn nodded. "And save we defeat them here, they'll go on—to Ket-Ta-Thanne and all the countries of this world." He smiled wanly. "We must find this river and follow it, for that shall lead us to Rannach and the others."

"I can help you." Flysse set down her cup, her pretty face determined. "I can lead you to the river, and the river leads to Grostheim."

"And the Breakers?" Yazte asked.

"We go to war, no?" Morrhyn looked at their faces. "We ride to save Rannach and Arcole and Davyd and Debo, but also to halt the Breakers. I think," his confidence faltered a moment, "that this shall be the last battle."

"How say you?" Yazte asked.

And Morrhyn answered: "I think that do we fail now, all shall be lost. Save we destroy the Breakers here, they shall destroy us and all those we left behind, and everything else in this world. And after go on to others and destroy them."

"Then," Yazte said firmly, "let us go find them and fight them, and be it the last battle then we shall die as warriors of the People and the Maker take us to Him in the Spirit World."

His sentiments were echoed by the others, and in a while the camp was struck and the great war band moved eastward.

Captain Jorge Kerik stared in alarm at Jared Talle.

"Are you sure, Inquisitor?"

Talle met the officer's nervous gaze with determined dark eyes. "Do you question me, Captain?"

"No!" Kerik shook his head vigorously. "Save . . ."

"Save what?" Talle asked, his voice brisk.

"It must leave the garrison mightily undermanned." Kerik hesitated to argue. The Inquisitor frightened him, but even so he felt a duty to his command. And now that Tomas Var was gone outlaw—presumed slain in the wilderness—he was, under Talle, the senior officer. And he thought the Inquisitor's plan insane. "What with the suicides . . . the ghosts . . . we've not so many men. Do we take all the marines out, then who shall guard the city?"

"There are sufficient of the God's Militia," Talle declared.

Kerik had far rather not disagree, but even so he said, "We cannot be sure of the enemy's position, Inquisitor; and do they outflank us to come against Grostheim . . ."

"I can *smell* them!" Talle rose from behind Andru Wyme's ornate desk in a swirl of black coattails. He strode around the bureau to stand before the nervous marine—and even must he look up into Kerik's face, still he frightened the man. "I shall lead you to them. They'll not outflank us!"

"But are we enough?" Kerik asked desperately. "You speak of a horde, and I've only two and a half hundred of my men."

"*Your* men?" Talle chuckled. "Surely *mine,* no?"

"Of course; forgive me." Kerik shaped an apologetic bow.

"To do with as I wish, no?"

"Yes, Inquisitor."

Talle said, "Excellent. We understand one another."

Kerik wished Tomas Var had not gone.

"So." Talle hooked his hands behind his back and leant against the desk. "You've two hundred and fifty marines not tainted with this ghostly curse."

Kerik, standing instinctively to attention, ducked his head. "Two hundred and fifty able men, Inquisitor."

"And sufficient powder, shot—all arms—for a campaign?"

"Yes, Inquisitor."

"Artillery?"

"Ten horse guns, Inquisitor. Unless we strip Grostheim of cannon and take them."

"Could we?"

"It should be mightily difficult, Inquisitor. The cannon are heavy and would surely slow us—besides leaving the city defenseless."

"Save for my hexes!"

"Of course, Inquisitor. I did not mean to imply . . ."

"No." Talle waved a dismissive hand and for an instant Kerik feared he shaped a hexing spell. It was an effort to remain at attention as his heart raced; then he stifled a sigh of relief as the hand fell back and the Inquisitor smiled his ugly smile. "So, we've ten horse guns?"

"With canister and grape shot," Kerik said, "and trained teams."

"Good." Talle nodded. The ducking of his head made Kerik think of the carrion crows he'd seen picking over corpses. "Then we shall go out to meet them. And do they . . . disagree . . . we shall destroy them."

Kerik said, "Yes, Inquisitor." And then: "When shall we depart?"

"The sooner the better, no?" Talle said. "How soon can you be ready?"

Kerik swallowed bile. He was mightily tempted to delay, to make excuses that should grant him more time—perhaps ships might arrive from Evander with reinforcements—but Talle fixed him with those piercing black eyes and he could not dissimulate.

"Three weeks, Inquisitor," he said, making a swift calculation. "Perhaps four."

Talle frowned and Kerik felt sweat run down his back. "We must requisition horses," he said. "Riding animals and stock for the limber guns. I'll need to send out parties. . . ."

Talle said, "Do it, on my authority. I'll sign the papers, and can you do it in less time, I shall commend you in my next report to Evander." He smiled. "Perhaps a promotion? After all, someone must take that traitor Var's place."

Kerik nodded. "I'll do my best, Inquisitor."

"Excellent." Talle beckoned a silent servant forward. "Brandy! We drink to victory, eh?"

Kerik nodded as the glasses were filled. "To victory!"

The servant, whose brand stood pale and stark on the skin of his cheek, said nothing as Talle raised his glass and drank, and Kerik did the same.

"Report at dawn," Talle ordered, draining his glass, "and at sun's set. Neither delay."

Kerik said, "Yes, Inquisitor," and then, "No, Inquisitor," and felt mightily grateful when Talle waved him away.

He quit the room wishing his duty had not brought him to Salvation. He could not understand what transpired here—ghosts riding the streets? An officer of the God's Militia betraying his command to rescue a ne'er-do-well convicted by an Inquisitor? An Inquisitor intent on stripping Grostheim of its defensive forces to go out and meet an unknown enemy? It made no sense. But Jorge Kerik was a mere captain of marines and it was not his place to question or argue with an Inquisitor, so he only wished and went about his duties, preparing for Jared Talle's campaign.

Davyd woke from restless dreams to find himself in a place he did not, for a while, recognize. Dreams and reality intermingled: the shooting of Bryn and Morrhyn's voice inside his head, images of the Horde and a great mass of the People riding out of the wilderness; fire and clashing blades; bloodshed and defeat and victory, all entwined. He groaned and looked about, sitting up.

He lay in a rumpled bed that stood beside a window, allowing in the pale light of early dawn. The bed was wide and took up most of the small room, which was timbered and plain, furnished with little else than a chest and a washstand. Memory returned: he was in the indentured servants' quarters of the Vitale holding, and Sieur Vitale was dead. And Bryn. He rose and went to find the others.

They sat around the table he remembered—Maker, but had he slept the whole day away? There was not time for that.

"So," Arcole greeted him with a smile, "you wake at last."

A woman handed him a tin mug filled with aromatic coffee and he sipped before he spoke, smiling his thanks.

"You dreamed?" Rannach asked.

Davyd nodded.

Abram Jaymes said, "You bein' a Dreamer, maybe you should tell us what to do."

Davyd felt his smile falter as he found Tomas Var's eyes on

him. The man was—no doubt of this any longer—a friend, but still he wore the uniform of a marine officer in the God's Militia, and Davyd could not forget what the Autarchy did to Dreamers.

Then, as if to put him at his ease, Jaymes said, "We were holdin' a war council. But we figured we need your advice."

"We've buried Bryn and Vitale," Arcole said, "and riders are out to alert the other holdings. But do we go on to Grostheim, or . . ."

"The People are coming," Davyd said. "They've come through the mountains with the Grannach, and they traverse the wilderness in search of us and the Breakers." The room fell silent, save for the scuffling of the children who played excitedly with Debo. "Morrhyn leads them, with all the warriors." He glanced nervously at Arcole. "Flysse is with them, and Arrhyna."

"What?" Arcole gaped. "In God's name, why?"

Davyd shrugged. "I don't know, only that she is."

Arcole translated for Rannach and the Commacht assumed the same expression of amazement and concern. In the language of the People, Davyd said, "I think they insisted—I can't be sure; only that they *are* with the band."

Urgently, Rannach said, "I must find her. I must take Debo back and see them both safe in the mountains."

"Nor would I," Arcole said, "have Flysse come here. There's too much danger."

"I think," Davyd said slowly, ponderous under the weight of the Dreamer's responsibility, aware of the eyes upon him, all waiting on his words, "that you have little choice in the matter. They are here, and will not go back until we are all safe."

He hesitated to add, "Or slain."

Rannach said, "Tell me where they are!"

"Moving toward us," Davyd said. "I know no more than that. I think . . ." He paused, sipping coffee, unwilling to meet their eyes, ". . . that it can do us no good to seek them. They shall find us, or not; but we must go on."

How to explain dreams all clouded with confusion and doubt? He wished he owned Morrhyn's certitude, but Morrhyn was the Prophet and he a mere acolyte. He fingered the warrior's braids stranding his hair and wondered if he was even that still.

Rannach said, "I'd not leave Debo in harm's way."

In Evanderan, Abram Jaymes asked, "What we talkin' about here?" And when Davyd explained: "It might not be so bad an idea. Listen—we already got word goin' out to the holdings, an' I'm taking word to Grostheim . . ."

He broke off as Var interrupted, "With me."

"So maybe if Rannach here contacts his people, we can get together. Rannach can tell your . . . Matawaye? . . . where we're goin', and we catch the Breakers between us."

"*Us?*" Var asked. "Who's this *us?*"

Jaymes grinned and gestured at the indentured servants listening to their conversation. "The branded folk," he said. "Them and others of the same persuasion. Maybe even your marines, are they of the same mind as you."

"Which is?" Var asked, suspicious.

"That we need to defeat the Breakers," Jaymes said. "That first, else they slay us all."

Var nodded, frowned, and asked, "And second?"

"Second?" Jaymes set down his cup and smiled. "That we need to defeat that little black crow bastard, Talle, an' make Salvation independent. Like we talked about, eh?"

Var hesitated. "You speak of secession and civil war."

"Yes," Jaymes said calmly, "that's why I'd like your marines on our side."

Var said, "*Our* side?"

"I reckon," Jaymes said. "Which side *are* you on?"

Var hesitated a moment longer before he said firmly, "Yours!"

"Good." Jaymes grinned and lowered the hammer of the pistol he'd held cocked beneath the table. "So let's make plans."

No military band played them out, which Jorge Kerik thought was somewhat of a pity, but all the bandsmen were dead, either by their own hand or slain in the rioting, so only frowning redcoats and sullen exiles watched the departure.

Kerik thought there should likely be a cheer as Jared Talle

quit the city, for he knew the Inquisitor was hated as any savage or ghost-rider, but only silence followed them as the gates opened and they went through to what he felt was likely his death.

Talle rode at the head of the column—a black-suited figure slumped uncomfortably on the mildest horse Kerik had been able to find—leading a column of two hundred and fifty mounted marines. The hinterland to south and north of Grostheim was stripped of animals, and Kerik knew the farmers and millers and traders resented the loss, but what could he do save obey the command of the Inquisitor?

They rode with the ten horse guns: light weapons that could be carried swiftly to battle, loaded with the canister and grape that weighted the wagons behind, and withdrawn at speed. Kerik wondered if they should be enough. Each marine carried a musket and pouches of shot and powder in addition to the long bayonets that might be attached to the muskets. Kerik himself wore a brace of pistols and, as befit an officer, a sword. He let his eyes swing sideways to glimpse Jared Talle, who rode saddle-slumped and black-coated, his lank black hair drifting in the warm spring breeze, with no more defenses than his hex magic. Kerik prayed that be enough, for he somehow could not believe that powder and shot alone might be sufficient to defeat the enemy.

They rode on through what the People would name the Moon of Dancing Foals. Salvation's grass grew fresh and green, and the sky shone blue and swallow-filled, lit by a warm yellow sun. They bivouacked around holdings and empty ground, pursuing the course of the Restitution until they came to a place where open country stood wide between low ridges that stretched down to the river, set atop with oaks and maples.

And Jared Talle raised his hand and shouted for the column to halt.

"We shall meet them here." He turned to Kerik. "Set up your guns for slaughter. Do they argue, we shall slay them."

"And if they do not argue?" Kerik asked, confused.

"Then," Talle said, "we shall make such allies as the Autarchy's never known."

Kerik saluted and set to positioning his guns.

36

Into the Fire

The Horde swept like wildfire across Salvation,
Akratil at its head with Chakthi following behind
like some sullen dog, unwilling—or unable—to
quit its cruel master. And was Chakthi the dog, then Hadduth was the jackal, cringing for favor, seeking to please both
his masters, so that amongst the Tachyn, men spoke of ignominy and lost dignity. But never loud, for fear of their terrible
allies. They remembered Chappo's fate, and kept their complaining low: none would fall foul of the Breakers. They came
out of the wilderness forest and descended on the tilled lands
beyond like some locust horde, and even the Tachyn were
horrified by what the Breakers did.

"We slay them all." Akratil sheathed a bloody sword, setting
a fresh skull on his saddle. "Men and women and children—
all!"

Chakthi said, "But the children might be raised as ours."

Akratil laughed and shook his head. "None live."

Chakthi nodded, unwilling to disagree, afraid to argue. He
felt sickened by the slaughter—not so much the slaying of the
pale-faced intruders on his lands as at the killing of the children.

Akratil said, "You'd have sacrificed your grandson, no?"

"That was different." Chakthi shrugged. "That was necessary—to bring you here."

"And now we are come." Akratil leered down at the
Tachyn. "Do you regret it?"

"No," Chakthi shook his head quickly, aware of how swift

that curved blade could lift from the scabbard, "I am your servant, and do your will."

"As should you, worm." Akratil laughed again and summoned Bemnida to him. "Listen, do you take half our force northward and destroy what you find. Meet me back on the river, eh?"

"As you command." Bemnida tossed away the morsel she'd gnawed. The child's leg fell to the ground and was gulped up by her mount. "How long?"

"Seven settings of the sun." Akratil reached across to fondle her long blond hair. "Deliver them to blood and destruction, eh?"

Bemnida smiled. "Is that not our way?"

Akratil said, "Yes. Now let them know that."

Anton Groell threw his musket aside and stooped to the body of his wife. A shaft of bright yellow wood jutted from Liesli's shoulder, and she moaned in pain as her husband lifted her in his arms.

The room stank of blood and gunpowder and smoke. The roof was burning and all the branded folk were dead; Anton had no more powder save the horn on his belt, and only enough shot for the pistol holstered there. He feared his wife was dying, and he'd not see her consumed in the flames of abomination's making: he picked her up and staggered through the smoke to the rear of the holding. He ignored the cuts on his own body, the pain of the two arrows grating on his ribs. He kicked down the burning door and walked out through the smoke.

A painted face confronted him and, unthinking, he drew his pistol and fired. The face went away as Liesli screamed, and he mouthed apologies as he picked her up and tossed her over his shoulder. He ran, as best he could under the burden of her weight, toward the river.

There was a cornfield there, and the trunks were high enough to hide them. It came to him that he'd not reloaded his pistol, and he prayed none of the savages or the demons find them before he could settle his wife into the little dinghy and cast loose. He was no longer sure God stood on his side.

It seemed almost impossible in light of what he'd seen: demons come riding on weirdling beasts to attack his holding, and led by a woman who had screamed her name as if in challenge of all that was good and true and ordered.

"I am Bemnida, and I bring you death!"

That alone had chilled Anton Groell, for he could not imagine such horridly lethal intent in a woman's mouth any more than what she had done after.

He had seen her strike down men and women and children as they fled for the safety of his house. And then seen her take up the body of a child and toss it to the thing she rode—which had chewed on the little corpse as if it were a tidbit. He had known true fear then.

But none so bad as this as he stumbled through the corn with Liesli across his shoulder. He dropped her twice, stifling her agonized cries even as he bit down on the pain of his own wounds. He wanted only to reach the dinghy and escape the awful carnage, but he could hear the shouting behind him, and the throaty crackle of his home burning. He began to cry, and staggered onward.

Then he was tumbling down the riverbank, Liesli screaming as the shaft imbedded in her body broke and drove deeper, he whimpering as pain flooded his body from his own fall.

He rose onto his knees and reached for his wife as he saw the dinghy, hope there in the little craft. And then a thing that was a lion and a lizard combined with other animals came charging down the slope. The rider wore armor of shining green and held a sword high.

As it swept down to take off Liesli's head, Anton Groell heard the wielder shout, "I am Bemnida!" He could not see her face beneath the helmet, but he recognized that voice, and shuddered.

He saw his wife's head go rolling down into the water and wished he'd recharged his pistol. He might then, at least, have fired one shot before the sword clove in his skull.

Even had Flysse not guided the Matawaye warriors out from the wilderness forest to the river, still they had likely found the trail the Breakers left, for it was as if flame ran across the land and they need only follow its swath. It sickened them, and firmed their purpose, and had any doubted the wisdom of this dread venture, then what they saw along their way confirmed the need to confront and defeat the Breakers. Nightly they prayed to the Maker for strength and victory.

"How can they do this?" Dohnse stared aghast at bodies sundered and burned, some spitted and carved like deer. "It shames me that the Tachyn ride with these folk."

"It should not," Morrhyn said. "It shames Chakthi and Hadduth, and those who ride with them, but it should not shame you."

Dohnse shrugged and turned away. Kahteney asked, "Can we defeat them?"

Morrhyn in turn shrugged and answered, "We can only try."

Yazte stared at the corpse of a child, roasted and gnawed like some suckling pig, and said grimly, "Must I die in the trying, then I give my life willingly."

"And I," Colun declared. "We *must* fight them."

"Then let's go on." Morrhyn turned from the sorry relics. He felt a tremendous sadness that such evil came again, nor less than the others a grim resolve that this be settled one way or the other. He did not think he could live in a world that also held the Breakers and their Tachyn acolytes. "Perhaps tonight I'll dream of Davyd."

Davyd watched Rannach mount the horse taken from Sieur Vitale's stock. It was a fine animal: a deep-chested bay with the legs of a runner. Debo was settled on a piebald mare that reminded him of his own horse, smaller than his father's mount, but still, the branded folk assured, fleet of hoof and possessed of stamina.

Rannach said, "Are you sure of this? I'd not leave you to fight alone, even though . . ." He glanced at Debo, who beamed to be once again ahorse.

"Yes." Davyd ducked his head and spoke with far more conviction than he felt. "Do you go back and see Debo safe, then tell the People where we go—that way they shall find us swifter. Tell Morrhyn I shall do my best to dream."

Rannach nodded. Arcole said, "And tell Flysse I love her. And are you able, send her back."

"I doubt," Rannach said, "I shall be able to do that, nor persuade Arrhyna, but no harm shall come to either one whilst I live. You've my word on that."

Arcole said, "I know," and they clasped hands.

"We'll meet you where the Maker chooses," Davyd said. "Farewell."

"Farewell." Rannach raised a hand in salute to all of them and beckoned Debo to follow, driving heels against the bay's flanks so that the big horse snorted and began to run.

"So now it's our turn." Abram Jaymes shouldered his rifle and spat tobacco onto the grass. "An' if Davyd's right, we don't have much time."

Davyd said, "No," and they went down to the landing stage, where Vitale's folk had provided them with a dinghy.

They loaded what little gear they carried and Arcole and Var took the oars, bringing the small craft out to the current. Jaymes manned the tiller and Davyd sat at the prow, his eyes blank with apprehension.

"God, but this reminds me," Var said.

Arcole grinned. "We faced an easier enemy the last time."

Var smiled back. "I was afraid then."

"And you're not now?" Arcole asked.

Var whistled. "I think that this time I am even more afraid."

"And I," Arcole returned.

"The guns are all in place." Jorge Kerik gestured at the wooded ridge that boundaried the eastern perimeter of the shallow valley. "Anyone entering here will be in easy shot. And must we withdraw . . ."

The chopping of Talle's hand cut off his words. "We shall parley," the Inquisitor declared, "and if they refuse my terms, we shall slaughter them."

Kerik held his face rigid as he nodded. And if we cannot, he thought, then I shall order my men to run for Grostheim, for I wonder if you're any longer sane. But all he said was, "As you command, Inquisitor."

And they waited for the Breakers to arrive.

Davyd woke confused, opening his eyes on a sky all pocked with twinkling stars and the fat crescent of the burgeoning moon. Water slapped restless against the planks of the dinghy, punctuated by the rhythmic creak of the oars. Abram Jaymes manned them alone, with Var sleepy at the tiller and Arcole snoring softly in the thwarts. Davyd wondered an instant what had woken him, and why he felt such a terrible urgency.

It was not anything he could put into words—only a certainty, a conviction he could not explain but must obey. He sat erect, sleep sloughing off as he stared around.

"Turn in!"

"What?"

Abram Jaymes looked back from his oars so that the dinghy wallowed in midstream. Var grunted and set firmer hands on the tiller; Arcole stirred, clutching at his musket.

"Turn in!" Davyd gestured wildly at the north bank. "Here; now!"

"Why, for Godsakes?" Jaymes demanded. "We're not more'n a couple days from Grostheim. Why here; why now?"

"Turn in!"

Jaymes stared at him awhile then shrugged, motioning that Var bring the tiller over. Var obeyed, but as he did, Davyd saw his expression: such as he might bestow on a madman.

Perhaps I am, he thought, save I . . . *know*.

"What's going on?" Arcole woke, coming upright with his musket cocked and raised to his chest. "Are we attacked?"

"No." Jaymes spat a long streamer of tobacco over the river. "Davyd says we have to beach."

"Why?" Arcole, in turn, stared at Davyd.

Maker, grant I'm right; please.

He swallowed, which was difficult with a mouth so dry. "We must," he said. "I can't explain, but we must."

"There's nothin' here," Jaymes said. "No holdings, only open land."

Davyd rubbed at his temples. "There's a valley," he said. "A wide valley with timber along the ridges."

"An' a stream along the bottomland that gets real marshy when it rains," Jaymes said. "Sure; it's about two days' walk from here, but what of it?"

"It shall happen there," Davyd said.

"What shall happen?" Arcole demanded.

"The last battle. I have to go there."

They all stared at him as the dinghy grounded on a stretch of sandy shore overhung with low-branched alders. He clambered wearily over the bow and held the little craft as Jaymes sprang into the water and manhandled the boat farther up the sand. He felt exhausted, and his old wounds throbbed as if in recognition. Arcole and Var jumped into the river to aid Jaymes. Water birds screeched a protest and splashed away. He looked at the river, rippled by starlight, silvery under the moon's glow. It was, as best he judged by the moon's position, close on midnight.

"Two days?"

Jaymes nodded. "If it's the valley I'm thinkin' of. But what're you goin' to do?"

"Go there." He shrugged. "I don't know."

Arcole said, "I shall come with you."

"You don't need to. I can go alone."

"And die?" Arcole shook his head.

"All right." Davyd looked at Jaymes, at Var. "But not you—you go on to Grostheim."

"And?" Jaymes asked.

"Raise this army you spoke of," Davyd said, not sure where the words came from, only that he must say them else the world fall down under the Breakers. "Bring all the folk you can to this valley. Armed for battle. Find us there, and so shall the People."

"And then?" Var asked.

"And then," Davyd said, "we shall either defeat the Breakers or die."

There was a silence before Tomas Var said, "Do you forget Jared Talle?"

"No; he's there already." Davyd shook his head as Var's

eyes framed a question. "I don't know how I know, but I do. He's there, waiting."

"For what?" Var looked at him out of eyes that now wondered.

"The Breakers," Davyd said. "He'd ally with them."

"He said as much to me." Var swallowed. "But would he, truly?"

"Yes." Davyd looked out at the night, the river. The water flowed like passing time and he felt again the certainty. "He would."

"Shall he succeed?" Var asked.

"I don't know." Davyd shrugged. It felt as if he raised a weight with his shoulders, a terrible weight that lay upon the certitude of his abstract knowledge. "Only that we must do what we can to defeat them all."

"Then we'd best get goin'." Abram Jaymes glanced at Var, then at Davyd. "It'll take a while to reach Grostheim, an' longer to raise folk—if we can."

Var said, "I thought you guaranteed that?"

"Against Talle, yes." Jaymes grinned; in the moon's light his smile looked hollow. "But we're talkin' about a different enemy now."

Var said, "Shall that stop us?"

"No; let's go." Jaymes shrugged and turned to Davyd. "Can you find the valley?"

Davyd nodded; the knowledge sat inside his skull like a lodestone pointing him to his destiny.

"Then we'll meet you there soon as we can. Come on, Tomas."

They shook hands, and then Var and Jaymes manhandled the dinghy clear of the strand and went away downriver. Davyd sighed and took up his musket and began to walk northward.

Arcole fell into step beside, not sure where Davyd led him, or to what; only that he must go.

He wondered if he was to die in Salvation, for it seemed a forlorn hope that the many strands of fate Davyd spoke of should come successfully together. How could the People find them in time, and even did they, were they enough to defeat the might of the Breakers? And how could Jaymes and Var raise an army of indentured folk to fight such horror? And Flysse was with the Matawaye—would she live? He glanced sidelong at his companion, no longer the gangly boy he'd brought out of Grostheim. Moonlight reflected silvery off Davyd's white hair, and the long scar running down his face shone pale against the tan. He could see that Davyd was mightily weary and guessed the old wounds hurt him, but there was an expression of grim resolve on his face that forbore questions, so Arcole only cradled his musket and went with his friend to meet their destiny.

Almost, their horses collided, but Rannach swung his around at the last moment and brought the bay in a skittering circle to come alongside Arrhyna's. They leant across to embrace. For a moment he held her and kissed her and smelled her hair, and wanted nothing more than to snatch her from the pad saddle and take her to their lodge. But she pushed him away and reached for Debo, taking the child into her arms, and they rode together as around them all the Matawaye warriors shouted their approval and danced their weary mounts in acclamation.

Flysse came up, questions in her blue eyes, and Rannach said, "He lives; and Davyd. They go to that city you came from, to warn the people there."

"No." Morrhyn joined them. "Davyd and Arcole go to meet the Breakers and another enemy, and we must hurry."

Rannach stared at the Prophet, doubt in his eyes. "They were . . ."

"I know," Morrhyn said, "but since you left them, Davyd's dreamed of other things. There's a valley . . ."

"They come." Jared Talle smiled into the night. "I can smell them. You're ready?"

Jorge Kerik nodded. "As you ordered, Inquisitor. But are you sure?"

Talle frowned, irritated. "Do you doubt me, Captain?"

"No!" Swiftly, Kerik shook his head. "But alone?"

"Not alone," Talle said with a certain degree of satisfaction. "After all, you shall be with me, and your ten best men."

Kerik said, "Yes, Inquisitor," and wished he were safe behind Grostheim's walls. Wished, no less, that he owned the courage to deny this madman, who thought to commune with demons and win them to his side. He doubted that was possible; and knew that he did not dare deny Talle: he had no choice save to obey.

"I shall speak with them," Talle said, "and convince them to join us—to join with the Autarchy. And then we shall both be hailed heroes, eh?"

Kerik said, "Yes," wondering if his affirmation sounded as hollow to Talle as it did to him.

"And do they disagree," Talle said, "then you and your men shall cover my retreat and your horse guns shall destroy them, and again we shall be heroes. Do you not understand, Captain? We cannot fail. After all, what chance can they hold over our modern weaponry? They fight with swords and lances, no? And we have cannon and muskets—and God on our side. We cannot lose!"

Kerik said, "No, Inquisitor, surely not," and felt sweat run cold down his spine.

Along the ridge dim fires burned, hidden amongst the pines, and he could hear the faint sounds his men made as they waited for the enemy—or the allies. He heard the nickering of restless horses and the mutter of low-voiced conversation. Kerik felt afraid. He thought the Inquisitor insane and could not bring himself to argue with the man. God knew, but they'd surely better waited in Grostheim, behind high walls, where reinforcements might soon come, rather than here. But Jared Talle was the Inquisitor and commander, the highest authority in all Salvation, and Jorge Kerik was not prepared to disagree with a man who might bespell him, or even slay him with a gesture. So he saluted and went to check the positioning of his force.

After the captain had departed, Jared Talle sat warming his hands beside the fire, staring at the western ingress to the valley. He wore the hex signs on his chest and on his hands, and he was confident that he must survive, no matter the final outcome. That, he anticipated with such enthusiasm as he'd not known since the War of Restitution. He knew the Breakers were powerful—but so was he. God was on his side, and the strength of Kerik's guns, the discipline of the marines. The Breakers possessed great magic, but still they fought like savages, their weapons simple, and did they look to use their magicks against him, why he'd his own for protection.

He studied the arcane sigils decorating his palms and smiled. They'd surely not harm him—and must some of the marines die, that should be a small price to pay in demonstration of the Autarchy's strength. He thought perhaps there should be some fighting, but after a volley or two of cannon, the Breakers must see the impossibility of defeating so mighty a power as the Autarchy—and then they would surely parley. And he could learn so much from them.

He nodded in approval of his own mad reasoning, telling himself that was how it *must* go. There would be an alliance formed: the Breakers and the Autarchy thought too much alike to disagree.

It did not, of course, occur to Talle that he was insane.

"Do you understand any of this?" Tomas Var glanced sidelong at his rowing companion. "For God knows, I don't."

Abram Jaymes shrugged as best he could while manning an oar and said, "I understand we better get to Grostheim fast as we can an' raise us an army. Then get it back to the valley. I believe in Davyd, eh?"

Var thought awhile, then nodded. "I suppose I do. But how do we bring him aid? Even if Talle's quit the city, he'll have left troops on guard, and they'll not let branded folk march out."

"Perhaps they'll be persuaded," Jaymes said.

"Perhaps," Var allowed, doubt in his voice, "but even so, how do we get back to this valley in time for—what was it Davyd said?—the last battle?"

"We'll find a way," Jaymes said. "We have to."

Var sighed and bent to his oar.

∎   ∎   ∎

Speed was of the essence. Morrhyn felt it in his blood and the marrow of his bones. It was as if the Maker spoke to him in the patterns of the night, and the play of the sun over the grass of this different land. He could smell the Breakers in his nostrils like an evil taint, like the foul spoor of a wolverine, and when he dreamed it was of war and fire, of destruction and conclusion. But the Maker did not vouchsafe him the knowledge of which side the scales should fall on, or of who should prove victorious; he could only hope. And because he was the Prophet, the warriors followed him.

He pushed the war band hard, riding through the dark hours when warriors made camp, refusing them respite until Rannach or Yazte or Colun urged him to halt, pointing out that exhausted horses should be useless in battle. Only then did he allow them or himself to rest, and only a few hours, so that they were mounted and moving before the sun rose, pushing steadily onward, eastward, toward the place he could now see so clearly in his mind.

It was a broad and shallow valley bordered with wooded ridges, and he *knew* that it was more than just a valley where a battle might take place. It was the melting pot of worlds, of the future. He could, even without dreaming, sense Davyd coming ever closer to that place, as if destiny throbbed in the air, and he knew he must make haste—that the Breakers not go by the valley.

"Even do we find it, what can we do?" Arcole sat across the fire, frowning less in confusion than concern for Davyd. "Just the two of us, what can we do?"

Davyd looked up from his contemplation of the flames. His hair shone white under the moon and his face was hollow. He looked mightily weary, and at the same time exhilarated. "I don't know," he said. "Only that we must be there—get there as fast we can." He shrugged. "I'm sorry, Arcole, I truly cannot explain it better. I only *know*."

"Well, you're the Dreamer." Arcole shrugged back. "Do you say it, then we'll attempt it."

Davyd nodded. "The People shall find us there, I think; and we shall fight."

"The Breakers?" Arcole wondered.

"Them, yes," Davyd said. "Perhaps also the Inquisitor and his soldiers."

"Then best pray Tomas and Abram find that army they spoke of," Arcole returned, "for we shall need all the strength we can muster."

"Yes," Davyd replied, "best pray."

The dinghy beached in the shadow of a landing stage and they sprang ashore. Var dragged the little boat deeper into the shadows as Jaymes cradled his rifle and scanned the walls of Grostheim. Var followed him inland—only a little way, so that they remained sheltered by the wharf—and studied the walls.

Cannon showed on the ramparts, and swivel guns, but not many men. Indeed, far fewer than he'd anticipated, as if the garrison were depleted.

"I reckon the madness took them," Jaymes murmured. "I reckon Talle's stripped the city for his war."

"Even so," Var said, "how do we get in? And if we do, what then?"

Jaymes grinned and said, "Follow me."

Frowning, Var did as he was bade.

They crept forward, shadow to shadow, until they reached the north gate, then Jaymes halted and stabbed a dirty finger at a patch of darker darkness where water swirled beneath the wooden wall.

"Arcole told me about it," he whispered. "That's how he got out. It used to be a runoff from the latrines."

Var said, "Oh, God!"

"Don't worry, it's not used for that now," Jaymes said. "You'll only get wet."

"Thank God for small mercies," Var murmured, and followed Jaymes into the water.

"Indeed, and remember the tide's low now," Jaymes lifted his rifle that the powder not get wet, "and keep your head down."

They waded up the trench. The walls hung low overhead, but the water level was low enough they need not submerge themselves. Jaymes slithered along until they were clear of the walls, then rose dripping to slide up the bank. Var came after him, thinking that he could even now smell the stench of the ditch's original purpose. He felt afraid and invigorated, the sensations familiar from experience of war. He looked toward the walls and saw the red tunics of the God's Militia dark under the moon, the glitter of light on bayonets. The walls were scarcely manned and he wondered how many men had fallen to the ghost madness, and why Jared Talle would leave Grostheim so poorly defended.

"Come on."

Jaymes beckoned him and they ran across open ground to the shelter of an alley. Walked down that to a side street where Jaymes turned left, deeper into the city, then halted before a lantern-hung doorway.

Var frowned. Surely this was the same alley where he had once seen branded folk give food to refugees. He watched nervously as Jaymes tapped on the wood and the door opened.

Soft words were spoken, and then Jaymes motioned him forward and he stepped up onto the sidewalk, into a room where lanterns burned and indentured folk attended ovens.

"This is Rychard." Jaymes indicated a small, balding man whose brand seemed to occupy most of his cheek. "Rychard, this is Tomas Var, once a major of marines in the God's Militia."

Rychard eyed Var awhile, suspiciously. "I know you," he said. "You were the Inquisitor's dog."

Almost, Var blushed, but Jaymes grinned and said, "He's surely not any longer. Dammit, he broke me out of prison an' saved me from hanging. Don't doubt him, Rychard—he's with us."

"All the way?" The man remained suspicious.

"All the way," Jaymes said, and turned to Var. "That's right, no?"

Var said, "Yes; all the way."

Rychard said, "Well, if Abram vouches for you . . ." He

studied Var a moment then smiled. "Best I find you both dry clothes, eh?"

"Food would be welcome, too," Jaymes said. "And talk."

Rychard nodded. "Follow me."

Davyd said, "We must go careful now, for we're close."

"To the valley?" Arcole asked.

"Yes; to that and the Inquisitor. And we must not . . ." Davyd hesitated. He was unsure what he wanted to say, or what he meant to say; he knew only that some inner voice spoke: one not his own but gifted him. "We must not . . . hurry. We must go wary, else . . ." He shrugged. "I don't know, Arcole; only that we must watch and wait."

Ahead, the land rose up a gentle scarp that ended on a ridge where trees stood windswept. The night was warm and a soft breeze blew, rustling the oaks and hornbeams that decked the ridge. The faint glow of fires showed amongst the trees to the north, and as they crept closer Arcole saw horse artillery set along the ridgetop.

"God, but they're marines." He indicated the blue-uniformed figures beside the guns. "Var's men."

"And the Inquisitor is down there." Davyd thrust a finger at the valley. "He's waiting for the Breakers."

"He's mad," Arcole said.

Davyd said, "Yes."

"What do we do?"

"Wait." Davyd settled onto the grass. "We wait for the Breakers to come, and—the Maker willing!—the People and Abram's army."

"And if they come late?" Arcole asked. "Or not at all?"

"Then," Davyd said, "we shall likely die."

37 Encounter

Jared Talle had somehow known they would come in the night, for that seemed their time, best suited to their purposes. He sensed them long before they arrived, like the prickling of a storm wind on the skin, the stillness in the air before the hurricane begins. He *felt* their imminent presence in the protective hex signs painted on his body, and smiled confidently as he rose from beside the fire and looked at Jorge Kerik and the captain's ten nervous soldiers.

"Stand ready!"

Kerik nodded, swallowed hard, and turned to his men. "At the ready! Fire only on my command."

"Or mine," Talle said.

"Of course." Kerik nodded dutifully. "My command or the Inquisitor's, eh? And remember"—this for the frightened eyes that stared at him—"we've the cannon to support us, and they are only savages."

"Indeed," Talle echoed. "Only savages, eh? Remember that!"

He rose to his feet, stretching his arms so that his coat flapped about him like the wings of a crow. He smiled, anticipating his triumph, and gestured that Kerik stand back.

Kerik drew his saber and perched the blade on his shoulder, playing the part of the confident officer for all he felt terribly afraid, which was strange. He had fought his share of battles and although he had known fear then, this was different. It was as if the night held presentiments, portents of doom. He had seen the ghosts stalking the streets of Grostheim, and

seen red-coated Militiamen turn on one another, even slay
themselves, and knew that the enemy he faced now was different from any other. He wondered if the Inquisitor did not
outreach himself. Talle was sheathed in powerful hexes, and
Kerik recognized his magical strength, but even so—the captain wondered if the Inquisitor was any longer entirely ra-
tional, or had fallen into such madness as must destroy them
all. But still he *was* the Inquisitor, and Jorge Kerik was an
officer of the God's Militia, sworn to service of the Autarchy
Talle represented, and not yet ready to question that command.

He sheathed his sword and licked his lips and checked the
loading of his pistols, nervously eased his sword a little way
from the scabbard, adjusted his tricorne, and scratched his
cheek.

"Are you afraid?" asked Jared Talle.

And Kerik answered honestly, "Yes, Inquisitor, I am."

Talle frowned, then chuckled, which sounded to Kerik like
a crow's cackling. "God, man! I've hexed this valley and all
your guns. Nothing can harm us! Do you think their magic is
stronger than mine?"

Kerik was tempted to answer yes, but he said instead,
"No, Inquisitor."

Talle said, "Good; have faith, eh? God is on our side."

Then why, Kerik thought, do you look to deal with demons? But he said nothing, only watched the western approach to the valley and mouthed a silent prayer that he and
his men survive Talle's madness.

Then, where the moon shone down on the ingress to the
valley, there was light, as if moon and stars reflected off
prisms, crystals of bright colors, and the sound of many
hooves, or clawed and padded feet, that tramped the earth of
Salvation as if thunder walked the ground.

Jorge Kerik felt his mouth go dry even as his hands
clutched instinctively on his pistols as he saw the Horde enter
the valley.

They were at first indistinct, as if light played games on
their armor to trick the eye and make them phantom, rainbow figures. The only solidity seemed to be the things they
rode, which were amalgamations of lions and lizards and

other creatures Kerik could not define. Clawed and fanged they were, with lashing tails and ugly eyes. But somehow worse was the horse their leader rode, for that was recognizable, akin to the mounts tethered up the slope, save that this was skinned in midnight's darkness, and its shifting head carried great curled horns like some monstrous ram's. From its forehead sprouted a unicorn horn, and its teeth were fangs and its hooves clawed, and it was both a horse and unlike any horse Kerik had ever seen.

Nor less impressive or dreadful was its rider, for he wore magnificent golden armor that sprouted spikes and great clawed gauntlets, and shone in the moon's pale glow as if bathed in sunlight. A massive sword was sheathed at his waist, and skulls clattered about his saddle: some old and clean, but others fresh and still haired, and from beneath his winged helmet red eyes shone like beacons calling Kerik's soul to hell.

Jorge Kerik wished badly to piss, but he steeled himself and cried in as firm a voice as he could manage: "Stand firm, men."

Jared Talle smiled confidently and raised his arms in greeting as the rainbow Horde came closer, stepping out to meet the leader, who reined in his dreadful horse to stare down at the Inquisitor.

"I am Jared Talle, and you are Akratil. Welcome."

"You know my name." Akratil's voice was deep and mellow, curiously friendly, as if acknowledging a kindred spirit. "How is that?"

"I, too," Talle said, "own magic. Perhaps as great as yours."

Akratil chuckled. "Perhaps." He loosed the strappings of his helm and raised the winged casque to reveal a loose-flowing mass of fiery hair. "But how do you know my name?"

"I took it from the dead," Talle said.

"Ah, necromancy." Akratil nodded as if approving. "Did you eat them, after?"

Even Talle hesitated at that, and shook his head. "No. They were savages, like those." He gestured at the Tachyn riding behind the Breakers.

"And I am not a savage?" Akratil asked.

Talle said, "I think not."

"Why not?" There was amusement in the mellifluous voice.

"Because," Talle said, "you are something greater. You own power . . ."

"That you'd have?" Akratil interrupted.

Talle said, "Yes! Together we might . . ."

His voice strangled off as Akratil reached down from his skull-hung saddle to clasp the frontage of Talle's coat in a gauntleted hand and lift the Inquisitor from the ground.

"Together?" Akratil spat the word into Talle's face. "You'd join with us?"

Talle struggled for breath. Found it and said, "Yes! Do you only ally with the Autarchy we might conquer worlds together."

"I already conquer worlds." Akratil loosed his hold so that Talle fell sprawling on the ground. "I destroy worlds."

Jared Talle struggled to his feet. Jorge Kerik wondered if he should order his men to open fire, but Talle waved him back.

"Listen, I beg you. Do you but ally with me, we can . . ."

"You are a worm," Akratil said. "You are a crawling thing that I crush under my feet. These"—he gestured at the Tachyn, at Chakthi and Hadduth—"are worms. But they summoned me, where you would only use me for your own sad purpose. You think to trick me, eh? To form me to your designs. You think those petty signs you paint on your body can protect you from me? No! You are the puppet, Jared Talle, not I."

Jorge Kerik motioned his men back. Damn the Inquisitor; he'd brought them to this crazed impasse, and could Kerik get his men out alive then he'd leave Talle to his fate. He paced backward, far enough that he could whisper to his sergeant: "On my order fall back to the ridge."

The sergeant nodded, eager to be gone from this weirdness, and together they eased away.

∎   ∎   ∎

"Barges." Abram Jaymes grinned at Tomas Var. "We take barges. That way we might reach the valley in time. Anyway, we don't have enough horses for everyone."

"Everyone?" Var set down his mug and stared at the lank-haired scout. "How many are you talking about?"

"How many branded folk do you think there are in Grostheim?" Jaymes returned.

Var shrugged. "I don't know: I never . . ."

He paused; he had never thought about it before. Branded exiles were commonplace, beneath consideration. They were simply there, to serve as bid. He sought to hide his embarrassment behind his mug.

"Hundreds," Jaymes said, his voice becoming earnest, "an' all faceless. Servants who bring you ale in the taverns; servants to warm your food an' shoe your horses. Maids to clean an' change your sheets; grooms an' farriers an' stablehands. Laborers an' dockhands; oarsmen on the barges. You name it, there's some branded man or woman doin' it. An' they have no say—only obedience to the masters. You think that's right, Tomas?"

Var shook his head. "No." Then asked, "But shall they be with us?"

"I reckon they will," Jaymes said. "The word's out—Rychard's seen to that."

"And the garrison?" Var toyed nervously with his mug. "What of the Militiamen?"

"That," Jaymes answered, "is your problem. Either you convince them to let us loose, or we fight them."

Var said, "I'll do my best to convince them."

"You're with us then, all the way?"

Var looked at the scout and lowered his head in acceptance. "Yes," he said, "even to secession."

"Survival first," Jaymes said, "then secession. But I'm glad you're with us."

Var raised his mug in a toast. "To Salvation."

"To Salvation," Jaymes echoed, "and to freedom."

Jared Talle loosened his collar that he might breathe better. He felt suddenly less confident: the hexes painted on his body should have protected him from such ignominy. He brushed at his coat and began to wonder if the magic of these strangelings was, perhaps, greater than his own. He began, for the first time, to feel somewhat afraid. But even so, he forced himself to confidence and said, indignantly, "I am not a worm. I am an Inquisitor of the Autarchy, and the Autarchy is the greatest power in this world. I am confident you cannot harm me."

Akratil rose up in his saddle, head thrown back as he roared laughter at the night sky. The strange sable horse pranced, and Talle moved farther away from the clawed hooves, the snapping mouth.

"You are very proud, little man, but I have encountered prideful little men like you before and I have no time for them." He brought the horse to rest, looking down at Talle, then drew his sword and brought it down in a sweeping arc at the Inquisitor's skull.

Jared Talle ducked, raising his hands as he voiced a hexing spell. For an instant the sword was slowed, halted in its descent as Talle flung himself aside. Akratil cursed and swung again, and again Talle blocked the cut.

"Listen to me!" he shouted. "Do you only listen to me, we can conquer worlds together. Join with me—with the Autarchy—and we can form such an alliance as shall own the heavens, all the worlds."

"I destroy worlds," Akratil roared as the sword swung down again. "I've no need of alliance, and less of you."

"I've power," Talle screamed, rolling across the grass. "The Autarchy has power. Join with me—join with the Autarchy—and together we shall own the universe. Join your magicks to mine and we can . . ."

His plea choked off as Akratil's blade touched his throat. He looked up into red eyes that held no more mercy than his own, and for the first time knew true fear. Death shone from those eyes, and he recognized that there was no bargaining with this creature, and that all his hopes were gone and doomed.

So be it: he had endeavored to win the Autarchy such an alliance as should have made that god he served all-powerful.

But if that was not to be, then let destruction reign. Even now, these Breakers should learn the might of the Autarchy.

He shouted, "Fire!" But Jorge Kerik and his ten marines were gone, running now to the ridge and the fragile safety of the guns. Talle risked a backward glance and snarled as he saw himself deserted.

"They've more wisdom than you," Akratil said, and swung the sword again.

Talle raised his hands. God knew, but his hexes were the strongest he could manufacture, yet even so he could feel the pressure of Akratil's magic vying with his own. He screamed as two fingers were cut from his left hand, and for an instant stared in horror at the twin fountains of blood that sprouted into the night. Then he shouted a spell that should have torn Akratil from the saddle and sent him tumbling and bloody over the starlit grass, but Akratil only grimaced and heeled his horrid mount forward.

Talle staggered back, avoiding the probing horns, the clashing teeth. He voiced another spell, and turned the sword aside.

"You've surely magic." Akratil's voice was mocking. "Even stronger than I'd thought. But . . ."

He drove the horned horse on, herding Talle like some frightened animal, and Jared Talle felt all his confidence slip away: an ebb tide that left him stranded on a lonely beach, bereft of hope. He cowered, no longer the proud Inquisitor but only a frightened, mortal man.

"Listen! Please!"

Akratil said, "No," and swung his blade down against Talle's skull.

From the ridge, Davyd and Arcole watched the drama. They saw the curved blade cleave through the Inquisitor's pate, dividing his face so that he danced awhile like some mad puppet, the two halves of his visage flopping wild as blood gouted from his neck in a great spray that shone black under the moon. Then he fell down and they watched the golden-armored man urge his dread mount onward to trample the body, and laugh and sheathe his sword.

Davyd felt chilled. His wounds ached and he felt an awful weariness. He wished Morrhyn were with him to advise him, or he in some other place; some haven, safe from the evil he felt emanating from the rainbow-armored Horde. But he was not and could not be: only here, where the Maker placed him to do . . . He could not say. He could not envisage defeating these slayers of worlds, only dying in the attempt.

He heard Arcole ask, "What do we do?" And shook his head helplessly.

"Do we fight?" Arcole grasped his shoulder. "Or do we run?"

All Davyd could say, and that only with difficulty, was "I don't know. I think we must wait."

"To be slain?" Arcole's voice was urgent. "For God's sake, Davyd—for the Maker's sake!—what do we do?"

Davyd shook his head.

"There are cannon on the ridge—horse guns." Arcole pointed to where the artillery was placed. "Var's marines, I'd guess. Do they open fire . . ."

"They'd not be enough." Davyd spoke thickly through the pounding in his skull. It was as if the Breakers' presence filled him with a numbing lassitude, as if their evil clouded his thinking. He rubbed at his temples and his eyes. "We must wait for the People to come. Them and Abram's army. Without them . . ."

"And if the battle begins before they come?" Arcole gestured at the men clambering up the slope toward the hidden guns. "Does that officer order his men to fire?"

"He must not!" Suddenly conviction filled Davyd. Suddenly the dreams he'd known, in Ket-Ta-Thanne, in the oak wood and after, came flooding back. "We must fight together. All of us!"

"All of us?" Arcole frowned. "What do you mean?"

"Them." Davyd looked to where the marines waited. "Them and the People and the folk Abram and Tomas shall bring. We must fight together! Otherwise all shall be lost. Do you understand?"

Arcole said, "No."

Davyd sighed and stared down into the valley. "We must fight together—all the people of this land—as one force against this evil. Separately, we shall be nothing. Separately, we shall all be conquered and destroyed. But do we fight together—everyone, the People and the branded folk, the masters and marines—then we can defeat them."

"Save they kill us first," Arcole said.

"We must speak with the marines," Davyd said urgently. "They must hold the Breakers until the People and Abram's folk come."

"Then I think," Arcole returned, "that we had best tell them that."

Jorge Kerik was glad to reach the ridgetop: he felt safer amongst his men, amongst the guns. He was about to order that they open fire—flay the valley with canister and grape—when two wild figures appeared. Both were clad in buckskins, like savages, their hair tied in braids such as the hostiles accompanying the weirdlings wore, and carried muskets. One was tall and handsome, the other smaller, his hair a startling white that emphasized the ugly scar scoring his cheek. And both, on their tanned skin, carried the brand of exile. Kerik drew his pistols; his men leveled their muskets.

"Friends!"

By God, the man spoke Evanderan: Kerik hesitated.

"Hear us out, eh?"

"Who are you?"

"I am Arcole Blayke; this is Davyd Furth. May we approach?"

The accent was that of the Levan, cultured. Kerik wondered what new strangeness was delivered him and held his pistols leveled as he said, "Slowly, eh? And with your hands in sight."

They came forward with their muskets raised high above their heads, to be snatched from them on Kerik's order. He stared at them: a strange pair.

"Runaways?"

Arcole nodded. "But not your enemies. Your enemy is down there." He gestured at the valley.

Kerik said, "There are folk like you down there."

"The Tachyn," Arcole said. "They are led by a warrior

called Chakthi; the others are known as the Breakers. God, but there's so much to explain."

"And you are not with them?" Kerik set a pistol hard against Arcole's belly. "Why should I not execute you now?"

"Because"—it was Davyd who spoke—"you would then be slain. You and all your men. If you listen to us, you've a chance."

There was something in those ageless eyes that persuaded Kerik to trust the ragged figure. "Ach, what chance?" He shook his head. "I can run or I can fight." He glanced down the slope. "There are too many of them to fight, and do I run, I suspect those creatures can outpace me. What chance there?"

"You can wait," Davyd said.

Kerik studied him curiously. There was an aura about him; not visible, but palpable—as if some undefined power resided in him. It sat in his eyes. Kerik felt it and ducked his head. "Explain."

"They are called the Breakers," Davyd said, and told Jorge Kerik all he knew of the Horde, and of the People and Ket-Ta-Witko and Ket-Ta-Thanne, and of Abram Jaymes and Tomas Var.

"You've been with Major Var?" Kerik asked when he was done. It was all he could think of to say: the enormity of the account left him benumbed and frightened.

Davyd nodded. "He goes to Grostheim with Abram Jaymes. They'd raise an army. And the Matawaye are coming, also. Do you only wait . . ."

"Why should I believe you?" Kerik demanded.

"Why should you not?" Davyd shrugged.

"Listen," Arcole said, "we wear the brand on our faces, no? Would branded exiles come willingly to soldiers of the God's Militia?"

"There's that," Kerik allowed. But what convinced him was the look in Davyd's eyes. "And you know Major Var, it would seem. So—what do we do?"

Davyd said, "Hold them. Wait for the People and the others, and fight together. We must hold the Breakers here in this valley, and destroy them if we can."

Kerik stared at him and lowered his pistols and his head. "All right—yes, I shall. And God grant I'm right."

"You are," Davyd said.

Akratil said, "We camp here. I like this place." His mount lowered its horned head to gnaw on the corpse of Jared Talle. "We shall rest awhile and then go on."

"And the warriors we saw?" Bemnida asked. "What of them?"

"*What* of them?" Akratil returned. "They ran like frightened rabbits, no? They'll be long gone, nor able to harm us if they remain."

"Even so."

"Even so." Akratil fixed the woman with a cold glare. "I'd rest awhile. Do you disagree?"

She shook her head, thinking it might well be loosed from her shoulders did she argue.

"Do I take my warriors and scout the ridges?"

Chakthi thought to curry favor.

"No." Akratil chuckled. "None can harm us. They fear us, no? Did you not see them run? They'll be off, and I've decided—we rest here awhile." He raised himself from the saddle and shouted to the Horde, "We make camp here."

It was close. Morrhyn felt it like a pressure on his soul, as if the Maker urged him on, pushing him toward the fining of destiny.

Hard as he'd driven them before, he urged them harder now. They rode down the days and half the nights, halting only to rest horses too weary to go farther. He urged them on when any sensible man would halt and rest and sleep, but there existed in his mind—in the flowing of his blood and the aching of his tired bones—the knowledge that they rode to such conclusion as must shape the future forever. Not only of this land called Salvation, or that of Ket-Ta-Thanne, but all the worlds he'd dreamt of on the Maker's Mountain—all the worlds down all the roads of time and space—and he knew that did they fail, then the Breakers must prevail and deliver their foulness to children unborn, to worlds not yet shaped.

He could not accept that, and so he acted the role of Prophet and took the warriors of the People hard and swift to where he sensed Davyd waited for the final battle.

He could see the valley now, as if Davyd spoke inside his head as once he had spoken into Davyd's. It stood clear in his dreams, and in his waking mind: a wide, broad place, wood-ringed and centered on a stream. And there, he knew, the future should be won or lost.

38 The Last Chance

Captain Francys Emmit stared at the outlawed marine over the barrel of his pistol and regretted his quandary. "I've my orders," he said carefully. "And you're proscribed."

"You're outnumbered." Tomas Var faced the garrison commander. "The Inquisitor is gone, and likely dead. A force such as you cannot imagine comes against Grostheim, and if it arrives, the city shall be lost. Salvation shall be lost! Open the gates and let us go. Dammit, come with us!"

"I've my orders," Emmit repeated.

"From Jared Talle," Var returned. "Do you bear such love for him?"

"He's the Inquisitor," Emmit said doggedly. "He speaks for the Autarchy."

"And I speak for Salvation," Var said. "For Salvation and all the folk who live here."

"Branded folk," Emmit said, glancing across Var's shoulder at the crowd filling the streets.

"No." Var turned, ignoring the leveled gun, to indicate the mass behind him. "See? There are freemen there! Owners alongside their servants; servants marching with their masters."

"You'd overturn the world," Emmit said.

"I'd see Salvation saved," Var replied. "Listen! You've seen the ghosts, no? You've seen them ride the streets?"

Emmit nodded reluctantly: that was a memory he'd sooner forget.

"Well," Var continued, "they're fleshed now, and coming here—save we halt them."

"Let them," Emmit declared, firmer than he felt. "We've

walls hexed by the Inquisitor, and cannon to use against them. They'll not take Grostheim."

"They'll take it and burn it down and eat your flesh," Var said. "And are they to be halted, then it must be soon, and in the right place. God, man! My marines are there and I'd go join them."

"I've my orders."

Var shrugged. "You've what? A hundred or so men left?" He again indicated the crowd at his back, restless now, even under the muskets of Emmit's soldiery. "Not enough to prevent us leaving, do we wish. You can shoot me, but what then? Do you want a bloodbath?"

Emmit frowned. Then: "No. But still . . ."

"There's no time to waste," Var said, and raised his arms so that he stood totally exposed to the Militiaman's pistol. "Either shoot me and have done with it, or open the gates. Better, come with us."

Emmit hesitated. Before him stood Major Tomas Var, clad in buckskins like some frontiersman—like the draggle-haired fellow holding a long Hawkins rifle across his chest that Emmit did not doubt but he'd use—and behind him all the branded folk in Grostheim and half the masters. He knew Var's reputation: a hero of the War of Restitution, the Inquisitor's dog, an officer elevated by the Autarchy for his knowledge of Salvation. Francys Emmit was young and inexperienced, and none too happy with his command. He'd thought the Inquisitor crazed to take Var's marines out and leave Grostheim stripped of defenses, and wondered what drove the man to go out hunting the ghosts. He'd heard the rumors—all had—that Jared Talle would form an alliance with the ghosts, and wondered if such communion was right. Now Var told him they were fleshed and come looking to conquer, and it appeared that most of the city agreed and was prepared to fight. Emmit thought that if he shot Var and ordered his men to open fire on the crowd, as duty dictated, then he and all his command must be overwhelmed and Grostheim left empty. Var stared at him, and slowly he lowered his pistol.

"You're sure, Major?"

"As God's my witness," Var said. "Yes: I'm sure."

There was such conviction in his voice that Emmit nodded and holstered the gun. "I pray I do the right thing," he said, and turned to the sergeant behind him, shouting that the Militiamen open the gates and let the people through. "What shall I do?"

"Open the armory," Var said, "and give us weapons; powder and shot; supplies. Then come with us."

"Sir!" Emmit saluted formally. "I place myself under your command."

"So far, so good." Abram Jaymes came up to join Var as Emmit ran to unlock the stores. "I thought maybe I'd have to shoot him."

"I thought he'd likely shoot me," Var said.

"No one," Jaymes remarked, grinning, "lives forever. Now let's get our people onto those barges."

They set to organizing the evacuation. Not all had agreed to Jaymes's plan, but enough stood with the man that the dissidents had no real voice. Those who agreed believed in liberation, in freedom and free choice, and their voice was the loudest, so that Grostheim emptied as they marched out to the river and the waiting barges, which filled up with folk armed with muskets and pistols and swords, all intent on defending their country and winning their liberty from invasion and the Autarchy, both.

"It's grand, no?" Jaymes remarked as the barges were poled out into the stream. "Look at that."

Var turned, staring back down the long deck at the flotilla of barges that followed them westward. It was a sight he'd never thought to see: branded folk manned the sweeps alongside freemen and soldiers of the God's Militia, all willing to work together for the future of their chosen land. "There'll be no turning back now," he said.

Abram Jaymes chuckled and spat tobacco into the Restitution. "There never was."

Var said, "No, I suppose not." Then: "Shall we be in time?"

"We'd best be," Jaymes replied evenly. "Is Davyd right,

then we win or lose in that damn valley. And I believe in that boy."

"Yes," Var said, "so do I."

And in Salvation's holdings, in the farms and mills and vineyards, men and women woke to the dawning of a new day, a new world. They did not properly understand it, only that a compulsion—a geas—lay upon them and summoned them to the valley. Masters looked at servants and smiled and handed out weapons. Indentured folk took up axes and sickles, and their owners nodded in approval and took up their guns and went with the branded folk to that conjunction of destiny, all hoping they come timely; none knowing if they should, only that they must, as if the world's future pulsed in their veins and filled them with shared purpose.

The valley stretched from north to south, a wide bowl contained within the curvature of the wooded ridges. The moon lit the grass, shining off the colorful tents of the Breakers, duller on the lodges of the Tachyn. Fires burned down there and the night was loud with the snorting of the lizard creatures and the nervous whickering of horses. The smell of dung was strong. The western entrance was broad, the only exit to the south, where the stream that flowed across the bottomland ventured out to meet the Restitution through narrowed walls. Save the Horde come over the eastern ridge, it must go out that way.

"We can take them there," Jorge Kerik said, angling a finger at the pass. "Two guns, and they'll be slaughtered."

"Save they come up the ridge," Arcole gave him back. "They've numbers enough to mount a frontal attack and overwhelm us." He pointed along the ridge. "Or outflank us. And likely they've strong magic."

Kerik nodded thoughtfully. "You've seen battle before."

"I fought in the War of Restitution," Arcole said, and grinned. "Against the Autarchy."

"An old war." Kerik chuckled, liking this man. "Two guns

overlooking the pass, then. The others on the ridgetop. What of these allies of yours?"

"The People come from the west," Arcole said. "Most likely they'll come in through the far pass. Can Abram and Tomas raise their army, then I'd guess they'll enter from the river side."

"And these Breakers be contained within the valley." Kerik scratched his head. "Shall we be enough?"

"Not alone. You've what—two hundred and fifty marines? The Horde could sweep over us—we need the others."

Kerik took a hip flask from his coat and swallowed brandy, passed the flask to Arcole. "Perhaps we should run."

"They'd outpace us," Arcole said, confirming Kerik's fear, "and go on to Grostheim. No, are we to win this fight, it must be fought here. Davyd says so."

"There are some redcoats still left in Grostheim," Kerik said. "And the city's strong walls."

"Even so." Arcole shook his head. "Davyd says we must make our stand here. It seems that's important, and so we must hold them here."

"If we can," Kerik murmured.

"Davyd says it must be so." Arcole shrugged as if that were the end of any argument.

"He's a strange one," Kerik remarked. "You trust him, no?"

Arcole said, "Absolutely."

Kerik sighed. "Then I suppose I must, too; though God knows why."

"You feel it, don't you?" Arcole said.

Kerik said, "I feel very frightened. I feel trapped—I cannot run and I've too few men to fight. But also . . ." He hesitated, frowning. "I feel . . . that worlds collide here, and I had best heed you and Davyd."

"And pray," Arcole chuckled, "that help reach us in time."

"Yes," Kerik said earnestly, "that, too."

Davyd lay restless. The night was warm and a breeze rustled the timber topping the ridge. He dreamt of battle and it was as if he again saw the images that had come to him in the oak wood. He saw armies locked in combat, and fire walk the land—and all was confusion. He saw the Breakers prevail and the Breakers defeated; friends die and friends survive. He knew, even asleep, that the future must depend on the morrow when surely the Breakers would move, and knew that were they not held and halted, then all was lost. He knew that did not the disparate peoples of this new world come together the Breakers could not be defeated—that all depended on that conjunction of forces—and that if that alliance was not made, the Breakers should prevail.

He cried out in his sleep to Morrhyn, seeking communication, and saw the wakanisha's face briefly before flames hid it. He wondered if the words he heard truly spoke of the People coming or were only a cry of anguish.

He woke dry-mouthed and sweat-beaded, opening his eyes on a sky that shone with the pearly light of burgeoning dawn. Birds sang and squirrels chattered, the grass along the ridge was dew wetted and the air promised a warm day, the sun already lighting the eastern horizon. Davyd wondered if it might not be his last day. From the marines' positions came the smell of coffee and frying bacon, the muted conversation of men aware they faced a fight they might not survive. Davyd rose from under his blanket and checked the priming of his musket. He realized that his wounds no longer ached and wondered if that was some kind of sign. He bathed in the dew and combed out his braids, re-tied them. He no longer cared whether he was wakanisha or warrior: it seemed unimportant on this day. He stood, staring down the ridge at the wondrous colors of the Breakers' tents, and knew the future of Salvation and Ket-Ta-Thanne, and all the worlds, hung in precarious balance. Then he made obeisance to the Maker, praying for victory, and went to find Arcole.

"We must hurry: I dreamed of Davyd."

Kahteney nodded. "And I, brother. But shall we be in time? Can we be?"

"We *must* be!" Morrhyn rubbed at eyes reddened for lack of sleep. It was not yet even close to dawn and all around men lay beneath their blankets. He clapped his hands and shouted, "Wake! We ride!"

And because he was the Prophet none argued, but only rose and saddled weary horses and followed him to the east, to the valley.

"We can ride no faster." Rannach held his mount to a gallop, shouting into the windrush. "The Maker knows, Morrhyn, but we'll kill the animals at this pace."

Morrhyn stared fixedly ahead. The night shone bright with stars, lit by the glow of the New Grass Moon. His unbound hair flung out behind him and it seemed to Rannach, as he caught the Prophet's blue eyes, that the cold brilliance of that moon shone there. He wished they might halt and set up their camp and he go lie in Arrhyna's arms, Debo asleep across the lodgefire, and knew that could not be until this thing was settled. And then, he wondered, when it is settled, shall there be lodges and wives and children? Or are we riding to our deaths?

As if in answer to his thoughts, Morrhyn shouted: "What else? Shall we abandon Davyd and Arcole? Abandon the world to the Breakers?"

"No!" Rannach shouted back.

"Then ride," Morrhyn told him, "and must we kill the horses, then we shall go on afoot and fight on foot. But fight we must!"

The oyster gray translucence of the early dawn grew sunlit. Light rose from the east and sent shafts of brilliance dancing heavenward. The horizon there grew bright, blue washing back the gray like a rising tide, and then the sun itself showed, leaping up to fill the sky with blue and gold, hot and heady on the men who waited on the ridge.

It was a while longer before the radiance lit the valley, and by then the Breakers were striking camp, folding their tents and stowing them on pack animals. The Tachyn did the same, stowing their lodges and mounting horses that fretted and stamped in the presence of the Breakers' beasts. Chakthi was painted for war, stripes of yellow and white daubed across his vulpine face. He wore a hatchet and a knife on his belt, and a quivered bow was strapped across his back. He carried a lance decorated with the hair of men and women he'd slain.

He looked at Hadduth and asked, "Is Rannach up there?"

Hadduth said, "Even is he not, still you'll have his head."

"Your promise? Else I'll take yours."

"Akratil's," Hadduth said. "His and mine: we cannot fail."

Chakthi stared at his wakanisha and nodded. "Best we do not, eh? Else your life's the forfeit."

Hadduth smiled, confidently. "We've all the strength of the Breakers with us, my akaman. We shall be mighty and ride down the world until all hail the Tachyn and their chieftain, and know us as conquerors."

"It had best be so," Chakthi said, and heeled his horse to where Akratil mounted his strangeling beast.

"We attack them?"

Speech was somewhat difficult, for Chakthi's mount skittered and pranced in such proximity to the animal Akratil rode. The Breaker smiled, reaching out to stroke the serpentine neck of the horned horse. "Are they still there and not fled," he allowed, "yes. Why not? Do you send your warriors against them first."

Chakthi hesitated a moment, remembering the thunder that had greeted his assaults on Grostheim and the border forts, the damage those long-firing guns had inflicted.

"They might have . . ." He recalled the owh'jika's words. "Cannon."

"Are you afraid?" Akratil donned his helm, staring mockingly at Chakthi, who snarled under that red-eyed stare and shook his lance in defiant negation and shouted, "No!"

"Then attack them," Akratil said, languid. "And we'll follow you. And do you fail, we shall destroy them."

"I shall not fail," Chakthi declared. "I am Tachyn, and I am not afraid to die."

Akratil raised a gauntlet to indicate the eastern ridge. "Show me then," he said, "how brave you are."

"I shall!" Chakthi raised his lance, shouting that his warriors join him.

They grouped around him and he set out his battle plan, which was a simple charge up the slope to whatever waited there. He raised his lance again and pointed the head at the ridge.

"We ride!"

They charged.

"They're coming!" Sergeant Ordan bellowed. "Man guns and stand ready!"

The limber guns were already loaded, fine powder in the priming tubes, waiting only for the touch of the slowmatches to ignite the charges and send the shot out against the enemy. Two were placed as Kerik had advised to fire down into the southern egress from the valley. Two more were set to cover the northern approach against flanking attack. The remaining five were angled down the slope, against such frontal assault as now came.

"Wait!" Jorge Kerik shouted. "On my order, eh?"

He watched the riders come out from the valley, across the bottomland, and up the slope. It was, he thought, insanely brave. Did they know there were horse cannon on the ridge? Were they only foolish? Did they understand modern warfare? No matter; they came to his killing ground and would die under the weight of his guns. Perhaps then he could ride away and be gone from this portentous valley. Save now he had a battle to fight and knew he must win it. Davyd and Arcole—though mostly Davyd—had convinced him of that, and so he gritted his teeth and watched the horsemen come screaming up the slope and waited until there was no chance at all his gunners could miss and dropped his hand and shouted: "Fire!"

The salvo ripped the Tachyn from their horses like wheat torn by a storm wind. Grapeshot flailed them and canister burst in terrible explosions. Men and horses screamed together, and fell down all bloody; bodies rolled down the slope or lay with mangled limbs on the stained grass. Birds rose in panicked flight from the timber. Chakthi's horse was blown from under him and the Tachyn akaman found himself stretched facedown, scrabbling at the ground as the firestorm of shot raged overhead.

When it ended he looked up, cursing through gritted teeth, and shouted for his men to rise and follow him. His lance was gone, so he strung his bow and sent a shaft flying to the ridgetop. The arrow passed over the heads of the gunners, busy reloading the deadly cannon, and was answered with musket fire that crackled down the slope to slay more Tachyn. Some turned and ran; others rallied around Chakthi, who vented his rage in a shrill scream and charged.

The cannon blasted again, and more Tachyn died; Chakthi saw his clan decimated. He was not sure whether the blood on his face and chest was his own or some slain warrior's. He was consumed with rage and chagrin as he saw that he could not hope to take the ridge.

"Back!" He waved at his surviving men. "Back!"

"By God, but we beat them!" Kerik beamed at his men. "Well done, boys."

"They were the Tachyn." Arcole spat a ball into his musket's barrel and rammed it down. "The Breakers play no part yet."

"Even so!" Kerik was sanguine with his first victory. "They'll find this ridge hard to take."

"Hard," Arcole agreed, "but not impossible."

"No." Kerik sobered, staring at the warriors massed below. "Shall your friends be long?"

Arcole shrugged and looked to Davyd, who stood grim-faced, his musket held at the ready. "I don't know," he said. "I pray they come in time, but . . ." He shrugged. "We must hold them here, in this valley. We *must,* no matter the cost!"

Akratil looked down at Chakthi and smiled contempt. "You failed."

"Had you ridden with us," Chakthi snarled, "it might have been different."

"Indeed." Akratil chuckled. "*My* people might have died."

Chakthi's face was a blood-washed mask of rage, furious eyes staring out from the gore and the streaking of his paint. "Are you afraid, then?" he grated.

Suddenly, Akratil's sword was at his throat. "I am afraid of nothing," the Breaker said, his voice no longer amused. Chakthi backed away and found himself surrounded by armored warriors who eased their dread mounts close so that he was ringed with scaley hides and gnashing teeth and could not escape the blade. "Heed me." Akratil pressed the sword's point home, so that a thick bead of blood ran down Chakthi's neck. "I will show you what we do—I'll take that ridge, and you shall ride beside me. Now find yourself another horse lest you go afoot. Bemnida!"

"Akratil?" The woman came from the crowd. Beneath her helm, her eyes were troubled as she glanced up at the ridge, at the bodies of the slaughtered Tachyn.

"These new weapons disturb you?" Akratil demanded.

"They seem . . ." she hesitated. "Very powerful. And— do I not miss my guess—protected by some magic."

"The magic is of no account." Akratil waved a dismissive hand. "What power it had died with that foolish man, Talle. Only its memory lingers, and now they've only those things our cringing ally here names . . ." He looked to Chakthi. "What are they called?"

Sullenly, Chakthi said, "Cannon."

"Cannon," Akratil repeated, smiling confidently. "We shall overcome them, no?"

Dutifully, Bemnida nodded.

Akratil's smile grew broader at the prospect of fresh slaughter. "We waste time here," he said. "There's killing to be done in this land and I'd move on to this city our friend has spoken of. But I'd not leave this troublesome group in our rear, so do you, Bemnida, lead the Horde out through that pass"—he pointed to the southern egress—"and I'll join you when I'm done. It should not take long."

Honored by such trust, Bemnida ducked her helmed head in acknowledgment and turned away. Akratil selected warriors.

∎   ∎   ∎

"They're moving." Arcole crouched beside a hornbeam. "It looks as if they divide their force."

Davyd stared down into the valley. "They'll look to destroy us," he said. He seemed possessed of an awful certainty. "The bulk will go to the river, and some will remain to attack us. We must hold them here, Arcole."

Arcole said, "We must do our best," thinking that sheer weight of numbers must surely overwhelm them. Was Davyd right, then save the impossible happened and *all* the folk of this new world came together in common purpose, the ridge must soon be only the Breakers' killing ground. But he could not imagine the People and the branded folk and the masters and the redcoats of the God's Militia joining in such intent—surely not in time. He wished he entertained no such doubts, but when he looked at Davyd's haggard face, he saw his own pessimism reflected there.

"I know," Davyd said, as if he read his comrade's mind. "But what else shall we do? We must hold them as long as we can, else all is lost."

Arcole nodded, smiling grimly, and studied the disposition of the enemy. The Horde moved now, the larger bulk flooding like some ghastly rainbow tide toward the eastern end of the valley, hundreds more massing at the foot of the ridge, preparatory to attack.

Kerik said, "I'd best move men to the pass." He no longer seemed so sanguine.

Arcole watched the captain stride away. "What think you?" he asked Davyd. "Can we survive?"

"That's of no account," Davyd replied. "Only that we hold them here long enough. Do the others come . . ." He shook his head fretfully. "It all depends on that, Arcole—that the others come."

"We could surely use their numbers," Arcole said.

"Not only that." Davyd stared down the slope at the shifting Horde. "More than that. It's not only numbers shall win this battle, but . . ." He shook his head again, as if he pursued some half forgotten thought, or the memory of a dream. "Does not all Salvation and Ket-Ta-Thanne come together here—all the folk who live in this land, on both sides of the mountains—then we shall lose. Save the People join with the branded folk, and the masters with their servants, then we are lost."

"Masters fighting alongside their indentured exiles?" Arcole shook his head in turn. "Is that likely?"

"It must be," Davyd said. "Save all the people join together, we shall lose this new land to the Breakers. Do you not understand?"

Arcole said, "No. I'd thought we might look for Abram's army of branded folk, and the aid of the Matawaye. But to think that the masters fight alongside their servants . . ." He rubbed the scar decorating his cheek.

Davyd said, "It has to be so. There must be a joining. Otherwise . . ."

In the valley below, a horn sounded and the Breakers formed into ranks. Arcole calculated there were perhaps a thousand remaining. Sunlight glittered on their armor, and as the wind veered round, he could smell the charnel reek of their mounts, the headily sweet scent of dung. He spat and crossed his fingers and said, "At least we've the horse guns."

Davyd said, "Yes; and hope."

The horn sounded again and the Breakers charged.

"By God, put your backs into it!" Abram Jaymes stalked the deck of the barge like some ancient galley-master. "Row, damn you! We've got a fight ahead we don't want to miss, so *row*!"

The oarsmen cursed him roundly and soundly, and bent the harder to their labors, propelling the lead craft swifter up the Restitution, the boats behind picking up their speed so that the flotilla ran like some pack of heavy dogs to its quarry.

"Shall we be in time?" asked Var.

"God knows." Jaymes shrugged. "We best be, is Davyd right."

The first wave was thrown back in confusion as the guns barked their terrible thunder and spread the slope with smoke. But then the second wave came, the monstrous beasts emerging from the gray fog of the cannons' discharge like fleshed nightmares, and before the gunners had chance to reload, the Breakers topped the ridge and came amongst them. Swords and axes swung against bayoneted muskets, and men and animals died in bloody fury.

Arcole saw a Breaker top the ridge and fired his rifle into the armored chest. He saw the rider toppled backward from the weirdling beast he rode and the beast charge snarling on. He lurched aside, reversing his rifle to smash the stock against the scaly snout that swung toward him with snapping fangs long as the bayonets of the marines. Foul breath gusted in his face and he flung himself away, scrabbling for the safety of a tree. He ducked behind its cover and the lizard-thing came after him, clawing at the trunk like some vast and maddened bear. Then Sergeant Ordan stepped forward and fired his musket directly into the creature's gaping mouth. The thing jerked back, blood erupting from its neck as its eyes dulled. It swung its head and spat blood, and clawed the sergeant down even as he drove his bayonet into its chest. Arcole drew a pistol and fired into a dulling eye and the thing collapsed over Ordan's body. Arcole reloaded and looked for another target.

Davyd fired as Arcole had taught him: aim steady and squeeze gently, center the shot on the chest. He fired and reloaded with automatic precision, saw Breakers fall, and beasts, and all the while prayed to the Maker that the People come in time, and Abram Jaymes's army. And that Kerik's marines hold the Horde long enough in the valley that all come together. Else . . .

He pushed the thought away. No time for that; only to fire and reload and fire again. He could not, he thought incongruously, be a wakanisha now. A wakanisha did not kill, and he could not remember how many he had slain. He saw a screaming Tachyn run toward him, hatchet raised to cleave his skull, and triggered his musket to drive a ball into the man's belly, sending him spilling over the momentum of his own run so that he somersaulted and landed at Davyd's feet. Unthinking, Davyd slammed his musket's stock down against the Tachyn's face, and drew a pistol as a second charged him, and shot the man cleanly through the right eye.

A dreadful calm owned him now. He felt given up to destiny, and accepted that what he did was all he could do. And was it wrong then the Maker had set him here in this place, and he could do no more save hope.

He crouched, reloading musket and pistol, and heard the cannon roar again.

"Back! Fall back!"

Akratil turned his dread horse, its horns all sticky and red, and waved his bloodied sword. This ridge was harder to take than he'd anticipated. He'd not faced such weapons as these folk used before, and they had wreaked carnage on his warriors. He took his mount at a gallop down the slope, thinking that the enemy was sore hurt. There could not be more than a few hundred of them—far less than the numbers he'd faced in that other valley in Ket-Ta-Witko—but they owned thunder and lightning, and he should have listened harder to Chakthi. The thought irritated him and he looked to find the Tachyn.

Chakthi sat blood-boltered on his borrowed horse and without thinking about it, Akratil swung a gauntleted hand to strike him from the saddle. Chakthi fell down and spat out blood, a broken tooth. He reached for his hatchet and Akratil kicked him in the face.

"I should take your head." He walked his dread horned animal toward the Tachyn. "I should slay you and set your skull on my saddle with these others for what you've done." He looked back at the slope. It was littered with the bodies of Breakers and their beasts. "I should kill you now."

Chakthi darted away from the probing horns. "No! Listen!" He felt afraid. "Do we only go around them . . ."

"*No!*" Akratil roared. "I do not go around things. I go over them and through them; not around them."

"Please." Chakthi cringed. "Let me take my warriors north and come against them from their flank. Then you charge upslope . . ."

The crash of cannon diverted them both.

■   ■   ■

Bemnida rode hard for the egress. She had far sooner fought with the others, but Akratil had commanded and she obeyed, and so she led the bulk of the Horde toward the pass and the river beyond.

Then the thunder came again and the ground around her exploded. Her mount began to prance. She was reminded of that other valley where rock had fallen, hills erupted, and knew this was different. This came not from the shifting of stone, which was magic and understandable, but from weapons she did not comprehend, that appeared to be set on the ridge above. She looked up, wondering at such strange creations, and saw the flash of flame and heard the roar, then a great whistling sound, and in the sunlight saw lines traced across the sky.

Then nothing.

The first burst of grapeshot pierced Bemnida's armor, her helm. It shot her through so that she fell from her saddle as the beast reared in its own pain and fell down across her as she screamed, and crushed her as she died.

The guns fired again, and muskets, angled down into the pass, and the Horde halted and swirled and fell back.

"By God!" Kerik shouted. "Keep firing, boys, and we'll hold them."

The gunners, thankful to be free of the carnage on the ridge—and angered by the destruction of their comrades— bent with a will to their work. They loaded and primed and fired as the supporting infantry volleyed musket balls into the riders massed below. It was a slaughter—did these rainbow-armored folk own magic it was not such as knew the power of musketry and cannon, of lead shot. The Breakers were thinned and slowed by the valley's bottleneck pass, and all the marines need do was fire down until the track was filled and blocked with bodies.

Bemnida slain, the Breakers fell back in confusion. But even so there remained sufficient of them none on the ridgetop might hope to survive unless help arrived swiftly.

Kerik looked at the carnage and then at the sun. It was not yet far over the horizon. He wondered if he would survive this day, and pasted a smile across his face.

"Hold the pass, boys. Help's on its way."

"Bemnida!" Akratil roared. "Where's Bemnida? I'll take her head for this!"

A warrior whose name was Beltyn told him, "She's dead," and in his rage, Akratil swung his sword and took off the man's head. "We attack again," he screamed. "Follow me!"

And again the guns flung them back in bloody carnage, and the Breakers chafed and cursed and knew the frustration of defeat.

The day aged: the sun traveled the sky and came toward its zenith, and in the valley and down the slope and on the ridge, the smell of blood was strong, the stench of death filling the air.

Akratil rallied his depleted Horde.

"They've power," he acknowledged, "but still not so great as mine, nor so great as our god's. We must bespell ourselves against these new weapons, and then we shall ride over them."

He ordered a fire built and the body of a man set on the blaze, alive and screaming. Chakthi objected that it be one his Tachyn, but not for long, and chose a warrior. Akratil called on the dark god he served, who was the antithesis of the Maker, dark to light, and bought strength. He raised his hands and sent that darkly summoned power out over his warriors, arming them against the hitherto unknown power of cannon and musketry, against black powder and lead shot.

"Now," he roared, "we are invincible. Destroy them!"

The Horde charged, and even did the cannon on the slope roar out and slaughter Tachyn, and even some of the Breakers, still the dread warriors came amongst the beleaguered defenders to deliver terrible slaughter.

Davyd fired his musket and saw the ball deflect off the armor of the blue-clad rider. He braced the gun against the down-swinging sword and flung himself clear of the gnashing fangs of the lizard-mount even as Arcole fired into the woman's back—the lead slug made no more impression than Davyd's earlier shot, and the rider went by, laughing as her blade carved a path through Kerik's marines.

"They use magic," Davyd shouted. "By the Maker, Arcole, they've armored themselves against bullets."

Arcole grimaced, reloading his musket. "Then what do we do?"

"Hold!" Davyd spilled powder down the barrel of his own gun, wondering if it be any use. "Hold them as long as we can. Do the others come . . ."

"Dear God, we can't hold them much longer," Kerik gasped. "We're running short of powder, and we're almost out of shot."

"We must," Davyd said. "Even if we must fight them hand-to-hand."

"Them?" Kerik barked a sour laugh. "Fight them with bayonets? Bullets bounce off them, no? What can we do, save die?"

Davyd said, "If we must. It's the world's only chance."

39   The Last Battle

Davyd wiped a face blackened by powder and listened to the moaning of wounded and dying men. A breeze had gotten up soft and malodorous with the stench of death—and it seemed to him that its song was mournful, counterpointed by the wailing of the hurt and the frightened snorting of the marines' surviving horses, the low-voiced conversation of men who believed they should die on this ridge. He wondered how many had already died—surely Kerik's men were sorely depleted—and if sufficient remained to hold the Breakers and the Tachyn penned in the valley. He wondered at the Breakers' magic, which allowed them to charge headlong into the volleys of musket fire and ride through unscathed. The cannon made some difference—as if the Horde's dark magicks were not quite enough to overcome that greater firepower—but still insufficient to halt the mass of beast-riders. Another charge, he thought, and likely the Breakers should ride over Kerik's men and leave them all dead behind as they went on to conquer all Salvation. And after that, deliver untold worlds to destruction.

He looked at the sun, high and hot now, and wondered where the People were—if they'd come timely. Then he made the ritual gestures Morrhyn had taught him and asked the Maker that it be so, asked that the Breakers be halted here, even must he give his life to that end. He realized that he no longer cared whether he lived or died, only that the Horde be halted and their threat forever ended. He wondered if Morrhyn had felt the same when the Dreamer climbed the Maker's Mountain. But there, so Morrhyn had told him, the Maker had vouchsafed him dreams, and therefore purpose. Davyd had no dreams to sustain him; it was as if the presence of the Breakers filled up the world and clouded the nocturnal images. He wondered why he did not feel afraid, and then if Taza was with the Tachyn, and then thought on the betrayals that had led to this last battle.

Had Taza not envied him so, he wondered, might these events have been denied? If Chakthi had not taken his clan away, or Vachyr not kidnapped Arrhyna, or Rannach not slain the Tachyn . . . The thoughts whirled around his restless mind and he decided there was no answer, only the determination that it end here.

He glanced up from his musing as Arcole joined him. "Here, best eat."

Arcole passed him a tin plate on which rested cold meat, a biscuit. Davyd nodded and took the food. He felt no appetite, but knew he should need all his strength.

"How are Kerik's men?"

"Angry. Angry and afraid." Arcole shrugged. "God knows, but they've reason. And you?"

"It's strange," Davyd smiled grimly, "but I don't feel any fear."

"It can sometimes be that way." Arcole settled beside him. "When you've a true purpose." He sighed. "I wish I could see Flysse again."

"Perhaps you shall." Davyd could not taste the meat. "Perhaps Rannach found the People; I think that Morrhyn knows we're here."

"And can find this place?"

Davyd shrugged. "At least Abram knows of it. But alone, his folk shall not be enough."

Arcole nodded and was about to speak, but shouts rang from the north, and the rattle of musketry, the blast of the two cannon placed there. "God, they look to flank us!" He sprang to his feet.

Davyd followed him and they ran to the north, where shadows moved amongst the trees and the cannon's flame outlined the Tachyn who sought to come up stealthy.

Arcole fired and a warrior screamed and fell. Davyd took aim, then flinched as an arrow thudded into the tree beside him; perhaps he was not so resigned to dying. He fired instinctively, and the archer coughed and toppled back into the bush that hid him.

The cannon roared again, the effect of their shot augmented by the trees ahead, so that terrible splinters and spinning chunks of jagged bark joined the discharge. Few Tachyn made it through that dreadful storm, and those who did were spitted on the bayonets of the marines.

The flanking attack failed, but even as it did, the Breakers came again up the slope, and toward the southern pass. Empowered by Akratil's magic, they rode oblivious of Talle's fading hexes, and the fire of Kerik's men sprang off their armor like raindrops from waxed cloth. They seemed impervious, and only at close quarters—as if honest steel prevailed over dark magic—could the defenders halt them. And even were the attackers finally thrown back, still more shot was used, more powder, and more marines left dead. They were down to only a few men now, surely not enough to halt another charge.

"We should consider withdrawal." Kerik winced as a bandage was wrapped about his wounded arm. "Perhaps we could slip away and get to the river."

Davyd said "No!" in such a tone as prompted the officer to stare at him.

Arcole said, "They'd find us, anyway. And were we on open ground . . ."

Kerik nodded and with his good hand, reached for his flask. His left was by now strapped to his chest and he fumbled with the flask before handing it to Arcole.

"Would you?"

Arcole grinned and unscrewed the stopper, passed the vessel back to Kerik.

"Well, it appears we stay and fight. So here's to . . ." He hesitated. "A clean death?"

"Victory," Arcole said.

"At some cost," Kerik returned. "I've but a handful of men left." He looked at Davyd. "But we'll hold them long as we can. So—to victory, or death!"

He drank and passed the flask to Arcole, who sipped and held it out to Davyd. Davyd shook his head: it seemed to him that he should have clear senses this day. He asked, "How long can we hold them?"

"I doubt we can withstand another charge." Kerik shrugged, grimacing as the movement shifted his wounded arm. "That at the best. Do they attack en masse . . ."

"You failed." Akratil stared contemptuously at Chakthi.

"We fought." The Tachyn glowered sullenly. A bruise decorated his cheek where the Breaker had kicked him, and his mouth was swollen. "Nor did worse than you."

Akratil nodded thoughtfully. "These folk are harder to take than I'd anticipated. These weapons they use are powerful."

Chakthi said, "I warned you of that."

"Yes." Akratil smiled as might a man at a fawning dog. "And meanwhile, we are held here. We cannot go through that pass."

"We might go back," Chakthi said, "to the west, and skirt around this valley."

"That," Akratil declared, "is not our way. No; I shall overcome this obstacle."

"How?" Chakthi demanded.

"That is for me to decide." Akratil waved a languid hand in dismissal. "Now go away and leave me to think."

Chakthi grunted and quit the silken pavilion, returning to his own lodge, where Hadduth waited.

"He treats me as if I am nothing." He snatched at the tiswin the wakanisha proffered. "I am akaman of the Tachyn, yet he speaks to me as if I were . . ."

He shook his head, snarling in outrage. Hadduth said, "You fought bravely."

"Ach, I know no other way!" Chakthi raised a hand and Hadduth cringed back. "Nor did I see Rannach. Indeed, I begin to wonder if he's here. Tell me where he is, Dreamer."

Hadduth swallowed nervously. "Perhaps," he said carefully, "he has taken his son back to the People."

Abruptly, tiswin was hurled in his face and Chakthi's hands were on his throat.

"You gave me your word." Chakthi's voice was a growl, his eyes red with fury. "I'd find him here, you said."

"Wait," Hadduth choked, "listen to me, I beg you." Chakthi eased the pressure on his windpipe a little. "If he's not here, then we can find him. Later, when we own this land."

"Later? I want him now!" Chakthi snarled. Spittle flecked his lips, saliva dripping from his jaw. "Where is he?"

"I don't know," Hadduth croaked.

"You don't know?"

As best he could with Chakthi's powerful hands tight on his throat, Hadduth shook his head. "No, but . . ."

"What use such a Dreamer?" Chakthi asked. "You promised me Rannach, but where is he? You promised me victory, but we're held like penned buffalo in this cursed valley. You promised me allies, but I am treated like a dog!"

Spittle fell onto Hadduth's face and the pressure on his windpipe increased. He tried to speak, to scream, but all that came out was a strangled moan. Chakthi straddled him, staring down as he drove his thumbs harder against the yielding flesh, his fingers gouging into Hadduth's neck. All his frustration, all his anger, focused on the wakanisha. It seemed to him that Hadduth had delivered him to this impasse, the Dreamer's promises false, leading only to disappointment and humiliation. He tightened his grip.

He saw Hadduth's eyes blur and begin to bulge. A red mist pervaded his vision as he watched the Dreamer begin to buck as lungs denied their fill of air protested, and felt Hadduth's hands grasp at his wrists. Chakthi was the stronger and held the wakanisha down, so that Hadduth felt a terrible pain in his chest and in his head. His mouth opened wide in a desperate search for air. Chakthi saw his hands fall away and flop uselessly at his sides, and in a while his struggling ceased and he only lay staring blankly at Chakthi's outraged face.

Hadduth's final thought was terrifying: that likely now he must face the Maker and be judged for all he'd done. Then there was only darkness.

Chakthi held the dead wakanisha a long time, and when he loosed his hold there were livid bruises on Hadduth's throat, and a swollen tongue that protruded from the gaping mouth.

Chakthi rose and took hold of Hadduth's hair and dragged the body from his lodge. He ignored the amazed stares of his warriors as he hauled the corpse across the grass to where the Breakers' dread beasts were penned. A black-armored beast-master stood there and Chakthi deposited the body at his feet.

"Here, let your animals feed on this."

Not long after, the Breakers attacked again. Somehow, as if sheer purpose and honest intent were enough to defeat their magicks, a score or so of marines still survived, and the Horde did not take the ridge. The Breakers retreated, but none still standing on the rim of the slope any longer entertained much hope save that they should die there.

Even so, none any longer spoke of retreat, but only that they must hold the dread attackers and ask whichever god they worshipped that help come in time.

Arcole wore a stained bandage about his head, where a sword had cut him, and another about his arm, where an arrow had pierced flesh. Davyd was one of the few lucky ones, as if the Maker Himself warded him against harm, for even though he stood in the thick of battle, no blade had touched him yet, nor arrow, nor beast. He wondered if he was saved for some greater fate.

"By God, they'd best come soon." Arcole wiped blood from his knife's blade and set a whetstone to the edges of the Grannach steel. "We cannot last much longer."

"No." Davyd tilted his head back, staring at the sky. The sun westered now, throwing long shadows from the trees. There was no birdsong, because in this bloody valley all the birds were fled, as if driven off by the presence of the Breakers and the awful carnage. The loudest sounds were the growling of the Breakers' beasts; even the wounded were quiet now. "But last we must."

"Or die," Arcole murmured.

"Or that," Davyd agreed.

"Here." A marine came with coffee and a meager luncheon. "Captain Kerik's compliments."

"Where is he?" Arcole asked.

"With the wounded." The marine eyed them curiously, as if he wondered at their origins, their presence here. Then he saluted and turned away.

Arcole chuckled. "No doubt he wonders what branded exiles do here, fighting alongside the marines of the God's Militia."

"Likely." Davyd sipped the coffee. It was bitter and lukewarm. He longed to sleep. "And do the others come, he'll wonder the more. But he'll fight with them—with us—and that shall be a fine thing, no?"

Arcole nodded. "Like your dreams? All the folk of Salvation and Ket-Ta-Thanne come together?"

"Yes." Davyd nodded in turn. "To save the world."

"And do we," Arcole murmured, "what after? You know that Abram and his folk shall declare independence, and then the Autarchy will send armies to claim back this land."

"Then I suppose," Davyd said, "that we shall fight another war."

"I think," Arcole said, "that I've had enough of war."

Davyd only shrugged, unable to answer. Instead, he emptied his mug and forced himself to eat, then lay back on the grass and watched the sun, wondering if he should see it rise again.

Akratil said, "This shall be the end of it. This sunset shall see them swept from that ridge and slain. We shall avenge all our dead; Bemnida and the rest." He raised his great sword and shouted, "Forward!" And in a great rainbow tide that shone and glittered, prismatic, in the light, all the Breakers charged to the attack.

"There!" Morrhyn pointed ahead, to where a broad avenue afforded ingress to the valley. The air above the surrounding ridges was misty, as if a multitude of fires fed smoke to the sky. "Swift now!" He urged his tired horse to a gallop, bringing the warriors of the People with him.

Rannach flanked Arrhyna, Debo agog with excitement at her side, Flysse beyond, her blue eyes wide with concern. "Hold back," he said. "This is work for men." He heeled his mount up to join Morrhyn, hefting a borrowed lance.

Flysse said, "I cannot: I must find Arcole. Arrhyna, do you keep Debo safe," and set her own horse to a lathered gallop before the Commacht woman had chance to answer or argue.

"Come on!" Abram Jaymes raised his Hawkins rifle and stretched his long legs in a furious run. "Can't you hear them?"

"God, but that sounds ferocious." Tomas Var paced him, his own rifle cradled across his chest.

Behind them came a stream of folk—masters and branded men and soldiers of the God's Militia, traders and tavernkeepers, servants, all Grostheim, all Salvation, represented. They had left the barges moored on the Restitution's north bank and made a forced march across country. Folk had joined them from the outlying settlements, as if some common purpose, felt but not properly understood, brought them together. And now they could hear the crash of cannon and the rattle of musketry, see the pall of smoke that clouded the valley. Var prayed they be in time.

Akratil, cursing foully, shouted for the hornman to sound retreat and fell back down the slope to regroup at the foot. He could not understand such defeat—he was the conquering blade, the servant of oblivion and death, and he had worked powerful magicks to protect his people. But still they died—it was as if some concatenation of forces worked against him. He sensed destiny heavy in the smoke-sullen air, and vowed that his dark god *should* be served, and these paltry obstacles be swept away.

∎   ∎   ∎

"By God, but we held them off!" Kerik waved a bloodied saber in triumph.

"They'll come again," Arcole said. Sweat ran down his face, cutting runnels through the powder stain, and blood oozed from a sword cut across his ribs. "But there'll be fewer of them."

"And of us." Kerik's elation dissolved as he looked around at the dead marines, the wounded. Then he forced a brave smile and shouted, "Well done, boys! Hold hard, and remember we fight for Salvation!"

Arcole noticed that he did not say, "For the Autarchy," and smiled. Then: "Where's Davyd?"

Kerik shrugged and Arcole turned, seeking his comrade. He saw Davyd slumped against an oak, spilling powder into the frizzen of his musket. He was pale under his own coating of powder, and it seemed to Arcole that his eyes were haunted.

"You're hale?"

Davyd nodded. "It's odd, no? I've taken no wounds."

"You're lucky." Arcole shrugged. "Or blessed."

Davyd smiled wearily. "How much longer can we hold them?"

"Not long. Another charge, perhaps."

"We must try to slay their leader," Davyd said. "The one on the horned horse."

"He's charmed, like you." Arcole regretted the unthinking words as he saw Davyd's face tighten, and sought to redress the mistake. "I mean that he rides unscathed—I've taken shots at him, but always some other rider blocks my aim, or his magic deflects the bullet."

"He serves his own god." Davyd stared down the slope to where Akratil rallied his forces. "And his god's dark, but powerful."

Then the horn sounded again and again the Breakers charged.

Chakthi held his warriors back. Let Akratil and his Breakers take the brunt of those thunder-blasting cannon. They owned magic, and his Tachyn were sore hit by this battle, his clan reduced—so let the Breakers go up that ridge and he'd follow after. He reined his horse and watched as the Breakers urged their awful mounts onward.

The bulk of dead littering the slope slowed the Breakers' charge. Only a few succeeded in climbing the bloody obstacle, and they were met by gunfire and bayonets.

For a while.

"Oh, God, we're out of shot! Stand firm!"

Jorge Kerik slashed his saber at a dismounted Breaker. The blade clattered on bright red armor and the Breaker swung a crescent-bladed ax at the marine. The curved head took Kerik's legs from under him, and he screamed as he felt bone break, but even as he fell he cut at his assailant, deflecting a blow that should have taken off his head. Then Arcole was there, musket blasting flame directly against the armor, and the Breaker gasped and was thrown back.

The lead slug dented the armor, but did not penetrate. Arcole wondered if these creatures might be slain and swung the musket like a club against the crimson helm, hurling the warrior—man or woman?—back, and drew a pistol that he pressed against the slitted eye sockets. He squeezed the trigger and saw blood erupt from within the casque. The Breaker fell down and was still; Arcole turned to Kerik.

"I'm slain." Kerik stared at his left leg, blood gouting from the stump. His foot lay close to the Breaker's corpse. "But it was a fine fight, no?" His voice faltered.

"It was a fine battle." Arcole knelt beside the dying man. "You and your men fought well."

"We're marines." Kerik chuckled bitterly and reached for Arcole's hand. "It was an honor to know you, Arcole Blayke."

"And to know you." Arcole took the hand and held it firm.

"Do what you can for my men, eh?" Kerik's voice grew thick, his eyes glazing.

Arcole said, "Yes," thinking that they should all die this day, and watched the light go out of Kerik's eyes. He loosed the dead man's grip and took up his musket and went back to the fight.

Morrhyn halted where the pass fed into the valley. For a moment he sat his panting horse with widened eyes as he stared at the battle raging up the far slope. He recalled the Meeting Ground in Ket-Ta-Witko, and the slaughter there, and wondered if he had brought the People to destruction. But Davyd was on that ridge, and he could feel the presence even through the Breakers' clouding magic, like a bright beacon shining out of fog, and *knew* the Maker had led him here. Worlds turned here, and was this battle lost then worlds should die.

He looked to Rannach.

"This is our work now." Rannach raised his lance. "To me!"

Yazte sided him, Kanseah and Dohnse. Colun slid down from the horse he shared, and the Grannach bunched around him as Rannach outlined his battle plan.

"See?" He angled his lance down the valley. "Chakthi holds his Tachyn back—we take them first, then the Breakers in the rear."

"An uphill charge?" Yazte frowned. "Do they turn, they'll run over us."

"Shall we leave brave men to die?" Rannach asked, and Yazte shook his head, saying, "No!"

Dohnse said, "This is a good day to die."

Morrhyn said, "The Maker grant we don't. The Maker grant we prevail."

Colun said, "A moment," and called for torches to be made and lit. Then he grinned wickedly and added: "Even do we die, they'll sleep rough this night."

Rannach said, "We attack!" And set his mount to trotting across the grass, picking up speed as all the warriors grouped beside and around him and the earth began to thunder with the pounding of their hooves and the blood-scented air grew loud with their battle cries.

■　　■　　■

Chakthi heard their shouting and swung his horse around. He cursed as he saw the great mass of warriors charging, the Grannach running like fleet boulders amongst the horses, their torches slapping at Breakers' silken pavilions and the hide lodges of his own clan. Flame began to fill the valley as he saw Rannach at the head of the People and snarled, vowing to take the Commacht's head. He couched his lance and bellowed for his men to follow him.

Rannach saw him coming and urged his mount to a swifter pace, so that both akamans ran out in front of their warriors. Rannach screamed, "He's mine!"

Chakthi carried a hide shield, Rannach none, and Chakthi smiled wolfishly as he recognized his advantage. He crouched low on his saddle, his lance held firm between ribs and arm, angled to strike into Rannach's exposed belly. As they came together, he drove forward, looking to gut the Commacht and lift him from the saddle.

Rannach swung aside at the last moment, feeling the Tachyn's lance score across his ribs, his own deflected by the shield. He ignored the flash of pain and snatched his horse around to stab at Chakthi's back, but the Tachyn turned and danced his mount away.

"For Vachyr! For my son and all you did to him!"

Rannach shouted, "For Debo and the People!" And they charged again.

Closer now, their pace was slower, and as Chakthi's lance probed at his gut, Rannach shifted on the saddle and flung his own spear at the Tachyn's chest. Chakthi raised his shield to fend off the missile, and as he did, Rannach caught his pole beneath his left arm and kicked his horse to the side, so that the lance was torn from Chakthi's grip. He screamed a curse and drew his hatchet. Rannach drew his own from his belt and they came again together, the larger fight forgotten as they clashed, each man intent on revenge.

Chakthi's hatchet slashed air as Rannach ducked, reaching across to smash his blade at the Tachyn's ribs. Chakthi flung back, the movement disturbing his balance, so that his horse whinnied and began to rear. It was a Tachyn pony—battle-trained—and it flailed its hooves and snapped its teeth at Rannach's bay. The bay was no more than a riding animal, and it shied from the smaller horse's attack. Chakthi brought his mount down and aimed a blow at Rannach's head. The Commacht twisted away and the swing lopped hair from the bay horse's mane. It screamed, panicking, and began to buck. Rannach cursed and heeled it away, then swung it round and forced it directly at Chakthi's mount.

The bay was terrified, but still it charged, smashing into the other horse so that the smaller animal was hurled back and sat down on its hindquarters. Rannach came out of the saddle in a reckless leap that carried Chakthi down onto the grass. They rolled together, locked in an embrace fierce and furious as any lovers', and came apart with upraised hatchets, and stared snarling at one another, knowing that one must die.

Chakthi still held his shield; Rannach drew his knife. Chakthi swung his ax and Rannach dropped under the blow, driving Grannach steel at the Tachyn's belly. Chakthi halted the stab with his shield and brought his hatchet down at Rannach's head. Rannach hurled himself aside, tumbling over the grass, and Chakthi roared and sprang forward, ax upraised.

Rannach came to his knees and flung his hatchet at the Tachyn. Chakthi brought his shield up, and as he did so, Rannach propelled himself forward, his knife outthrust.

The blade entered Chakthi's stomach and an expression of stark surprise bloomed in his eyes. Rannach twisted the blade and rolled away. Blood spread over Chakthi's shirt, spilling over his breeches. He chanced a glance at the wound and snarled and moved once more to the attack. Rannach ducked another blow—Chakthi, for all his insensate fury, was slower now—and slashed across the ribs. Chakthi grunted and swung again. Rannach caught the Tachyn's wrist and brought his knife up in a sweeping arc that severed the underarm tendons so that Chakthi cried out in pain and dropped his hatchet. He tried to bring his shield across, but before he could, Rannach smiled and drove the knife upward, under the Tachyn's ribs into the heart.

"For Debo and my father!"

Chakthi gasped. "I damn you, Rannach!" Then his eyes went blank and he fell down on the grass and spat blood and died.

Rannach stared at him a moment, then sheathed his knife and retrieved his hatchet and his lance, found the frightened bay and vaulted into the saddle.

Around him, the valley burned. Where the Grannach had torched the pavilions and the lodges flame rose high, taking hold of the grass so that all the valley blazed. The sky above was dark with smoke and the air filled with the sickly stench of burning flesh.

"The Tachyn are destroyed." Yazte came out of the dancing light. "Now we attack the Breakers."

Rannach ducked his head and they rode through the flames to where the People and the Grannach waited to charge.

"God!" Var stared in awe at the bloody barricade filling the pass. The bodies of animals and Breakers were piled there, ravaged by grapeshot and canister, pierced by musket balls. He looked up at the high walls and saw marines crouched there. Not knowing their ammunition was expended, he shouted, "Hold your fire! I'm Tomas Var."

"Major?" A man stood, peering down. "By God, sir, but you've come timely."

"Who's in command?" Var shouted.

"Captain Kerik's dead, sir. I'm not sure who commands now."

Var frowned. "What of the Inquisitor?"

"Dead, sir. Slain by them savages in armor."

"And Arcole Blayke? Davyd?" Var called.

"They fight with us, and bravely."

Var smiled his relief. Then: "We're coming through. Where's the enemy?"

"All over, sir. We held them off this pass, but now they're coming up the ridge."

"Contain the pass," Var ordered, for all he no longer held any command recognized by the God's Militia. "We'll take them on the flank."

"Sir?" the soldier called. "I think there are more savages coming across the valley."

"They'll be friends," Var shouted. "Save they attack you, don't fire on them."

"Sir!"

"Let's go." Var turned to Abram Jaymes, and they began to clamber over the horrid pile of ruined flesh.

The Breakers topped the ridge. Muskets were useless against them, but bayonets thrust into the joints of their armor to find the softness of yielding flesh succeeded, and they died. Not so many as the few remaining defenders, who now fought only to survive. To hold the ridge long enough that Davyd's promised support might come. No more than thirty marines remained hale. Nineteen more lay sorely hurt, unable to take part in the battle, but each one clutching a pistol they'd use on themselves: they understood the Breakers better now.

It all seemed lost.

"We're done." Arcole wiped at the blood of a fresh cut. "We're finished."

"No!" Davyd squinted through the smoke. "See, they've come."

Arcole followed his comrade's gaze and saw the fire that filled the valley. It spread over the grass, but between the conflagration and the foot of the ridge, he saw the warriors of the People massed to charge. He recognized Rannach there, and fat Yazte, Morrhyn and Kahteney behind, Dohnse and Kanseah siding Rannach, and Colun with his sturdy Grannach.

The Breakers were gathering for their last charge, which must surely overwhelm the defenders. Akratil pranced his horrid mount before them, confident now, as he rallied his warriors and promised them victory. He raised his bloody sword and pointed at the ridgetop.

Then shouting came from the southern pass and Arcole turned to see Tomas Var and Abram Jaymes leading a great mass of folk over the necrotic barrier there to come running down the valley. He began to smile, then saw Flysse amongst the Matawaye.

"God, what's she doing there?"

He stood, shouting that she go back, and a long, brightly painted arrow drove into his right shoulder. He grunted and found himself stretched on the grass. For a while there was no pain; then it seemed fire filled him, and he cried out as it burned down his arm and across his chest. He was unaware of Davyd dragging him back until he felt a pistol set in his hand and opened his eyes to see Davyd's worried face.

"I must leave you."

"I'll come with you." Arcole struggled to rise; could not, and fell back.

"Rest still," Davyd urged. "I've not the time to remove the arrow, so lie still."

Arcole groaned and tried to find his feet. They seemed detached from his body, he floating in some limbo world of pain and fire. He wondered if the Breakers poisoned their shafts. "Can you," he moaned, "look after Flysse. And do I die, tell her I love her."

"She knows that," Davyd said, "and you'll not die."

Arcole laughed and reached for Davyd's hand. Like poor Jorge Kerik, he thought. Am I dying? For an instant, they clutched hands, then Davyd was gone, running back to where the Breakers came again.

The People charged, and from the southern pass the army of Salvation attacked.

Akratil heard the shouting and swung his dread horse in a prancing circle. He sensed the conjoining of forces he could scarce understand, save they combined to deny him victory— save there was power come here that defied his own dark god's. It was as if minds once disparate—the Breakers' prey—now mingled; as if beliefs and hopes united to confront him and defeat him: he felt his magic dissipate.

He cursed, wishing he'd not come to this valley. For the first time he faced numbers he sensed he could not defeat. It was not so much the mass of them as their shared purpose. It was, he felt, as if opposing forces had joined together to deny him, to defeat him. He *felt* the strength of that conjoined intent, the weight of its purpose, like a blade crashing against his shoulders. He screamed an imprecation at his malign god and raised his sword and shouted for his warriors to charge the ridge.

The People rode hard up the slope. The Grannach ran with them, and when they reached the hindmost Breakers, they began to hack at the weirdling beasts with their axes as the Matawaye sent showers of arrows against them, and closed with lances and hatchets and knives on the dread riders.

Then the folk of Grostheim were there and muskets and rifles clattered an awful tattoo, and—Akratil's dark-earned magic fled under that joining—all became bloody chaos.

Breakers were pitched from their saddles to fall under the axes of the Grannach. Men with the brand of exile stark on their cheeks fired pistols at beasts and Breakers alike, and closed with drawn swords and knives and axes and sickles and mattocks—whatever weapons they bore against the common enemy—even as the red-coated soldiery of the God's Militia fired precise volleys and fixed bayonets and drove in alongside the indentured folk and the masters. The people of Salvation fought together, and Davyd saw his dreams come true.

Then nightmare rode out of the carnage.

It was the golden-armored rider, mounted on his dread midnight horse, fury shining like hell's furnaces from under the ornate helm as Akratil rode toward him.

"You!" The Breaker angled his sword in accusation. "You are the one."

Davyd leveled his musket and squeezed the trigger. The ball struck the golden armor and fell useless on the stained ground—whatever magic quit the Horde seemed still to pertain to Akratil. Who laughed and heeled the horned horse onward. Davyd flung the musket away and drew a pistol. Like the musket's shot, the ball echoed off Akratil's armor, and the Breaker swung his blade at Davyd's head even as the lethal unicorn horn of his horrid mount darted at Davyd's chest.

Davyd danced back, evading horn and sword, aware that the rider drove him into the woodland along the ridgetop. Suddenly they were separated from the rest, apart from the battle and moving amongst darkening trees, as if this final confrontation must be theirs alone. Horn and tusks probed at him even as fangs snapped close to his face and Akratil's blade swung deadly at his head. He threw himself to the side and the sword embedded in a tree. It was an oak, he noticed with a strange clarity he assumed was born of the knowledge of his own death, like those in the wood, where Taza had sought to kill him and perhaps brought on these events.

He swung around the tree, hiding and suddenly very afraid. He sensed, not knowing how, that this fight was his and none other's: save he slayed Akratil, the Breakers might still prevail.

He could not imagine how he might defeat so savage a warrior.

He saw, incongruously, that the day aged now. Shadows hung darker and deeper amongst the timber. He realized that he wore the wolverine skin poor, dead Tekah had given him, and that granted him some strength.

"You're beaten." He ducked under a second swing, darted clear of the horse's probing horns. "See? Your people die."

Akratil glanced an instant back and snarled, for it was the truth. The Breakers fell down under the guns of the Grostheim folk and the weapons of the People, the axes of the Grannach. Their pavilions burned in the valley below and only a few were left now. The Matawaye pressed in, and the Grostheimers, and the Grannach swarmed like limber rocks over the lizard beasts.

"Even so." Akratil swung from his saddle, limber on the ground even as he motioned his dread mount onward to flank Davyd. "I shall kill you. I shall take your skull and hang it on my saddle to show in other worlds."

Davyd thought it must be so—he was driven back from the ridgetop and there were no friends close enough to aid him in the shadowy wood. He bore no weapon other than the knife he drew, and that was small defense against Akratil's great sword, the horns of the horrid sable horse.

Save the Maker grant him strength.

He ducked as the Breaker's sword chipped wood close over his head, and Akratil drove him back, deeper into the trees.

"Why?" he shouted. "Why do you destroy?"

"Because," Akratil replied, "that is my duty. Do you not understand?"

"No!" Davyd sprang behind a hornbeam as the blade shivered bark and the horned horse trotted, probing hungrily, forward. "Why destroy us?"

"*Us?*" Akratil's voice was mocking. "Of which *us* do you speak?"

Davyd said, "The Matawaye—the People—and the folk of Salvation. The Grannach, and all the others you've reived."

"Because you deserve it." Akratil hefted his blade in both hands. "Because you summon us with your betrayals and envies and we are that dark side of you that lusts for death; that only lusts—after another man's wife, or his horses, or for anything you do not have—but will sell your soul to own. Can you deny that? Can you deny me?"

Davyd thought on how he'd lusted after Flysse and shook his head.

"Not that I lust. Only that I respect my friends."

Akratil's laughter rang mocking through the trees as his blade sent fresh shards of bark and twigs dancing around Davyd's head.

"Betrayal brought us to that sorry land you know as Ket-Ta-Witko," Akratil said. "When one man lusted after another's wife. What did that bring, save us? And what brought us to this new land, save envy and betrayal? Shall you expunge that from your souls? Can you?"

Davyd said, "No! But we can rise above it," even as he danced, avoiding horns and blade alike in a desperate gavotte he knew he could not maintain. He thought he must soon falter and die. "And now folk come together to defeat you. Can you beat that joining?"

Akratil snarled afresh then, and swung his sword in a great curving arc; and Davyd felt a sudden flood of hope.

"Morrhyn defeated you," he said.

"And Vachyr stole Arrhyna and raped her," Akratil returned. "And Rannach slew Vachyr; and Chakthi betrayed

Racharran." The curved blade flung fresh splinters from the trees. "And Taza stole Debo; and Chakthi would have his revenge—and could you, you'd have Flysse."

Davyd said, "Yes; save she's Arcole's wife, and so I . . ."

"Do not want her?" The blade cut hair as Davyd ducked. "What if Arcole's dead, eh? What then—after she's mourned awhile. Would you not go to her, all lusty and forgetful of your friend?"

Davyd allowed, "Perhaps. But only did she welcome me. And even so . . ."

"And even nothing," Akratil laughed. "Only all lustful and glad of your friend's death."

Davyd said, "No!"

And into his mind came a vision of Arcole lying wounded and helpless, and of Flysse when he'd seen her in her under-things, and he knew that in a way, Akratil was right. And in another wrong, for there came also an image of Morrhyn and the wakanisha's unrequited love for Lhyn, and so he was able to say again, with utter conviction: *"No!"*

And then it was as if fire leapt up inside him and filled him with burning purpose, and he was able to deny Akratil's se-ductions, for it was as if Morrhyn spoke inside his head, and Rannach, and all his beliefs, and he knew Akratil for the liar and seducer the Breakers' god had made him. He felt the Maker's purpose fill him up and give him strength, and knew beyond doubting that his life did not matter—only that he end this threat to all he believed in.

He shouted *"NO!"* and darted under the sweeping blade to drive his knife upward, between the joinings of the armor, into Akratil's dark heart.

It was odd to see blood come from such a being, but it flowed copious from the joindure of armor where the Gran-nach steel had gone in, and Akratil's smile dissolved into a grimace of pain and disbelief.

The sword swung a last time at Davyd, and then Akratil fell to his knees and the blade dropped from his hands. He clutched at his belly and stared, amazed, at the red flow that decorated his gauntlets.

"Are you so strong?"

Davyd said, "No."

"Then how?" Akratil's voice faltered. Blood came out of his mouth and nostrils, spilling down his golden armor to color the metal with the stains of his dying. "How can you slay me?"

"I've friends," Davyd said. "And a god stronger than yours."

Akratil stared at him, uncomprehending; even now unwilling to believe.

"That cannot be." Laborious, he rose to his feet, taking up his sword. He raised the blade, the movement bringing fresh floodings of crimson from between the plates of his armor. "No god is stronger than mine, nor any purpose."

He raised the heavy blade and swung it in an arc at Davyd's head. Davyd ducked and closed with the Breaker. It no longer mattered whether he lived or died—only that he slay Akratil.

He felt the Breaker's sword arm crash against his shoulder, almost driving him down on his knees, and the other close around him in a horrid embrace that set the talons of the gauntlet in agonizing scratches down his back. The pain reminded him of the wolverine's claws. He cried out, "In the name of the Maker," and thrust his knife upward into the gap between Akratil's helm and neck brace.

The blade found flesh, piercing the Breaker's jaw to drive up through the roof of the mouth into the brain beyond. For a moment the two men stood embraced, then Akratil's sword fell from his hand and the talons gouging at Davyd's spine let go.

Davyd pushed the Breaker away and watched as the red eyes went blank and Akratil fell down on his face like any other dead man, and twitched awhile and then coughed out his death rattle and was still. He seemed smaller then, and the golden armor not so lustrous.

Davyd shoved his blade into the honest ground to clean it and rose weary to his feet. They're beaten now, he thought, and still I don't know what I am—wakanisha or warrior? Shall Morrhyn tell me?

Then the horned horse came charging angry from the trees.

Davyd felt a tusk rip through his shirt as he sprang aside. Fresh pain scored his ribs and he began to laugh: it should be ironic that he die under the horns of the dead Breaker's beast when he'd slain its master.

Still laughing madly, he scrabbled away from the probing horns, finding the temporary safety of an oak. Oaks, he thought, are strong, and I'm too weary to fight any longer.

The horns scattered twigs over his face and drove down against him. He sank to his knees, clutching at the oak, no longer caring whether he lived or died: only that Ket-Ta-Thanne and Salvation be safe.

Then a shot rang out and the sable horse tossed its head and went down on its knees. A second pitched it sideways to roll kicking amongst the trees, and Davyd saw Flysse standing with a smoking musket, a pistol in her right hand.

Davyd rose up weary. He felt tired now, and sickened by the bloodshed. Was this the way of the warrior, he'd no liking for it; but neither, he thought, could he be any longer a wakanisha. He'd blood on his hands now, and even was it forced on him, still he regretted it. He turned away, aware that the sounds of battle were ceased, and all he heard were victorious shouts as all the folk of this new land came together in friendship. He walked slowly back to where Flysse held Arcole.

"It's over. The Breakers are finished."

"And Arcole's dying," she said.

40 Epilogue

The fires burned out before they reached the ridges surrounding the valley. Smoke stank up the warm air, heavy with the ghastly perfume of the bodies consumed there, but the Breakers and their awful beasts were destroyed—and the Tachyn—and there were no more enemies save what lay across the Western Ocean and the Sea of Sorrows. And the Autarchy was an enemy to face another day.

For now, it was a time to celebrate.

Matawaye, Grannach and branded folk, soldiers of the God's Militia and masters, all joined together, sharing tiswin and brandy and ale, and vowed to stand together in perpetual friendship to make Salvation a free land.

And Davyd sat with Flysse and Arcole as Morrhyn took out the arrow and declared the wound clean. Tomas Var and Abram Jaymes waited outside the lodge with Rannach, who had his arm around Arrhyna and his left hand held by Debo. And Yazte, Kanseah and Dohnse and Kahteney, Colun, as if they were old friends concerned for another, a beloved companion.

"Shall he live?" Flysse asked.

And Morrhyn smiled and nodded and said, "He'll live. He'll hurt awhile, but he'll not die. Indeed, he'll hold you in his arms again before too long."

Flysse said, "Praise the Maker."

"Praise the Maker," Morrhyn echoed, and looked at Davyd.

Davyd's face was drawn, as if all the horror of the last battle were etched there.

"What's amiss?" Morrhyn asked.

"I killed," Davyd said. "I've slain men and not regretted it."

"I think they deserved to die," Morrhyn said.

"But what of the Ahsa-tye-Patiko? How can I be a wakanisha now?"

Morrhyn shrugged. "I think the Maker changes the Ahsatye-Patiko," he said slowly. "I think that this is a new land, and that things change. I think that you *can* be a wakanisha; surely you're already a Dreamer such as the People have never known."

"But . . ." Davyd said.

"Would you become my pupil?" Morrhyn interrupted. "Would you learn the lore and dream for the People?"

Davyd nodded.

"Then it shall be so," Morrhyn said, "and you shall be the first to be both wakanisha and warrior, and likely the greatest of all."

"Thank you," Davyd said.

"No." Morrhyn shook his head. "My thanks to you. The People owe you a great debt, for what you've done."

"No," Davyd echoed. "I owe the People a debt, for making me what I am."

Morrhyn beamed his approval.

"I suppose it's settled now," Tomas Var said. "Salvation's independent."

"Declared so, I reckon," Abram Jaymes answered. "You regret it?"

"No." Var shook his head.

"We'll need an army," Jaymes said. "Sooner or later, the Autarchy's bound to send troops against us."

"Then we'll meet them," Var returned, "and defeat them. We've friends now, eh?"

Jaymes grinned as he looked out at the celebratory fires and the folk dancing there. "Curious friends," he remarked, "but good friends. Yes, I think we'll do all right."

Rannach and Davyd approached them. Colun was with him, and the Grannach held an empty bottle of brandy. "This is almost as good as tiswin," he said. "Is there any more?"

Davyd laughed as he translated.

Abram Jaymes could not understand the words, only the gestures, and said, "Plenty. All you can drink." He thought he should like this squat manling.

"He can drink a great deal," Davyd warned. "I have never seen a man drink so much."

"That so?" Jaymes said. "We should have a contest."

Colun said, after Davyd translated, "I should like that," and belched. "I should like that very much."

"And you must visit Grostheim," Var invited.

"And you our mountains," Colun replied solemnly.

"And even Ket-Ta-Thanne," Rannach added.

They began to laugh.

From where he lay on his blanket, Flysse at his side, Arcole said, "I think all shall be well now. Eh, Davyd?"

Davyd looked out at the feast. It was like a Matakwa, save now all the folk of Salvation and Ket-Ta-Thanne were come together in friendship. He ducked his head and said, "Yes, I think it shall."

About the Author

Angus Wells was born in a small village in Kent, England. He has worked as a publicist and as a science fiction and fantasy editor. He now writes full-time, and is the author of The Books of the Kingdoms (*Wrath of Ashar, The Usurper, The Way Beneath*) and The Godwars (*Forbidden Magic, Dark Magic, Wild Magic*). *Lords of the Sky,* his first stand-alone novel, debuted in trade paperback in October of 1994, and was followed by the two-book Exiles Saga: *Exile's Children* and *Exile's Challenge.* He lives in Nottingham with his two dogs, Elmore and Sam.